PRAISE FOR

SHADOWS OF TEHRAN

"An exceptional read; truly honoured to have been one of the first to read this book."

—PATRICIA M WENNELL, author of
Because It Didn't Stop When It Ended

"A literary masterpiece that weaves captivating storytelling with profound insights, making it a must-read for anyone seeking both entertainment and enlightenment."

—PETER E SAUNDERS, author of the
highly acclaimed *The Truth: The Whole Truth,
and Nothing but the Truth, so Help Me . . .*

"Contains all the elements to succeed, as its very core is a consideration on life itself—of family, of past, and choices for the future—and a lesson that no matter how many times you find yourself at the gates of Hell, you can still get out of there! A traumatic read at times, but a rich and inspiring book."

—KAREN SLATER, best-selling
author of *My Journey Through Hell*

"An eloquent tapestry of words that not only transports readers to another world but leaves an indelible mark on the heart, proving that some stories linger long after the final page is turned."

—MADISON ALEXANDER DAY,
best-selling author of *Despite It All*

"A poignant and insightful glimpse into life during the Iranian Revolution and beyond. Its powerful storytelling brings the struggles of conflict and oppression to vivid, relatable life."

—JOHN WEST, author of *The Psychiatrist*,
Hemingway Award short list, Booker Prize entrant

SHADOWS

OF

TEHRAN

FORGED IN CONFLICT: FROM IRANIAN REBEL TO AMERICAN SOLDIER

NICK BERG

FORTIS PUBLISHING

This is a work of fiction. Although most of the characters, organizations, and events portrayed in the novel are based on actual historical counterparts, the dialogue and thoughts of these characters are products of the author's imagination.

Published by Fortis Publishing
Altea, Spain

Distributed by Greenleaf Book Group

For ordering information or special discounts for bulk purchases, please contact Greenleaf Book Group at PO Box 91869, Austin, TX 78709, 512.891.6100.

Design and composition by Greenleaf Book Group
Cover design by Greenleaf Book Group

Publisher's Cataloging-in-Publication data is available.

Print ISBN: 979-8-9919714-0-9

eBook ISBN: 979-8-9919714-1-6

To offset the number of trees consumed in the printing of our books, Greenleaf donates a portion of the proceeds from each printing to the Arbor Day Foundation. Greenleaf Book Group has replaced over 50,000 trees since 2007.

Printed in the United States of America on acid-free paper

25 26 27 28 29 30 31 32   10 9 8 7 6 5 4 3 2 1

First Edition

To the ones we lost along the way—
In the dance of light and shadow, you moved silently, a
whisper between worlds. Though the light may fade, and the
shadows stretch long, your spirits guide us still. This story,
crafted in the contrasts of our shared past, seeks to honor your
memories, the silent sacrifices, and the unspoken dreams.
May this stand as a monument to your journeys, bridging the
dusk of yesterday and the dawn of tomorrow. May we meet
again in the light beyond the shadows.

CONTENTS

PREFACE

E very story begins with a whisper, a subtle invitation to enter a world unseen, to walk in the shoes of another.

Shadows of Tehran is no different. It is a tale whispered in the shadows of a turbulent Tehran, where the lines between right and wrong, friend and foe, are often blurred by the mist of war and the complexities of familial ties.

While inspired by true events, this novel is an exercise in fictional storytelling set against the backdrop of historical upheavals that shaped nations and destinies. Ricardo's journey from the narrow, bustling streets of Tehran to the expansive landscapes of America is more than just a physical transition—it is a voyage through the trials of a soul caught in the storm of cultural and personal conflict.

The character of Ricardo, though born of my life experiences, embodies the spirit of many who find themselves torn between two worlds. His struggles are not intended to represent every Iranian or American experience but rather to offer a lens through which we might better understand the resilience required to navigate such lives. In crafting this story, my hope was to delve into the emotions and decisions that define us in times of crisis and calm alike.

In the early chapters of his life, Ricardo had to mature swiftly, navigating his youth with the limited tools at his disposal yet never yielding to despair. He wasn't cast from the heroic mold celebrated in tales of lore; rather, he was a person who faced numerous challenges and made mistakes. These very imperfections and struggles are what render his story authentically human.

Within these pages lies a deeper narrative about the timeless battle between good and evil and the profound sacrifices made by those who choose to confront darkness with light. Ricardo's story highlights the personal costs of fighting for justice and the heavy burdens of those who dare challenge the status quo. This battle, fraught with peril and steeped in sacrifice, tests the mettle of our protagonist and serves as a stark reminder of the price paid by those who strive to tip the scales toward good.

At its core, *Shadows of Tehran* explores the pivotal role of life choices in shaping our destinies. It illuminates the stark reality that we—not the events in our lives—decide whether to be victims or survivors. This book is a deeply personal story drawn from the wells of my own experiences and reflections. Assisted by my very talented writing coach, Ken Scott, I have endeavored to present a narrative that not only entertains but also resonates with the truths I have faced and we all face. As you turn these pages, you may find echoes of your life's uncertainties and the shadows you have faced or fled. Whether in the throes of revolution or the quiet battles of the heart, the essence of Ricardo's story is universal. It is about survival, identity, and the indomitable human spirit that persists through the chaos of history. It is about his pivotal decision to be a survivor and not a victim.

Though time has taken the characters of this book from this world, make no mistake: They are real. In the pages of this book, they live on, just as they live on in the memories of those who knew and loved them. They will never be forgotten, for they are truly not gone. As long as these words are read, they will continue to walk among us, unbound by the limits of time and mortality.

Shadows of Tehran is not just a recounting of events; it is an exploration of the human condition under pressure, a testament to the enduring quest for freedom and a place to call home. It is my sincere wish that Ricardo's story resonates with you, offering both a window and a mirror into worlds both foreign and familiar.

With every shadow, there is light—and it is in the interplay of both that our stories truly unfold.

Nick Berg

1

WHISPERS OF DIFFERENCE

Be yourself; everyone else is already taken.
—Oscar Wilde

The boy was from two different worlds. From an early age, he felt he never belonged to any one part of society.

Ricardo was born in 1967 to an Iranian mother and an American father; his life was destined to be a unique blend of cultures and a crossroads of identities.

David, his father, a naval intelligence officer, was returning from the Vietnam War. His ship had docked in Abadan on the southern coast of Iran in the Persian Gulf.

According to Samira, his mother, it was love at first sight. David was a dashing young American in a pristine white uniform, and she was an Iranian woman with an enigmatic figure, a gentle charisma, and a striking appearance. David described her as the most beautiful creature he had ever seen, with a flirtatious but also rebellious character.

After just a few short months, he asked Samira for her hand in marriage.

"Impossible," Samira had said. "My family would fight tooth and nail to prevent the union, and anyway, securing a work permit will be impossible; my brother said it will take more than a year."

"I'll make it happen," David had said.

His confident demeanor had surprised Samira, and her family had ridiculed his claim. Sure enough, the work permit came through within a few short months, and they were married soon afterward. Very few of Samira's family members attended the small ceremony. Nobody was in attendance from David's side; there was no family or even a single friend.

—

Ricardo was born twelve months later, and his sister, Hannah, was born two years later.

It was a fairy tale come true. Samira couldn't have been happier, so they moved to Samira's mother's house.

Why not? The house was huge, an ancient Iranian house built in the mid-1800s in one of the more affluent areas of Tehran near the skirts of the Alborz mountains in the north part of the city.

Ricardo's grandmother had passed away, and his Aunt Sudabeh was always rattling around the house on her own. Sudabeh was the youngest of Samira's siblings. She was the embodiment of grace and compassion, and whenever Ricardo was in her presence, she brought a sense of calm and solace, like a gentle breeze on a warm day, her voice as soft as a whisper. Sudabeh epitomized gentleness; no soul could recall a moment when she raised her voice. To Ricardo, she was more than an aunt; she was a sanctuary. She filled the house with the aroma of her soothing teas, and the faint hum of a kettle often accompanied their late-night conversations.

It seemed like the ideal solution: the type of house that needed a family to make it a home, the sound of children's feet, the toys strewn around the floors, chaos, bedlam, meals shared, a place where memories were made and cherished, never to be forgotten.

The house was built over two stories. The stairs to the second floor were accessible via the garden, with the kitchen on the side of the house. It was a grand affair. The house had servants, though Ricardo never looked upon them as such; they were more of an integral part of the family and even shared mealtimes together—one big family.

Nanny Belgase was a kind woman who had been with Samira since Ricardo was born. She was one of the kindest women Ricardo had ever met, from a village north of Tehran. She took care of the children and acted like a second mother. Now and again, she'd bring one of her younger children to the house, and Ricardo and Hannah would play with them for hours.

Belgase's eldest son was called Ali. He was the family driver, a very well-mannered, educated young man. He worked to help support his mother and father while attending college. The kids loved Ali; he always brought them sweets and played with them in the garden. The garden had a fountain and ponds surrounded by lush greenery. There were colorful pomegranate trees and lemon and orange trees with fragrant blooms. The maple trees were tall and elegant, evergreen the whole year round, and jasmine and lavender bushes gave the garden a heady aroma.

The grounds were tiled with decorative blue tiles, and flower beds bordered the length and breadth of the house. In the middle of the garden was a large marble birdbath that stored water for watering the garden.

The house's basement had a large, now empty reservoir. It had been worth its weight in gold for generations long past, supplying all the water they needed in the long, hot summer months. The public water system installed in Tehran in the 1920s confined the reservoir to history, a relic of a bygone era. The downstairs of the house had four large rooms with a covered patio where the family spent most of the summer evenings.

High brick walls and a large wrought iron gate separated the house from the busy Tehran streets and led to the garden's entrance.

It was the dirt part of the garden that Ricardo loved best. He tingled with excitement as he wandered into the roughest, most unkempt part of the property with his father, where the air hung heavy with the scent of damp earth and decay. Here, they transformed the earth into a vast battlefield, the once-vibrant flower bed now a cratered moonscape, meticulously sculpted with determined hands.

Plastic army men, hand-painted green and camouflage; tanks and trucks; and tiny rocket launchers were strategically placed for maximum impact on the make-believe enemy. And that look in his father's eyes as he was transported into another world, mumbling snippets from the Vietnam War as he rambled on about napalm, a village called My Lai, and the tunnels underground called *Cù Chi*.

The intensity of the play battle concerned Ricardo, even at such a young age. His father took it too far; he got carried away.

"What are you doing?" Ricardo asked as he watched his father douse some of the plastic soldiers with lighter fuel.

"Making it a little bit more realistic, my boy."

A small rocket in his father's hands. He watched as his arm was at full stretch, and he made a whistling noise as he drew the rocket toward the ground where the soldiers were. "BOOOOOM!" He stretched the sound out, struck a match, and threw it into the mix.

There was a far-off look in his father's eyes as the plastic soldiers burst into flames, and they both watched as they melted away into nothing.

A slight smile crossed his father's lips, and then it was gone

"Dad, was it like this when you were in the war? I mean . . ."

"It was like this, but much more serious. We had choices and decisions to make; taking a wrong turn could mean death. I lost a lot of good friends out there." David smiled. "Ready to see if your sniper can hold the ridge?"

Ricardo laughed, and the tension eased slightly. "Let's do it. I bet he'll last longer than your tank brigade!"

Ricardo loved every precious second he spent with his father in the dirt of their backyard battlefield. His father seemed to enjoy it at and was at his most animated and talkative. His mother once said David was a riddle wrapped up in a mystery inside an enigma. She'd stolen the quote from some book, but Ricardo understood.

—

His father spent most of the time in an upstairs room that he had claimed as an office. No one was ever allowed in the room; it was strictly "off-limits."

"I'm preparing some schoolwork," he'd say as he disappeared upstairs. He had taken a job as an English teacher at the Iranian Air Force Base.

Some nights, Ricardo passed by the room and saw it shrouded in total darkness. His father would be sitting quietly in the shadows, a microphone headset with earphones perched on his head, the glare from a screen cast a faint silhouette against the blackness, and his father talking in a language Ricardo couldn't understand.

—

The highlight of the school week was when the weather was good and his father would take him to school on his powerful Harley-Davidson motorcycle. As David pulled up to the school gates, he would open the throttle while slowing to a stop. The deep, throaty rumble from the exhaust pipes turned heads, and the other children were in awe of the green-eyed, cool kid with the American father.

His mother was the polar opposite of his father: kind, loving, and, at the same time, a powerful, strong-willed, determined woman. She was also a teacher and specialized in math and science. It was never lost on Ricardo that she was a teacher first and a mother second, so obsessed with what she called . . . her *vocation*.

2

SHADOWS LINGER WHERE LOVE FADED

If you're going to do something wrong, at least enjoy it.
—Leo Rosten

Samira walked in after school one day and proudly announced to her family that she had a driving license—the first woman in her family to do so.

Within a few weeks, Samira announced she would visit a car showroom in Tehran; she was determined to buy her first car.

Reza owned it. He introduced himself: "I'm from Khomeyn," he said.

"I know of it," Samira replied, "but are you going to show me some cars?"

He watched as Samira walked over to a shiny new Renault.

"I'm not sure that car is for you," Reza said. "Those French curves are a little ugly, if you ask me."

"Well, you know what they say: Beauty is in the eyes of the beholder."

Reza chuckled; his gaze lingered a little too long. "Well, a woman like you would certainly know about that."

Samira straightened up. "Reza, you're very kind, but I'm just here for the cars, and it may pay you to know that I'm a happily married woman."

"Of course. Let me know if there's anything specific you are looking for."

As she turned back to the cars, Reza studied her intently.

Although confident, Samira was initially unaware of the depth of Reza's attraction toward her; he was fascinated to the point of obsession.

She purchased the shiny new Renault. Reza gave her a generous discount and said he would personally take care of the aftercare service and attend to the mechanics, servicing, and additional paperwork. He'd need to visit her several times to ensure everything was in order.

—

But Samira's attention was firmly focused on her family. She was strict and disciplined, especially regarding her children's education. Both Ricardo and his sister knew that they could not skip their studies. She forecast quite prophetically that they had to be prepared for life in general, "that there were turbulent years ahead."

For all her discipline and intelligence, she was very naïve regarding Reza's real intention. When it came to her husband, she trusted him without question. She never asked him about his many hours alone in his dark office or his two- or three-day trips away on "school business."

During dinner one evening, Samira told the family that she wanted to speak English. She wanted to be able to converse in David's native language.

"Is there any need?" David said. "I speak Farsi perfectly well."

Samira shrugged her shoulders. "Why not?"

—

A few days later, David entered the living room. Samira was engrossed in an English study book.

"I think Spanish might actually be more beneficial," he announced. "It's the second-most-spoken language in the world, you know."

"Spanish?" Samira said. "But I was quite set on English, David. Why the change?"

"Well, I just think Spanish could open up different opportunities for you."

Samira was confused. "Surely English is the obvious choice; after all, it is your language, and it will help if I ever meet anyone in your family."

"Spanish," David insisted.

"I want to learn English," Ricardo chimed in. "I will be able to watch the American movies."

David glared at him and returned his focus back to Samira. "Don't you see? I speak English, Russian, German, and Italian. We can teach the children Spanish, too, and as a family, we'll be able to speak to most of the world. If you learn a Latin-based language, then picking up French and Italian will be as easy as falling off a log."

Samira shook her head. She stood and started to walk out of the room. "I really don't understand you sometimes, David."

—

David walked into the house the following day. "I've bought you some Spanish books," he said, handing Samira a package. "There's some children's books in there as well."

"Fine, we'll learn Spanish," she said. "It looks like you've decided for us."

"It makes sense, Samira; you know it does."

"What's the big deal?" she muttered as she walked from the room. "Why is he so determined to stop me from learning English?"

—

A month later, David announced he was leaving for the United States. "I think we should possibly consider relocating as a family; what do you think?"

America—the very word sent shivers down Ricardo's spine, a thrilling mix of nerves and anticipation. The skyscrapers that stabbed the clouds, Hollywood, the bright lights of New York, the roller coasters that looped and corkscrewed, cowboys riding across dusty plains. Yes, yes, yes! If his father wanted to take them to America, that was fine with him.

—

Within just a few days, David had left, leaving the family behind with their dreams and expectations. On his regular phone calls those first few weeks, David explained that it was all part of the process. Ricardo couldn't wait to speak to him. He told his son all about America, how wonderful it was, and how they would all have a wonderful life together.

As the weeks turned into months, his father's phone calls became fewer and further between, and even as a young boy, he couldn't help noticing his mother's anguish and some of the arguments she had with her husband when he did call.

—

Six months after David had left, the family dynamics had changed completely. The calls had stopped. Samira put on a brave face and maintained a positive façade, saying that the calls from the United States were costly—David still hadn't secured employment.

Sudabeh also moved out, which was a devastating blow to Ricardo. She had married and moved into her husband's house.

There was a pleasant tranquility for a while, until one evening,

Bahman, Samira's younger brother, arrived. After the passing of Samira's mother, he had inherited the house that Samira and the kids lived in.

Samira made dinner, but she could see that Bahman had something on his mind. "Spit it out, Bahman," she said. "I can see you want to say something."

"Yes, you are right, Samira, and this isn't easy to say."

"Tell me."

"Well, as you know, I own the house, and I have decided to sell it. I have a buyer lined up, and we have agreed on a price. He wants to complete the purchase within the month."

Samira was dumbstruck.

Bahman held up a hand. "But don't worry, Samira, I have made arrangements for you; you can move in with Masood, your older brother. He said he has plenty of room for you."

—

The tension in the new house was built from day one. Samira did not see eye to eye with Masood's wife, an older, traditional woman who had never attended school. Ricardo overheard arguments.

On one occasion, Masood's wife stood nose to nose with Samira as they shouted at each other. "And don't think I don't know about that secondhand car salesman; he's up to no good, believe me. And with your husband in America, it's scandalous. You bring shame to our family."

"I bring shame to nobody," Samira screamed. "I am a good woman. I don't believe it's my fault my husband cannot find work. The sooner I'm out of this place, the better."

—

Hannah was also taking her father's absence badly. During the first winter, she was sick with a high fever that wouldn't go away. Ricardo decided he had no option; he'd need to step into his father's shoes, be the man of the house, and protect the family.

Ricardo was reading her a bedtime story one night. Her brow was wet with sweat, and she coughed and sniffed.

"You're always ill," he said as he tucked her in.

"I know, it's Daddy's fault; he has abandoned us."

"Don't be silly," Ricardo said. "He'll be back. It's your birthday soon; he'd never miss that."

—

David never attended Hannah's sixth birthday party at Uncle Masood's house. There were no phone calls, birthday cards, or presents, and when Hannah asked to call him on her special day, her mother said she no longer had a number for him.

Ricardo felt his mother's pain. On the surface, she appeared to cope, but inside, Ricardo sensed her heart had been torn in two.

She focused on her children and determined that their father's absence would not affect them. She told herself to keep the children well-grounded and instill morals and values. Discipline and conversation would be the cornerstones of their world.

Each evening, Samira made a point of putting Hannah to bed, but she was oblivious to the mayhem going on around her. Samira's voice was gentle and soothing as she told her stories about old Persia, the stars that sparkled brightly in the vast Persian sky, and a wise old weaver who spun threads from the silver light of the stars.

Ricardo would talk to his mother about his father's absence and school. He'd complain about his education, how it wasn't so much of a challenge, and how he struggled with the monotony of his studies.

"First and foremost, life is about education," she'd say.

"But my father, when is he coming back?"

"Soon," Samira said.

"Really?"

His mother smiled. "Yes, I think we should go and look for him."

"In America?" Ricardo questioned.

"Yes," she said.

His eyes lit up, and a wide grin pulled across his face. "When? When can we go to America?"

"I've booked the flights. We leave next week," she said.

3

GHOSTS IN
THE WIND

You can run, but you can't hide.
—Joe Louis

Ricardo, Samira, and Hannah landed in Detroit.

Ricardo could not have been more excited. He'd read everything he could about Detroit being the powerhouse of the car industry and having a vibrant music scene. While racial tensions existed in the city, the new, innovative architecture reflected a city on the move. There was a flourishing art scene and a sense of community.

They were met at the airport by his cousin Baback, who was just a few years younger than Samira. They climbed into Baback's shiny red car, a '76 Cadillac DeVille with leather upholstery. As soon as he started the engine, Motown music filled the air, and Ricardo grinned from ear to ear.

Baback leaned over and turned the volume down as he spoke to Samira. "I have hired a private investigator. He is already on the case, as you instructed. He seems fairly confident that we will be able to find

David through the system; the Americans are very particular about their records."

They drove through the city, skirted the city of River Rouge to the east, and then headed northward to the small suburb of Harper Woods. They stayed at Baback's house with his American wife and younger brother, who had come to America just a few years earlier to attend college.

Although the house was not very big, Ricardo was excited about the different architecture, the grass in front, and the giant trees that grew everywhere.

He listened intently to the conversation between the two adults and realized that this was not just a two- or three-week trip; Samira intended to stay for as long as it took to find her husband.

That was precisely what Ricardo wanted to hear. They'd find Dad, he'd be fine, and they'd settle down in a big house in the suburbs and fall into the American way of life.

———

Yet it was clear that Baback had no idea where David was, and America was a big place. Ricardo's face fell when Baback described it "like looking for a needle in a haystack."

Baback's wife had prepared an Iranian herb-based stew, *ghormeh sabzi*, with meat and kidney beans served with rice. It had been slow cooking in the oven and was ready to eat. Ricardo was disappointed. "I wanted American hamburgers," he said.

Baback laughed. "Tomorrow, Ricardo, I promise I will take you to a Burger Chef, and we can all have fast-food hamburgers."

The family was tired. It had been a fifteen-hour flight, and they were all ready for bed.

Baback showed them upstairs to the solitary room they were all sharing. Ricardo and Hannah thought sharing a room with their mother would be a great adventure. "It's a little small," Samira said when Baback left. "Still, it will have to do."

—

The following day, around lunchtime, Baback came to the house with an American private investigator called Mike. Ricardo had read a lot of books about PIs in America. The concept of a PI was very American; there were no private investigators in Iran. Reading the PI books in Iran nearly got him into trouble. Ricardo had been only around six years old at the time. "Mother, what's a *brothel?*" he'd asked innocently.

His mother had looked at the book in her son's hand. "Did you borrow that book from your uncle's shop?"

"Yes."

A frown. "I'll need to have a word with that uncle of yours."

—

The adults sat around the table discussing tactics and options. Samira said she had never had contact with David's family since their marriage; he seldom talked about them or where they lived. The private investigator said it would be difficult, but they had to start looking for relatives. That was the starting point.

The investigator took notes, and Samira gave him recent photographs of David, which he placed into a folder. After a couple of hours, he left and said he would return when he had any further news.

—

Mike returned after about a week, and the news was good. He had located a sister and an aunt who had raised David as a child. He explained that David's mother had died when he was very young, and his mother's sister had raised him, along with his seven brothers and sisters. Samira was amazed. She said that David seldom spoke about his siblings; she had had no idea, but it was a glimmer of hope. Undoubtedly, one of them would know where David was. Mike agreed. He said it was a breakthrough and that he was "on the case."

The private investigator traveled to the house every week. Eventually, the weeks turned into months.

During another weekend meeting with Samira, Mike said he had met with the aunt and the sister. During discussions, they said they had no idea that David had married an Iranian woman or had any children. They claimed they had not heard from David since the mid-'60s, when he left New Jersey for the Navy. The aunt said that none of the family knew what David did in the Navy, but the other sister joked that he was very secretive and she "was convinced he was a CIA spy."

Ricardo felt a shiver run the length of his spine. He knew precisely what a CIA man was; he had read about them, especially since the family had traveled to America. He'd read Graham Greene's book *The Quiet American*. It explored the world of espionage and covert operations in Vietnam during the early years of the war with America.

"No way," he whispered to himself. "Could my father be a spy?"

———

Ricardo recalled the day with clarity.

It was a Sunday morning, and it was raining quite hard. He had awakened as he heard knocking at the front door. He'd listened to his mother running down the stairs, and as she opened the door, the unmistakable sound of Mike and Baback. Ricardo sat up, jumped out of bed, walked into the hall, and listened at the top of the stairs.

Mike was talking. "We've found him. He's at an address in Phoenix, Arizona."

Mike said he had booked flights, and the two men were leaving at lunchtime. After half an hour, they left, and the house bristled with excitement.

Ricardo whispered to his sister, "This is it—we're going to see Daddy again."

—

The following day, Samira took a phone call. Mike and Baback had found the address, a rented apartment in the Glendale district of the city. They had called in and knocked on the door. It was clear that David was not at home; the next-door neighbor said he had left earlier in the day.

The two men staked out the apartment for a week. It was clear that David was not coming back. They persuaded the neighbor to contact them, for a small payment, should David return, and they had no option but to fly back to Detroit.

—

They received a phone call from the neighbor two weeks later to say that the apartment's owner had arrived with new tenants. David had contacted the landlord and told him he was leaving the city.

They were devastated; they had been tantalizingly close, and none of it made any sense.

Ricardo studied his mother's reaction for several days. He couldn't quite explain her demeanor, but it certainly wasn't one of disappointment—more of realization. While Ricardo and Hannah shed tears of frustration and lay awake for hours at night thinking about what might have been, their mother carried on as usual.

—

Three weeks after the trip to Phoenix, the private investigator had another lead: an address in Los Angeles's Arcadia district; David had signed a lease agreement two weeks prior.

Mike was at the family home within an hour, and at the same time, Baback had booked the flights over the telephone. Mike was very optimistic, and as he left, he said, "This time, there's no escape; we've got him."

———

David had settled nicely in his new Los Angeles apartment. The block was in an affluent area, with a swimming pool within a gated community. He had been sorry to leave Arizona behind, but perhaps it was for the best; after all, he could work anywhere in the world.

He was relaxing by the swimming pool when the concierge disturbed him. He said there was a phone call for him at reception. "Who is it?" David asked.

"They wouldn't say."

David dried himself off, pulled on a shirt, and walked into the building. The phone was off the hook, waiting for him.

He picked it up—a familiar voice. "I'm sorry to do this to you again, David, but you've got to get out of there. They're on a flight from Detroit as we speak."

———

The private investigator and Baback had missed him again. The concierge couldn't explain it. "Mr. Williams seemed so happy here and had only been a resident for a few weeks. A nice man," he said. "A little quiet, but lo and behold, he took a phone call earlier that morning, and within the hour, his bags were packed, and he'd handed in the keys."

"Did he say where he was going?" Baback asked.

"Not a word. He gave me a little tip and said he hoped to see me soon."

"So, he may be back?"

"I wouldn't count on it," the concierge said. "When they hand in the keys like that, it generally means we won't see them again."

"But he'd paid the rent."

"Three months in advance."

"Do me a favor," Baback said as he slipped a $20 bill across the desk. "This is my phone number. Will you give me a call if he comes back?"

The concierge looked alarmed. "Who are you guys, the cops? What's this man done wrong?"

"He hasn't done anything wrong other than abandon his family."

The concierge nodded in approval and slipped the $20 into his pocket. "I hate guys like that. I'll give you a ring if he turns up again," he said.

The private investigator and Baback walked out of the building. Somehow, Baback sensed that he would never hear from the concierge again.

—

It was all doom and gloom in the small living room area of Harper Woods in Detroit as the private investigator explained the latest happenings in Los Angeles. "I don't like it one bit, because somebody is watching us; they know our movements. As soon as we get close to him, he gets a call." He looked at Samira. "I think there's something you're not telling me, because your husband has friends in high places. Who is he?"

"I told you," Samira said. "He was a teacher on an Air Force base, nothing more than that."

—

As the two men left and Samira prepared some food for Ricardo and Hannah, she wondered about those conversations from David's office. Obviously, she didn't understand a single word, and now it became clear why he hadn't wanted her to learn English.

There were other things, too: phone calls in the middle of the night, meetings at strange times, and sleeping over at the Air Force base on more than one occasion. There was no doubt about it: His working life was cloaked in secrecy. She knew that now.

After eating, Samira put her son and daughter to bed.

Ricardo complained, "It's too early. I want to watch TV."

"Not tonight," his mother said. "You need to study; this is a great opportunity for you to learn English, and by the time we return home to Iran, I want you to speak it fluently."

After thirty minutes, Samira tiptoed up the stairs and stood outside the children's bedrooms. She knew Hannah would be fast asleep; she was worried about Ricardo. After about a minute, she heard the faint sound of her son snoring gently. She turned and crept down the stairs. The telephone was at the bottom, in the hallway, and she picked up the receiver and punched the numbers. It rang four times before he picked up the phone.

"Hello, Reza," she said. "It's me. How has your day been?"

4

AN UNSEEN FATE

The only thing we have to fear is fear itself.
—Franklin D. Roosevelt

After the Spanish Conquistadors departed Mexico and the country gained independence, the area east of the Arizona desert and north of Chihuahua became known simply as Nuevo Mexico.

During the Mexican–American War, the territory was acquired by the United States and eventually became the forty-seventh state.

Mike and Baback tracked David down to Albuquerque, New Mexico, six months after Samira and her family had landed in Detroit.

"This is it," Mike told Baback as they sat drinking coffee in Old Town Albuquerque, at a street café near the Botanical Gardens. "This time, we have him; he can't run away."

Mike's investigations had led him to a man called Jesus, and he knew where David was. Although Mike was anxious, he was also optimistic. He had even called Samira. The conversation ended with Mike telling her she would see her husband soon.

After two cups of coffee and a stiff shot of tequila, Mike told Baback it was time to go. He was meeting Jesus in the "Barelas" part of town.

As he got up and left the table, he joked with Baback that "it was not the place to be seen after dark."

—

Mike, Baback, and Samira sat at the kitchen table back in Detroit. Everything about the PI had changed. His confident demeanor had been replaced by a worried look, etched on his ashen face. Mike told his client that he was off the case.

"What do you mean you're off the case?" Samira said.

"You don't understand; I've done everything I could."

"Of course I don't understand; you told me yesterday that you nearly had him, and then you couldn't wait to jump on the first flight back here. You must tell me what happened; otherwise, you're not getting paid."

Mike nodded. "I value my life, Samira; it's as simple as that. Jesus told me that David didn't want to be found. He had David's address on a small piece of paper in his hand, but he refused to give it to me. I tried to grab it from him, and almost immediately, two men in dark suits climbed out of a car. They wrestled me toward the restroom, and let's say they told me things I didn't want to hear. David doesn't want to be found; it's as simple as that. I advise you to get back on a plane to Tehran and forget all about him."

—

Samira and the two children discussed their future. Everyone agreed that America was the land of opportunity, and it was where their future lay. Ricardo loved everything about it, even the school they attended. Ricardo had had his problems; the fact that he was an Iranian who hadn't entirely picked up the language meant he was singled out, teased, and bullied from time to time. But he told his mother he could handle it, and it hadn't been so bad after he had dumped one of the bullies on his backside.

Hannah jumped up from the table and said she was going upstairs to write a letter to her friends, leaving her mother and son alone.

"We need to make it official," Samira told him. "You and I can go along to the offices tomorrow, and I can register to work, get my green card, and enroll you in school permanently. I don't know why your father doesn't want us to find him, but he has his reasons, and at least if we stay in America, when he does want to find us, we'll be here."

"And Reza?"

His mother furrowed her brow. "What about him?"

"I hear you talking to him on the telephone. You talk to him quite often."

"He's just a friend, Ricardo, who cares about me, but he'll never replace your father; he's not half the man your father is."

"But . . ."

"But nothing. You are a nine-year-old boy. Where do you get your intuition and curiosity from? I swear, you're an adult in child's clothing. Now, no more of your idle chatter; get upstairs, brush your teeth, and put yourself to bed, because tomorrow we will start a new life."

—

The Immigration and Naturalization Office was located on Jefferson Avenue. Samira took a ticket from the machine and waited her turn. The offices were busy; at least two dozen people were before her. After around thirty-five minutes, her number was called, and she gave Ricardo a nudge. They walked toward the designated interview room.

The woman looked up. "Take a seat. This must be your son, Ricardo?"

Samira smiled. "So we are in the system."

"Well, your son, Ricardo, is in the system, as is your daughter, Hannah.

Your husband has registered them with the authorities, but I'm afraid there's no record of your marriage."

"There must be some sort of mistake," Samira said. "My marriage certificate is here." She handed across the piece of paper.

The woman studied it. "Yes . . . but this is your marriage certificate from Iran; nothing is registered here in America."

"As I say, there must be a mistake; David said he had registered the marriage a few weeks after we were married in Iran."

"There's no mistake, lady. As far as we are concerned in America, your marriage doesn't exist, and he never applied for your green card."

The meeting had started badly and went downhill quickly.

Samira said that her husband had applied for a green card for her. The woman shook her head.

"So I can't work?" Samira said.

"You certainly can't," the woman said. "Furthermore, you are in danger of deportation because you have overstayed the permitted period."

In a strange twist, the woman said that Samira's children could stay, but they would need to be placed in foster care.

Samira exploded. "That's never going to happen!"

She fought hard but could not control the tears running down her cheeks. Reaching for Ricardo's hand, she left the office. The interview lasted no longer than ten minutes.

—

Samira decided it was time to go home to Iran. She had done everything she could to find her husband and spent a small fortune doing so. At least in Tehran, she could pick up where she left off, working as a respected teacher. The salary was good, and she could stay with her older sister Parvaneh until she found a place to live.

Over dinner that evening, Samira told Ricardo that Reza was coming from Iran. "He's a good man. He has offered to help us get organized for our trip back to Tehran. He's the nice man who sold me the car."

Ricardo thought he was anything but a nice man. Reza smiled when they met him at the airport; he tried to be charming and talked fast. He wasn't very tall, Ricardo thought, and he had a noticeable slouch and a slight pot belly that seemed to hang just a bit too comfortably over his belt, but there was no doubt Samira was pleased to see him, and that was all that mattered.

—

Reza told the children where he was from: a small farming village south of Tehran called Khomeyn. When it came to cars, he was the fountain of all knowledge and owned a grand car dealership. Ricardo wondered if he would be better suited to sell fruit in the markets. Ricardo didn't like the way Reza looked at his mother or touched her when he thought the children weren't looking.

The first night Reza stayed at the house in Harper Woods was tense. Baback clearly had a problem with the car salesman, while Samira went out of her way to try and create a pleasant family atmosphere.

Samira sent the children to bed early and told them to be as quiet as possible because Reza would also be in the room, sleeping on the sofa because there were no other beds in the house. Ricardo couldn't quite put his finger on it, but the thought of that man sleeping in the same room sent shivers running the length of his spine.

Ricardo couldn't sleep. He was on edge; there was something about Reza that he didn't like at all.

Samira and Reza came into the bedroom close to midnight. Ricardo closed his eyes and pretended to be sleeping.

He heard his mother make the sofa into a bed. She turned off the light and slipped into her bed.

Ricardo still couldn't sleep. After thirty minutes, he heard foot-steps—a man's footsteps walking over toward his mother's bed and a laugh and a giggle, whispered voices, words he couldn't make out.

And soon after, those awful noises, adult sounds that would live with him forever. He put his hands over his ears as a solitary tear fell onto his pillow.

5

WHERE WORDS BREATHE MAGIC

There is no friend as loyal as a book.
—Ernest Hemingway

Reza met the family at the airport; he had returned to Iran the previous week. Ricardo was exhausted; he hadn't slept on the flight.

The feeling of abandonment was now genuine, and his mother had made it clear that she had done everything she could to find their father and bring him back home.

It was bad enough that his father had left the family behind, but David knew they had come to America looking for him, and he had run. It was difficult to describe the emotion, confusion, and bewilderment. He was old enough to realize that husbands and wives could have issues, but what had Ricardo and his little sister done that had caused him to act this way?

Reza spoke and brought Ricardo back to the present. "Welcome home, Ricardo."

Reza's hand was outstretched, and he had no choice but to shake it.

His skin crawled. *Who was this man?* he thought. *What was he doing here? What were his motives?*

Reza embraced Samira, said hello to Hannah, and helped load the luggage onto a steel trolley. They walked out into the bright sunshine, starkly contrasting the gray, wet evening they had left behind in Detroit.

Ricardo sat in the back of the car; thoughts of his father were permeating his brain again.

He was angry, and he felt betrayed and resentful now. He wondered about the real reasons for his father's decision to walk away. He wrestled with self-doubt. *Were his son and daughter so worthless to him?*

He gazed out of the window. Driving through the Tehran streets felt very different now; it was another cultural shock as Ricardo realized how much he had enjoyed his time in America. Tehran was vastly different from Detroit, yet a certain familiarity sank in. The intricate blue tile work on the mosques and domes, the hustle and bustle of the crowded streets, and the chaotic traffic.

As they drove into the city's heart, street vendors lined the streets selling traditional Iranian snacks, fruit juices, Persian ice cream, and kebabs. Some stalls were filled with handmade crafts and clothing, and as he opened the car window, the old smells of spices and foods cooking in open-air cafés filtered in.

But he still couldn't shake the loneliness and isolation; he barely shared a sentence with his sister in the car. He had attended an American school for a short period and had been known as the "foreign kid." Most of the kids had never heard of Iran; those who did couldn't find it on the world map. Now, back in Iran, he would be the "foreign kid" again, but at least he could speak the language. He'd stay positive; his family was here, Uncle Masood's bookstore.

But Reza talked. Reza couldn't stop talking, and his voice was beginning to annoy Ricardo. He closed his eyes, praying that sleep would come soon.

—

He awoke with a start as the car came to a stop. Reza and his mother were already out the doors, unloading the luggage.

They were at a taxi stop, not at Parvaneh's house. Ricardo was confused as they unloaded their luggage into the taxi. Then, a beautiful sound—Reza was saying goodbye.

They drove no more than a few kilometers, and the taxi stopped in front of Aunt Parvaneh's house.

Parvaneh was the eldest of Samira's sisters. She was a warm, loving person but very much set in her traditional ways. She was eighteen years older than Samira. Her daughter had been pregnant at the same time as Samira had been pregnant with Ricardo.

Parvaneh lived on the outskirts of the city in a very affluent area. The house had two entrances at the front, opening onto a beautiful street with tall trees. The garage was at the front; Ricardo's Uncle Nassar's immaculately polished car was always parked outside. Nassar was a very meticulous man. As an executive, he worked for the Iranian tobacco company, leaving the house every day at 4 a.m. and returning home in the evenings. He worked six days a week.

The house had seven bedrooms, more than large enough for Samira and her family. Parvaneh's children were all adults and had their own families, so it was just Nassar and Parvaneh in the house. They had a large garden in the back and a gray-painted, wrought iron door that opened into a dirt road. Across the road was a farm with cows and goats roaming wild. The farm was a relic left behind from the days before the developers moved in.

Ricardo walked into the house with a rucksack on his back, carrying a large, heavy suitcase.

Samira helped Hannah into the house. His sister was almost sleepwalking, her eyes half closed. The flight had been long, uncomfortable, and turbulent at times. Ricardo placed the suitcase in the hallway and took his sister's hand. "C'mon, let's get you to bed. It's been a long trip."

Hannah nodded, closed her eyes, and leaned into her brother's chest. He whispered under his breath, "Don't worry, little sister, if our father won't protect you, I will. I swear to God I will."

—

The change in family life was huge; Samira was spinning plates, working two different school shifts, looking after her children, and at the same time giving her sister and her husband the space they needed in their own house. Even though a blend of familiarity seeped back into his life, Ricardo realized that he missed America and had enjoyed the short time they had spent there. For a start, the school day had been much more exciting, and even though he had struggled with the language, he had understood most of it. Some of his teachers had picked up on his level of intellect and asked him to solve math problems at the highest school level possible. They had taken a keen interest in his ability, and even though he was "the foreign kid," they had cared.

—

He had missed one place so much: his Uncle Masood's bookstore. He was always in awe of that place. It was amazing how many books such a small bookstore contained, where time seemed to stand still amid the musty scent of aging paper, leather, and glue and the gentle creak of the wooden shelves packed to the brim with tomes of every size and shape.

He'd missed the heady atmosphere as he wandered through the maze of narrow passageways and hidden nooks amid the rows of leather-bound books and weathered hardbacks. He couldn't help but feel a sense of wonder and awe at the sheer knowledge contained within the walls.

During long summer days, when most stores in Tehran closed around noon for a few hours due to the oppressive heat, Ricardo regularly visited his uncle Masood's store.

Masood was an early bird. He arrived at his shop around 6 a.m. and spent most of his day repairing old antique books.

Masood's grandfather had established the bookstore in the city's heart in the early 1900s. Masood kept his unique books on the top floor, which few people saw. Ricardo had exclusive access.

Some books had been there since the store opened, mostly first editions, some even handwritten. They were not for sale. Masood said they were not his books; he was simply holding them. They belonged to customers who brought them for repair and were in his care until they returned to claim them. It didn't make much sense to Ricardo, because some books were one hundred years old, and most clients were dead. Masood said it mattered not; he felt responsible for keeping the books safe and loved. They were natural treasures and would be there forever and a day. They were not for sale.

Ricardo read Dante's *Trilogy*. The book fascinated him because Christianity's teachings were similar to Zoroastrianism, but also so different. He always wondered if what was written could be true and how Dante could see and describe unseen worlds with the help of his guide.

Books became a big topic of discussion with his uncle, who was very pragmatic about religion. He said that just because something is written in a book does not mean it is true. "I'm an agnostic," Masood said.

"What's that?"

"It means I don't know if there's a god."

"Explain, Uncle Masood."

"Belief in a god, any god, relies on faith, tradition, or authority—nothing more. When a religious man tells me there is a god, I say prove it."

"But they can't," Ricardo said.

Uncle Masood nodded. "Exactly. Books are there to tell you stories of the past; sometimes they act as your best witness to history, but you have to understand that they were written from the author's perspective at that point in time. We once believed that Earth was the center of our universe, that all celestial bodies, including the sun, revolved around us."

Most of the books were in Farsi, but there were also many books in other languages, including Russian and English, and some in Polish and Hebrew.

—

That night Ricardo went to bed with his head filled with old memories of the bookstore. He wondered how he had survived in America without it. He couldn't wait to see Uncle Masood.

He recalled a few years ago when a book with many Jewish symbols had caught his eye. He spoke regularly with his uncle about books and their stories.

Ricardo had asked him why so many books were in Russian, Polish, and Hebrew.

Masood had closed the shop, taken Ricardo to the top floor, and told him to make himself comfortable.

He started to speak. "There were a lot of Jewish children who were brought to Iran from Poland and the surrounding areas during World War II. They had nowhere to go; we called them the 'children of Tehran,' and the whole community felt a responsibility for these poor children. Some stayed with Iranian–Jewish families, but others lodged in schools. None of them spoke a word of Persian, but somehow, the host families managed to communicate with them. We supplied them with food, and I collected books for them. I bought children's books in Hebrew, Polish, and Russian so the children would have something to read. They had escaped the concentration camps, most of their relatives had been murdered by the Nazis, and they were on their way to Israel to settle with Jewish families there, but some never left Iran. Some of them are still here today; their children and their children's children still live in Iran."

Ricardo recalled a man stopping by the bookstore to see Masood. He was a small-statured, older man who spoke with a slight accent. Ricardo remembered him telling stories about when he was not much older than Ricardo, how he watched as the Nazis killed his family, how he escaped Poland during WWII, and the endless train rides that brought him to Tehran as a child.

—

Masood's words and stories about the books had profoundly affected his nephew. At age ten, Ricardo had started reading *The Rise and Fall of the Third Reich* by William Shirer. He found a Farsi translation of the book and read it with such intensity that one night before his uncle closed the store, he forgot that Ricardo was still there, locked the door, and left.

When Ricardo realized he was alone in the shop's darkness, he called his uncle, who returned and rescued him. They laughed and spent the walk home talking about the war. His uncle explained that even though Iran was neutral during World War II, it was still invaded by the British. "The British and Americans used the railroad system to get supplies from the Persian Gulf, from the south to the north, and then into Russia."

Masood once showed Ricardo a famous WWII photograph taken in the Golestan Palace, where Rosevelt, Stalin, and Churchill met to solidify their alliance against Germany.

World War II always fascinated Ricardo; it helped him understand that no matter what odds were stacked against you, there was always a way out, always a glimmer of hope, and he read that on more than half a dozen occasions, it looked as if the Nazis and their allies would win and take over the world. He read that when Adolf Hitler invaded Russia in June 1941, it all looked over; but for a heroic resistance and the Russian winter, it would have been. Ricardo read books on how the Nazis had invaded France and established a government in Vichy. However, some men and women refused to give in, and as a result, the French resistance was born. For five years, the French Resistance battled against all odds, against superior numbers, and with little arms and ammunition, but they fought; they never gave up hope.

One quote from Winston Churchill always resonated with him: "When you are going through hell, keep going."

Lying in the darkened bedroom less than twenty-four hours after returning from America, Ricardo would never know how poignant that quote would be during the years ahead and how he would hang on to Churchill's words forever and a day.

Ricardo's final thoughts before sleep eventually came to him, and they were of Hannah. He felt the weight of responsibility for his little sister; he had to step into his father's shoes and keep Hannah in check. Hannah was only seven, but she was fire, and with his mother focused and occupied with so many other things, Ricardo was the only person who could reason with her. He was determined to oversee every aspect of her life, particularly her education. He'd read somewhere that education was a knowledge that nobody could steal.

He whispered under his breath, "Don't worry, little sister. I'll ensure you study; I'll check your homework every night, even though you'll probably hate me for it."

6

RUMORS ARE FLEETING BUT EVER PRESENT

Whoever gossips to you will gossip about you.
—Spanish proverb

Ricardo wasn't exactly sure when his relationship with his mother had changed. It had occurred between his father leaving the family home and Reza taking a more prominent part in his mother's life.

His mother was always on his case when it came to education, and one evening, during a minor disagreement, she told him, "I am your teacher first, your mother second. I am here to teach you that the world is unfair, and you must learn how to survive when I am long gone."

—

Parvaneh had just retired and announced one evening that she intended to spend a few months with her son and his new American wife in the States. Her husband, Nasser, would stay home in Iran; he couldn't take the time off work.

Ricardo noticed things after Parvaneh left. His mother was a little distant now, not as affectionate as she had once been, and he also noticed stuff between her and Nasser. There was a difference in their interactions: laughs and jokes, intimacy, a brush of hands occasionally, an arm around Nasser's shoulder, a brief kiss on the cheek. These were the things she used to do with his father. Samira had stepped right into Parvaneh's role. She ran the house, shopped for groceries, and cooked.

—

Parvaneh had planned to stay in the United States for six months but arrived back home in Iran three months earlier than scheduled. Ricardo could feel the tension between his aunt and his mother as soon as she walked through the door.

Previously, Parvaneh's daughter had spent the weekend at the house and called her mother, telling her to return home immediately to save her marriage.

Soon after, Parvaneh demanded that Samira find somewhere else to live, and they moved out of Nasser and Parvaneh's home within the week.

—

Samira picked up the pieces and acted as if nothing was wrong. Ricardo was horrified when she started to introduce Reza to the family. He overheard an argument between Samira and Parvaneh's daughter; she accused Samira of having an affair with Reza for more than a year. Samira said she had only begun a relationship with Reza when she realized her husband was gone for good.

"Reza is a decent man," she said. "He intends to marry me."

As the words left his mother's lips, a chill ran down Ricardo's spine, and his stomach twisted into a knot. He stared at her, his young mind reeling, unable to comprehend the enormity of what he had just heard. The man she spoke of embodied everything he loathed—a looming shadow that had already begun to darken the corners of their lives.

He wanted to scream, shout, and tell her this was wrong.

Parvaneh's daughter wouldn't let the rumors lie, and the rest of the family took her word as gospel. Samira was shunned.

However, the family crisis did not phase Masood. He was still the same uncle Ricardo had always known.

Ricardo sat in the bookshop one day as his uncle clarified everything. "It matters not to me," he said, "and it should not matter to you either. The bonds of blood go deeper than any action. I do not know if the rumors about your mother are true, but she is doing her best to navigate a tough world while taking care of her children to the best of her ability, and I will never turn my back on her. Never turn your back on your mother or sister, no matter what they do. Promise me."

Ricardo nodded. "Yes, Uncle Masood."

—

The new house was much smaller than any other house they had lived in. It had just two bedrooms, and Ricardo had to share one with Hannah.

The neighborhood was primarily upper working class. The house had a small fenced-in yard that opened to the street and a slightly bigger garden at the back of the house. Nevertheless, Ricardo and Hannah felt a sense of freedom in the house because they no longer relied on relatives. They'd lost their only home when their father left; Samira had spent the better part of her life savings looking for him. No matter how hard Ricardo tried not to blame his father, it was clearly his fault.

7

VOICES OF REBELLION, ECHOES OF CHANGE

Religion is regarded by the common people as true, by the wise as false, and by the rulers as useful.

—Seneca

The Shah, Mohammad Reza Pahlavi, had come back into power after the 1953 coup d'état and faced increasing criticism for his authoritarian rule. He had introduced censorship and suppressed political dissent, banned opposition groups, and targeted intellectuals and religious figures through the government's secret police, the SAVAK, who had a brutal reputation.

Iran was a country of the haves and have-nots. Social inequality and economic disparity fueled tensions in Iranian society. While the Shah and his associates enjoyed immense wealth and privileges, people in rural areas and urban slums faced hardship and poverty.

The religious opposition was also voicing its disapproval of the Shah's regime, particularly within the Shia clergy. Ayatollah Ruhollah Khomeini, a prominent Shia cleric, openly denounced the Shah's rule and called for the establishment of an Islamic government and the end of Western influence, which he said supported the Shah's regime.

Things were changing in Tehran.

One evening after dinner, Ricardo quietly lingered in the doorway as his mother and Aunt Sudabeh conversed in hushed tones.

His mother leaned closer to Sudabeh, her voice barely above a whisper. "Last night, I saw something unsettling: A man was painting graffiti on the wall leading into the city's old part."

"What did it say?" Sudabeh asked.

"It read *Death to the Shah*."

Ricardo wasn't stupid. He knew what was happening on the streets of Tehran, but that was the least of his worries. He was more concerned about what was happening inside their home.

—

Reza was a devoted Muslim; he always spoke in a low tone about the tapes he had of sermons from the man called Khomeini and how he believed in what he was saying: that the West was ruining the culture of Iran and that the country should go back to its Muslim roots. It reestablished Ricardo's belief that Reza hadn't read a decent book in his entire life. Muslim roots indeed; hadn't Reza heard of the Arab conquest of Persia in the mid-seventh century and the Rashidun Caliphate? Persia didn't have any Muslim roots!

Reza's faith and religious beliefs went against everything Ricardo had discussed at Masood's bookstore. Ricardo couldn't make any sense of an invisible man in the sky, and no matter how much Reza pontificated, he would never be able to prove it.

His family never attended religious ceremonies, although they celebrated significant Persian days, like New Year's Day in the spring or the winter solstice. His father had always celebrated Christmas, but certainly never from a religious perspective.

It was no big deal in school, either; they had a light course on Islam, but if you were not Muslim, it was optional. That is precisely how it should be. Ricardo had nothing against religion or faith, but it should not be forced on anyone.

Even at the New Year celebration table, when most Muslim families placed the Quran at the table, Samira placed the Persian Book of Kings, *The Shahnameh*. The book of poems was credited for saving the Persian language from the Arab invasion.

—

Ricardo spoke with his uncle in the bookstore. "I was talking to Reza the other day, and he mentioned his religious practices. It seems like his faith influences his political views," Ricardo began.

Masood closed the book he held with a soft thud, a thoughtful frown creasing his brow. "Ah, Reza and his beliefs. I've always felt that religion has its place, but it shouldn't meddle in state affairs."

"You mean keep religion out of politics?"

"Exactly," Masood said.

"Weren't you involved in politics during Prime Minister Mosaddegh's time? When there were tensions between the United States and Britain?"

"Yes, I was. Mosaddegh wanted to nationalize our oil and take it back from foreign powers. I supported him because I believed in our nation's right to control its resources. But foreign interference and religious opposition were formidable. Religion can inspire beautiful things in people, but when mixed with politics, it can become a tool for manipulation. That's why it's crucial to keep them separate. Everyone should be free to believe as they wish without it dictating government policy."

Ricardo absorbed his uncle's words, understanding the depth of his convictions. "It seems like a difficult balance to maintain, especially here."

"It is, Ricardo. But remember, true faith should empower individuals, not limit them."

The conversation lingered in Ricardo's mind as he browsed through the books, and he appreciated the complexity of the issues his uncle had grappled with in his political past. Masood had fought for what he believed in and even served prison time after the 1953 coup d'état.

Masood ruffled Ricardo's hair. "I can't believe we have discussions like this, boy; you are way more advanced than any other eleven-year-old boy I know. They study the World Cup football teams while you read politics and sociology. Now run along; your mother will be home soon."

"I will, Uncle."

As Ricardo opened the bookstore's door, Masood said, "Remember, Ricardo, a real man must have the courage to stand firm in his beliefs. True manhood is defined by the courage to uphold what is right, even when the path is difficult."

"Yes, Uncle, I will remember."

—

Samira wasn't at home, just Reza.

It had started as an innocent game, a wrestling match where Reza had managed to get Ricardo in a playful headlock, but he'd twisted himself around, escaped, and faced Reza head-on. As they squared up to each other and Ricardo prepared for another confrontation, the look on Reza's face concerned him—a look he had never seen before, a look beyond description. Reza's bulk overpowered him as they came together, and he threw Ricardo on the floor. Momentarily winded, he saw stars for a second or two and then froze as Reza climbed on top of him, pinning his arms above his head.

It happened in a flash. It wasn't that Ricardo didn't know what was happening, but the shock took over, and just for a minute, he didn't know what to do. Reza giggled. "What do we have down here?"

Reza's left hand held Ricardo's wrists tight above his head while his right hand was fumbling around between his legs.

It was over as quickly as it had started, Reza treating it all as a joke. During the next few days, Ricardo convinced himself it was an isolated incident and Reza hadn't meant any harm. Perhaps it was the sort of thing adult men did with each other? Ricardo didn't know because he didn't have a father to ask.

—

It happened again a week later, Reza initiating another wrestling match even though Ricardo didn't want to participate. This time, Reza went further, attempting to unbuckle Ricardo's belt and pull his trousers down.

Ricardo managed to break free and get away, but not before Reza's horrible fat hand had made it inside his trousers. A swift slap across the face shocked Reza enough to break his concentration, and Ricardo ran to his bedroom and locked the door.

He vomited into the wastebasket at the side of his bed. He was trembling with fear and confusion and didn't know what to do.

Reza had already warned him about disclosing their intimate wrestling games to Samira. Reza said his mother wouldn't believe him, that Reza would convince her that her son was a liar, and he'd have him evaluated and sent away. It was an adult's word against that of an eleven-year-old boy, and he wouldn't stand a chance.

"I know influential men in Tehran," Reza had said, "policemen and judges. It wouldn't be so tough to have you thrown in jail."

—

Ricardo lay awake in bed for weeks as the abuse escalated, culminating one day with Reza trying to join him in the shower. That was it: Ricardo had had enough, it had gone too far, and with all the strength he could muster, he pushed Reza out of the shower cubicle onto the floor.

"I won't do it," he screamed.

Reza stood up as a grin pulled across his face. "Well, young man, if you don't enjoy our little games, I'm sure your sister will."

Ricardo couldn't believe what Reza had said. "You don't mean that!"

"Oh, I mean it. If you won't give me a little fun, I'm sure Hannah will."

Ricardo was his sister's protector. He'd committed to that the day they had returned from Detroit. As long as he had breath in his body, he would never let any harm come to her, and he would do anything in his power to stop her from getting hurt. Anything.

Ricardo made a sickening pact that day, a pact with a sexual deviant. They sat down and discussed the situation like two adults; they debated the boundaries and the consequences if Ricardo didn't adhere to the terms and conditions. As Reza left the room, he stopped at the door and turned. "Boys or girls," he cackled, "it makes no difference to me."

—

As Samira returned from work and Reza left to spend a few days with his family, Ricardo told his mother he wasn't hungry and wouldn't eat with the family.

"You don't look too well," his mother said. "Perhaps you're coming down with a virus."

"Perhaps," he said. "I'm going to my room."

"Just a couple of hours of study tonight," Samira said. "Get some sleep, and you'll feel better in the morning."

Ricardo doubted he ever would.

—

Ricardo had never experienced feelings like this; he had withdrawn from social activities with his school friends, and he was becoming increasingly irritable and sometimes even aggressive.

Reza wasn't just abusing him; he was changing his character. He had not always been the boy who walked with his head down, his shoulders hunched as if carrying the world's weight. There was a time when he laughed easily, his eyes bright with curiosity and wonder, a thirst to learn. The world that once seemed full of possibilities was now a battleground, where each day was a struggle for survival.

—

He stood at the entrance of his bedroom, which he shared with Hannah. Once, it was a sanctuary where he could read what he wanted and let his imagination run wild. The walls were painted a vibrant sky blue, reminiscent of endless summer days. It was a room that breathed life, a reflection of the boy who had once lived in it—a boy full of hope and boundless energy.

But his world had darkened; the bright colors that had once made him feel safe now seemed out of place, mocking him with their cheerfulness. It was as if they no longer belonged to him but to someone he used to be, someone he could barely remember. He couldn't change the pact he'd made with Reza, but he could change the space where he spent so much time. He found several paint pots outside in the corner of the garage. It took him most of the day, but by nightfall, the main wall in his room was painted black, the wall opposite a deep, ugly blue, and the wall by the door was bright red. He painted the wall that looked onto the backyard a sickly slime-yellow and blacked out the windows with aluminum foil.

A few days later, he built an electronic music light system with four red, blue, yellow, and green lights in the corners of the room's ceiling. It was connected to a homemade stereo system he had built with old electronic parts.

The room became pitch black because that was how he felt about the world around him. In the dark room, he would play Pink Floyd tapes with the colorful lights flickering in time to the music.

The room was no longer his sanctuary; it was his hell. But one day, he would change it.

He wrote Churchill's words into his notebook: *When you are going through hell, keep going.*

He tore out the page and slipped it under his pillow.

—

It was his father's fault—none of this would have happened if he were still there. His father should be there to protect him, and his father should be there to protect Hannah, too. He had deserted them; he had locked them both in a prison cell, but they'd get out one day. Ricardo would make sure of that.

—

The Shah's regime was well known for its strict rule and repression of dissent, but voices were beginning to make themselves heard. The Shah oppressed the opposition parties, the activists, and the intellectuals; they faced imprisonment and torture meted out by the Shah's secret police.

Voices were also being heard from abroad: The religious leader Ayatollah Khomeini was living in exile. He had voiced his opposition to the Shah and called for an Islamic government. Reza said it would be a great day for Iran when the Ayatollah returned.

Ricardo had mixed feelings. He wasn't an admirer of the Shah, but he took the chants of "death to America" personally. His friends at school would participate in the chants, and he would feel completely isolated . . . again!

On the way home from school one day, a group of boys who knew his father was American approached him. They had menace in their eyes.

"You, American boy," the ringleader said, "we are going to teach you imperialists a lesson."

There were too many of them to fight. They were older and faster, there was nowhere to run, and he knew he was facing an inevitable beating.

He tried to appease them. "I'm not an imperialist. I was born in Iran; I'm a proud Tehran boy."

"You are a fucking Yankee; you're not welcome here." The ringleader took a step forward. "And when we see that bitch of a sister of yours, she will get the same."

Ricardo saw red and launched himself at the leader with a flurry of punches to his head and knocked him to the ground. But the odds were hopeless; within seconds, the mob was on him, and they punched and kicked him to the ground and continued kicking him as he covered his head with his hands.

When it was all over, Ricardo was writhing in pain on the ground. He had a fractured rib, a fractured cheekbone, two black eyes, a broken nose, and a cut in his head that he knew would need stitches. But the boys seemed satisfied with their five minutes of abuse against the American infidel.

Ricardo eased himself gingerly to his feet. He eyeballed the ringleader. "If anyone goes anywhere near my sister, I swear I'll come after every single one of you, and the beating you've just given me will seem like a walk in the park."

Ricardo felt a trickle of satisfaction as the blood drained from the face of the ringleader.

—

The street battles between the Shah's army and the revolutionary forces escalated. In January 1978, a peaceful demonstration at Tehran

University turned violent when security forces opened fire on the protesters, killing several students. If the Shah thought his actions would quell the protests, he got it spectacularly wrong, as it galvanized opposition to the regime and made it even stronger and more noisy. Mass demonstrations and further protests in different cities all over Iran occurred throughout 1978. The security forces continued to use live ammunition and tear gas, resulting in numerous deaths and injuries. Still, despite the crackdown, the protests grew in size and intensity and garnered attention worldwide. The scale of the brutality was televised live on foreign TV screens, increased scrutiny, and put pressure on the Shah's government.

The events of 1978 set the stage for the Iranian Revolution. Unrest and protests continued, and despite attempts to implement reforms, crackdowns, and even martial law, the Shah's regime began to crumble.

It was clear that the monarchy was on the verge of collapse.

—

The men of religion had gauged the people's feelings well, seized the moment, and called for Khomeini's return and the establishment of an Islamic Republic.

—

As Ricardo walked to school in the mornings, it was not uncommon to see the streets covered in blood and an occasional dead body from the previous evening's battles. He did his best to guide Hannah away from the worst of it.

He recalled that when he had been in America, some of the American boys had taunted him about Iran being a third-world country. But even those boys could not have imagined anything like this. Once again, even though it was the country where he had been born, the streets were no longer familiar to him; they were almost unrecognizable.

The Shah had brought in curfews and lockdowns, and the sound of machine guns filled the air almost every night. Samira sat with her children close to her as they cowered in the corner of the living room until the chaos passed.

—

Eventually, the Shah left the country, seeking medical treatment abroad, and a temporary government was set up. The people vowed he would never set foot on Iranian soil again, and for a time, there was jubilation on the streets and a temporary lull in the violence.

"Death to America" was a familiar chant in the streets and at school; one day, Ricardo and his fellow students were forced to walk over the American flag. It cut Ricardo to pieces; this was a symbol of his father, and even though his father had deserted the family, he still loved him and cherished America during the short time he had stayed there. The majority of Americans were good people, and the revolutionaries who were chanting "death to America" had never been there, never met an American, so how could they judge? What gave them the right to impose their beliefs on the students?

—

In time, Khomeini returned to Iran from France and took full control of the government. He established the Revolutionary Guards and a paramilitary group called the Basij. The Basij was created for young people who were not quite old enough to join the Revolutionary Guards. They were like the Hitler Youth Ricardo had read about in the WWII books.

The Revolutionary Guards carried out executions on the Shah's military commanders and people connected to the royal family.

It seemed to young Ricardo that the lessons of history were quickly forgotten. He'd read books on the Russian and French Revolutions and also what the Nazis did during the Holocaust, and here it was, happening all over again, on the streets of his city.

Night after night, as he closed his eyes, he hoped that he'd wake up in the days of prerevolution Iran. Even the Shah's regime had been better than this.

8

THE SPARK
IS IGNITED

Liberty, when it begins to take root, is a plant of rapid growth.
—George Washington

Soon after the revolution succeeded, Samira drove to Reza's house to collect a desk. As Ricardo walked into the backyard, he noticed Reza standing with his sons, loading some signs into the back of a truck.

"What are you doing?" Ricardo asked.

With a big beaming smile, Reza announced that his sons had joined the Basij.

It was a defining moment that horrified Ricardo because he hated everything the revolution stood for. In one of Khomeini's tapes, he had declared that the Holocaust was a lie invented by Zionists, and yet Ricardo had spoken to the people who had lived through it. They told stories about entire families who had been wiped out in concentration camps like Auschwitz and Dachau. Khomeini was evil; he was nothing more than the reincarnation of Adolf Hitler.

—

Life would only get worse as the Revolutionary Guards set up checkpoints throughout the city, manned mainly by the illiterate Basijis who couldn't read a single word. Some of them had never been to school. But they had uniforms, badges, and machine guns, so they had power and were not to be disobeyed.

At school, Ricardo and Hannah were forced to join in Islamic lessons and prayers even though they were not Muslims. More tensions followed with Reza's family, and one day at a checkpoint, one of Reza's sons was with the group who stopped Samira's car.

It was clear to Ricardo that Reza's son hated everything about his family; he even called into question Ricardo's name and said that very soon, he would need to change his name to a Muslim one. "I was talking with my father," he goaded. "He said your family would be converting to Islam very soon." He laughed. "I can choose your name for you; how about Mahdi or Mohamad? Anything is better than that stupid Mexican name."

Without thinking, Ricardo bit back. "I'd rather die than change my name."

Reza's son grinned. "I'm sure we can arrange that," he said.

Samira scolded him once they had driven away from the checkpoint. She said it was dangerous to speak out, and it was not his place to reply. The next time, at a checkpoint, she would do the talking, because she was afraid of the consequences if Ricardo opened his mouth again.

From that day, Ricardo became a very different person and found countless parallels between the supreme leader and Adolf Hitler: Both men preyed on the weak and the uneducated and force-fed their empty promises of glory.

—

The revolutionaries talked about the golden days of Islam and how wonderful it was as they conquered countries and occupied Spain for more
than six hundred years. They wanted to export the revolution around
the world and, in their words, "free the oppressed" and "one day, Islam
would rule the world."

But this was not how it was. His uncle Masood said that Islam was
forced on Iranians in the seventh century, so why on earth would they
want an Islamic government?

"Don't these people read history books?" Masood said.

—

After an initial period of slaughter and executions, the streets became a
little calmer, and some people tried to live their everyday lives. There was
talk of a referendum for the new government. Ricardo had done a lot of
reading and wondered if it would be like the US elections he had learned
about when he was in America. Surely a democratic election would put
an end to the dark days?

In time, he would be sorely disappointed, because there would be
only one form of government, and the vote was a simple yes or no for the
Islamic Republic. Because of the terror on the streets, most people had
no option but to vote yes and support Khomeini and the revolution. It
was not a democratic vote, as he knew it, but simply a vote to legitimize
what had already been decided.

—

After his mother married Reza, under the new Islamic law that allowed
him to have two wives, Ricardo fell into a depression. His world was
crumbling around him; he was still being abused, and his father had
deserted him. But what could he do?

In the darkness of his blackened room, his heart felt heavy with the weight of everything he had endured. The shadows surrounding him felt like they were closing in, suffocating the last remnants of the boy he used to be. The taunts, the cruel words, the blows, and the abuse by Reza had left their mark, carving deep scars into his soul. He had retreated into himself, hiding from a world that seemed bent on breaking him. Yet, somewhere deep within, buried beneath the layers of pain and fear, there was a flicker of something he hadn't felt in a long time.

It started as a whisper in his mind, a quiet voice that refused to be silenced. *Keep walking, keep walking, and fight.*

At first, he tried to ignore it. After all, hadn't the world taught him that he was powerless?

But the voice persisted, growing louder with each passing day. It reminded him of the stories he used to love, tales of the heroes he'd read about in Uncle Masood's bookshop. And Uncle Masood's words: *A real man must have the courage to stand firm in his beliefs.*

His pain was not a sign of weakness but a testament to his resilience. He had survived the worst Reza could throw at him and was still standing. If he could survive that, then what else was he capable of?

He had to fight; he would fight for his freedom and that of his little sister, and he would find a way out of hell. He'd fight Reza and his uneducated, revolutionary family.

—

He began planning as he lay awake in his darkened bedroom early one evening.

Sabotage—that's where it would start. Reza loved his cars, so he'd start there and practice sabotaging Reza's vehicles.

The following day, he returned to his uncle's bookstore and learned about mechanics, electronics, and how cars worked. He even learned how to make a Molotov cocktail, send and receive secret information, and create code books and messages, and he wrote everything down.

The French resistance fighters were his heroes now; he couldn't read enough about them. He read *The Resistance: The French Fight Against the Nazis* by Matthew Cobb and *A Train in Winter* by Caroline Moorehead. Her book focused on the role of women in the French Resistance and told the extraordinary story of 230 women who were arrested by the gestapo and deported to Auschwitz. The women fought for freedom, which was something they believed in.

The wise scribes and philosophers had said that revenge was wrong, but Ricardo didn't care. He would fight against Reza, and he would fight on the streets. First, he'd make Reza's life hell, drive him away from his family, and then take the fight onto the streets of Tehran.

9

TEHRAN'S UNWELCOME GUESTS

Uninvited guests are often most welcome when they leave.

—Aesop

Ricardo's conversations with his mother had changed. They talked about the history of Iran and its past and present politics. Even though Samira had never been a political person, she explained to Ricardo that she liked the freedom provided to women under the Shah.

Ricardo also noticed how Samira and Reza's relationship had changed and how their political opinions could not have been more different. They argued a lot. Samira said how repressive the new regime had become.

Ricardo took in every word of Samira and Reza's quarrels, trying his best to suppress a smile.

Like her older brother Masood, Samira was a free soul and critical thinker, not blindly devout.

Reza was utterly different. "What this country needs is a Muslim government without outside influences," he said, banging his fist on the table.

"Hah!" Samira smirked. "Do you think the Mullahs know anything about governing a country? Only a fool will buy into what they are selling. They tell you anything you want to hear about the afterlife, and since no one can come back to prove them wrong, you believe it."

"I'm no fool!"

"They are selling you a promise, Reza, and by the time you are ready to collect, you will be dead, so what's the point? The world is a wonderful place; life is wonderful. You have your family, and I have my family. We eat well and have fun. Why not enjoy what your so-called god has given us and forget about the afterlife?"

Reza was lost, and Samira's words were cutting and challenging to respond to.

She continued. "You do what you want, Reza. You bow down to the Mullahs and your god, but I'll concentrate on my family and what I can do for them now. Life is too precious to waste on your knees praying to something I can't see or hear."

They were a million miles apart when it came to intellect. Reza opened his mouth to counter, but Samira was leaving the room. Ricardo wondered how Samira had fallen for Reza in the first place.

—

The mandatory *hijab* and head covering were now firmly in place, enforced by the Morality Police, a division of the Revolutionary Guards. Music and any parties were outlawed and strictly enforced. Checkpoints monitored the people's movements day and night.

The Basij would raid houses for no reason, and even owning a dog was outlawed. If you were caught walking a dog on the streets, you would be arrested and the dog shot on the spot. They said a dog was a Western influence that had to be terminated. Ricardo couldn't quite understand the logic; he had read in a book in his uncle's store that evidence of domesticated dogs could be traced back to the Stone Age and were kept by early Neanderthals and early *Homo sapiens* as hunting companions and pets.

—

Ricardo sensed Samira was tired of Reza; they were opposites of each other, and she sat Ricardo and Hannah down one evening and made an announcement. "I'm considering returning to the United States. If I can register my marriage there, I can apply for a green card. I'm sick of this religious revolution, and this is no place to bring up a family. I've discussed it with Baback. I need to go to the US Embassy in Tehran, and I've already made an appointment."

"And Reza?" Ricardo asked.

Samira shook her head just once.

Ricardo was ecstatic. He could not wait to get back on a plane and leave the pain of Reza's abuse and the revolution behind him. He was thinking about school and how he would fit in much better with the older kids in high school. He couldn't wait to hear the new music he had missed since the revolution.

"We are going back to America," she said. "I'll walk over broken glass to get there, and I'll do anything I can to support our family."

—

Samira made an appointment at the US Embassy on November 4, 1979, to plead her case and get a visa to return to the United States.

Samira and the kids woke up early and had a small breakfast of tea, bread, and feta cheese. The taxi arrived soon after, and Samira ensured Hannah's hijab was in place. She had just turned ten; the hijabs were mandatory.

As they approached the US Embassy, it was more crowded than usual, and many people were walking with anti-American signs. Ricardo kept talking to Hannah to distract her from what was going on outside the car. Samira was getting very nervous about the traffic as her appointment time of 11 a.m. approached.

As the embassy building loomed into sight, the streets were filled with people shouting anti-American slogans.

"This isn't right," the taxi driver said. "Something is going on, something is happening; I can feel the tension out there."

Samira gasped; her face had turned white as she pointed. "Look!"

People were scaling the walls of the embassy. The giant American flag was on fire, and as the taxi driver stopped the car, they heard gunshots. He acted quickly and turned the car around. "We need to get out of here as fast as we can; it's not safe."

Samira was nodding in agreement, but it would only get worse.

The sound of gunfire was getting louder and happening more often as the taxi driver turned into a side street. A man ran across the road and then fell to the ground.

"He's been shot," the taxi driver screamed.

Ricardo reacted by throwing his sister full length onto the back seat and then lying on top of her. The streets were chaotic, with people running and shouting, trying to find a hiding place as the driver sped through the narrow streets.

It seemed like forever before they finally arrived home, and at last, Hannah stopped crying. He looked into his mother's eyes, and her face was etched with disappointment, tears rolling down her cheeks.

She had always been the rock, and it seemed nothing would ever get her down, but he saw a different side of his mother, a look he had never seen before.

The taxi driver apologized to Samira and refused to take her money. "I hope they sort this mess out and you get another appointment quickly; this is no place for children to live."

Ricardo opened the door, took Hannah's hand, and walked inside.

His mother put her arm around him. "You have no idea how proud I am of you, Ricardo; you were the only one in the car who did not panic and knew what to do."

He couldn't put his finger on it, but he had been calm, and strangely . . . he had almost enjoyed all of the drama. It was the first adrenaline rush that he could ever remember.

—

Reza came to the house soon after. He had a broad grin on his face and announced that militants supporting the Iranian Revolution had stormed the US Embassy in Tehran and taken dozens of hostages.

"Madness," Samira said. "This is just madness. We were there, and we barely got out in one piece."

Reza looked puzzled and asked what she was doing in that part of town.

"I had to do some shopping," she said quickly. "I just happened to be there."

"They want the Shah back," Reza said. "He needs to stand trial; we demand his extradition and his execution."

"You make demands on America," Samira said, "you and your Mullahs?"

"They will listen," Reza said. "The hostages, the barricades—the Americans will have no choice."

Ricardo studied Reza carefully, the excited beam that had pulled across his face, the genuine excitement that his country had given America a bloody nose. At that moment, despite his youthful years, Ricardo realized that the man who stood in front of him, the man who had forced his way into the family fold, was nothing more than a fool. His face was etched with lines of ignorance rather than wisdom; he believed in himself and was a beacon of enlightenment.

Ricardo knew where Reza had come from, and while he boasted loudly of his supposed expertise on matters far beyond the horizon of his small village, his knowledge was as barren as the fields he had once tilled. He believed he was the epitome of intellect and sophistication, yet he had the brain cells of a newborn piglet. Ricardo despised him, and judging by the look on his mother's face, she was slowly but surely beginning to drift in the same direction.

—

The American Embassy siege divided the country even more, as had the election, which was a sham. Various factions in Iran wanted to overthrow the government and fight for free democratic elections. Some even campaigned to have the Shah brought back and the royalty reinstated.

But while the men of religion were firmly in control of the government at present, Ricardo sensed that there were too many divisions within the country to bring any form of stability.

Still, Reza and Samira argued, and Reza tried to urge Samira and Hannah to "cover up" even when another male came into the house. Ricardo laughed; his mother would never bow down to that. She was pretty and happy to flaunt it.

"It preserves your honor and dignity," Reza ranted, "and it's a submission to Allah, a sign of respect."

Samira shook her head. "I'm submitting to nobody, and I do not believe in your Allah anyway."

"You bring dishonor to our families." He turned and pointed to Hannah. "She must cover up, too."

"It's not going to happen," Ricardo said, surprising himself at his outburst. He reached for Hannah's hand. "Come on, let's go out," he said.

"It's a beautiful sunny day; we don't have to listen to this nonsense. Let the sun give your face some color."

As Hannah stood and took her brother's hand, he glanced casually at Samira and knew that she stood side by side with her son.

10

A CONVENIENT ARRANGEMENT

The secret of a happy marriage remains a secret, but a loveless marriage is no mystery at all.

—Henny Youngman

Not even Reza would have believed that more than six months later, the American Embassy would still be under siege, with fifty-two American hostages held by Iranian students and militants. Anti-American propaganda filled the TV and the radio.

But Ricardo read between the lines. He could see through what they were trying to do: distract the people from inflation and the shortages that had taken hold of the country, the mess, and the chaos. America was to blame for everything, they said, since the United States had placed sanctions on Iran due to the Embassy siege. They were rationing rice, sugar, cooking oil, and fuel, and even the people with money could not find the essential items to buy on the black market. On hot summer days, they had to stand in line for up to six hours to buy sugar.

—

Reza's contempt for America and everything it stood for was evident as he gleefully described the events of April 24 and 25, 1980.

Samira sat at the table with Ricardo and Hannah.

"Hah! They sent in their Special Forces against a bunch of Tehran students, but they didn't even get there."

Samira stood with her hands on her hips. "So, what happened?"

Information was still sketchy, but Reza claimed to know everything. "They sent helicopters and flew into a sandstorm; one of the imperialist's helicopters turned back, and another got lost on the way." Reza laughed out loud. "There was a cargo plane waiting on the runway in the desert. The plane was going to take the hostages back to America once they were rescued, but one of the helicopters crashed into the cargo plane, and they both went up in flames."

Samira scowled at Reza's antics, hugging his eldest child as they danced joyfully around the room.

"This is God's will," he said, smiling. "He is watching over us, and not even America, with all its might, can stand in front of God. They might have weapons, but we have God on our side."

Ricardo saw the disgust in his mother's eyes and felt the tension between them.

A little later, there was an argument about money.

Samira did not attempt to lower her voice; Ricardo could hear her from his bedroom. He knew Reza's car dealership had closed within a few months of the revolution, and his mother told Reza exactly why.

"You are a fool," she said to him. "You had a good business selling cars from the West and at the same time backed a revolution against Western values and everything to do with America. They've closed cinemas and stopped all imports, your dealership can't get a hold of a wheelbarrow anymore, you've nothing to sell, and yet you backed the Imams and the Mullahs."

Reza protested, "Who was to know?"

"But you know everything, Reza; you claim to be a man of the world," she said sarcastically. "Don't you understand, before the revolution, you were a rich man, your business was booming, and now look at you, you are the turkey who has voted for Thanksgiving."

Reza frowned. "I don't understand."

"No, I didn't think you would."

Ricardo understood and thought his mother summed him up rather perfectly.

—

Ricardo watched the news reports on Iranian television, what was being described by State TV as "the hand of God that created the sandstorm to defeat the infidels." The TV reporters and commentators were no different than Reza in their unadulterated joy and celebration for the American operation that had gone so badly wrong. They showed the dead bodies of the American soldiers on TV, and it didn't sit comfortably with the teenager. It had only made the streets of Tehran and Iran more dangerous to live in. Couldn't they see that?

As Ricardo watched Reza proudly polish his Peugeot 504 through the living room window, he realized that he hated everything Reza and the religious revolution stood for.

He was tired of sitting back and doing nothing; he knew he had to take action. He had to wreak havoc, and he'd start right now.

—

The books on engines and car mechanics he'd read from Uncle Masood's shop had served him well. He started devising a plan to rebel against Reza and make himself feel better by doing something. He could not stand by and be a victim any longer.

As Reza slept that evening, Ricardo snuck out of the house in the darkness and replaced the steel plug in the bottom of the engine with a loose-fitting cork from a bottle.

—

Samira took the phone call around 10:00 the following morning, and while Ricardo buried his head in his latest book, he smiled, as it was obvious from the one-way conversation he could hear that the cork had dislodged from the engine of Reza's car as intended. The oil had run dry, and Reza's car had stopped.

Ricardo acted innocently as his mother explained. "His engine is ruined; he'll need a new one."

"What happened?" Ricardo asked.

"The plug in the bottom of the engine worked its way loose, and as Reza drove to work, every drop of oil ended up on the road. He didn't know; he kept driving until the engine blew up on the highway. He has no transportation now, so he won't come here until he can figure it out."

Ricardo couldn't have wished for a better result. It was his first sabotage, and it wouldn't be his last.

—

There was only one occasion where Ricardo felt genuine sadness for Reza's family, and that was when Reza's wife was killed in a car accident. However, his sympathy for Reza was soon lost when he announced to Samira that his three young children needed to be looked after, and he would be moving them into her house.

Ricardo knew from the outset that it was never going to work. Amir, his oldest son, was fifteen; Behrooz was thirteen; and his daughter, Maryam, was nine. The culture and political attitudes at even such a young age had been drilled into them at home and from the *minbar* as the Imams had delivered their *Khutbahs* during Friday prayers.

It was a million miles away from the values and views of Samira and her family. There were fights almost immediately, as Amir came home from the checkpoints and bragged about stopping music and parties and arresting helpless teens. He would laugh about how he would watch the boys and girls get flogged, and he aspired to the day when he would join the revolutionary guards so he could do the flogging himself. He would talk about how they had to carry a girl to an ambulance to get her to a hospital after the flogging and how he enjoyed watching her cry the whole time.

Amir tried to make Hannah wear long garments and cover up whenever he was around since they were not blood-related. Poor Hannah feared him, and when he threw a long black dress at her one day and demanded she wear it, a punch on the nose from Ricardo ensured he would never act that way again.

Reza was livid. Although his son was older and bigger than Ricardo, he had run crying to his father like a five-year-old child, and Reza's reaction was to be expected. He had cornered Ricardo in the kitchen and pushed him against the wall. "You ever lay a finger on my son again, and you'll regret it, I swear to Allah."

It had been the moment Ricardo had been waiting for, and the words tumbled from his mouth as if spoken by another. "Ah, Reza. Holier-than-thou Reza. The fine, upstanding man of Islam. I wonder what your son would think of you if he knew what you are doing to me; what would the Imams think?"

Reza's eyes opened wide, and his grip on Ricardo's collar tightened. "You . . ."

"And your god, Reza: *Fear Allah and know Allah is seeing what you do.* Isn't that what it says in your book?"

Reza was lost for words.

Ricardo reached for his wrist and pulled it from his collar. He edged closer and spoke in a hushed whisper. "You think you can break me, don't you, that your twisted games would be enough to tear me down? You don't know the fire that burns inside me, though. Everything you did left a mark, but not the kind you hoped for. You see, those marks—they hardened me, Reza. Whenever you tried to push me under, I fought my way back to the surface; you thought you could drown me in fear, but you only taught me how to breathe underwater. Do you think you can still hurt me after everything I've endured? You don't even know the meaning of pain. I've walked through hell and faced demons you can't even imagine. And you, you're just another shadow trying to darken my path, and I'm done with you." He edged a little closer to Reza. "So listen to me and listen well—it's over. You don't have any power over me. Your threats are empty now. I'm beyond them, beyond you. I'm done being your target, your victim. This ends today. You won't hurt me anymore because there's nothing left for you to hurt. I've faced more than you'll ever know, and I'm still standing. So take your cruelty, your anger, and find somewhere else to bury it because you've lost your hold on me. It's over, Reza; you come near me or my sister again, and I'll beat the living daylights out of Amir and Behrooz. I'll take them both at the same time, and if you want to join in, I'll take you on, too."

Reza stepped back, his mouth opened just slightly as if to speak, but no sound emerged. The words, thoughts, and emotions that had driven him this far all conspired against him, abandoning him at the final moment. His breath caught in his throat, and he swallowed hard. Ricardo brushed past him. "You may have wounded me, Reza, but I'm far from broken; no man on earth will ever break me." As he reached the threshold of the doorway, he turned. "And get your family out of this fucking house by the end of the week."

—

The arrangement lasted three months. Reza and his family were gone; however, what happened next was unimaginable in Ricardo's eyes.

Reza had found a new wife from his village of Khomeyn. She was seventeen years of age and couldn't read or write, but by paying her father a dowry, Reza had secured her hand in marriage. Under the terms and conditions of a verbal agreement, the young girl would become Reza's unpaid homemaker and, no doubt, sex slave. It was an arrangement that Ricardo was disgusted with, and he voiced his opinion to his mother in no uncertain terms.

"Doesn't it bother you?" he asked.

"Yes, the situation bothers me, but it doesn't worry me either."

"Aren't you jealous?" Ricardo asked.

"Jealous?" his mother questioned. "Of an illiterate village girl?"

"But she is seventeen."

Samira sighed and pointed to the kitchen table. "Sit down, Ricardo," she said. "There are a few things I think you should know. Life hasn't been easy for me since your father left, and there are certain things that a woman must do to protect her family. I had to have respectability, and I also needed to show that I had a husband. Reza gave me both of those things, and I thank him for that. But as you know, he has a village mentality. He has been brainwashed from an early age, and we cannot judge him too harshly. Sadly, we are from different worlds, and sometimes opposites attract, and sometimes those marriages work out."

Ricardo and his mother spoke for some time. Samira shared things that a mother wouldn't normally share with her young son, but she did. She talked about love and sex, economics and shame, and family values. "If it hadn't been for the family turmoil at the time, I would never have married Reza. He can take numerous wives under Islamic law, and I gave him permission and my full blessing."

As Samira stood, she beckoned young Ricardo forward and hugged him. "Never forget, my boy, who the real man of the house is. When your father decided to leave me, I knew you would step into his place.

I guess Reza was a convenience then, but we both know those days are gone, and he's at his house now. He's welcome to stay there as long as he wants."

Ricardo could feel his mother's pain. She had been a single parent in a society that did not accept the way she wanted to be. He understood the pain of relying on Reza because she had to have a man in her life to have peace from the gossip.

He would keep his dark secret from her.

She was dealing with enough in her life and did not need that burden.

11

THE CRUCIBLE
OF KNOWLEDGE

Talent hits a target no one else can hit; genius hits a target no one else can see.

—Arthur Schopenhauer

icardo was in his last year of high school. Over the previous year, he had worked hard on his schoolwork, skipping as many grades as possible and collecting credits to graduate early.

But school was tedious, as he had studied most of the material in his uncle's bookstore years earlier. In his final year in high school, he completed seventeen math classes despite some teachers claiming it was impossible.

He applied to Tehran University, but before he could attend, he had to pass the entrance exam, find people who would vouch for his character, and confirm that he was a good Muslim and didn't have anti-revolutionary tendencies.

The entrance exam was the easiest; the second hurdle was much more complicated but required under a new Islamic law.

The university's capacity was very low, and they would only take a limited number of students each year. Demand was high: around twenty thousand applicants for just four thousand places.

After the initial application, a background check was carried out; each student had to prove their revolutionary credentials.

Ricardo devised a plan. He started attending the local mosque and playing along with the nonsense the people there were peddling. He had one friend, Ali, from a progressive but deeply religious family. Ali's world was a world of conflicts between his beliefs and the government's actions. He was well educated, and his uncle was one of the ayatollahs who graduated from the Shiite seminary school in Qom, the center of the Shiite Muslim world.

Ricardo would call it the Eagle's Nest, Hitler's mountain retreat in the Bavarian Alps of Germany. Ali would tell Ricardo stories about how his uncle was trying to change the government from the inside and that this was not true Islam.

Ricardo spoke with Ali about needing a reference and asked if he would help. Ali was more than happy to help, but the problem was that Ricardo was not a Muslim.

"Yes, but I want to be. I am a regular at the mosque."

"You'll need to learn the Quran."

"I've read the Quran."

"You have?"

"Yes."

He wanted to say he'd read the Bible and the Torah, too, and completely understood the teachings, but decided against it.

Ali offered to introduce him to his uncle to help Ricardo learn more about Islam. It was exactly the break that Ricardo was looking for, and he started the pretense of working with the ayatollah. He would ask profound questions, and the ayatollah would happily answer them while Ricardo would pretend to accept the answers at face value. Ali and the ayatollah were impressed with his dedication to Islam, and they both agreed to be references for him as long as he continued his learning and converted at some point in the future.

—

The five-hour exam covered all subjects, including math, science, and religion. As he finished, the adjudicator informed the students that the results would be published in the newspapers in a month.

Ricardo was quietly confident; he knew he had done well, and on the day in question, he waited patiently at the store for the newspaper truck to arrive.

There were more than three thousand names—the students listed according to their marks—and he ran his finger to the first page of eleven, which settled on number 1, a boy named Amir Hossein.

To his absolute astonishment, his name was second on the list, the second-highest recorded mark among more than three thousand students.

He was ecstatic and ran all the way home to tell his mother.

As he burst through the kitchen door, he could not contain himself. "I had the second-highest marks in the whole school," he said with a smile as wide as a river.

"Congratulations," Samira said as she looked at him. "That's good . . . but why were you not number one?"

12

ALLIANCES IN
THE FIRE

A common danger unites even the bitterest enemies.
—Aristotle

Ricardo met some boys on the street handing out anti-government flyers. They called for a democratically elected secular government, which appealed to him. Before he approached them, he noticed they had various lookouts on the corner of the streets, watching for the Revolutionary Guards and the plain-clothed Basij.

Ricardo couldn't believe how stupid the guards were as he studied the streets, because they stood out like sore thumbs. They wore loose-fitting dress shirts that were buttoned to the top, untucked, and usually khaki-colored pants. They had short haircuts, and most had long beards. As soon as they ventured too close, the lookouts would simply shout "Run," because if these young men were caught handing out anti-government literature, they would be arrested, beaten, and tortured. There was a chance they'd even be executed.

It was a dangerous occupation, and Ricardo respected them as he approached the boys. They were two or three years older than Ricardo, and they chatted for a few minutes before one of the lookouts screamed, "Run!"

The boys threw their leaflets to the ground and sprinted in all directions. Ricardo had no choice but to run too as several members of the Basij ran across the street.

He ran fast, occasionally turning around to see where they were, and darted through the streets and alleys he knew so well.

One of the Basij guards got within a few yards of him at a point, but Ricardo found that his legs propelled him even faster. It was another adrenaline rush, and as it coursed through his veins, he wanted more of it; he loved how it made him feel.

By the time he shook off the last guard, he was out of breath but euphoric—he was alive again.

A few minutes later, two of the other boys from the street arrived in the same alley. They all hid behind a rubbish bin. They spoke in hushed voices, still wary that the Basij were in the vicinity.

"We need to do more," Ricardo said. "We need to do more than hand out leaflets; we need action."

The oldest of the boys looked at him suspiciously. "And who are you telling us how to run our organization?"

Ricardo shrugged. "I'm telling you that we need to do more than hand out pieces of paper. If the Basiji find us, they will beat us to a pulp and throw us in prison, and you believe pieces of paper will defeat them?"

The other boy spoke. "Who is this child who speaks to us like this?"

"I'm no child," Ricardo said. "I'm happy to be part of your group, but only if we step up this campaign."

"You mean terrorism?"

Ricardo stole the quote he'd read from one of his uncle's books. "*One man's terrorist is another man's freedom fighter*, and yes, I believe in freedom for Iran, freedom for my family and our people from these religious zealots who know nothing. The government leaders and their followers are brainwashed; they are led like sheep. They preach simplicity and religious devotion while taking over the best hotels in the city. The bastards live a life of luxury, and it's their fault that we are now the pariah of the world. The sanctions are killing us, and we cannot find basic life necessities."

"Wow!" one of the boys said. "Some fucking speech."

Ricardo continued.

"They have divided the country, and if we all thought the Shah was bad news, then this lot is one hundred times worse. Look around you: The morality police are taking freedom away from our sisters, forcing them to cover their femininity, and we can't play music or dance anymore. This cannot continue, and I will do my very best to oppose it, but I won't oppose it by waving sheets of paper in the air."

—

The boys invited Ricardo to a meeting, and he was asked to address the group of about thirty young men, women, and students. He told them to build alliances with other groups, like the MEK and the Fedayeen. The MEK was a traditional Islamist, Marxist organization that emerged in the 1960s as a militant opposition group against the regime of the Shah of Iran. Following the revolution, tensions were high between the MEK and the new Islamic government because the MEK had opposed the establishment of an Islamic state under the leadership of clerics.

Ricardo was on fire with excitement. He had finally found his people. Most of them were much older than Ricardo and felt betrayed by the current government; the revolution had been hijacked and stolen from them. They wanted freedom in the way the Western countries had freedom, not to be transported back to the sixth century.

Ricardo had been rehearsing this in his head for a long time. This was his moment and a chance to lead.

One of the boys objected. "But the MEK are Marxist religious zealots, and the Fedayeen are communists."

Ricardo corrected him. "Not religious zealots—they just subscribe to religion, and it's a doorway we need to walk through because now we all have a common enemy. The MEK got their hands on a lot of weapons during the revolution, and we have nothing. How can we be expected to fight against a heavily armed government when we don't possess as much as a peashooter?"

The group listened, impressed with what the young boy had to say.

"They want nothing more than to control us," Ricardo said. "They stop our sisters in the street, and if we want to listen to Michael Jackson, we have to arrange an illicit meeting with a dealer in the same way we would buy drugs." He took a deep breath and cast his gaze around the room. "They have outlawed parties and imposed curfews. We might as well be under martial law. This is no way to live."

Ricardo paused, the weight of his words hanging in the air like a charged storm. He scanned the faces around him, searching for any sign of doubt or hesitation. But all he saw in their eyes was the fire he had lit, the same fire that had been smoldering in him for years.

"Enough is enough," he continued. "We are the generation that will take back what was stolen from us, but we need to unite."

He allowed his words to sink in, and then, with a final, unwavering glance, Ricardo said, "This is our time. We either take it or let them take everything from us."

As he stepped back, he heard the murmur of voices and saw the quiet nods of agreement, the spark of a shared resolve.

"The revolution has been hijacked once," he said. "If we stick together and fight, we can take it back from them."

Suddenly, the crowd was on their feet applauding him; there were even a few cheers. A stranger stepped forward and embraced him. Ricardo had found his people, but more importantly, they had found their leader.

13

BAHAR

Love is composed of a single soul inhabiting two bodies.

—Aristotle

He tried to shake himself from the strange trance. What was this? He wasn't the type to lose himself over a stranger. Love at first sight wasn't real, at least not for him. Yet he stood, heart pounding, his mind racing with questions. Who was she? Where did she come from?

It was a moment that could have been fleeting and insignificant—a simple glance between strangers, but when her eyes found his, something deep and wordless passed between them. He could almost feel it, an invisible thread of connection, fragile yet undeniable.

Her name was Bahar. She seemed almost surreal in her beauty, like a vision from a dream he desperately didn't want to end. Her hair was jet black and flowed down to the small of her back, each strand shimmering under the sun. Her eyes were deep and dark; they held a mesmerizing depth as if they contained ancient Persian secrets. Her skin was strikingly pale against her dark features, giving her an almost luminous quality. She moved with an utterly effortless grace as if she were gliding rather than walking. Her slender figure was poised, blending delicacy with an underlying strength. To Ricardo, she was perfection personified, and he found himself captivated.

There was an intensity about her, a fire within that seemed eager to break free. Ricardo could feel this fiery spirit whenever he caught her gaze or saw her passionate expressions—it drew him in, an unspoken energy between them. He wanted to learn more about this girl and understand the force behind her serene exterior and the story her eyes longed to tell.

—

He had noticed her at several meetings and had plucked up the courage to speak to her. When their paths collided that afternoon, it was as if something electric had come between them. It started with a simple glance, a fleeting moment where their eyes met, and the world around them faded into insignificance.

From that moment on, their hearts beat as one as they stole moments of intimacy on the rooftops of Tehran, hidden away from prying eyes. Their love was a secret, known only to the stars that watched over them in the stillness of the night. They were two souls bound by the threads of a desire for change.

They spent time together, secretly carving out their hidden sanctuary amid the chaos of their daily lives. They would meet under the cloak of dusk in the shadowed corners of the city and share dreams of a future free from the shackles that bound them.

Every stolen moment was a breath of fresh air in a suffocating world, and he felt a profound peace enveloping him whenever he was by her side.

Ricardo found love and resolute strength to face whatever lay ahead. He was overwhelmed by the enormity of their cause and the risks they faced. But with gentle words and a reassuring touch, she reminded him of the importance of their fight for justice. Together, they plotted courses of action, her strategic mind complementing his passionate resolve. Her emotional and practical support gave Ricardo the courage and clarity to continue their clandestine resistance.

—

As their bond deepened, she learned of Ricardo's dark secret.

His voice breaking slightly, he turned to her and said, "Bahar, there's something about my childhood, about Reza. . . . I've never told anyone this before. When I was a kid, Reza . . . he had a much darker side."

She reached for his hand.

"I was powerless and alone and didn't speak out because I had to protect Hannah."

At first, Ricardo was lost for words; Bahar's grip on his hand tightened. "Tell me; rid yourself of this burden."

"He . . . he . . . he abused me, he touched me, made me undress, and . . . there was more. He did things to me, Bahar, disgusting things, and said that if I refused or told anyone then he would replace me with Hannah."

Bahar's hand covered her mouth. She touched his shoulder softly. "I can't imagine how hard it must have been to carry this alone."

"I just wanted you to know, Bahar. He hurt me, but he didn't break me. I didn't tell you this earlier because I did not want you to think I am broken; I am not. It's strange, but talking about it now, it feels like I can finally breathe a little easier. I never really accepted him as part of our family to begin with; there was always something very unsettling about him. Hannah hates him, too, and I found it hard to reconcile how a man who prays three times a day can have such a dark side."

Bahar spoke and kissed him on the lips. "I'm glad you feel you can share this with me. I cannot imagine how difficult that was for you. You are not broken; I know that."

He looked up. "I don't know what I did to deserve someone like you, Bahar."

"I love you, Ricardo, and that is all that matters. Together, we can overcome anything . . . even this."

—

Her presence became a refuge for his tormented soul. She offered an unwavering ear as he shared his harrowing past experiences. Her understanding and acceptance gave him a safe haven to express his deepest fears. Through her compassion, she helped him begin the challenging process of healing. As they shared secret whispers, Ricardo gradually started to release the shadows of his past; he told her how he had confronted Reza and threatened to beat his two sons. "He's a man of religion; I quoted from the Quran and told him, *Fear Allah and know that Allah is seeing what you do*."

"I bet that worried him."

"He's never bothered me since."

—

Ricardo went everywhere with Bahar, and when she mentioned a secret teenage get-together one evening, Ricardo didn't hesitate to agree. "I'll bring Hannah, she's dying to meet you."

"I can't wait," Bahar said.

It was a tame party—nothing more than a dozen young people playing a little music. The atmosphere was pleasant, and Ricardo loved every second he spent with his sister and Bahar.

But the party was about to end abruptly.

There was an explosion of noise outside; the front door was kicked in as the morality police stormed into the house, batons drawn, hitting people and pouncing on the teenagers as they handcuffed every single one of them and announced they were under arrest.

The leader, a young man in his mid-twenties, stood in the center of the room and announced, "This is an illegal mixed-gender gathering, restricted under Islamic law. The dress code in line with Islamic regulations has also been violated, and the music has corrupted everyone here, contravening public decency. You are all under arrest in the name of the Ayatollah Khomeini."

Ricardo shook his head in disbelief.

—

Within a few hours, the teenagers were in front of the Mullah for sentencing. Ricardo was mightily relieved when the Mullah delivered a strict moral lecture to his young sister but told her she was free to go. "Don't let me ever see you here again."

Hannah stood in the dock, shaking her head as the tears ran down her face.

Ricardo and Bahar were next. They faced the stern figure of the Mullah, seated on a raised platform. His traditional garb, a flowing robe, and a white turban emphasized his authority.

Bahar, her nerves visible, glanced at Ricardo before addressing the Mullah, her voice shaky but audible. "Honorable sir, we meant no disrespect. It was just a gathering of friends, nothing more. Please understand, we didn't think it would upset anyone."

Ricardo squared his shoulders and met the Mullah's eyes steadily. "We were there to socialize, nothing illicit. It was simply a celebration of friendship."

The Mullah stood and leaned over his platform. "You are both old enough to understand our laws; they must be respected. Gatherings like that have been outlawed; they go completely against the will of God and Islam, of decency, self-respect, and morality."

"But, sir," Ricardo begged, "might there be leniency? Perhaps we could make amends that contribute positively to Islamic ways. We are ready to demonstrate our respect for our traditions."

The Mullah spoke. "Your plea for leniency is heard, but the moral Islamic fabric must be upheld. Chief Justice Ayatollah Mohammed Beheshti has been consulted, and you will each receive fifty lashes. This punishment will remind you of the boundaries you must not cross."

"But, sir," Ricardo cried out.

"Take them away."

—

Ricardo's wrists were bound tightly, the rough rope digging into his skin as two officers gripped his arms and dragged him toward the center of the courtyard. His mind was numb with the certainty of it: There was no escape.

His crime? He had been caught at a party—an innocent gathering of friends. It seemed impossible that something so ordinary could lead to this, but in this place, under the cold gaze of the religious madmen, ordinary things were dangerous.

The officer stood a few feet away, uncoiling the whip slowly, methodically, as if savoring the tension. The leather was dark and heavy, its end frayed from countless punishments before this one. Ricardo braced himself for the impact he knew would come. He had heard stories: the whip-cracking sound and the way it felt like fire lacing across your back.

But none of those stories prepared him for what was about to come.

The first lash came without warning, a sharp crack and then the pain. It was immediate, searing through him like a flame ignited across his back. His body jerked forward instinctively, his muscles contracting as he tried not to scream. But the pain was relentless, traveling through his skin and into his bones, setting fire to every nerve it touched. Another crack, then another. The air tore from his lungs in short, ragged bursts, and his vision blurred. With another crack, he could feel the warmth of blood rising to the surface, seeping through the fresh welts that had begun to form.

The pain became a rhythm, a terrible, inescapable beat that pounded through his body with each strike. Those first few seconds turned into endless, agonizing minutes. Each lash was worse than the one before, each crack of the whip another wave of agony that sent him spiraling deeper into darkness, and no matter how much he wanted to, he couldn't pass out. His body refused him that mercy.

On the final lash, he wasn't sure if he was still standing or being held up entirely by the guards. His legs trembled violently, threatening to give way beneath him, but the ropes around his wrists kept him in place. The ground beneath him was slick with blood, a dark stain spreading across the cracked stone.

At last, it was over. The whip fell silent, the courtyard settling into an eerie stillness.

As the officers untied him and let him fall to the ground, the world around him blurred, distant voices faded into the background, and all he could think of was Bahar's turn. Next, she was about to suffer the same torture and humiliation. Despite the pain, if he could have, he would have taken every one of her fifty lashes himself.

—

But amid the darkness, there was resilience and a thirst for revenge. As they told him he was free to go, he looked into the eyes of the morality police and studied their faces. An unwavering desire to hurt them coursed through every fiber of his body. The morality police and the Mullahs had crossed a line. Ricardo was up for the fight; life would never be the same again.

—

As he recovered from the brutal punishment, his thoughts sharpened toward exacting revenge; the pain that still lingered was a reminder of the pain and humiliation he and Bahar had faced.

As he lay beside her under the stars, on the rooftop, his mind mapped out plans for retribution to weaken the foundations of the government and the morality police's authority. He'd never forget their faces.

Together, they made their plans, hatched schemes, and plotted late into the night.

—

Only days later, Ricardo addressed the meeting. "We must attack the morality police and the Revolutionary Guards with everything we have," he told the assembled group.

"What can we do?" asked one of the boys. "We have no weapons."

"We must use what we can get our hands on," he said. "I vowed that I would make them pay, and that's exactly what will happen; we are going to rid our city of these maggots."

Ricardo's plan was simple: He would offer himself up as bait and lead them into a trap. One of his friends had a 600cc motorcycle, which had been made illegal in post-revolution Iran. It was simple enough to borrow his friend's bike, hidden and covered with a tarp in a garage nearby. "I will drive to the nearest checkpoint, and they will follow me. There's no doubt about it," he said. "I will lead them into a trap where you will be waiting. You guys"—he pointed at half a dozen of his comrades—"will hit them with everything we've got."

—

Despite the risk, Ricardo was ready to execute the operation. A few days later, he climbed on the motorcycle, his face covered with a scarf, and roared out of the shadows.

Ricardo couldn't believe the stupidity of the Revolutionary Guards in the two Toyota Land Cruisers who took the bait and sped after him. The streets were narrow, and he was always a few seconds ahead of the Land Cruisers, but it didn't stop them from shooting at him. As arranged, he roared into a side street in the city's heart, and the guards followed directly behind.

He drove his motorcycle toward the stairwell, pulled up the front wheel, and roared up the stairs, along a small passage, and down the stairs on the other side. The guards in the Land Cruisers stopped, realizing there was nowhere to go, and as they started to reverse out of the street, the second part of the plan came into effect as Molotov cocktails, bricks, and glass bottles rained down on top of them.

While the first few bombs exploded harmlessly on the street, one of them scored a direct hit on the first Land Cruiser, right in the middle of the front windshield. The flames lit up the night sky as the doors opened, and the Revolutionary Guards scattered in all directions, weapons drawn and shooting aimlessly at the rooftops. Still, the bricks and petrol bombs rained down onto the street. One of the guards was now in flames, his colleagues desperately trying to put the fire out, and they retreated hastily as they poured into the second Land Cruiser. The Revolutionary Guards didn't know how many people were on top of the roofs and didn't hang around to find out. Instead, they scurried away like rats as cheers and flames filled the night air.

—

The following evening, the team of freedom fighters met secretly and, encouraged by their success, decided to do it all over again. Ricardo would wait for the cover of darkness and for Samira to retire to her room. When he was sure she was sleeping, he would sneak out of the house and assemble his team. He would plot a different route and select a different street, and the team would take up their positions, armed with as many Molotov cocktails as they could carry.

It would be a routine that Ricardo would repeat four or five times a week, each time getting more skilled on the motorcycle with an inevitable confidence of indestructibility.

—

He was on a mission, determined that his actions could one day overthrow the government and bring Tehran back to the type of city he once loved. During an MEK meeting one evening at the safe house in the city, he heard some of the older, more experienced members talking about making a bomb and told them in no uncertain terms that he wanted to be involved.

14

CONSEQUENCES
AND REFLECTIONS

Sooner or later everyone sits down to a banquet of consequences.
—Robert Louis Stevenson

B y now, Ricardo had a reputation as a fearless street warrior. The guards had named him the Shadow Rider of Tehran. Despite his youthful appearance, he was highly respected, as he had caused chaos on the streets for many months.

Dozens of Toyota Land Cruisers had been destroyed, several Revolutionary Guards killed, and more than twenty hospitalized.

Fueled by a burning desire for revenge and justice, Ricardo's resolve only hardened in the days following their successes. The lashes they received were not just marks on their bodies but emblazoned on his spirit, each scar a call to action. The attacks on the morality police were good, but he wanted something bigger—something that would make a mark at every level of the government.

As he plotted his next moves, his thoughts turned toward a bold, audacious plan—an intelligence-gathering mission targeting the headquarters of the Islamic Republican Party, the nerve center of the very apparatus that had inflicted their suffering. He knew that senior members of the ruling party had their meetings there every month; the next one was at the end of June.

It was 1981.

—

Precise, accurate information was essential, more powerful than any weapon in their arsenal of resistance.

He began meticulously planning the infiltration; the success of such a mission could significantly impact their fight against the regime. This was now not just about personal vengeance; it was about striking a blow that could loosen the government's grip on the people.

He spent countless nights poring over maps, gathering intelligence from sympathetic insiders, and crafting a network of informants that provided real-time data from within the party's stronghold.

He infiltrated the building and bribed and hoodwinked surveillance people for information. Bahar was with him, refining his tactics and ensuring that every angle was considered and every risk assessed.

—

Ricardo laid out the intelligence before the MEK leader as he spread the maps, documents, and photos across the dimly lit table. The leader leaned forward, a mixture of surprise and admiration.

"Ricardo, this is impressive," he said. "How did you manage it?"

"I had help, and we knew where to look. It was risky, but it paid off."

The leader looked directly at Ricardo, his expression turning serious. "This is unbelievable; we have enough information to hit them where it hurts them the most. We could cripple their operations significantly."

Ricardo knew the stakes were high and the risks even higher. "It's a big decision," he said, "but I say we can get in. I say we should bomb the shit out of the head of the snake. Ayatollah Mohammed Beheshti is the one responsible for what happened to me and Bahar. He's why we're in this fight; it's personal to us."

The leader nodded. "I know how you feel, Ricardo, but this is more than personal. We can strike at the very heart of the government."

—

They planned and plotted for six weeks leading up to the attack. The operation was clouded in secrecy, and the primary target, Beheshti, was followed, his movements tracked daily. He was protected well, his body-guards never far away, and yet, on several occasions, Ricardo was able to slip inside the headquarters of the Islamic Republican Party and take more detailed notes and photographs.

Ricardo was told to stand down as darkness fell over the city on June 28. The bomb was in place; carnage would surely follow.

—

The explosion devastated the IRP headquarters, and the television news channels speculated about a suicide bombing carried out by individuals opposed to the regime and, unsurprisingly, blamed America.

The bomb caused widespread destruction and massive loss of life. Ricardo and Bahar watched on television as it was announced that Chief Justice Ayatollah Mohammed Beheshti had been killed.

There were no joyous celebrations or cries of glee; they both knew they had crossed a line. They held hands, hands that were now stained with the blood of many men.

Several other high-ranking officials of the Islamic Republican Party and government officials were also killed in the attack; the total number of casualties was substantial.

The MEK, Ricardo, and his team had struck a devastating blow to the government. Ricardo dared to believe that by taking out the head of the snake, a coup d'état would surely follow, and the government would be no more.

—

It was not to be; the Iranian government launched an extensive investigation to identify and apprehend the perpetrators, increased security, and cracked down on the opposition groups. On the same evening of the bombing, Revolutionary Guards were on the street rounding up suspects, and a dozen executions were carried out in Tehran's Evin Prison alone. Anybody connected to opposition groups was picked up, doors were kicked down, and arrests were made. Many were never seen again.

In a sickening twist of cruelty, the family of those who were executed were contacted and asked to pay exorbitant prices for the bullets that had killed their loved ones. Only when the execution account had been settled were they allowed to collect the corpses for burial.

Ricardo felt a reinforced commitment to the fight and reflected on the ramifications of the bombing. He couldn't help but draw parallels to Operation Valkyrie, the famous assassination attempt against Hitler during World War II. Like the German officers who plotted against the Nazi regime, Ricardo and his group had stepped into the realm of high-risk, high-stakes resistance, where the objective was to cripple a powerful and authoritative leadership structure. Much like Operation Valkyrie, their efforts were driven by a desperate necessity to restore freedom and dismantle a regime that thrived on oppression and fear.

—

The bombing marked a turning point in his teenage years, and he fully embraced his leadership role within the resistance movement. The successful execution of such a high-stakes operation significantly elevated his status and credibility among his peers. He rallied more support and resources for their cause, galvanizing a once-wavering faction into a more cohesive and determined force.

Because of his relationship with Ali and his ayatollah uncle, he didn't draw any attention to himself.

He had perfected the hoax well and still pretended to study the Quran. At university, Ricardo ensured he was the perfect student and never participated in political discussions. Instead, he had his head down and kept his nose clean, staying clear of anything that resembled Westernization. He also always wore loose-fitting clothing.

They were tough times; some of his friends were taken away and imprisoned, and some were even executed, but Ricardo was very philosophical because he knew that he was fighting a war, and just like in World War II, there would be casualties.

—

Ricardo was more determined than ever to bring down the government. It was his destiny. He was in hell—the hell of his own country, the hell at the hands of his countrymen—but like Churchill had said, when in hell, keep going until you get out of there.

—

Ricardo and Bahar's rendezvous on the rooftops of Tehran took on a more profound, more poignant significance. The meetings became their sanctuary. Seated under the vast night sky, they talked for hours about a vision of Iran, a nation thriving with freedom and openness.

In their private moments, their affection was expressed in whispers, tender touches, gentle kisses, and a language of love that needed no words. Ricardo felt a kind of completeness when he was with Bahar; her presence made the outside world momentarily fade away.

They sat together, the city lights a distant shimmer below their rooftop sanctuary. Ricardo took a deep breath. "Listen, Bahar," he said, his hand finding hers in the dim light. "The more I think about everything, about us, the more I realize we might need an escape plan."

Bahar turned to look at him. "Escape plan?"

"Yes, if things get too dangerous, too unbearable here, I want us to leave, to go somewhere we can be truly free. We could live without looking over our shoulders, express ourselves without fear . . . wear what we want, listen to whatever music drives our soul."

"It sounds like a dream," Bahar whispered, "but to leave everything behind. . . . Do you think we could do it?"

Ricardo squeezed her hand. "I know it's a lot to ask. It's not just about surviving out there; it's about living. I promise I'll do everything to make it happen if it ever comes to that. But only if you're with me."

She nodded. "With you, yes. If it means a chance at freedom, at a life where we can be ourselves," she said, "I'll go anywhere with you, anywhere at all."

15

A SECOND FRONT OPENS UP

If you chase two rabbits, you will lose them both.

—Russian proverb

In September 1981, as Ricardo was walking home from school, he heard the unmistakable sound of aircraft engines in the sky. As he looked up, to his horror, half a dozen military planes were releasing bombs into the early evening sky. His only thought was for the safety of his mother, sister, and Bahar, and he ran home as quickly as his legs would carry him. Bahar's house was just a few houses down from his.

When he got home, Samira was glued to the television news as a reporter gave details that everyday life in Iran had been brought to an almost impossible point. The neighboring country, led by Saddam Hussein, had launched a full-scale invasion.

Iraq had been involved in border skirmishes for three days, and the Iranian government hadn't even noticed. There had been minor border disputes between Iran and Iraq for many years, especially over the Shatt al-Arab waterway, which served as the border between the two countries, but the Iranian government had been caught with its pants down and totally missed the escalations on the border.

Masood had said the Iraqi president was trying to dominate power in the Persian Gulf and wasn't happy with Iran under the leadership of Khomeini. He saw it as a threat to Iraq, as Khomeini had mentioned in many broadcasts that Iraq should also have an Islamic government. Masood had said quite prophetically that Hussein was frightened Iran would export its revolution to Iraq. Masood said that, despite the Iranian government broadcasting and boasting of a position of strength and unity, Iran was weak, and it was only a matter of time before Hussein threw down the gauntlet.

Uncle Masood was the wisest man Ricardo had ever met, and Iran, as Masood had forecast, was now at war with Iraq.

—

The government of Iran was ill-prepared for war, and during the early days of the revolution, they executed hundreds of Army officers they had seen as loyal to the Shah. Thousands of soldiers had deserted or laid down their weapons, the military was in disarray, and Saddam had seized the moment.

The first bombing raids were over Tehran's Mehrabad Airport, which was close to Aunt Sudabeh's house. After getting home and ensuring that Samira and Hannah were OK, Ricardo tried calling his aunt, but the line was down. He decided to take his mom's car to go and check on her. At that age, he did not have a driver's permit, nor had he ever driven a car alone, but a mere detail like that wouldn't stop him.

He took the keys and started the ignition. He had a bit of trouble with the gears, but having watched many people synchronize the accelerator and the clutch, he got the hang of it quite quickly.

The streets were relatively clear of traffic—the checkpoint guards were no longer there—and he quickly reached his aunt's house. His heart sank as he noticed the commotion and so many injured people being carried into cars and ambulances from nearby houses. As he got a little closer, he realized his aunt's house was intact; it was an apartment building nearby that had been hit. He exited the car and banged on his Aunt Sudabeh's door. When she opened it, he fell into her arms and said he was so glad that she was alive.

"Where is Sara?" he asked.

Sudabeh explained that her five-year-old daughter had been hiding under the bed.

Ricardo walked into the apartment on a carpet of glass. Every window in the house had been blown in, and it looked like a tornado had powered through the house. His aunt was shaken, and there was no electricity.

As he spoke to his aunt, he could still hear the sounds of explosions nearby. He told her they would have to leave and go to Masood's house. He crawled under the bed, persuaded Sarah to get out, and tried his best to calm her down. They were all in the car, driving toward Masood's house within a few minutes.

Sudabeh looked at Ricardo, confused. "When did you learn to drive?" she asked.

"Thirty minutes ago," he replied.

Sudabeh and Ricardo had a special bond. She had been there for him since birth, and he often visited her for in-depth conversations. She always sensed that there was something deep and dark in Ricardo's life that he was not telling her, but she figured he would talk about it when he was ready.

As they pulled outside Masood's house, his uncle was already at the door. He was amazed when he saw Ricardo, because he had planned to go to Sudabeh's house, too. "You've beaten me to it," he said. He looked at the car. "When did you learn to drive?"

"Forty minutes ago," Ricardo replied.

—

The bombing raids continued; it was clear the Iranian government had been surprised. It beggared belief, Ricardo thought; how could the people be so stupid as to trust a government that was so incompetent?

During the bombing raids at night, the power went out immediately, so the planes had difficulty finding the city in the darkness.

Samira, Hannah, and Ricardo would hide in the basement.

In the dim light of their basement, as the distant wail of the air raid sirens faded, Ricardo sat close to his mother and sister amid the clutter of stored household items and the awful smell of diesel fuel. Ricardo glanced nervously at the large diesel tank adjacent to the boiler. He turned to his mother, his voice tinged with concern. "Not the safest place in the world, Mom," he said, eyeing the tank warily.

Samira, who had been folding a blanket, paused and looked around, her gaze settling on the tank. "You're right, Ricardo. I hadn't thought about the tank in all this chaos." She stood. "Let's get the hell out of here."

—

As the raids became routine terror, the numbing familiarity bred a strange boldness among Tehran's citizens, including Samira and her children. They took to venturing outside, joining their neighbors each time the sirens went off, and looked up into the night skies.

"It's almost like a show to us now," he remarked. "Gathering in the streets, watching the antiaircraft guns firing into the night. It's surreal, but it is better than hiding in the basement with a diesel tank for company."

"It's how people cope, Ricardo," his mother said, "finding a bit of control or normalcy amid this chaos. We look up because it's better than feeling helpless in the basement."

"I guess you're right," he conceded softly. "It's just strange how quickly we adapt."

"Yes, it is," she agreed, pulling him into a reassuring hug. "But we'll keep adapting together, no matter what life throws at us."

Their conversation drifted off as they listened to the distant thumps of antiaircraft guns, a grim soundtrack to their resilience.

16
BREAKING POINT

*Torture produces more misleading information
than actionable intelligence.*

—John McCain

Tehran was in chaos, with almost daily and nightly air raids by the Iraqi Air Force. However, this did not stop Ricardo, whose determination to overthrow the government and attack the morality police and the Revolutionary Guards was as strong as ever. He blamed the Iranian government, which had weakened the country so much that the Iraqis had invaded and were now taking over cities in the south of the country.

The street talk was of a freedom fighter on a motorcycle, a youth who was taunting the Revolutionary Guards and the morality police at checkpoints, and no matter how hard they tried, they couldn't catch him. The motorcycle was a powerful superbike that led the pursuers into traps. They were met with bricks and bottles and Molotov cocktails, and no matter what they did, they could never catch the motorcycle, which sped up the stairwells of the buildings and escaped out the other side.

So when Ricardo was walking down the street one day, thinking about hope and the future and somewhat daydreaming, and a Toyota Land Cruiser screeched to a halt beside him and demanded that he get in the car, he was sure the game was up.

He didn't mind admitting that he was terrified as they bundled him into the back of the vehicle, a potbellied, middle-aged Revolutionary Guard punching him around the head, telling him he was under arrest, and heading for a detention center.

Ricardo knew all about the notorious detention centers run by the Revolutionary Guards. They systematically abused detainees, and he knew that he was in for a hard time; there was a chance he wouldn't make it out alive.

They drove him to a nondescript building on the other side of the city. As the vehicle pulled into the heavily fortified compound, he looked up at the high walls and barbed wire fences. Armed guards were stationed at various checkpoints, and access to the facility was strictly controlled.

The guards led him to an interrogation room and hurried him inside. Five minutes later, two burly guards walked into the cell and, without uttering a single word, attacked him with batons and beat him senseless. One of the guards used his boot, repeatedly kicking him in the ribs. By the time they had finished, the pain in Ricardo's rib cage was unbearable, and he could hardly breathe. His eyes were blackened and swollen, and as he managed to open them, he noticed one of his front teeth lying on the cold concrete floor.

Ricardo lapsed in and out of consciousness for what seemed like ages. There were no windows in the small room, and when he eventually managed to sit up, every inch of his body cried out in pain. He couldn't think; he was in a daze, and his vision blurred.

A voice brought him back to reality. "Now we will start your interrogation. You are a friend of Mohsen's." The interrogator leaned in, his voice stern and demanding. "Focus and listen very carefully. You are a friend of Mohsen's, correct?"

Ricardo, coughing and wincing in pain, barely managed to respond. "I . . . I know Mohsen, yes."

"He was arrested last night," the interrogator continued. "He has already confessed to being a member of the MEK. We have his statements. Now, you must tell us everything you know about him and his associates."

"I don't know what you're talking about. Mohsen is just a friend from high school . . ."

The interrogator's patience seemed to wear thin. "Boy, we are not here to play games; do not waste our time. The more you hesitate, the worse it will be for you. We need you to cooperate fully if you want any leniency."

Ricardo tried to muster the energy to sit up straight against the cold, hard wall, his body aching with every movement. He squinted through swollen eyes, trying to make sense of the situation, his mind foggy from the pain and fear. "I don't know anything. I have known him since high school; that's all."

The interrogator sighed heavily. He signaled to one of the guards. "We can do this the easy way or the hard way, boy. It's your choice," he said as the guard stepped forward, baton in hand, an ominous reminder of the consequences of noncooperation.

In the grand scheme of things, Ricardo realized he'd just gotten a lucky break. He'd been arrested for no other reason than association. His detention had nothing to do with the mystery motorcyclist.

Over the next four days, they beat Ricardo every few hours, used electric shock treatment, and threatened to harm his family members.

His entire vocabulary had been reduced to three words: "friend from school."

—

There was no bedding in his prison cell, no sanitation facilities, and no access to clean water. The screams of other prisoners echoed through the building twenty-four hours a day.

Ricardo thought of only Bahar, his young sister, and Samira; they would be frantic and worried. The Revolutionary Guards were not in the habit of notifying the families of detainees. It was all part of the mental torture.

On the third day, two guards entered the room with an interrogator. Ricardo sat at the plastic table, his hands in cuffs, in the middle of the small, windowless room.

"We'll start all over again," the interrogator said. "Tell us everything you know about Mohsen."

"Friend from school."

The interrogator had adopted a casual demeanor, trying to coax information from Ricardo with a tone of friendly persuasion. "Ricardo, we're just trying to get to the bottom of this," he started. "You know Mohsen, and that's a start. We need to know who he's been meeting with and what plans he's discussed. It's in your best interest to help us."

"Friend from school."

The guard sighed. He put his hand into his pocket and pulled out a pair of pliers, which he placed on the table. Ricardo knew precisely what they were and how they were used.

He had never known anything like it, as the pain in his two broken ribs paled in comparison, but still, he maintained his denials. "Mohsen is a friend from school."

The interrogator questioned him pleasantly while the guard continued extracting the nail from Ricardo's finger with the pliers.

"You can stop this at any moment, Ricardo," he said calmly. "All you need to do is tell us what you know about Mohsen and his connections."

Ricardo shook his head weakly. "Friend from school."

"Think carefully; this can all end now. You're not protecting anyone by taking this pain."

"Friend from school." He looked at his hand. The nail had been pulled out; it was hanging with blood and flesh at the end of the pliers.

The interrogator sighed and motioned to the guards, and they paused and stepped back. "We will continue until you remember something," he stated.

Out in the corridor, one of the guards turned to the other. "You know, I think we may have made a mistake with this one; I think the boy might be telling the truth."

"You think?"

"Yes, they normally break long before now. Have you noticed anything else about him?"

"What's that?"

"He hasn't shed one tear. I normally have them crying like a baby within thirty minutes. This boy has lasted three days."

"Give it another go. The information was good from a boy from the village of Khomeyn; he said that he and Mohsen are thick as thieves."

The guard nodded, and they walked back into the room.

It took the guards two hours to tear out two more of Ricardo's fingernails. They beat Ricardo again and threw him in the corner of the room in a pool of his own blood.

He closed his eyes and begged a god he didn't believe in for sleep. He wanted to close his eyes but not to die; he'd get through this, and they wouldn't break him. He'd resist, he'd remain defiant, he wouldn't betray Mohsen or the cause. Didn't the imbeciles realize that by beating and torturing him they had made him stronger and more determined than ever? He thought about the beautiful music he played in the privacy of his bedroom. The Pink Floyd song "Comfortably Numb" played in his head; the lyrics about fading away, numbing the pain, were particularly poignant.

—

Ali and his uncle walked into the interrogation center, and the uncle demanded to see the chief of interrogation. Thirty minutes later, the two men sat in an office.

"You've made a terrible mistake," the uncle said. "This boy is one of my top Islamic students; he has nothing to do with being a rebel. He is well respected and would not get caught up in any of the anarchy happening in Tehran. He is guilty of nothing more than association with another student. I demand he be released immediately."

The chief of interrogation was reading a report. "For once, I must agree with you; the boy hasn't said a word despite two of my top interrogators' efforts."

Ali's uncle was influential; the chief was worried and agreed to his immediate release.

"Take me to him," the uncle said.

—

On day four of his incarceration, the two guards walked into the cell and told Ricardo he was free to go. He had been drained of every ounce of strength; his legs were black and blue from the ankles to the hips. He had not moved from the corner they had thrown him in the previous day, but as they walked over to help him to his feet, he noticed a change in their demeanor. They made him stand and dragged him toward the cell door, and then he heard a familiar voice.

"Ricardo, what have they done to you?" It was Ali.

"I'll see someone pays for this," the uncle said to the chief.

The chief was defensive. "We have a difficult job to do, and don't forget we are carrying out God's work."

Ricardo said nothing as Ali stroked his bloodied hair and told him Samira had contacted him. "She was frantic and worried; she said you had not returned home. My uncle found out where you were."

They took him straight to the hospital; Ali called Samira and told her he was safe.

At the hospital, less than an hour later, Samira gasped at the sight of her son lying on the hospital bed, his body a map of bruises and wounds, hooked up to tubes and a drip.

"My dear boy," she murmured as she approached the bed, tears welling in her eyes.

"Mom," he whispered.

Samira took his hand, holding it gently between hers. "I'm here now, Ricardo. You're safe."

Ricardo squeezed her hand weakly as he drifted in and out of consciousness. "I never said anything. I did not betray anyone; we stood and fought together."

"What are you talking about?"

"He's rambling," the nurse said. "It's normal; we had to give him morphine for the pain."

"My motorbike, get my motorbike," Ricardo said. "We'll hit them harder than they've ever been hit."

The nurse shrugged. "He's talking nonsense."

His words trailed off, and soon, his breathing deepened, and he slipped into the steady rhythm of sleep. His mother watched him for some time, her heart swelling with a mix of relief and tenderness. Though absurd, the nonsense he had spoken was somehow a comfort—proof that her boy was still in there, untouched by the fear and pain that had brought him here.

"How could they do this to you?" Samira's voice was choked with anger and pain. "You are just a child."

Samira brushed a lock of hair from his forehead. "It's over now, my son. Get some rest."

17

INTO THE ABYSS

If you gaze long into an abyss, the abyss gazes also into you.
—Friedrich Nietzsche

The interrogation had left its mark; his mother believed he was in a state of fear, of paranoia, in the midst of a breakdown. She had never seen Ricardo in this condition—he was angry; he was furious with the world. But his mother knew that his injuries had to heal, and the only way to recover was to sleep. She nursed him through three sleepless nights. He was like a demon, possessed, but then a change seemed to wash over him, and he started to sleep like a baby.

—

It was two weeks before his mother allowed any visitors; the first to arrive was Bahar. Samira led her to his room. She pushed open the door, and Ricardo lay motionless on the bed.

"Ricardo, look who's here to see you."

Ricardo opened his eyes and focused. His eyes lit up, and a smile crept across his lips. "Hey, Bahar. I thought I'd never see you again."

"I'll leave you to it," Samira said as she closed the door.

Bahar stepped closer. She set a bunch of flowers on a nearby table. "I brought these for you . . ."

"Thank you, they're beautiful."

"How are you really feeling?"

"Getting better. What those bastards did to me, I—"

"Shhh, don't talk about it; they're not worth it."

"Seeing you . . ." Ricardo said. "It helps more than you know."

Bahar reached out gently and squeezed his hand. "I'm here, Ricardo. No matter what."

"How are you?"

"I'm fine, but I thought I'd lost you." She wiped the tears from her cheeks. "I can't bear the thought of losing you. You are my world."

Ricardo gripped her hand. "I'm fine. Believe me, I'm recovering. You should have seen me two weeks ago."

—

Bahar visited daily, and her presence became the cornerstone of Ricardo's recovery. Her love and strength sustained him through his long journey toward full fitness.

It was difficult because Bahar had to lie to her parents; they knew nothing about their relationship, and it was forbidden. While her parents were not religious extremists, there was still a cultural stigma around a young girl associating with a boy.

Hannah played her part, befriending Bahar as part of the deception so Bahar could "come by" the house to see Hannah regularly.

—

After a month in the house, Ricardo announced he was ready to resume operations. He wanted revenge, and Bahar insisted on being part of the team.

"That will be difficult," he said. "You know how some of the group members feel about females getting involved in frontline operations."

"But you would argue for me; you know how strong I am."

"I would. All I'm saying is we'll have an uphill battle."

What Ricardo had gone through at the hands of the Revolutionary Guard interrogators would never leave him; he would never forget, in particular, the two guards who beat him and tortured him so much. And yet, it was the psychological torture that affected him the most. He could take the beatings and the pain and even the humiliation they inflicted upon him, and on several occasions when he would not tell them what they wanted to hear, they said to him that he would be executed within the hour. Because there was so much word on the street about executions, part of him was convinced they intended to carry out the threat. He'd never forget those feelings as he sat alone in his cell, sincerely believing he would never see his mother again or his little sister and, of course, Bahar. A rage burned inside him like an inferno whenever he thought about it.

Later that day, he called his friend. "Is the motorcycle still in the same place?"

"It is, Ricardo, and it's all yours. It's good to have you back."

—

The Shadow Rider brought back his two-wheeled mayhem to the streets of Tehran. He had a new determination and convinced himself that he had come back from his interrogation and near-death experience tougher than ever. He became more ruthless. He took the motorbike out more often, daring and taunting the Revolutionary Guards even more. He embraced the shadows that hunted him and became one with his rage. The regime introduced an unprecedented reward for catching the Revolutionary Guards' "enemy number one."

—

"I want to work closer with you," Bahar announced one evening.

"What do you mean?"

"I want to come on the back of the motorcycle. I want to help you; I want to be with you. Two sets of eyes are better than one."

"Do you know how dangerous it is, Bahar? They shoot at me; I swear I've lost count of the number of bullets that have nearly removed my ears."

"I don't care; we will be stronger together. I want to feel your passion and be a part of what you are trying to achieve."

Ricardo argued, but he argued unconvincingly because he wasn't convinced himself. He wanted Bahar there with him; he wanted her with him because there was no more incredible feeling than his soulmate close when the adrenaline rush was in full flow. He'd never tried drugs, but surely there could be no high anywhere in the world that could match that.

—

Overnight, "public enemy number one" became a pair. They were a modern-day Robin Hood and Maid Marian. The English folklore heroes had fought against injustice and oppression; Ricardo and Bahar were no different. The corrupt sheriffs and nobles of Sherwood Forest had been replaced by the fundamentalist Mullahs of Iran, and just like Robin Hood and the love of his life, they would continue their fight until they could fight no more.

—

They played cat and mouse with the morality police and the Revolutionary Guards two or three evenings every week. But now it was so much better because it was clear to the authorities that it was a girl taunting them from the back of the bike. In their eyes, females were second-class citizens. Before Bahar joined Ricardo on the motorcycle, he sometimes struggled to instigate the chase, but now, the guards were raging. How dare a female bring the fight to them!

To rub salt in the wound, Bahar recruited an all-girl team and prepared the traps. They were as good as, if not better than, the men and boys, and she was proud of them.

Ricardo had just celebrated his sixteenth birthday with Bahar, and a few days later they were back on the streets, the motorcycle fueled and ready for action. They had already completed a successful run, luring two Toyota Land Cruisers into a part of the city where Bahar's team lay in wait on the roof. As he rode up the steps of the apartment block, Bahar hanging on for dear life around his waist, the assembled team sprang into action and struck the guards before disappearing into the darkness of the night. Once again, Ricardo and Bahar had escaped, tearing down the main street in the darkness.

After a few miles, Ricardo pulled into a small side street. They climbed off the bike and hugged each other.

"Let's do it again," Ricardo said. "The night is young."

Bahar wasn't so sure. "That was good," she said. "Let's not chance our luck."

"No, let's do it again. I'll make a phone call, and we'll assemble a new hit squad."

Eventually, she agreed and climbed back onto the bike. The thrill of the chase was addictive.

As Ricardo approached the first checkpoint, the Revolutionary Guards stood on the pavement several meters from the vehicle. As they spotted the motorcycle, they sprinted toward their vehicles, giving Ricardo a precious few seconds to gain several hundred yards on them.

But this night would be different, and as he sped up the street, two Toyota Land Cruisers pulled out in front of him, blocking his way. He didn't panic; he was now highly skilled on the bike, and as he pulled and leaned sharply to his right, he steered the bike through a gap, pulled a wheelie, and roared away.

There were four vehicles in pursuit of him; one of them was danger-ously close as he heard the gunfire behind him. This time, he needed to use the speed of the powerful bike; there would be no side streets tonight. He knew they were close but was confident he could outspeed the heavy Land Cruisers. He pulled onto a big roundabout and made for the freeway. As he took the motorcycle up to top speed, Bahar tightened her grip around his waist and buried her head into his neck. He glanced in his mirror: Just one vehicle was left on his tail, and the sound of gunfire was heard as he approached a part of the city he knew so well. He turned off the main street and maneuvered through a labyrinth of narrow streets and down an alleyway where he knew the vehicles could not follow. He drove on for a few miles until he knew they were safe.

"We've made it," he shouted at Bahar. "We've made it, we've escaped."

He was concerned at a warm, wet feeling flowing down his neck.

"Bahar, don't you hear me?"

There was no reply

"Didn't you hear, we've escaped, we've outrun them?"

Ricardo pulled into a small garage by an empty shop. Bahar's hands were still locked around his waist as he reached down to feel them. They were cold, and something about the feel of her skin wasn't right. A sick-ening feeling washed over him as he turned around.

In that heart-stopping moment when Ricardo felt Bahar slump against him, his world came crashing down. The abrupt shift in her weight and her sudden stillness filled him with an immediate, deep dread.

He reached around to hold her and let the motorcycle drop to the floor, and as he looked at her, the sight of blood spreading across her clothes confirmed his worst fears. His heart pounded with a raw mixture of grief and panic, each beat a harsh reminder of the grim reality.

Her eyes were closed, her beautiful smooth skin a deathly pallor, and as he reached around to the back of her head, he felt the crater in the back of her skull where the bullet had hit her.

She was gone, and the stark, unbearable truth settled over him with a crushing weight as his legs buckled and he sank to the ground, his two arms still wrapped around her dead body.

The sounds of the city seemed to fade into a distant murmur, replaced by a deafening silence.

Guilt clawed at him, a relentless torment. He had been trying to protect her, to flee to a safer life together, and now she lay lifeless because he did not make that decision to go home. He had failed in his promise to protect her. He felt the shadows laughing at him.

Ricardo knelt in the dirt, his arms trembling as he cradled her limp body against his chest. Her head lolled unnaturally to one side, strands of her hair clinging to his bloodstained hands. Her eyes—those warm, familiar eyes that had once looked at him with such trust—were now lifeless. A shuddering breath escaped his lips, but no sound came. There was only silence, the crushing silence of a world that had come to a halt.

It shouldn't have ended like this.

He had failed her.

This was his fault.

They should have gone home. Why hadn't they gone home?

Now look at her.

A sob tore through his chest. He tightened his grip on her, as if holding her close could somehow pull her back from the edge of oblivion. He pressed his forehead against hers, the salt of his tears mixing with the blood on her face. His tears dripped onto her cheeks like raindrops, but they did nothing to bring her warmth back. Nothing could.

"You trusted me," he whispered, the guilt crashing over him in powerful waves threatening to drown him. He had promised her they'd be safe. He had promised that nothing would go wrong, that he would protect her. He had lied to her.

His mind raced, replaying every second that led to this moment. The sounds of the gunshots. Had she known, in that final moment, that he couldn't save her?

"I'm sorry," he whispered, over and over, like a mantra, a desperate chant to ward off the crushing reality of her death. But the words felt hollow, meaningless. What was he sorry for? Sorry that he had been too stubborn to listen to her, too blind to see the danger? Sorry that he had dragged her into this nightmare? Or sorry that he wasn't the hero he thought he was?

None of it mattered. She was gone.

Her blood soaked into his clothes, warm at first but quickly cooling, leaving a sticky residue.

Ricardo couldn't move or think beyond the moment's suffocating weight. All he could see was her face, pale and still, framed by the nightmarish contrast of the blood.

—

Reality settled in as the first hints of dawn broke the darkness. Ricardo knew he had to move to make decisions he wasn't ready to make. The city stirred, and with it, he mustered the strength to seek help.

At 7 a.m., when curfew had ended, he walked out into the street, found a phone booth, and called his friends. Within thirty minutes, they arrived in a car and took Ricardo and the body of Bahar to a safe house. They had been there for twenty-four hours when Bahar's father came and stood over the dead body of his daughter. Like Ricardo, he was devastated.

Her father knew that she'd been working against the government. "What happened?" he asked.

"A stray bullet," one of the boys said.

Bahar's father nodded. He knew the boy was lying, but what could he do? It wasn't as if he could report the incident to the police; that would lead to a full investigation and put his family at risk.

—

It was the worst day of Ricardo's life as he looked down at the cold floor where Bahar lay. The lifeless form, once vibrant and full of laughter, was motionless, robbed of its vitality by the merciless hands of the government forces. Her father cradled her in his arms as his tears flowed freely. The sight and the pain that ran through his body left him gasping for air. Each breath was a struggle, each heartbeat a painful reminder of all that was lost, his soul shattered beyond repair.

18

THE VOID

Success is not final, failure is not fatal: It is the courage to continue that counts.

—Winston Churchill

Time stood still for many hours as the father and friends of Bahar, who had also arrived, stood over Bahar's lifeless body, paid their respects, and grieved.

Nobody could quite believe the pale, lifeless form of the once beautiful girl, her face now drained of color.

Bahar was dead, and that in itself presented a considerable problem.

Under normal circumstances, the police would have been contacted, a doctor would have been summoned, and then hasty arrangements would be made for the funeral. But Iran wasn't normal; the regime was brutal and ruthless.

Ricardo spoke to their mutual friend Behnam. "She has been shot by a bullet—you know what that means. We cannot report the death because if we do, they'll come after her family. They will make her father's life a misery even though he had nothing to do with what has happened because they'll know she was part of the resistance."

Bahar's father looked up and caught the conversation. He nodded slightly. Ricardo knew he was in complete agreement. Although his life would never be the same again, he also had to think about his family and even his secondary family—his brothers and sisters, cousins, and nephews—because the regime didn't care. Any family member was a target. They ruled on fear, and they were proud of their reprisals. Nobody was safe.

Bahar's father spoke. "We must take her body to Karaj; my brother has a farm there. That is where we will bury my daughter, where nobody can find her."

—

It was a two-hour drive to Karaj. Ricardo and his companions feared being stopped at the roadblocks manned by the Revolutionary Guards. Thankfully, the traffic was light, and the guards appeared to have better things to do as they smoked cigarettes and talked among themselves.

A man was waiting by the gate as they drove toward the farm entrance. The car stopped, Bahar's father stepped forward, and the two men embraced. Bahar's father waved at Ricardo, who climbed out of the vehicle. The man, Bahar's uncle, asked them to follow him, and they walked fifty meters to a small space in a wooded area where a grave had been marked out. He explained to the friends that they would need to dig the hole and that Bahar's mother and her sister were on their way to wash the body in the traditional Muslim tradition.

Ricardo was in a daze, barely comprehending what he was doing. Each shovel of dirt he heaped on the ground drained him like nothing he had ever felt. His hands were raw and blistered from gripping the old wooden handle of the shovel, and his fingers throbbed. The air was heavy, thick with the scent of earth, damp and unyielding as he repeatedly drove the blade into the ground. Each thrust sent a jolt up his arms, but he barely felt it. He was numb to the pain, numb to the world around him except for the crushing weight of what he was doing.

She deserved better than this; she deserved so much better.

He paused, leaning heavily on the shovel as he gasped for breath, his chest heaving. His body felt like it wasn't his, every movement sluggish, as though his limbs were weighed down with lead. He couldn't remember how long he had been digging; time had dissolved into nothingness.

A hand on his shoulder. "Stop, Ricardo. It's enough; that is sufficient."

———

The uncle returned and beckoned everybody toward the farmhouse to a room at the rear of the house.

The small, dimly lit room was filled with the scent of rosewater mingling with the smell of freshly laundered white cloth. Bahar's mother and her sister stood near the corner, their faces a mask of stoic determination, but their eyes betrayed the depth of their grief as they prepared Bahar's body for its final journey.

Ricardo could not help but be impressed by the mother's precise and practiced movements. He had witnessed the ceremony countless times before but never one so heartbreaking as this one.

She stepped forward and began to untangle the soft fabric that covered her daughter, knowing that her grief must not cloud her duty. It was a sacred act, a final gift to her beloved child. Gently, she began to wash her daughter's hair; cool, pure water flowed over her daughter's skin.

Every inch of skin was cleansed, and every body part was honored. Finally, her cold, still feet completed the journey of their earthly walk.

They dried the body with clean towels, the white shroud was brought forward, and with great care, mother and sister wrapped the body layer by layer.

The prayers were held in a courtyard, and friends and family, united in grief, stood shoulder to shoulder.

Ricardo remembered little about the burial, his entire being wracked with pain and guilt and, yes, anger that such a beautiful soul had been taken at such a young age.

After the ceremony, the crowd drifted away, and Ricardo lingered by the grave.

He stood there with the fresh dirt under his feet; he couldn't move and felt weighed down by his feelings. It was hard for him to accept that Bahar was gone forever. Everything said seemed to float around him during the ceremony; he felt empty. Tears had made it hard for him to see, but he stood firm, filled with feelings of loss and love.

As darkness fell, Behnam returned to the grave. "Ricardo, it is time, we must return to the city—the curfew, we must . . ."

He nodded.

Behnam settled into the passenger seat, his face somber as Ricardo started the car. The ride was quiet for a while; each man was lost in his thoughts.

—

Ricardo occasionally glanced in the rearview mirror, half expecting to see Bahar's smiling face looking back at him, but only the empty road stretched behind him. The thought of days ahead without Bahar was daunting; every routine and every familiar place would remind him of her absence. His heart was heavy with the knowledge that life would move on, but for now, his grief was a quiet companion.

As he approached the city, the noise and lights seemed overwhelming, a stark contrast to the quiet and peace at the farm. Despite being surrounded by people, he felt utterly alone.

He kept his eyes on the road, his jaw clenched as he fought back emotions.

He spoke. "It's tough, Behnam. It feels like there's a hole where my heart is."

"She was your world," Behnam replied, turning slightly to face him. "Words don't help much at times like these, but I'm here for you, my friend. Whatever you need."

Ricardo gave a sad smile, a single tear escaping down his cheek. "Thanks, Behnam. It means a lot, but I do not think I will ever be able to get over this feeling."

"Then let's keep talking. Let's keep her memory alive. She will always be in your heart. She would have wanted that, wouldn't she?"

Ricardo nodded as he pulled the car over in front of Behnam's house. "She would, yes. I'll try to remember the good times."

As Behnam opened the door to get out, he paused. "Call me anytime, Ricardo. Day or night, all right? We'll get through this together."

Ricardo managed a grateful nod. "I will. Thanks, Behnam, for all your help. Goodnight."

"Goodnight, Ricardo," he said as he closed the door gently behind him.

—

Ricardo stopped venturing out, except for the bare necessities. The outside world held no attraction to him; he no longer felt a part of it. He locked himself in his dark room. It was just him, his Pink Floyd albums, and books about better times and struggles that ended in happier days.

Bahar's death consumed him.

The few times he did leave the house, he moved through the city like a shadow, his eyes downcast, every step a struggle against his grief. He avoided places they had frequented, the cafés and parks, especially the rooftops. He had no desire to go anywhere he had once been with Bahar.

—

The bombings of Iranian cities continued. Now, it was not just the planes but rockets that flew overhead. Some people called them the "flying water heaters" because that's what they looked like.

And the repression of the Regime got more potent by the day, as if Bahar gave her life for nothing.

For Ricardo, the days blended with the nights; time was meaningless. Samira often found him sitting in his dark room, staring at nothing . . .

His mind replayed moments of their life together on an endless, painful loop. He recalled her voice's sound, how her hands felt in his, and how her scent lingered everywhere. She haunted him. In a way, it was beautiful but unbearable.

His friends tried to reach out, but their messages and phone calls were ignored. When they did manage to visit, he was a hollow shell, going through the motions of conversation but never really there. He could see the concern in their eyes, hear it in their words, but he was too far gone to respond.

They offered help, but he couldn't summon the energy to care. He wanted to curl up in a ball and die.

And he lied; he had to lie. Most of them had no idea what had really happened. They were told that Bahar had left the country in the middle of the night.

—

It took Ricardo months to return to the world, but he eventually regained the will to live. He told himself Bahar would not want him to be like this. He knew she wanted him to be a survivor and not a victim.

Hannah was undoubtedly the catalyst that sparked the recovery.

He owed it in no small part to the dynamics around the house and the complications surrounding his explanation to Hannah and Samira about Bahar's mysterious disappearance.

Hannah had become very close to Bahar and couldn't understand why she had gone without telling her.

"But you must know, Ricardo," she said. "You two were very close. She must have told you where she was going and when she was coming back. All you ever tell me is that she went on a trip."

"Do you know how many families are trying to leave Iran?" he said. "Don't you know there's a war on?"

"Yes, but—"

"It's not so unusual that people want to flee a city where bombs are dropping daily."

"But she would have said something to me, or she would have said something to you."

"Well, she hasn't, and I'm just as upset as you are, so just leave it."

But Hannah wouldn't leave it, and she fired the same questions at her mother. The atmosphere in the house was tense, and Hannah was getting rebellious. To make matters worse, his sister now had a boyfriend, and Hannah called on the same favor that she had bestowed on Ricardo.

The ridiculous cultural ruling was still in place: Young men and women who were unmarried could not be seen on the street together and instead needed a family member to accompany them whenever they went out.

Farhad was charming and handsome, with Persian looks, dark eyes, fair skin, short, curly black hair, and a neatly trimmed beard. He was well spoken and from an affluent family in Tehran. However, the more time Ricardo spent in Farhad's company, the more he disliked the boy and realized that Hannah's boyfriend was controlling and jealous. Before his eyes, Hannah's character was changing, and it seemed there was nothing he could do about it.

—

It was a terrible evening, a fight like Ricardo had never witnessed before, as his sister and Samira shouted and screamed at each other. Hannah had told her mother that Reza had reached across and squeezed her breast and commented that she was "developing nicely."

"I won't stand for that man touching me, do you hear?"

Ricardo couldn't believe what he was hearing, but Samira was in denial.

Samira had fought a long battle to keep her children safe during all the challenges that life had thrown at her. When David had left, some of her own family turned against her, and that's why she had married Reza, to silence the gossip mongers . . . to survive.

The fight culminated in Hannah storming to her room, packing a suitcase, and telling her mother she was moving in with her boyfriend because she couldn't stand it any longer. The problem was Reza. She hated him, and it was all her mother's fault for bringing him into their family. Ricardo wanted to agree; he hated Reza as much as Hannah did, but instead, he bit his lip, said nothing, and watched as his sister left the house.

—

A few days later, Ricardo called Farhad and Hannah. He wanted to talk some sense into his sister. She'd had enough time to calm down, and he needed to bring her to her senses. She was just fourteen and could not move out of the family home, no matter the circumstances.

It did not start well. He had tried to reason with her as she stood in the doorway of Farhad's house, but gradually, the two voices increased. Ricardo realized that his sister had spirit and determination, and he was losing the argument.

As Hannah exploded, she screamed, "I want you to leave me alone. This is my life, and I want you out of it. I don't need my mother, I don't need you, and I certainly don't need Reza." At that moment, Hannah turned around and slapped Ricardo in the face. He froze; he could not believe what had just happened. He never expected this from his little sister.

It was a knife through the heart; his sister's words and actions cut him deep, and all the emotions of losing Bahar came flooding back. At that moment, Ricardo realized he had failed Hannah as much as Bahar. Now he had lost his sister, and as he walked home just before curfew, the night sky of Tehran closed in around him, and tears ran down his face.

He had lost the two people in life who he had loved the most.

Someone would need to pay.

19

A BOXER ON
THE ROPES

Fall seven times, stand up eight.
—Japanese proverb

As Ricardo approached his house on the way back from school, he realized there had been an incident. The emergency services were there, crowds of people flocked around the area, and he heard screams and cries for help. Chaos ensued as he ran toward the melee of people. He realized that the focus was on his friend Comron's house. The family home, once bustling with warmth and laughter, was reduced to a shattered shell; it had been struck by an Iraqi rocket.

Debris littered what was once a beautifully manicured garden, and the air was thick with the acrid smell of smoke.

His heart pounded with dread.

"Ricardo, over here!" a voice called from the crowd. It was Sara, another neighbor, her face streaked with tears. She was standing by a small, improvised command center some locals had set up.

Ricardo rushed over, his voice hoarse. "What happened? Is it just . . . are they all . . . ?"

"The rescue team went through." She paused as she sobbed. "Comron, his mother, and all the kids. . . ."

"What, Sara, tell me?"

"They've been buried; there's no sign of life."

"No," he said. "I won't have it."

Ricardo ran toward the remains of the house. He fell to his knees and began to claw at the rubble. Other people were removing pieces of broken wall and twisted metal.

"He is a good friend, a good brother," Ricardo muttered to another helping neighbor.

After several hours, they had removed enough of the rubble to find the bodies underneath, and the medics confirmed that there was no sign of life.

He cradled Comron's corpse in his arms. His dead body looked remarkably intact, his face barely scratched, but his ribs had been crushed into his chest, and his lungs and heart had burst. He'd had no chance.

Ricardo walked away with tears running down his face. Someone, somewhere, was conspiring against him, and he had lost another person whom he loved dearly.

He was overwhelmed and confused. First Bahar, then Hannah, and now Comron and his family. *Why me? What did I do to deserve this?* he thought to himself.

Three painful losses left him reeling like a boxer on the ropes, vision blurred, knees weak. He leaned up against his front door and looked into the night sky. Once again, the cloud of depression descended, dark and suffocating, a dense, unyielding fog that seeped into every crevice of his brain.

—

He once again sought solace at Masood's bookstore. On the way home one evening, three vans and two military trucks suddenly pulled up. They closed both ends of the busy street, and two lines of troops marched down and met in the middle; they rounded up all the men in the street. He should have been on high alert, but he didn't care anymore.

"You are all required for military service," a bearded, middle-aged man commanded.

They started loading the men onto the trucks. Ricardo breathed a sigh of relief as he realized what was happening and fumbled in his pocket for his student ID card. "I'm a student, sir; I'm exempt."

"I don't give a fuck; get in the truck."

"You don't understand; I'm a student."

"Tell that to my commander," the man said as two well-built guards took Ricardo by the arms. Ricardo protested again, and one of the guards told him that any misunderstanding would be sorted out at the military base. The guards were aggressive, and he had no option but to climb aboard the truck. They secured the back doors and drove away.

The men were scared and nervous; they glared at each other as the darkening cityscape rushed past the small, barred windows. One of the boys, a skinny teenager with a look of stubborn defiance, leaned closer to Ricardo. "Hey, do you know where they're taking us?"

Ricardo shook his head. "No, I don't. They just grabbed me off the street. I tried to tell them I'm a student and shouldn't be here, but they didn't listen."

"Same here, man. I was heading home from college. This is crazy. They can't just take us like this."

Ricardo sighed. There was a strange sense of camaraderie amid the chaos. "They can, but we can do nothing right now except wait and see where we end up. What's your name?"

"Keavon," the boy replied. "Maybe they'll sort it out at the base and realize we're not who they're looking for."

"Yeah, I hope so."

They had been in the truck for over two hours when it stopped. As the back doors opened, he noticed a huge, illuminated parade square with hundreds of men lined up side by side.

Again, Ricardo tried to protest, "I am a student. I'm only seventeen, and my mother does not know where I am."

His protests fell on deaf ears as a man walked up and down the lines, asking potential recruits questions before announcing whether they would be enlisted in the Navy, the Army, or the Air Force.

The man approached Ricardo and asked him about his fitness. "Do you have any medical conditions or allergies?"

"No, I don't, but I shouldn't be here; I'm a student."

The man looked him up and down and then squeezed his bicep. "You're a fit young man; we could use you in the Army," he said, and before Ricardo could offer any more objections, the man had gone.

Ricardo and his fellow press-ganged recruits were fed and then taken to an army-style barracks, where they were allocated beds and told to rest.

—

In the dimly lit barracks, the air was thick with the murmurs of other recruits settling in for the night. Ricardo lay on his narrow bed, staring at the dark ceiling, his mind racing with thoughts of his sudden conscription. Beside him, Keavon shifted on his bed, the springs creaking slightly under his weight.

"I can't believe this is happening," Keavon whispered. "How are you holding up?"

Ricardo turned his head, his eyes adjusting to the low light. "I'm trying to figure out what to do. I kept telling them I'm a student. This has to be a mistake."

"I hear you, man. I said the same and told them my family expected me back soon."

"They just don't seem to care." Ricardo sighed. "Did you see the look on that guy's face when he assigned us? Like he was picking out livestock."

"Yeah, we're just numbers to them."

Ricardo propped himself up on his elbow. "First thing tomorrow, I will try talking to someone in charge. There has to be a way to explain my situation. Maybe they'll let me call my mom or at least send her a message."

"That sounds like a plan. Maybe I should do the same," Keavon said. "Stick together, yeah? Might make them take us more seriously."

The two young students were part of an estimated 100,000 boys under the age of eighteen who were unlawfully conscripted into the Iranian military. The boys, some as young as twelve or thirteen, were often recruited from schools, mosques, and the Basij militia. Some child soldiers signed up voluntarily, brainwashed from an early age that it was Allah's wish, but most were press-ganged from the streets, unfortunate enough to be in the wrong place at the wrong time.

—

In the morning, the uniformed man said they had an early start, heading for the desert city of Yazd.

Ricardo knew all about Yazd, which was at least five hundred miles away, in the desert of central Iran. It was famous for its unique Persian architecture and Zoroastrian heritage.

20

BENEATH
BLOOD-RED SKIES

In the end it is how you fight, as much as why you fight,
that makes your cause good or bad.

—Freeman Dyson

In the dusty courtyard of the military camp, Ricardo and Keavon stood shoulder to shoulder, their duffel bags at their feet, waiting for the military truck to take them to basic training in Yazd. As Ricardo boarded the truck, all he could think about was how worried Samira would be. She had already lost her daughter; her life would be turned upside down when she discovered that her only son was not in his bed when she awoke that morning.

A simple phone call could resolve her torment, but that was beyond the mindset of the men in charge.

Keavon kicked at the side of the truck, his voice low. "Looks like this is it, huh? No way to call home, no way to get out. We're really going to Yazd."

"Yeah, it's happening. But you know, part of me is . . . I don't know. I'm excited."

"Excited, huh? I wish I could say the same."

Ricardo shrugged. "I can't explain it. When we were lined up and they were talking about what lay ahead, something clicked. Like I could actually be good at this."

Keavon nodded slowly. "I get that. Finding purpose in this mess that we call life could help make sense of it. Maybe I can find something, too, something to keep me going."

Ricardo clapped him on the back. "We'll find it together, brother. We'll get through the training and the war and figure things out. Maybe it won't be all bad."

As the military truck rolled out of the camp, he glanced at Keavon. He had taken to him immediately; they would walk the road together and make the best of their unexpected journey.

—

As the truck rumbled toward Yazd, Ricardo's thoughts drifted to his family—his mother, Samira, and his sister, Hannah, who had left home. He also thought of Bahar, and a part of him wondered if this unexpected turn into the Army might lead him to where she was. *Perhaps,* he thought, *this was how his life was meant to end.*

He wasn't scared and couldn't shake off the feeling that maybe this was where he was meant to be. The fear of death seemed distant, almost irrelevant, as if he had accepted that whatever happened next in his life was part of a larger plan. He wondered if this was destiny, steering him toward an unknown but inevitable path where he might finally make sense of his loss.

—

It took a day and a half to reach Yazd, and as Ricardo climbed from the back of the truck, the heat hit him immediately. The recruits were taken to an office where they signed a series of forms. They were given a uniform and told they would start basic military training later that afternoon.

—

They underwent rigorous physical exercise to build stamina and strength and spent countless hours on drills to instill discipline and coordination. Ricardo felt a sense of unity among the soldiers, and after the third day, he got his act together and stopped protesting. However, he made a point each evening of asking the drill sergeant if he could write home to his mother. The request was always refused.

—

They were given instructions on how to handle weapons and how to maintain them. The recruits practiced loading and unloading rifles and underwent basic shooting exercises on a firing range. Toward the end of the first week, they were instructed on unarmed combat techniques and focused on self-defense and incapacitating an opponent. The second week consisted of military fieldcraft and learning to survive in harsh conditions, mainly the desert. There were lectures every day on the religious doctrines of the Islamic Republic of Iran and the importance of defending the country and loyalty to the supreme leader.

Ricardo switched off entirely as the lecturer whined on about honor, sacrifice, and the sanctity of the cause. His gaze drifted to the small window high on the wall. It was a narrow slit, as if the room itself was trying to keep the outside world at bay. Through it, he could see a patch of sky, a brilliant blue, and then beyond. He was with Bahar; she was there somewhere, and he was no longer in the stuffy room, no longer a soldier-in-training. He was back in her embrace, and they were running barefoot through the tall grass, the earth firm and cool beneath their feet. The air was thick with the smell of wildflowers and . . . her scent. It was as real now as it had been on that fateful last night. He wanted to hold on to it, to stay in this moment, but the shadow pulled at him, dragging him back—back to the present, back to the suffocating heat of the classroom.

—

On day fourteen, they completed a two-hour first aid course and learned how to treat wounds and splint broken bones.

Keavon and Ricardo sat against their tent's cool, sandy wall, cleaning their rifles after a long training day. Keavon glanced over at Ricardo, a wry smile spreading across his face. "Man, I gotta say, you've got a sharp eye. I saw you at the range today. You're a natural with that rifle."

"Thanks, Keavon. I don't know what it is—maybe I just got lucky. But it feels good to hit those targets, like everything clicks into place."

"It's more than luck; I can tell. You pick up things fast: You were the first to get the hang of loading and unloading under time pressure."

"Yeah, it's strange. I've never handled guns before, but it all made sense once I understood the mechanics. Kind of like solving a puzzle, you know?"

Keavon nodded. "Exactly. And it's not just shooting; you've been sharp about everything—spotting mistakes in formation during drills, keeping up with the fieldcraft lessons, and even developing those first aid skills. You're observant, which will serve us well. I'm sticking beside you, brother."

"You do that. We're going through this together."

"Absolutely. We'll watch each other's backs."

Ricardo smiled. "Yeah, we will."

As they continued cleaning their rifles, the quiet confidence between them fortified their resolve, readying them for the challenges ahead on the front line.

—

On the fifteenth day, they were put on another bus and told that their basic training was complete.

"What the fuck," Ricardo said. "They can't be serious."

"They're desperate, brother."

"It's madness." He looked at Keavon. "I mean, do you feel like you're ready to fight the enemy?"

Before Keavon could answer, a sergeant at the front of the bus announced that they were heading to the front line, near a village occupied by the Iraqis. As he walked the length of the bus, speaking to each soldier, he told the two friends they had been assigned to an antiaircraft gun: Keavon was the shooter, Ricardo on sight.

21

FEAR OF THE UNKNOWN

Fear of the unknown is the greatest fear of all.
—Yvon Chouinard

Samira was consumed with worry; every passing day without news deepened her fear that Ricardo had been captured by government forces and left to rot in some hidden government dungeon. Her mind raced with nightmarish images of her son in distress, fueling her determination to find him. Desperate for assistance, she contacted Ali again.

—

In the dimly lit corner of a local café, Samira sat across from Ali, her hands clasped tightly around a cup of tea that had long since gone cold. She waited for him to speak.

"Samira, I've been making some inquiries," Ali began. "I have some information. It seems government forces didn't capture Ricardo, as we feared."

"So, where is he? What have you found out?"

Ali sighed, choosing his words carefully. "From what I've gathered, it appears he was forcibly conscripted into the Army. This is unfortunately common these days, but I haven't yet pinpointed his exact location or which unit he's been assigned to."

"Forcibly? But he's just a student; he shouldn't be—"

"I know," Ali interrupted gently. "He should be exempt from military service, and my uncle is on the case, but he's safe for now; that's the main thing. You can rest assured we'll do everything we can to bring him home."

"Thank you, Ali," Samira said. "I don't know how I can thank you enough."

Ali nodded. "We will keep pushing and contact everyone we can. I'll update you as soon as I hear anything new. We'll find him, Samira. You have my word."

"Thank you, Ali. I don't know what I'd do without your help."

—

Reza was waiting for Samira when she arrived home; one of his sons had dropped him off.

Samira explained what she thought was good news and how Ali and his uncle had turned over every stone to find out where Ricardo was and bring him home.

"Well, Samira," Reza said, "while it's unfortunate, we must remember that everyone must do their part. The government must make tough decisions for the good of Islam and the country."

Samira's expression hardened. "Sometimes you are unreal, Reza. Don't you know that he is just a boy, a student? I'm afraid that's not right."

Reza shook his head. "I disagree. You know he is very much a man in a boy's body. Perhaps this will be an opportunity for Ricardo to grow up, to find his strength."

Reza harbored a hope that Ricardo might not return from the war. He hated the boy; he hated everything he stood for. And then there was their secret. That secret would be kept forever if he didn't return from the war. If God were good, perhaps he would remove Ricardo from their lives.

Samira's eyes flashed with anger, her voice firm and strong. "He's just a boy, Reza, a boy pulled away from his studies and family. How can you even suggest that this is good for him?"

"He is already on the government's radar, Samira. We all know that he was chastised because of the party he attended, and then there's his relationship with Mohsen. That's serious stuff. These kinds of associations can have serious consequences. His past mistakes might have put him on a watch list. Who knows what else he is involved in? These are exactly the type of boys the government wants to take off the streets, and what better place to send them than the front line? At least if they die, they will die with honor and restore some respectability to their families."

Samira's anger grew. The volume of their argument notched up a decibel or two. "You are unreal, Reza; you really are. Do you seriously believe that my boy deserves to be sent into a war zone?"

"I didn't say that," Reza replied. "These are troubled times. My sons are in the Revolutionary Guards, too; they are doing God's work, protecting our way of life."

"'God's work?' They're a bunch of uneducated thugs harassing women while my son is sent to the front lines to fight a war the Imams have inflamed."

Reza opened his mouth to respond, but Samira cut him off.

"You've blinded yourself with this ideology; you've ignored my pain while Ricardo is paying the price for this ridiculous government's actions."

She took a deep breath. "I think you should leave, Reza. I can't have this conversation anymore. I don't want you in this house anymore."

Reza was furious. "How dare you talk to me this way, woman! Don't you know your place?"

"My place is in this house. But not you, Reza. Get out, get out, and don't come back."

He stood up, walked out of the room, and slammed the door behind him without another word.

He muttered to himself as he walked out into the street. "There will be consequences. This is exactly why we need to keep women in their rightful place. They have too many freedoms, too much education."

Reza would report to the police first thing in the morning. He'd file a complaint against her disobedience under Sharia law.

22

BLIND FAITH

All religion, my friend, is simply evolved out of fraud,
fear, greed, imagination, and poetry.
—Edgar Allan Poe

Finally, Ricardo was granted permission to write a letter to Samira.
He wrote that he was in good health and supremely fit and that they were feeding him well.

He wrote:

Dear Mom,

I hope this letter finds you well. I miss you and Hannah so much, and the thought of seeing you both again is what keeps me going every day. Even though I was brought here against my will, I've come to find a sense of purpose in serving in the Army. It's strange, but I feel like I'm where I need to be right now.

Each day, as I wear my uniform, I feel a deep connection to our homeland. I imagine the rolling hills, the bustling markets, and the quiet evenings at home. I'm here fighting for those peaceful moments, for our family, for our friends, and for the freedom of our nation. The enemy has taken a lot from us, but they can't take our spirit or resolve to fight back.

Life here is challenging. The days are exhausting, and the nights are bitterly cold. The constant background noise of gunfire and explosions has become my new normal. But amid this chaos, I find strength in my comrades. We share stories of our homes and dreams of the future, and these bonds have become my refuge.

I often think about you, especially when I'm feeling overwhelmed. I remember your comforting smile and your warm hugs. You always knew just the right thing to say to make everything feel OK. I long for those days, and I wish I could be there to help you with everyday tasks. But for now, my duty is here. I am fighting not just for my future but for Hannah's too. I want her to grow up in a world where she doesn't have to worry about her safety.

I know things are not good between the two of you, but please tell Hannah that her big brother is doing everything he can to ensure her world will be safer. I miss the sound of her laughter so much.

I know you worry about me, and I wish I could ease your fears. But I promise you, we all look out for one another here; it's like having another family, a band of brothers united by a common cause. In a way that I never expected, I find I enjoy the camaraderie.

In the quiet moments, when the dust settles, and the sky is clear, I think about what life will be like when this is all over. I dream of returning home, sharing all my stories with you, and creating new memories together. I hold on to these thoughts tightly; they are my beacon in the darkness.

Please don't worry too much about me. I am strong and fighting with everything I have. This struggle is indeed tricky, but I believe it is worth it. I am proud to stand up for our home and our freedom, though my thoughts on our government remain distant. My loyalty lies with our people and our shared future.

I also find myself missing Uncle Masood and Aunt Sudabeh immensely. Uncle Masood's bookstore was like a second home to me, a place filled with stories and wisdom, where I spent countless hours lost in the pages of books. I miss those quiet, peaceful afternoons with them and the sense of calm and curiosity that filled every corner of his shop.

And I cannot lie to you: I have moments filled with darkness. The days here are long, and it feels like the weight of everything is pulling me under. There are moments when I can barely find the strength to keep going. The loneliness, the constant uncertainty— it all becomes overwhelming. I miss home, your voice, the simple comfort of knowing you're near. Some nights, I lie awake, wondering when it will end, and though I hate to say this, the end does not concern me; perhaps "the end" will be a better world than the one I'm living now.

I love you more than words can express, and I miss you every moment of every day. Stay safe.

With all my love,
Ricardo

He read his words several times before sealing the envelope and taking it to the duty sergeant. Just a few weeks ago, if someone had told him he would write a letter like that, he would never have believed them.

—

In the early, gray light of dawn, Ricardo crouched beside Mohammed, a fourteen-year-old Basiji volunteer, in a foxhole scraped out of the muddy earth along the front line. Around them, the quiet hum of tension filled the air as soldiers prepared for an imminent assault on an Iraqi position.

Ricardo observed Mohammad preparing his gear, the boy's hands steady despite the daunting task ahead: almost a suicide mission, crossing through a minefield to clear a path for the Army. Yet Mohammad's eyes shone with a zeal that spoke of his deep, unshakable faith.

"Aren't you scared, Mohammad?" Ricardo asked.

Mohammad looked at him with a slight smile, betraying a hint of pride. "Scared? No, brother Ricardo. I am ready to die for Allah and my country; it's the greatest honor. I believe in our cause, in our victory ordained by Allah."

"Mohammad, listen to me: Bravery isn't just about rushing toward death; it's about knowing why you fight, about hoping to return to those who love you. Don't you want to go back home after the war? It is not your job to die for your country; it is your job to make the enemy die for his country."

"I fight for what I believe in, for a better future for our people, but if I die, I will meet Allah knowing I did my duty."

The poor boy's mind had been made up for him, filled with the notion of martyrdom.

Ricardo sighed. "I pray you run carefully and stay safe, young brother. I hope you return to tell your story."

"Thank you, Ricardo. May Allah protect you in the battle as well."

———

As they readied their weapons and the first light of dawn broke over the horizon, signaling the start of the attack, Ricardo felt a protective urge toward Mohammad. Despite his disagreement with the ideology that drove these young fighters, he couldn't help but admire their courage.

As the boy got ready and prepared to go over the top, Ricardo grabbed his hand and shook it. "Take it easy, brother. Walk slowly, watch where you put your feet, and if you see the ground disturbed, walk away from it."

Mohammed nodded, but Ricardo knew he hadn't heard a single word. He watched as the boy sprinted in a straight line across no-man's-land. Twenty seconds later, there was a dull explosion, and then nothing but silence.

—

The Basiji boys on the front lines were a stark contrast to those who stayed back in Tehran, enforcing strict rules and harassing women. They were true believers, wholly committed to their cause and ready to sacrifice their lives. Ricardo witnessed these young fighters displaying unwavering conviction and courage throughout his time on the front. They died in the thousands.

—

The sun was setting over the battlefield at the end of the day, casting long shadows and a reddish glow on the sand. Keavon and Ricardo sat behind a crumbling wall, the sounds of distant artillery echoing through the air.

Keavon's eyes were wide, his expression a mix of shock and disbelief after what he had witnessed on the battlefield. "Did you see that kid? He couldn't have been much older than fifteen; he wrapped himself in grenades and rolled under a tank. How can that be? How can someone so young throw away his life like that?"

"It's hard to comprehend; these young Basiji, they're brought up in a culture steeped in martyrdom and sacrifice. To them, such acts aren't seen as throwing their lives away. They believe they're fulfilling a noble purpose, achieving the highest honor."

"But it's just . . . it's suicide. How does that become noble? How do you convince yourself that's the right thing to do?"

"Desperation and indoctrination. They prey on the weak, the uneducated. They believe that to die for their cause is to live forever in paradise. It's not just about convincing themselves; it's all they know."

Keavon shook his head, his eyes still fixed on the ground where the young Basiji had made his final moves. "And what do we believe in, Ricardo? What are we fighting for?"

"We fight to survive, Keavon. We want to return to our families and maybe improve things for those who come after us. Our fight might not be wrapped in the glory of martyrdom, but there are things in this world that are truly worth fighting for. Think about World War II—how many stood up against tyranny, against the horrors of Nazism. They fought for future generations, to preserve humanity."

"It just seems so senseless, all of this loss."

Ricardo sighed. "Yes, but every generation has battles, brother. The hope is that fighting for what you believe in leads to a better future."

Ricardo's thoughts drifted to Bahar, and he felt her presence beside him. He knew about heartbreak firsthand. As they sat in silence, the last light of day gave way to the coolness of the night.

Keavon leaned back in his foxhole. *Who was this boy, so wise beyond his years*, he thought, *this boy who speaks like a philosopher?*

"You are a strange one, Ricardo," Keavon said.

"In what way?"

"The way you speak, the way you weave your words. You guide me toward an understanding of how the world works; you make me question things."

"Well, that's good, Keavon. Where others settle for belief, we must seek clarity. It might keep you alive one day."

23

THE WEIGHT OF
A LIFE TAKEN

In war, there are no unwounded soldiers.

—José Narosky

The whole damned world was against Iran. Although it had been Iraq who had invaded its neighbor, world events—not least the American Embassy hostage siege—meant that although officially neutral, the United States provided significant support to Iraq. The United Kingdom was the leading supplier of military hardware and technology to Iraq. The French supplied advanced weaponry, including Exocet missiles and helicopters, and provided training and technical support to the Iraqi military.

However, it was the French Mirage F1 fighter jets that Ricardo and Keavon learned to identify quickly as they fired their antiaircraft missiles into the night sky. Their section commander could not have made it any clearer: "Make no mistake about it; when you are on that gun and you see a French Mirage F1 fighter jet, you get the hell out of there, because if you have seen the plane, you can rest assured that the plane has seen you, and within a few seconds you and your gun will be blown to hell."

The section commander explained that the planes carried precision-guided missiles, and as soon as one of the missiles locked on its target, it never missed.

For two months, the two friends fought hard, and they fought smart. Whenever the French jets were spotted overhead, they ran for their lives. After two months on the guns, their section commander said that they had served Iran well, and two months in such a high-risk environment, where death was a common occurrence, was more than any man should have to face up to.

They stood side by side, their uniforms dusty and worn from months of relentless battle. The section commander, a stern man weathered by war, called them forward. The other soldiers in their unit paused, sensing the moment's gravity.

The commander's gaze first settled on Ricardo. "We are sending you to Khorramshahr," he announced.

Ricardo's heart sank. Situated strategically on the Karun River near the Persian Gulf, it was not just any city; it was a significant battleground, reclaimed from Iraqi forces but always on the verge of conflict.

Ricardo looked over at Keavon, his expression grave. He had traded one front line for another.

Turning to Keavon, the commander continued. "You, soldier, will be posted to Halabja." Halabja, an Iraqi Kurdish town close to the Iran–Iraq border, was another critical area fraught with complex challenges.

—

As they walked back to their tent, their steps were measured, their minds occupied with thoughts of the battles to come and the uncertainty of survival.

"Stay sharp, Keavon," Ricardo said quietly, his voice tinged with concern. "We're both heading into the lion's den."

Keavon looked at Ricardo. "And we'll both come out of it, Ricardo."

Ricardo slapped him on the back. A dark feeling washed over him as he realized there was no real conviction in his friend's words.

They had become close during the tough times on the front lines, looking out for each other, but now Ricardo was worried because they could no longer do that. He knew the challenges they would face in their new locations, and the thought that they might never see each other again was hard to take.

The two friends hugged and said goodbye to each other, and within hours, they were put on buses heading in the opposite direction.

—

Trench warfare held no glamour; it was a living, sleep-deprived hell. As night fell, the battlefield would descend into darkness, and artificial light was kept to a minimum as the soldiers relied on moonlight and starlight. The quiet was often deceptive, masking the dangers lurking in the shadows as sentries kept watch along the trench lines, watching for enemy movement and listening for any unusual sounds.

A moment's lapse of concentration or a desperate desire to catch up on a few minutes' sleep could have grave consequences.

Ricardo had been in the trenches for about a week. He was tired and cold. That particular night dragged, and he longed to be relieved at 6 a.m. to crawl into his sleeping bag for a few hours of sleep. As usual, around midnight, he stood up and stretched his legs. He heard a rustle behind him and felt something cold and wet against his throat. Instinctively, he pulled up his rifle, and the barrel connected with the man's midriff. For one adrenaline-filled second, the light of the moon caught the insignia on the man's uniform, and he realized that he had come face-to-face with an Iraqi soldier.

It was an automatic reaction as Ricardo pulled the trigger, not aiming anywhere in particular, and as the rifle exploded, the man staggered backward and dropped to the ground. A cry went up. The Iraqis had attacked both flanks and somehow infiltrated the trenches on the north and south sides. Ricardo and his comrades were in a fight for their lives.

Shock and disbelief surged through him as he grappled with the reality that he had just taken a life. The world snapped back to life, but he remained frozen, staring at the motionless body. He wanted to feel relief, some sense of accomplishment. But instead, a hollow emptiness filled him, a dark pit opening in his chest. This was different from the drills and the practice targets. This was a life, and he had taken it.

The gravity of his actions weighed heavily on his heart, mingling with intense guilt, yet there was an undeniable rush of excitement, too, because this was real. He felt strangely energized by the immediate danger that sharpened his senses, in a heightened state of alertness, ready to respond to the ongoing threat as the fight raged on.

The battle lasted all night, and as the early morning light filtered into the trenches, Ricardo looked down at his uniform and realized it was soaked with blood. As he lifted a hand to his throat, it slowly dawned on him that the cold steel on his neck had been the Iraqi soldier's knife, and he had been a split second away from having his throat sliced open.

They fought the Iraqis all night, and as the sun cast its rays over the battlefield, the carnage was clear to see as dead and dying men were scattered everywhere.

Suddenly, there was a voice, a medic who told Ricardo to sit down and keep still. Without arguing, he allowed the medic to insert a dozen stitches into his neck wound.

Ricardo was in a daze; it had been the first time he had ever killed a man in such a direct way, and he knew how close he had been to being killed himself. The medic brought him back from his thoughts. "Soldier, get to your feet and help where you can." The medic handed him a first aid kit. "Remember your training: Just get out there and do anything you can."

For the next four or five hours, Ricardo bandaged head wounds, put splints on broken limbs, and much to his surprise, even stitched up wounds. There were no more attacks for the next few weeks, as both sides appeared to regroup, collect their dead, treat their injured, and do their best for those who had survived.

—

One morning, Ricardo was summoned away from the front lines and told to report to his military commander. As he stood at ease in the small office, the man told him he had news of his friend Keavon. Ricardo looked at the expression on the man's face, and he knew he wasn't about to deliver good news.

"There has been a chemical weapon attack on Halabja. That dog Hussein has used a nerve agent on our brave soldiers; thousands have died."

"And Keavon?" Ricardo said, but he already knew the answer.

"Your friend is one of Allah's martyrs; his family will be proud of him. I knew you and Keavon were very close, so I want you to take his body back home to his parents. We believe you have done enough for your homeland; it's time to go home."

The military commander got to his feet. "Both of you—both of you must go home together."

24

A GLIMMER
OF HOPE

We must accept finite disappointment but never lose infinite hope.
—Martin Luther King Jr.

Ali and Samira sat across from each other. Samira's eyes were anxious yet hopeful, a stark contrast to the last time they had met in this same café, under much more dire circumstances.

Ali leaned forward, a gentle smile breaking across his face. "Samira, I have good news."

"You found him?" she asked, her voice barely a whisper.

"Yes, we found him and managed to arrange his discharge. He's coming home, Samira."

The relief that washed over Samira was visible: Her shoulders slumped and tears welled up in her eyes as she absorbed Ali's words. "He's coming home? After all this time?"

"Yes, he's coming home. It took some doing, a lot of talks, and a few favors called in by my uncle, but it's all arranged. He's safe, and he'll be back with us soon."

Samira took a deep breath. "I can't believe it. Thank you, Ali. How can I ever repay you for this?"

"There's no need for repayment. Seeing you and your son reunited will be more than enough for me. He is a dear friend and has helped me a lot. He's survived so much; it's time for him to come home, to heal."

Samira nodded, wiping the tears that had started to spill over. "Yes, it's time. I want to hold my son again."

—

Ricardo and another soldier shared the ride in a small military truck and drove through the night to Arak, where they were met with Keavon's body. They loaded his corpse onto their vehicle, had a little food and some rest, and departed for Tehran soon after. Ricardo hardly spoke with the driver; he was in no mood for words. All he wanted to do was contemplate quietly and think about the bond he had shared with his friend.

For a fleeting moment, he believed in a god—a demonic, evil entity who, for some reason, had it in for him. This god hated him and was going to punish him with the death of every person he ever cared for.

—

In Tehran, Keavon's family were waiting at the military base. His mother and father stood solemnly with an older brother of Keavon's and his young sister. There were some cousins, an aunt, and an uncle. They were there to collect the body, which had to be prepared for the funeral the next day.

Ricardo stood back as a team of soldiers transferred the body to the family vehicle. He wanted to step forward; he wanted to tell Keavon's parents what a special man he was and what a special bond they had between them. He wanted to say that if only the Iranian military had kept the two men together, fighting side by side, Keavon would still be alive.

But he didn't. He remained motionless, lost in his own thoughts as he watched the vehicle drive away.

—

Ricardo stood on the familiar doorstep, raised his hand, and knocked. The door swung open after a moment that seemed to stretch into eternity, and Samira stood there.

"Ricardo!" she exclaimed, her voice cracking with emotion. She stepped forward, engulfing him in a tight embrace.

Ricardo buried his face in her shoulder. "I'm home, Mom."

Samira pulled back slightly, holding his face in her hands, tears streaming down her cheeks. "I prayed for this day, my son. I prayed every day. I can't believe you're here."

—

After a few hours at home, Ricardo wanted to reconnect with Hannah. He picked up Samira's car keys and drove with apprehension, but also hope, toward Farhad's house. Their last meeting had been fraught with conflict. The memory of that confrontation was crystal clear as he parked outside Farhad's house.

He remembered Hannah's harsh words and the sting of her slap, but he took several deep breaths and steeled himself to face her again. Determined, he stepped out of the car and approached the door.

He knocked tentatively. The door swung open. Hannah stood frozen in momentary shock, tears welling in her eyes.

"Hi, Hannah," Ricardo said softly.

Hannah's voice broke with emotion. "Ricardo, is that really you?"

She threw her arms around him, her body shaking with sobs. Ricardo hugged her back tightly.

"I'm so sorry, Hannah," Ricardo whispered. "I missed you so much."

Hannah smiled through her tears. "I thought I'd lost you forever. I was so angry, but I never stopped caring, Ricardo."

"Let's not lose each other again," Ricardo murmured.

They stepped inside together and sat down in Farhad's living room. They began to talk, eager to heal the wounds of the past and rebuild the close bond they had once shared.

Ricardo learned that Farhad and Hannah had been married for a few months, and she was planning to move to Denmark. It was a shock of monumental proportions. He didn't know what to say.

—

Keavon's funeral was an elaborate affair, so different from Bahar's. The funeral was a large, solemn event, following the traditions of a Muslim ceremony. Many people gathered and filled the streets, carrying his coffin through the neighborhood streets to the mosque and then the cemetery. As they walked toward the mosque, the crowd raised their voices, chanting *"Allahu Akbar"*—*God is great*—as they moved toward his grave.

Not so great that he took such a fine brother, Ricardo thought to himself.

Nevertheless, it was a powerful and moving scene—an entire community coming together to honor Keavon's life and say their final goodbyes.

As they laid the young man's body in the ground, all Ricardo could think of was Bahar. It brought everything back, as if it were yesterday.

As he listened to the solemn words spoken at the service, memories of their time together on the front lines surfaced, conversations that had forged a deep bond between them. He vividly recalled a specific discussion in which Keavon had shared his dreams of returning home, rebuilding his life, and starting a family, and then had asked him, "What are we fighting for?"

"For family," Ricardo had answered.

Keavon's dreams had been shattered.

25

THE SOCIAL DIVIDE

All animals are equal, but some animals
are more equal than others.
—George Orwell

icardo took a few weeks off and then picked up his studies where he had left off. He was about to graduate. Toward the end of the first week back at school, Ricardo caught up with his old friend Shahram. Shahram had an incredible tale to tell.

While Ricardo has been away fighting in the Army, Shahram had met the girl of his dreams, Lyla, and fallen in love.

He was happy for his good friend; he deserved to find true love.

"But there is a problem," Shahram explained. "I have asked her father for her hand in marriage, and he has refused. He told me to get the hell out of his house; he would rather die than see his daughter marry somebody like me."

Ricardo shook his head; he knew only too well about the class system that still held sway in Iran. Shahram's father was poor, an unskilled laborer who had struggled with poverty most of his life. On the other hand, Lyla's father was connected, a wealthy business owner with ties to high-ranking government officials.

"And there's another problem," Shahram said rather sheepishly.

"Go on."

"Well . . . we've been intimate . . ."

Ricardo placed his hand over his mouth. "No, you don't mean to tell me you've . . ."

"We've slept together, Ricardo; I'm afraid she is no longer a virgin."

Ricardo was well aware of the gravity and seriousness of the situation his friend had just explained. He said Lyla's father was the type of man who would readily agree to a virginity test for his daughter. While it was not an official state policy, virginity tests were conducted in some conservative and traditional circles due to cultural and societal norms around purity and honor. Failing the test could result in severe consequences. Any marriage arrangements could be canceled, significantly impacting the girl's prospects for future marriages, and in extreme cases, the girls could face violence or even honor killings.

"Oh dear," Ricardo said. "You've put poor Lyla in a real mess."

"Her father is a real religious hothead; I don't know what he'll do to her if he finds out."

As Shahram broke down in tears, Ricardo placed an arm around his shoulders. "Don't worry, my friend; I'll work something out."

—

They met again the following day. Shahram was sad and angry. "Her father is an asshole who still lives in the sixth century. He'll have her tested, and then she'll be punished. My god, how far will he take it? You know some fathers don't want—"

"Don't say it, Shahram; it won't come to that. I have a plan."

"What possible plan could you have?"

"I will marry her for you."

Shahram's reaction was to laugh uncontrollably for more than a minute. As Ricardo waited patiently for him to calm down, he eventually spoke.

"I am very well connected, Shahram. Before the revolution, my family was good friends of the Shah. Our family is well respected in Tehran and wealthier than Lyla's father and family. Marrying into my family would be a step up the social ladder for her, though it pains me to use such language. My family would not insist on a virginity test before the marriage, and therefore, your secret would be safe."

"Hah! Excellent planning, and then what happens? It's a ludicrous plan; in fact, it's the daftest plan I've ever heard in my life, and if you think I'm going to go through with that, then you have another thing coming."

—

Ricardo entered the kitchen. Samira was preparing dinner.

"Mom," Ricardo began, "I need to talk to you about something quite important."

Samira looked up, her expression shifting to one of concern. "What is it, Ricardo?"

"I've been giving much thought to my future, and I've decided it's time for me to settle down and start a family."

"Settle down? But you're so young; you haven't even been dating."

Ricardo took a deep breath. "I understand it might seem sudden, but this is the right time for me. There's someone . . . a girl named Lyla."

Samira's confusion deepened. "Lyla? I haven't heard you mention her before. Are you sure about this?"

"Yes, I am. We haven't spoken much, and I know it's unconventional for our family, but after the war and everything, I'd like us to meet her family and discuss marriage."

Samira paused, the signs of her anxiety apparent. "Ricardo, you're my son, and I want the best for you, but with someone you barely know?"

"She's a wonderful girl."

"We'll discuss this more, but if you're to make such a commitment, I need to know who this young woman is."

"Her family, I'd like you to—"

Samira held up a hand. "Yes, I'll meet her family; we can take it from there."

———

A week later, Ricardo, Samira, Aunt Sudabeh, and Uncle Masood arrived at Lyla's family home to a warm and enthusiastic welcome from her parents. Her father was particularly animated and joyful, greeting them at the door with open arms and expressing his delight over the families' potential union.

"Welcome, welcome." He beamed as he led them into the living room, where aromatic hints of saffron and rose water filled the air. "We are so honored by your visit today."

The conversation flowed easily; they discussed shared values and future aspirations. Lyla's father expressed his heartfelt joy and expectations for the union.

Lyla entered the room carrying a tray with tea and pastries. She began serving each guest with practiced precision. Though her movements were meticulous, her demeanor was noticeably restrained. When she briefly met Ricardo's eyes, her expression conveyed a subtle discomfort.

As the visit neared its end, Lyla's father suggested, "It seems like Lyla and Ricardo could benefit from getting to know each other better. Perhaps they should go out to dinner together?"

Ricardo and Lyla exchanged a look.

"That sounds like a great idea," Ricardo said.

———

Lyla's father had a grin as wide as the Karun River. After doing his checks on him, he realized Ricardo was a fine, upstanding man; he had played his part in the war against Iraq and even fought on the front lines. Ricardo had been fearless and wounded in action. He was also an Islamic student, and his family name was well respected and connected to all of the best circles. Ricardo would make a fine husband for his daughter.

—

Lyla sat across from Ricardo at a table adorned with fine linens and crystal glassware in the elegant setting of a five-star Persian restaurant in north Tehran. The restaurant's luxurious decor and the soft melodies of traditional Persian music in the background did little to ease Lyla's tension about the meeting her father had arranged with such enthusiasm.

Ricardo, dressed impeccably for the occasion, was acutely aware of the delicate situation. He initiated the conversation and leaned forward slightly. "There's something important I need to tell you."

"I'm all ears."

"I know you don't want to marry me."

Lyla leaned back in her seat. "And why would that be?" she said.

"Because you're in love with someone else. Moreover, you've been intimate with him."

Lyla's face flushed. "How dare you? I'm as pure as the driven snow; no man has ever—"

"Shahram told me; he is the reason I am here."

—

Ricardo explained the intricate details of the plan. He said it was a radical idea, but it would shield her from societal judgment and preserve her father's happiness. "Then, in time, we will separate and divorce. You and Shahram will need to be patient, but then he'll ask for your hand in marriage, and this time, your father will approve."

"You're suggesting a temporary marriage that only you, me, and Shahram would know about?"

"Yes. What do you think?"

"It's a ridiculous suggestion," she said, "the worst plan I've ever heard in my life, and if you think I'm going to go through with that, then you have another thing coming."

—

The wedding day finally arrived, and Lyla's big backyard was transformed into a festive venue. It was filled with lush trees and decorated with colorful flowers, creating a cheerful and inviting atmosphere.

Traditional Persian music filled the air with lively tunes as the guests arrived, and the yard buzzed with people chatting and laughing.

In the middle of the yard was a unique wedding spread called the *sofreh aghd*, decorated with various symbolic items including a mirror, candles, sweets, coins, rose petals, and a book of poetry, all intended to bring the couple happiness, prosperity, and love.

Ricardo stood by the sofreh in a well-made Italian suit. Lyla, wearing a beautiful, traditional white dress, made her entrance to cheers from the guests. She walked over petals scattered by the younger children.

The ceremony started with Ricardo and Lyla sitting in front of the mirror. A woman who was close to the bride and her family rubbed sugar cones together, showering the couple with sweetness and symbolizing a sweet life together. Family members decorated Lyla with gold jewelry, symbolizing the wealth and prosperity bestowed upon her by those who cherished her most.

The couple exchanged vows and rings, performed the honey ritual by feeding each other honey to symbolize sweetness, and listened to blessings and readings.

After the ceremony, the music got livelier, and everyone started dancing—mixed groups of men and women, allowed to celebrate together freely, away from strict public rules.

The feast followed, a lavish spread of Persian delicacies: fragrant saffron rice, succulent kebabs, various stews, and delicious desserts like baklava and Persian ice cream.

As the night continued, the yard was softly lit with strings of lights, and the music mellowed. Ricardo and Lyla spent the evening mingling and laughing with their guests, surrounded by love and good wishes in the beautiful outdoor setting they had created for their special day.

Shahram attended the wedding too, his expression clouded with concern. Ricardo excused himself from a group of laughing relatives and approached his friend, clapping him on the shoulder to get his attention.

"Shahram, my friend, you seem a bit distant tonight. What's on your mind?" Ricardo asked.

Shahram glanced around to make sure no one was listening. "Ricardo, I know what we agreed on, but I can't help feeling anxious about what happens after this . . . you know, after the ceremony."

Ricardo nodded. "I get it, Shahram, but remember, I gave you my word and intend to keep it."

Shahram looked down, fidgeting with his watch. "I know, but it's hard not to worry. It's all so unconventional."

"Listen," Ricardo said, leaning in closer, "tonight, after everything here winds down, Lyla and I will go to the hotel as planned. But I assure you, we're not going to do anything. We'll watch videos, maybe some films I missed out on while I was gone. Nothing more."

"You promise? It's just, she's so beautiful and . . . you have been away so long."

Ricardo placed a hand on Shahram's shoulder. "I promise, Shahram. You are like my brother, and I will never betray you. Tonight is a formality, a step toward fixing things so you and Lyla can be together."

Shahram exhaled slowly, his shoulders relaxing as he processed

Ricardo's words. "Thank you, Ricardo. I'm sorry for doubting. It's just a lot to take in."

"No need to apologize; I understand completely."

At that moment, Lyla walked by, smiled at both men, and joined another group of family members. Ricardo and Shahram's eyes fixed on her beautiful figure, accentuated by the close-fitting dress.

"Then again," Ricardo said, "a new husband has needs."

Shahram looked at Ricardo with a flash of momentary anger, until he saw his friend's wicked grin. Shahram punched him playfully in the stomach. "You're a bad man, Ricardo, to joke about something like this."

—

Ricardo and his bride drove away to the marital hotel suite, as both families looked on with admiration. *They make a beautiful couple,* Lyla's father thought. *My grandchildren will be the most handsome babies in Iran.*

—

But Ricardo and Lyla would never have any children, and there was no chance of any intimate relationship between them, because Ricardo had agreed with Shahram that he wouldn't even kiss his beautiful bride, wouldn't lay a hand on her, and would also find a solution for the virginity test. That was the easy bit.

The morning after the wedding, the first light of dawn filtered softly through the curtains of the hotel wedding suite. Ricardo stirred stiffly on the uncomfortable couch, stretching as he awoke from a night spent precisely as planned—watching videos on an old Betamax player. Across the room, Lyla was already up, sitting at a small table near the window, sipping a cup of tea.

"Good morning," Ricardo greeted her.

"Good morning," Lyla responded warmly. "We did it, didn't we?"

Ricardo chuckled softly as he stood up and stretched again. "Well, we didn't do it, just like we planned."

She laughed.

He glanced toward the bedroom where they had staged a small but significant act the night before. "Especially with that little bit of theatrics with the animal blood."

Lyla nodded, remembering the moment. "I still can't believe we did that, using the vial of animal blood you brought to stain the bedsheets—just to keep up appearances. It felt so bizarre."

"It was one of the more unusual things I've done," Ricardo admitted as he joined her at the table and poured himself a cup of tea. "But it helped cement our story, especially if anyone gets too curious. I'm just glad it's all over now, and we can go back to normal, or as normal as it gets from here."

Lyla smiled. "Thank you for everything, Ricardo. I know this wasn't easy for you and that it cost you a lot of money for the wedding and all the arrangements. You're an incredible friend."

—

The penultimate part of Ricardo's plan was put into action precisely six months later.

Ricardo sat across from Lyla's father in the same living room where they had first discussed the marriage. The room was quiet, and the tension was evident as Ricardo prepared to deliver the news that he had planned from the start.

"What is it, Ricardo? Is everything all right?"

Ricardo took a deep breath. "I'm afraid things aren't going well between Lyla and me. It's been a difficult few months, and, after much thought, I believe it's best if we part ways. We are getting a divorce."

The news hit Lyla's father hard. "This is quite sudden, Ricardo. What seems to be the problem? Is there anything we can do to help?"

"It's mostly about our plans . . . and children," Ricardo explained. "Lyla is ready to start a family, but I've realized I'm not prepared for children. It's not fair to her. She's been doing her best to make our relationship work, but our desires for the future don't align. I feel I'm holding her back. It's been tough with the war and things; I guess I have a lot of unresolved issues I didn't know about."

"It is regrettable, but I understand your position," Lyla's father said. "In Islam, the husband has the final say, and if this is your decision, then there is not much more I can do, is there?"

Ricardo shook his head and gazed toward the floor.

As the conversation concluded, Ricardo excused himself and left, confident that he had effectively set the stage for the final part of their plan.

—

The last piece of the grand deception slotted into place when Shahram returned to Lyla's father a few months later and, for the second time, asked for Lyla's hand in marriage.

Her father did not hesitate to agree. He viewed his daughter as soiled goods; indeed, no man with any self-respect would ask for his daughter's hand. Divorce was seen as an adverse event; divorced women were judged harshly by society and perceived as having failed in their marital duties.

This was a real stroke of luck, he thought. "Yes, you may marry my daughter, Shahram," he replied. "I've always thought you were a fine boy."

And strangely enough, he respected the man who stood before him. *He must truly love my daughter with all of his heart if he is prepared to marry her after another man has been there first.*

26

CHASING THE WIND

It is the obligation of every person born in a safer room to open the door when someone in danger knocks.

—Dina Nayeri

Samira answered the knock at the door. It was late, an unusual hour for a visitor. Ricardo had his head in a book but looked up as his mother spoke. She turned around, a worried look etched across her face. "It is Ali; he has some news."

Ali burst into the room, his face flushed, sweat on his brow. "Ricardo, I bring grave news; you must go, you must go now."

His good friend blurted out his story that Ricardo's anti-government friends had been arrested. "They tortured them, and one of them gave the government your name. They are on their way here now; they say you are the Shadow Rider."

Samira spoke. "Wait a minute, Ali, what are you talking about? I—"

"There's no time, Samira. He must go; he must flee the country. His execution paper is out; they will kill him on the spot if he resists arrest."

Ricardo trusted his good friend with his life; he had never seen him in such an animated, desperate state. Ali's uncle was involved in all the

top circles, and whatever Ali was saying had to have come from his association with high-ranking officials in the Revolutionary Guard.

Ricardo stared into his mother's eyes. He opened his mouth to speak.
"I . . . there's something I need—"

Samira reached for her purse. "There's no time to explain; you heard
Ali." She handed him everything in her purse. "You'll need money. Pack
a bag and then go to Masood's. He knows people."

—

Ali and Ricardo sat down at a table with Masood. He confirmed that one
of his friends had also told him of a big government crackdown; many
people had already been executed, and thousands were being interrogated in prison.

"We need to get you out of the country, Ricardo," Masood said.

Ricardo buried his head in his hands. "And how will I do that? Where
will I go?"

"I know people," Masood said. "We have money—money talks. I'll
make contact with the people smugglers."

—

In the early hours of the morning, Masood took a phone call. Ricardo
listened carefully to his uncle, but most of the conversation came from
whoever had made the call. It was clear the caller was giving Masood
instructions.

Ricardo sat up on the sofa. He was tired; he had slept fitfully. His
brain was too active, and yes . . . he was scared.

As the first light of dawn began to seep through the darkness,
Tehran stirred from its slumber. Masood handed him a coffee. "It is
time," he said.

Ricardo took the cup and walked toward the kitchen window. The sky began to lighten as he looked up at the Alborz mountains in the distance, their snowcapped peaks catching the first early morning rays of the sun. The streets were still quiet; the air was crisp and cool.

Masood handed him a note. "Here is an address. Make your way to Qods on foot. On no account take any public transport; they will have spies on every damn bus." Masood took a deep breath and sighed. "Ask for Chishti." Masood handed him an envelope. "This is his payment. He will get you to the Turkish border, and then you are on your own."

The sheer enormity of what his uncle Masood told him gradually sank in. He was about to flee the country, about to become a refugee, seeking refuge in a country he had only ever seen on a map. He couldn't speak the language; he knew nobody.

"Tell the authorities you are an American; tell them your father's name."

—

Chishti drove him to Qazvin, where he was put into a truck. The driver and his associate repeated what Uncle Masood had told him: All they could do was get him to the Turkish border, and then he would be alone.

They drove to Sanandaj, in Kurdistan, and then headed north. The journey took all day. The temperature dropped as the road twisted and turned and began its gradual ascent into the mountains toward the Turkish border. More people climbed into the truck: PKR fighters who were fighting for Kurdish independence.

They all had a story to tell, and Ricardo was horrified at their tales of mass arrests and executions. One man explained that because of the war, all the rules had gone out of the window, and the Supreme Leader Ayatollah Khomeini had issued a *fatwa*, targeting the MEK and other leftist groups. He mentioned secret trials that were closed to the public—trials consisting of Islamic judges—executions carried out within hours of sentence, and talk of mass graves.

—

At Orumiyeh, Ricardo met another group of people. Chishti told him they were the only people who could smuggle him into Turkey. Chishti handed them some money, shook Ricardo's hand, and wished him good luck.

From there, he took another truck that climbed into the mountains toward the Turkish border. After three hours, they arrived at a secluded base camp. It was already dark, and the Kurdish guides told him it would be a challenging, long hike to the border.

They trekked for several days through mountain paths, avoiding the Iranian border guards who were on high alert.

The paths were covered with snow, and the temperature fell below freezing. As they made camp, the guides told them they could not make any fires to keep warm, as the Iranian border guards would see the flames and smoke.

At first light, they were joined by more refugees on their way to Turkey.

Ricardo noticed a woman in the new group. Her face was marked with fatigue, and she was carrying a baby in her arms.

Ricardo approached her. "Hi, I'm Ricardo," he said, "I couldn't help but notice you and your baby; how are you managing?"

"I'm Shahla. Yes, it's hard, but we have no other option. I'm from Isfahan, and I'm part of the MEK group. It was too dangerous to stay behind. They executed my husband, and I fled with my daughter; she's all I have left in the world."

"I can only imagine how difficult it must be. If there's anything I can do to help, please let me know."

"Thank you, it means a lot to have your support."

—

They began their journey into the mountains. They walked for two days, and at night, they huddled together in caves that only their guides knew about. Their only food was dates and stale bread.

On the third day, they had been walking for no more than an hour when one of the men stopped and crouched down to his knees, indicating to the rest of the group that they should do the same. Ricardo looked up and saw a border patrol heading toward them in the distance. They clambered behind some rocks as the guards came nearer.

"We must stay quiet," one of the men said.

As if on cue, the baby started to cry. The man glared at the young mother. "Keep it quiet. If they find us, you know what they will do: They'll kill you, but not before they've had their fun. There are not many women in these mountains."

His statement wasn't lost on the woman as she clamped her hand over the infant's mouth. It had no effect; the shock of the cold hand on the baby's face had the opposite effect, and it started to cry even louder.

"Shut it up!" the man whispered. "Shut it up now, or we'll all be killed."

Shahla pressed harder and muffled the child's cries.

"Harder," the man cried. "I can still hear it, and the guards are coming this way."

Ricardo looked on as the mother, in a state of panic, pushed her scarf against the young baby's face, and, at last, its cries were stifled.

The guards came within fifty yards of their position but seemed in no hurry to leave. They stopped for a few minutes while they shared a cigarette.

After what seemed like an eternity, eventually, they left and made their way down the mountain.

The man stood up and smiled. "We are in the clear. We are good to go," he said.

Ricardo became aware that Shahla was panicking; she was shaking her child. "She's not breathing," she said. "She's not breathing."

Ricardo rushed over. The baby was still warm, but there was no sign of life. Shahla was crying hysterically. One of the other men was attempting to give the child mouth-to-mouth to resuscitate her, but there was no sign of life. They did everything they could, but it was clear that the child had died.

Shahla was inconsolable. The men took charge and dug out a shallow grave in the snow as Ricardo looked on helplessly. The stark reality of the baby's sudden death hit Ricardo hard; what had compelled Shahla to make such a dangerous trip? She had heard the stories whispered by those who dared speak of the regime's brutality, of women like her who had stood defiant, whose voices had carried too far, and who had paid the price with their lives. Why, he asked himself, why must men act this way? At first, it had seemed like a fight she could win. But then came the crackdown. Her friends disappeared, one by one. Some were imprisoned, others . . . she never heard from again. Her husband was dragged away in the middle of the night, the guards saying she would be next.

As he helped to pull her away from the shallow grave, she became hysterical. She clung to Ricardo and begged him to let her stay by the grave.

"We must go on; it's what your daughter and your husband would have wanted."

He sat her down. He told her about Bahar and the promises he had made in her memory. "We need to draw our strength from our despair, Shahla. Otherwise, they win."

—

They walked for hours. Shahla's tears never stopped.

Eventually, she collapsed to the ground. She didn't want to go on. "Leave me here; I have nothing to live for. I shall die here."

He talked again.

Shahla listened.

"I'm not leaving without you," he said. "I'll die here in the snow with you, if that's what you want."

Eventually, she stood and reached for Ricardo's hand. "Let's go. With you by my side, at least we'll have a chance."

—

Shahla had unearthed more painful memories of Bahar's death. He had tucked away those agonizing emotions, hoping time might dull their sharp edges. Yet witnessing Shahla's devastating loss, the old wounds of losing Bahar ripped open, as raw and overwhelming as the day it happened.

—

After days of trekking, the border was finally within sight. A group of Kurdish Bedouins approached them casually as they sat and rested. The men announced that the group would be separating and split into individuals. That way, they stood a better chance of crossing the border.

"This is goodbye," Ricardo said. "Take care, Shahla. I hope you find peace and safety. I will always remember you. I promise, from the depths of my heart, that I will do everything I can to make sure no other mother has to go through your pain."

Shahla nodded as she wiped away her tears. "Thank you, Ricardo. Be safe, my dear friend."

Ricardo was directed to follow an old sheepherder among the Bedouins.

The harrowing journey and the farewell to Shahla changed Ricardo forever. The stark realities of the choice she had had to make to keep the baby quiet reshaped his perspective on the cruelty of life and mankind. He pledged to do everything he could to protect the inno-cent for the rest of his days. That is what Bahar had fought for; this is what she believed in.

—

The Bedouins were herding two thousand sheep back and forth over the border through the mountain passes. They explained that the border guards seldom stopped them: Their faces were familiar with the guards, their nomadic lifestyle posed no threat, and they crossed the borders during daylight hours, as the sheep wouldn't walk in the darkness.

Ricardo asked the question: Then how are you going to smuggle me across the border?"

The Bedouin smiled and took a large knife from his belt. "Follow me."

The Bedouin selected one of the larger sheep, took a handful of wool on its neck, and held it between his legs. As Ricardo looked on in horror, the man positioned the knife to the side of the sheep's head and pulled the knife swiftly across its throat. The animal let out a brief squeal, struggled, and collapsed onto the ground in less than a minute. Ricardo couldn't imagine what the dead sheep had to do with him making his escape across the border, but he would soon find out.

The Bedouin began to skin the animal, and, little by little, the sheep pelt came away from the carcass. Eventually, the Bedouin, covered in blood, held up the sheepskin and then announced that Ricardo had a new winter coat. Still puzzled, it became apparent when the Bedouin made him drop onto his hands and knees and laid the pelt across his back. "You are a sheep now," he said, grinning. "You will walk with the sheep, you will eat with the sheep, you will piss and shit like the sheep. We will get you across the border this way."

Ricardo looked up toward the mountain pass and asked, "How far?"

"Three miles," the Bedouin said. "Not far."

Ricardo knew it would be the longest journey he had ever under-taken, but what other option did he have?

—

The biting wind howled through the craggy peaks; his hands and knees were numb as he inched forward between the sheep. The stench of sheep's wool mixed with blood overwhelmed his senses. Once pristine and pretty, the snow sapped his strength with each laborious crawl. His knees were bruised and bloodied as they scraped against the frozen ground. Strips of flesh had been torn away from his palms and knuckles, leaving a trail of crimson drops in the snow.

He allowed himself no more than an occasional glance up into the steely gray canvas and ducked his head down whenever he heard a voice. The border guards were everywhere.

Every breath was searing agony as the frigid air tore through his throat and lungs like shards of glass; it was only the sheer force of willpower that drove him forward. "Bahar, Bahar," he whispered to himself, over and over again.

He felt her presence urging him on; Bahar was with him, giving him strength. She was his silent guardian, pushing him onward whenever he wanted to give up. Her memory was a beacon of hope. "Bahar, Bahar, Bahar."

—

At last, the Bedouin announced they had made it.

Ricardo collapsed as the man poured hot tea into his mouth. He had never felt so cold, and wondered if he would ever feel his fingers and toes again.

They rested through the night. Ricardo was glad of the warm clothing he had been given and clung to the dead sheep's pelt as if his life depended on it.

He had made it across the border.

—

As instructed, he turned himself in to the first Turkish police station he found, announcing he was an American seeking political asylum.

There was a problem. "What sort of American can't speak English?" the official asked.

Ricardo persevered and told them his father's name and his last known address in Detroit.

Twenty-four hours later, he was transferred to a holding prison for refugees.

Ricardo noticed a man leaning against one of the walls inside the stark, crowded confines of the refugee holding prison. Unlike everybody else, he had a calm, reassuring demeanor, and they started a conversation.

He was called Abbas; a truck driver with a work permit, he said he would be released in a few hours.

Ricardo warmed to him immediately, and the truck driver surprised him when he handed him his telephone number. "Call me when you're out, and we'll figure something out for you."

Ricardo hoped the man was genuine. Was this the lifeline he sought?

"Thank you, Abbas. I appreciate this."

—

The first meeting with the consulate representative did not go well, because Ricardo could not speak English, and the representative barely understood what Ricardo was talking about. If only he could make them understand that he was an American by way of his father.

"So tell me again," the consulate representative said, "what is your father's full name?"

27

THE GOLDEN TICKET

The world is full of obvious things which nobody by any chance ever observes.

—Arthur Conan Doyle

The sun had barely crested the Cairo horizon, yet the relentless heat was already seeping into every crevice. The air hung heavy with humidity. It was going to be another sweltering day. In the less salubrious quarters of the city, the scene was a stark contrast to the iconic images of pyramids and bustling markets. Amid the warren of narrow streets, it was a daily struggle for survival.

The buildings leaned precariously, their façades graffitied and crumbling under years of neglect. Makeshift shops lined the streets; their owners touted their vegetables, secondhand clothes, and trinkets. The air smelled of uncollected garbage and acrid smoke from open fires, where low-income families cooked meager meals.

Children darted through the alleyways, their laughter a brief respite from the bleakness around them. Some were barefoot as they played amid the rubble and refuse. Women in faded hijabs haggled over prices at the market stalls, their voices blending with the distant honking of car horns and the persistent calls to prayer echoing from minarets.

In these parts of Cairo, the roads were little more than dirt tracks, riddled with potholes and strewn with debris. The electricity was unreliable; the water, when available, flowed sluggishly from corroded pipes. Life in these streets was a life lived on the edge.

—

In stark contrast, the Dutch Embassy stood just a few miles away. A fortress of glass and steel loomed imposingly over the city, its air-conditioned interiors a world apart from the sweltering streets. The embassy was an enclave of comfort and modernity, its immaculate grounds and pristine offices a testament to Western wealth and power.

Inside, the atmosphere was calm and serene. Diplomatic staff moved through the halls with purposeful strides, their faces reflecting none of the hardships faced by those outside. Meetings were held in plush conference rooms, where the hum of air-conditioning provided a constant, soothing backdrop.

Security was tight. Guards stationed at every entrance and surveillance cameras monitoring every corner ensured that Cairo's troubles remained at bay.

From the windows of the vast kitchen, David looked out over the sprawling cityscape.

The chef in residence was preoccupied with preparing a meal for the Netherlands ambassador—at least, they thought he was a chef. But David was much more than a chef.

He glanced at the simmering pots as an embassy staff member approached him. "David, you have an urgent call," he said, gesturing toward the office.

David wiped his hands on his apron and hurried over, picking up the receiver.

"David speaking."

"Lieutenant Colonel Stevens from the US Embassy in Izmir, Turkey. This is a secure line."

"Lieutenant Colonel, how are you?"

Lieutenant Colonel Stevens was in no mood for small talk. "We have a situation here."

"Tell me."

"We have a young man in a holding cell; he claims to be your son."

"In Turkey?"

"Yes."

"Impossible, my son is in Tehran."

"That's what we thought. He said he is a rebel, has been fighting the government, gave us some cock-and-bull story that he crawled over the snow-covered mountains on his hands and knees with a sheepskin on his back, and that if we send him back to Iran, he'll be executed."

David didn't answer. *It wasn't possible, surely not.*

Lieutenant Colonel Stevens continued. "He hardly speaks a word of English, surely he can't be—"

"What's his first name, sir?" David interrupted. He heard the rustle of paper.

"Ricardo."

David's legs weakened. He held on to the desk for support and slowly sank into a seat. "Tell me more."

Lieutenant Colonel Stevens read from a file for over five minutes while David sat back and took it all in. He never uttered a single word.

Eventually, the attaché spoke. "Well, David, are you there? What do you think?"

David paused, taking a moment to settle. "That's my son, sir; there's no doubt that's my son. I always knew that boy had my blood in him."

"He wants a US passport."

"Issue it."

"You sure?"

"Yes, issue the passport, but please ensure the boy doesn't learn anything about my whereabouts. He mustn't know."

"We'll handle it discreetly. Thank you, David. Have a good day."

David hung up, his mind racing with thoughts of the boy in a Turkish holding cell. *How old would he be now, and what the hell had he gotten himself involved in?*

And then the reality sank in: It was none of his concern. He had no son and no family. He had a duty to his country, and nothing else existed.

He picked up the phone and pressed three buttons. "Hi, Oscar, can you tell me the ETA of the Dutch ambassador?"

28

A FORTUNE IN
PATIENCE

*The price of anything is the amount of
life you exchange for it.*
—Henry David Thoreau

Ricardo had been in the holding prison for just over a month when the American official arranged another appointment with him and handed over the holy grail: an American passport.

"You can stay no more than thirty days in Turkey, and then you have to leave."

"Where will I go? " Ricardo asked.

The man shrugged. "You should have thought about that before you left Iran."

—

Ricardo had five dollars and a pocketful of Iranian money, which he quickly learned was useless in Turkey. He couldn't even change it at the bank, but he managed to phone Samira and tell her he was safe.

What she told him turned his blood to ice.

She said the authorities had turned up at her house within hours of him going missing. They ransacked her home, turned it upside down, and then went to see his uncle Masood and his aunt Sudabeh. They were interrogated for three days and three nights before eventually being freed. They fared better than most people arrested. The MEK crackdown had been brutal; it was said that more than thirty thousand people had been executed.

Ricardo hung up the phone and slid down the wall onto his backside. What a predicament he was in! How could he ever return home?

He had to get to America; that was the only way.

He used the last of his coins to call Abbas. He told him he was free but had no money and had thirty days to leave the country.

"And where will you go?" Abbas said.

"I need to get to America."

"That's going to cost you a lot of money."

"I know."

"OK, then you can come and work for me. I will pay you in cash. You have an American passport, which allows you to cross borders, and I need a strong, young man to load and unload my truck. You stay where you are. I will be with you in about three hours."

——

While loading a truck one day, Ricardo noticed that the crate's weight didn't match its listed contents. Driven by curiosity, he pried it open and discovered a hidden compartment of rifles buried beneath some agricultural machinery.

He guessed Abbas was deeply involved in the MEK network that Ricardo knew operated in the region. He was a supplier of arms and ammunition to MEK and PKE across the Turkish frontier.

Ricardo put two and two together and figured Abbas's routine involved transporting ordinary cargo from Turkey to various Western European nations, only to return with weaponry.

—

Ricardo and Abbas were taking a break. Ricardo thought it was time to bring up the topic of his discovery. "I hear you're into some heavy stuff; I've heard you're transporting weapons across borders. Pretty dangerous, huh?"

Abbas eyed him suspiciously. "It's dangerous, that's for sure, but it's important to me. You wouldn't understand."

Ricardo shook his head. "Hah! You're not the only rebel here, Abbas; we are fighting for the same thing. Why do you think I had to cross the border that way?"

Abbas pointed at him. "But you're just a boy; what the hell could you do?"

"I'm more than a boy, and I've been in from the beginning. I've also served on the front lines, killed Iraqi soldiers, and seen others die in front of me. I used to lead the Revolutionary Guards into ambushes on a motorcycle."

Abbas looked shocked; his mouth fell open. "That was you, the Shadow Rider?"

"That's me."

Abbas held out a hand, and Ricardo shook it. "It's a true honor to be in your company, man. Do not worry: I will ensure you have enough money for that ticket once this is all over."

—

From that day forward, Ricardo and Abbas began collaborating on the trips. The arrangement was perfect, because each time Ricardo left Turkey for another European destination, his visa was automatically renewed for another thirty days. All the while, Ricardo focused on saving money for his plane ticket to the United States. He wasn't exactly sure where he would go, but he had fond memories of Detroit.

—

Abbas arranged a job for Ricardo in Istanbul as a dishwasher in one of the city's restaurants. It was flexible enough to give him time off when Abbas needed him on the truck. Ricardo loved Istanbul; the city was always buzzing with life and an incredible mix of old-world charm and new-world hustle. It had everything, from lively markets and trendy cafés to ancient mosques standing alongside modern buildings. It reminded him a lot of Tehran—before the Revolution, before the curfews, before the madmen took charge. Istanbul's blend of the traditional and the contemporary—from the smell of spices in the air to the sounds of prayer mixed with music from nearby cafés—made him feel at home.

With his regular wages and an occasional tip, he was getting closer to the $600 he needed for his plane fare to America.

—

Abbas's brother burst into the restaurant one evening. Ricardo was washing dishes in the kitchen. "What is it, Akbar?" he said.

"I have grave news: Abbas has been arrested at the border, and they found weapons in his truck."

Ricardo's limbs turned to jelly, his knees gave way, and he sank into a chair, shaking his head. "This is terrible news. Is there anything we can do?"

"Well," Akbar said, "I have had a phone call from someone in Brussels who claims to know all about his arrest."

"Go on."

"He wants a lot of money and says he has the power to get him released."

"And do you believe him?"

"Do we have a choice?"

Akbar explained that the official had given him a week, and he had to get the money to Brussels; otherwise, the deal was off.

Akbar buried his face in his hands and let out a deep sigh. He looked up. "I'm $500 short, but even if I get the money, there's no way I can get to Brussels; there's visas to apply for and—"

"Whoa, calm down," Ricardo said. "We can do it. I have an American passport; I can travel freely to Brussels without any visas, and I have the money."

"You have?"

"Yes, my money for my ticket to America."

Akbar shook his head. "No, no, no. I know how hard you've worked to save that money. That's for your passage to America; there's no way I can take that money from you."

"You can and will because I know Abbas would do the same for me."

"Are you sure?" Akbar said.

"I have never been so sure of anything in my life."

———

Istanbul to Brussels would take several days and cross parts of communist Europe. The language barriers would add complications, but Ricardo settled in and became comfortable on the Bosphorus Express. He looked at his watch. The first part of his journey would take him through the Balkans to Sofia, in Bulgaria, which would last nearly twenty hours. The trip wasn't without its dangers. Each border crossing would be strict, especially in Yugoslavia and Hungary. He prayed that the border guards wouldn't conduct any searches, as he was carrying more money than some of them earned in a year, and he hadn't forgotten that he was a wanted man.

Once again, adrenaline rushed through his veins at each border check, but he surprised himself and kept calm. It was almost as if he were born to do this.

As he traveled through Hungary and Austria, the atmosphere was less oppressive, and the trains were more comfortable and faster. Traveling through Austria was stunning. Ricardo took in the alpine vistas, the snowcapped peaks, and the lush valleys. Every village they passed was like a picture postcard.

Everything changed in Brussels, and as he stepped on the platform, he knew he had to move fast and find the contact waiting for him to complete his mission. He navigated the unfamiliar city streets and walked into Central Park from the north side on a sunny June day as instructed. Despite the picturesque setting and children's laughter, Ricardo was enveloped in a bubble of nervous anticipation, acutely aware of every passing moment as he waited for contact.

A familiar voice cut through the peaceful air. "Ricardo."

He recognized that voice as it repeated his name. A young woman approached him, and the lines of her face were familiar.

Momentarily stunned, he could only utter one word. "Shahla."

"So, you recognize me?"

"Shahla," he repeated.

How was it possible that the woman who had tragically lost her baby during their arduous journey crossing the border into Turkey stood before him? It didn't make sense.

He stood up, held out his hands, and she took them in hers. She looked dramatically different. Her once dark, flowing hair was now cut short and dyed blonde. The change highlighted her fair skin and delicate features. She was much slimmer than he remembered her. It took him a while to gather his composure as he stared at her in disbelief.

"I'm not a ghost, don't worry," she said, her eyes twinkling with an affection that had always lingered between them.

His mind reeling, Shahla began to reveal layers of her life he had never known.

"Yes, I'm your contact here. After we separated, I crossed the border and eventually came to Brussels."

"But how are you involved with Abbas and Akbar, and why are you my contact?"

"I am a high-ranking member of the MEK. I now oversee all of our operations originating out of Western Europe, with the knowledge and discretion of the Belgian government."

Ricardo sank back on the park bench, and Shahla sat beside him.

He listened as she explained that she had arranged for Abbas to meet him in the Turkish holding cell, and the puzzle pieces began to fall into place.

"I've never forgotten how you protected me during our journey," she said. "You gave me and my baby your food, water, and even your coat to keep us warm on those cold nights." Her voice was thick with emotion. "When I lost my daughter, I was devastated, and you were there for me again; you never left my side. That speech of yours saved my life; I was ready to lie down in the snow and die. I never forgot your kindness. I know your whole life story, Ricardo. My team has told me about the bombing in Iran and the Shadow Rider of Tehran . . ." She paused, her expression solemn. "And you told me about Bahar and how she died. It was a tragic loss, which didn't go unnoticed. Her story deserves a voice, a chance to be heard in the chaos of conflict. Ricardo, we've all suffered and lost, but we can strive for something better to ensure those sacrifices were not in vain. I'm here to help guide you. We need your strengths to fight our cause."

Ricardo was in awe. His respect and understanding deepened for the woman sitting next to him.

But he was also conflicted. Even though he cared about Shahla and respected what she had achieved, he couldn't ignore the MEK's core beliefs. They were very different from his own—too many Marxists and Islamists with Imam-inspired agendas.

Ricardo looked at her. "I'm here to help Abbas, nothing more, and I need to get back to Turkey as soon as possible. I have the money that needs to be delivered to the diplomat."

"I understand," she said, taking him by the hand as they walked through the bustling city center. Her hand felt good in his.

—

As they neared their destination, they entered an apartment where two men were waiting. One of them stepped forward, extending his hand in greeting. "It's an honor to meet the Shadow Rider of Tehran. We've all heard so much about you."

The other man smiled. "The only Iranian in Tehran with a Spanish–Jewish name, and he is neither Jewish nor Spanish."

Ricardo was overwhelmed at the unexpected recognition.

Shahla got down to business immediately. She laid out the plan for Ricardo. "We've prepared the briefcase, which you will take to the lobby of the Hotel Amigo. It's a well-known spot in the city. You will meet the Iranian diplomat, but you must be careful. He will call you Hassan, but even then, you will tell him he has the wrong person and wait for his next move."

When she had finished, Ricardo picked up the briefcase and the directions to the hotel.

—

The lobby of Hotel Amigo was an elegant blend of old-world charm and modern luxury, with polished marble floors and rich, ornate tapestries adorning the walls. Soft, classical music played in the background, and opulent chandeliers hung from the high ceilings, casting a warm glow over the plush seating areas. The hotel was filled with guests engaged in quiet conversations or absorbed in newspapers. Potted plants added a touch of greenery, enhancing the sophisticated decor.

Ricardo moved through the lobby, his heart racing. He needed to find the right person, make the exchange smooth, and leave without drawing attention to himself.

Finally, a man approached him cautiously. "Hassan?" he inquired discreetly.

"No, you have the wrong person," Ricardo replied.

The man gave a subtle nod of understanding, and Ricardo sat down nearby. After a few minutes, the man casually walked over and sat beside him. Ricardo placed the briefcase between them on the floor. Ricardo stood, exited the lobby, and returned to the apartment.

—

Shahla stood as he walked through the door.

"How did it go?" she asked.

"It went smoothly. I did exactly as planned."

"Good work, Ricardo," she said. "Now we wait for a phone call to say Abbas will be released."

—

It was early evening when the phone rang, and Shahla jumped up to answer it.

Ricardo studied her face: concern, relief, and a flicker of a smile, and then she replaced the receiver on the hook.

"The money was delivered to the right person," she announced. "They've agreed to release Abbas within the next twenty-four hours."

A collective sigh of relief washed over the room, but Shahla's following words quickly tempered it. "But there's a problem; the diplomat recognized you and said you are a person wanted by the authorities."

"So what?" Ricardo said. "I've no intention of returning to Iran, no reason to ever see that diplomat again."

"It's too risky for you to return to Turkey," she said. "They know where Abbas lives, and their agents will be waiting for you."

"OK, so now what?" he asked.

"You can stay with me for a few days until we decide what to do. I have some contacts who might be able to help."

Ricardo was thinking only of getting to America, but he was stranded without the funds necessary for his journey. He had little choice but to accept Shahla's help and hope for a viable path forward.

—

The following day, Ricardo woke up late, his body heavy with exhaustion from the recent travels, the time changes, and the relentless waves of excitement and anxiety. He stumbled out of the small bedroom and into the kitchen.

"Good morning, Shahla," he said. "Is that coffee I smell?"

"Sure." She handed him a cup, a smile on her face. "Abbas was released this morning. His brother picked him up at the border. It's all gone according to plan."

Without stopping himself, Ricardo rushed forward, closing the distance between them, and hugged her tightly.

"Abbas wanted me to tell you he's safe now," she said, "and he wants to thank you for everything you've done."

The hug lingered a little longer than expected as Shahla continued to hold it. Ricardo stepped back to meet her gaze. Their eyes locked, and their lips touched. The kiss lingered, and the world around them faded as they found solace and understanding in each other's embrace. They kissed passionately.

Ricardo broke the embrace and stepped back. "I'm sorry, that shouldn't have happened; I don't know what came over me."

Shahla stood in silence, her face flushed with embarrassment.

"I'm sorry, Shahla, I shouldn't have . . . I haven't been with anyone since Bahar. I just . . . I need some time. I need to go for a walk to sort things out."

—

Ricardo walked the streets, lost in his thoughts and the weight of conflicting emotions. He could think of nothing but Bahar. He felt a solid attraction for Shahla, and their bond over their shared grief and trauma was undeniable. But deep down, Ricardo knew nobody could ever take Bahar's place; his heart would always belong to her.

—

He decided to return to the apartment. This wasn't fair to Shahla. She had done nothing wrong.

As Ricardo stepped inside, Shahla turned to look at him. "Are you OK?" she asked.

"Yeah, I'm OK."

"I am so sorry about what happened. I didn't mean to put you in a bad position."

"No, it's not you at all; it's me. I'm still trying to figure things out. I think it's a guilt thing."

"I know how you feel, Ricardo," she said. "I will never forget my husband, but remember your speech to me. You told me that if we give up on life, then they have won. We will never forget our lost loves, Ricardo, but would they really want us to be this unhappy?"

Shahla was right; Bahar would never have wanted him to feel this way.

He stepped closer, took her hand, and pulled her toward him. She opened her mouth to speak, and he kissed her. She responded instantly, wrapping her arms around him, her hesitations dissolving in the heat of the moment.

They slowly began to undress each other, moving toward the bedroom through the open door, and Shahla fell onto the bed.

His eyes gazed at her naked body; for a moment, he forgot to breathe, and his heart pounded like a drum.

"I've never done this before," he confessed.

His eyes traced the delicate curves of her body, the soft lines and gentle slopes, each detail a testament to the beauty of her form. He felt a profound sense of wonder, a deep appreciation of her naked beauty.

Her words broke his thoughts. "It's OK," she said. "There's always a first time for everyone."

—

Ricardo stayed with Shahla for three weeks. She helped him secure a temporary job to earn money and continued helping him work toward his goal of getting to America.

Throughout their time together, Ricardo learned a great deal from Shahla. He gained insights into her convictions and the sacrifices she had made for her cause, and their sexual encounters were experimental and intense.

As the weeks passed, they both recognized that their relationship was nearing its natural conclusion. Ricardo was focused on his journey to America, and Shahla was deeply embedded in her activities with the MEK.

—

In the fourth week of his stay with Shahla, Ricardo entered the apartment to find an unexpected but welcome guest: Abbas was waiting for him in the living room. Overwhelmed with joy, Ricardo rushed over, and the two friends embraced warmly.

"I can't believe it's you," Ricardo said. "I'm just so glad you're safe; it's wonderful to see you. How are you holding up?"

"I'm doing well, thanks to you. I can't believe you used your American money. You worked so hard to save that; I don't know how to thank you enough."

"You'd have done the same for me," he said.

"Well, my friend, sit down. Because I've got something to tell you."

A little puzzled, Ricardo did as he was told and sat on the sofa beside Shahla.

"I've got some news for you," Abbas began. "I was able to secure your fare to the United States for you."

Ricardo was stunned. "Really . . . How did you manage that?"

Abbas explained, "I connected with a friend; he's a chef in Cairo." Abbas paused; he hoped he hadn't given too much away. No, of course not. Ricardo didn't even know what country his father was in, let alone that he was masquerading as a chef at the Dutch Embassy in Cairo. He continued. "When I told him how you sacrificed your US savings to help me, he was moved by your generosity and insisted on buying your ticket. He wired the money to me this morning."

—

Abbas took Ricardo to a travel agency the following day, where he purchased Ricardo's ticket to Detroit. Ricardo turned to Abbas and embraced him. "Thank you so much for everything you've done for me."

America, the land of the free, was within his grasp. Yet, amid his rising excitement, his thoughts drifted to Bahar; it was a dream they should have shared. If only she were alongside him. The world was crafted from cruelty.

—

When they returned to the apartment, Shahla announced that she was heading to Paris that night. Ricardo showed her his airline ticket and said he would leave the following day.

Abbas said he needed to meet some friends and soon after left the apartment. As soon as the door closed behind him, Ricardo and Shahla looked at each other. They embraced tightly and kissed passionately. They knew their time together was slipping away.

In the quiet of the bedroom, their intimacy cemented memories that would last forever.

"I know I am not Bahar," she said. "I can never take her place in your heart, but I will never forget you. You will always be in my thoughts, and I will never forget the promise you made to me on our last day at the border. I know you will always honor that."

"I will never forget you either, Shahla. You are my first, and that's something we will always share. I will always cherish our time together. And be sure, I am planning on keeping my promise."

—

When Shahla left the apartment, he picked up the phone and called Samira.

Samira was thrilled that he was finally making his way to America. "Ricardo, that's amazing! I'm so happy for you. Your sister is also leaving this mess of a country; she is moving to Denmark with Farhad and his family. It seems like she's trying to move on as well. I'll miss you both, but I'm so happy for my son and daughter. You're starting new chapters of your lives at the same time. Take care of yourself, Ricardo."

"You too, Mom. Thank you for everything."

—

Samira hung up the phone and broke down.

She had known this day might come. The signs had been there for years, flickering like dim, distant stars: the unrest, the disappearances, the executions, the fear that crept into their home with every phone call, every knock on the door. Samira had tried to keep them safe, wrapping her love around them like a blanket, hoping it would be enough. But it wasn't.

The twisted clerical regime had snaked its way into every corner of their lives, turning their once vibrant homeland into a cage. It had taken their freedom and hope; now, it was taking her children.

Samira had watched them grow, and she had watched the light in their eyes dim as the world around them became more dangerous and suffocating. She had felt powerless to stop it, helpless to protect them from the twisted ideology that had turned Iran into something unrecognizable.

Iran. Her beautiful Iran. The country she had known as a girl, full of poetry, music, and laughter, was gone. The streets that had once echoed with the voices of children playing now hummed with tension and fear. The parks where she had picnicked with her family had become places of silence, where people walked with their heads down, afraid to be seen and heard. The government, the mad Mullahs, and their self-righteous henchmen had stolen it all.

Samira stood and walked to the window, looking at the city she had known her whole life. With its mountains in the distance, Tehran felt like a stranger to her now. She whispered a silent prayer for her children. She prayed they would find freedom. Hope. A future.

—

Finally, the day of Ricardo's flight arrived. He had spent a restless night, unable to sleep with the anticipation and anxiety of what lay ahead. Along with the money in his pocket, he carried a dream to build a better world.

Abbas accompanied Ricardo to the airport. They shared one last embrace. Abbas handed Ricardo a large envelope as they parted, his voice low and urgent. "These are blueprints for new Revolutionary Guard military bases in central Iran, where they plan to set up nuclear research facilities. Use them as bargaining chips in the United States if you ever find yourself desperate and in need of money," he instructed.

"Take care, Ricardo," Abbas continued, his voice choking with emotion. "We believe in you."

"Thank you, Abbas. Thank you for everything."

Filled with hope and uncertainty, Ricardo made his way to the gate. He thought he was leaving behind a life of hardship, stepping out of hell and into a new beginning. But the weight of the envelope in his hand was a heavy reminder that the shadows of his past might still reach out to him.

29

DETROIT

You can always count on Americans to do the right thing—
after they've tried everything else.

—Winston Churchill

etroit's airport was familiar, and yet it wasn't. Ricardo remembered many things from his first visit, but nearly a decade of change and modernization made him feel like he might as well be stepping onto the moon's surface. He was nervous and excited, but at the same time, fear was gnawing away at his bones. He had one suitcase, an American passport, and just $48 in his pocket as he walked toward immigration control.

The man on the desk seemed impatient, reeling off a lot of short, quick sentences that Ricardo barely understood. He did his best and tried telling the man he didn't speak English well.

The official shook his head. "But you have an American passport; why can't you speak English?"

Ricardo apologized.

"On your way," the official said, returning the passport. "Everything seems to be in order. Have a nice day."

Ricardo walked out of the airport and into the street. There was a massive line of taxis, and suddenly, the realization hit him like a hammer blow. Where would he go? How much would the taxi cost to wherever he was going? Where would he sleep?

He sat on a bench outside the airport, unable to even think. He didn't know any neighborhoods of Detroit, not even a street name. The enormity of his predicament slowly started to sink in. Ricardo sat for five minutes watching the taxis and buses, weighing his options.

"Hey, son!" A man sat beside him. "I've been watching you. Do you need a taxi?"

"Yes, I think so."

"What do you mean you think so? Where do you want to go?"

"I don't know," Ricardo stammered.

The man laughed. "Well, that's a first. I've never had a fare from someone who doesn't know where they want to go. So you don't have an address?"

"No."

"A hotel?"

"Yes, I need a hotel, somewhere to sleep."

The man nodded. "At last, we're getting somewhere; which hotel do you want?"

"I don't know?"

"OK, how much do you have in your pocket, son?"

"$48."

"That's it—$48 to your name?"

"Yes."

"You don't have a bank account?"

Ricardo shook his head.

The man picked up Ricardo's suitcase. "Well, I'm afraid that won't get you far, but we'll figure it out. Come with me."

The taxi driver walked him to his car on the other side of the concourse, and Ricardo climbed into the passenger seat. The taxi driver told him he was heading for Detroit's West Side, to Brightmoor. He said it wasn't the best area of Detroit, but he knew a YMCA hostel, and Ricardo could buy a bed for a few nights.

The taxi driver would only take $8 from him and explained that his remaining $40 wouldn't last very long. He bid him goodbye, and the taxi pulled away. Ricardo had never felt so lonely in his entire life.

He checked in at the YMCA. It was $10 a night, and he paid for two nights, keeping the remainder of his money for food.

—

Later that day, Ricardo wandered the neighborhood streets, lined with crumbling buildings and vacant lots choked with weeds. He walked past long-abandoned houses, their windows broken, doors hanging askew, and graffiti daubed across every available surface.

He stood outside a Wendy's. It seemed like a good place to start, so he walked in.

His English was still poor, but he was able to get by. He approached the counter toward a Black woman whose name badge read *Sandy*.

"I need work," he managed to communicate, and the lady smiled. She reached under the counter and handed him two sheets of paper. "This is a job application. Will you be able to fill it in?"

"Yes," Ricardo replied, "I write good."

"And your Social Security card, can I see it?"

Ricardo shrugged his shoulders. He had never heard those words before. He showed her his passport.

The woman explained that a Social Security number was essential in America, and it was impossible to find work without one.

She told him to sit down. An hour later, when her shift finished, she accompanied him to the Social Security office. Within an hour, he had his Social Security number, and the very next day, he started work at Wendy's, flipping burgers. Sandy said his English wasn't good enough to serve customers.

Ricardo felt a sense of achievement, but his remaining cash ran low. He asked Sandy when he would get paid.

"Two weeks."

—

On his third day at the YMCA, he was thrown out. He tried to explain to the manager that his paycheck would be with him soon, but the man told him that the YMCA did not extend credit.

Ricardo emptied his locker, put his belongings in the suitcase, and left the building.

This was not how he had planned it.

He started taking double shifts at Wendy's. Sandy was more than pleased, as employees in that neighborhood were hard to find. Even though he had no money, he could eat as much as he wanted at the restaurant, so at least he wouldn't starve.

When his shift finished that evening, he wandered the area. He knew he had no option but to sleep on the streets until his paycheck arrived. It was the height of summer, and Detroit was experiencing a mini heat wave. Rain was not in the forecast for several weeks. He wasn't going to freeze to death or get washed away. He'd be fine.

He found a spot under a bridge and put his head on his suitcase. Ricardo had slept in worse places. He cast his mind back to the sleep-deprived trenches of Khorramshahr. At least nobody was shooting at him. He would survive.

He slept surprisingly well, until the sun came up around 5:30 the following morning.

—

As he laid his suitcase under the bridge, toward the end of the week, he heard a familiar voice.

"I thought as much."

It was Sandy.

"I knew you were sleeping on the street, so I followed you. You pick up that damn suitcase, and you come with me. You're not sleeping here one more night."

Sandy took him back to the YMCA and paid for his bed for another seven nights. She told him he could pay her back when he received his paycheck.

—

Ricardo treated everyone he met as a fellow human being. He was especially touched by the kindness of Sandy, who, despite not being wealthy, showed immense compassion and whose kindness knew no boundaries.

As Ricardo adapted to life in Detroit, he began to grasp the racial disparities that characterized the city. His prior understanding of racism, shaped by academic readings from books in his uncle Masood's store in Iran, was purely theoretical. However, living in Detroit brought him face-to-face with the stark realities of racial tensions, influencing every-day interactions and opportunities.

The neighborhood was predominately Black. The aspirations and values of the residents mirrored those of the people he had grown up with, and the community welcomed him warmly, allowing him to immerse himself in the subculture of Black Americans. He learned the unique slang of the area and broader cultural insights. He observed, took everything in, and slowly but surely began to realize that while you can't choose the circumstances of your birth, you can choose whether you let those circumstances define you.

He witnessed the deep and enduring impacts of inequality and sys-temic pressures on the community; long-standing issues had left scars of hurt and distrust. Being one of the few White individuals in the area, he experienced the tension of racial dynamics, particularly during night-time walks. Prejudice and hostility were not unique to any one race.

And as always, he read books. He read about the 1960s, the civil rights movement, and figures like Martin Luther King Jr., whose relentless battle against segregation and prejudice profoundly inspired him.

—

Ricardo met Martha at Wendy's. She was a regular, and they quickly became friends. Martha taught Ricardo English, and one day, she shared her story with him as they sipped coffee at Wendy's.

"I had a son. . . . He passed away a year ago." She paused, wiping away a tear that rolled down her cheek. "He was just three; he died from sudden infant death syndrome."

Ricardo listened. "I'm so sorry, Martha," he said.

"It's hard, but talking to someone about it helps."

—

Ricardo felt a deep connection with Martha; her companionship became a source of comfort and understanding in his life. As they shared their stories, he appreciated the solace she offered and the strength she showed. Martha's presence helped mitigate his isolation, making the unfamiliar surroundings more tolerable, even if Sandy complained occasionally.

"That woman is always around here," she said. "You'd better be careful, she's out to hook a husband."

30

THE CALL TO DUTY

The larger the island of knowledge, the longer the shoreline of wonder.

—Ralph W. Sockman

Sergeant Collins was also a regular customer at Wendy's and a recruiting officer at a nearby Army recruiting station in the strip mall across the street. Always well turned out and polite, he was someone Ricardo warmed to immediately, and they often struck up a conversation when the sergeant was having his lunch.

One day, he brought some Army brochures to Ricardo. "You ever thought about the Army, son?"

Ricardo's English was improving; he could now hold a conversation. He told the sergeant about the Iran–Iraq war and how he had served in the Iranian military. He said he wasn't sure how the US Army worked, but it couldn't be very different.

Sergeant Collins was amazed. "Do you want to take the test?" he said.

"Sure," Ricardo replied.

—

Ricardo walked into the recruiting station the following Monday, but there was a problem. "You must have a high school diploma to join the Army."

"But it's in Iran."

"Great—get your mother to mail it to me."

Ricardo nodded but knew it wasn't going to be easy. When he called Samira later that day, she promised to call the school. A few hours later, his suspicions were confirmed: The authorities had seized his paperwork. His mother delivered the bad news. "You are a wanted man, Ricardo. They have removed everything; it's as if you never existed."

"Call Uncle Masood," Ricardo said. "See what he can do."

—

Ricardo's translated high school diploma and all his qualifications arrived three weeks later. Sergeant Collins was shocked to learn that Ricardo had a bachelor of science degree in electronics engineering at such a young age.

Twenty-four hours later, Ricardo took the Armed Services Vocational Aptitude Battery (ASVAB) test. It measured purpose and tested general science, including chemistry and physics, math, English knowledge, auto and mechanical comprehension, assembling objects, and verbal expression.

The sergeant explained that if Ricardo passed the test, his results would determine what jobs he could apply for in the Army.

—

Sergeant Collins appeared in Wendy's several days later with another man by his side. He delivered some good news: Ricardo had passed the ASVAB with flying colors, except for the English, which he was still learning. Because of the English part, the only job he qualified for was Infantry. He explained that the stranger was an Iranian interpreter and that Ricardo had to attend an interview because they needed to know everything about him, specifically his experiences in the Iranian army.

Ricardo asked Sandy for a few hours off to attend the interview the following day.

As Ricardo sat at the desk, several men faced him, all dressed in US military uniforms. Collins introduced them to the last man, Major Dunvegan, who had a gold oak leaf on the shoulder epaulets of his dress uniform. Ricardo knew enough about US military rank to know that attending such an interview was highly unusual for a major.

Through the translator, one of the men explained that they knew everything about him and that he shouldn't lie. Otherwise, he would not get into the Army. They said they knew all about Turkey and his flight across the Iranian border.

Ricardo took a deep breath and started to talk.

He told them everything, from his involvement with the MEK to his time as the Shadow Rider, Bahar's death, the bombing that killed the members of the Iranian government, and his service in the Iranian Army. He told them about the Iranian execution order with his name on it and running illegal guns across the border. The military men sat in silence. They were in awe; the interview lasted seven hours.

At the end of the interview, Ricardo surprised himself. He didn't know why, but he handed the military blueprints of the Revolutionary Guard bases to the assembled men.

"What are these?" Major Dunvegan said.

"See for yourself, sir," Ricardo said.

As the major opened the paperwork, his jaw almost touched the floor. He nodded at Sergeant Collins.

"I'm pleased to inform you," Sergeant Collins said, "that you have been accepted into the United States Army."

"And give this man secret security clearance on a need-to-know basis," Dunvegan said.

Sergeant Collins looked at the superior officer. "Sir?"

"Trust me, Collins, this man needs security clearance."

"But he's in the infantry; infantrymen don't get security clearance."

"He does."

—

At the Dutch embassy in Cairo, David took the phone call just before midnight. "Major Dunvegan, it's nice to hear from you," he said. "Is it good news?"

"Yes, David, your boy is on his way to becoming an American GI."

"Great, and he talked?"

"From dawn to dusk. David, that boy told me things that had my hair standing on the back of my neck. He also shared some documents with us, which you should see. I will send you copies."

"No need, I have already seen them. It was a test to see if he could get them into the right hands."

31

CATCH OF THE DAY

The worst prisons were not constructed of warped steel and stone.
They were carved out of expectations and lies, judgment and trust.
—Kelseyleigh Reber

Ricardo thought he and Martha were just good friends, but suddenly, she became more attentive, and their bond gradually deepened.

Martha was always around. Seldom did a day go by when she didn't breeze into Wendy's to announce that Ricardo needed another English lesson.

Sandy frowned, and Ricardo grinned; Martha was growing on him.

The countless hours of practice and conversation, the shared laughter over mispronounced words, and the warm encouragement during challenging lessons laid a solid emotional foundation.

Ricardo noticed a particular hostility between Martha and Sandy. It came to a head one evening when Sandy blew up after a particularly stressful day.

"Don't you see, boy, that woman is no good?"

"How can you say that, Sandy?" Ricardo replied. "I think she's great.

She can't do enough for me, and it's because of her that I'm speaking to you so well right now."

"She has ulterior motives, mark my words."

"*Ulterior?*" Ricardo said, looking confused. "I am not familiar with that word. What does it mean?"

"Look it up. Look it up in the goddamn dictionary."

—

Martha knew Sergeant Collins from Wendy's. He had joked that she was in there more than him. Martha wanted to know everything about Ricardo; she said she liked him. Sergeant Collins said he wasn't allowed to say too much because of official secrets, but with a wink, he said, "That boy is exactly what I am looking for. He's heading for a great career in the US military."

"And his English—he handled the exams OK?"

"Yes, thanks to you, Martha. You've been teaching him well, and he has some of the highest marks ever on his tests."

Martha left Wendy's without saying goodbye to Ricardo; she had arranged a meeting with her best friend.

—

Emma and Martha sat in a diner in Corktown.

"Did you get the information?" Martha asked.

"I did."

"Let me see."

Emma handed her a small pamphlet. "It's all in black and white; it seems like the US military looks after their own. Not such a great starting salary, but look at the benefits."

"Wow," Martha said. "There's an allowance for housing and health-care for all the family."

"Absolutely," Emma said, "and they cover dental costs and a monthly stipend for food."

Martha read on. "Education costs, tuition and fees for college."

"And life insurance, should anything happen to him, and paid leave for up to thirty days a year."

Martha leaned back in her chair. "Well, Emma, I'd better start laying on the charm, and if that doesn't work, I'll join the fucking Army myself."

32

TRUE FAITH AND ALLEGIANCE

Duty, honor, country: Those three hallowed words reverently dictate what you ought to be, what you can be, what you will be.
—General Douglas MacArthur

Ricardo was sworn in two weeks after the final interview. Raising his right hand, he swore the Oath of Enlistment that he would support and defend the Constitution of the United States against all enemies, foreign and domestic. He promised to bear true faith and allegiance to the Constitution and the president of the United States.

"OK," the drill sergeant said, "that's it, soldiers, on the bus. You're heading to Fort Jackson."

Around thirty men and women stood up and headed outside toward a bus, the engine already running.

Ricardo sat next to a Black man with a slender figure and glasses. Ricardo held out his hand. "Ricardo. Pleased to meet you, brother."

The man looked a little surprised. "Absolutely, man. I'm Malcolm, pleased to make your acquaintance."

The bus took them to the airport, where they flew to Fort Jackson, South Carolina. Ricardo talked to Malcolm the whole way. They spoke of their dreams, family, and what it meant to both of them to be in the US Army.

The drill sergeant met them at the airport and put them on another bus to the base.

Ricardo admitted to Malcolm that he was a little frightened but confident. "I've been through all this basic training once before, albeit with the Iranian Army. But I'm guessing this will be a little more intense."

—

Ricardo was two days into basic training when he turned to Malcolm. "This is an absolute breeze."

Malcolm looked at him in astonishment. "What do you mean *an absolute breeze*? They are shouting and screaming at us, we have to run everywhere, and they treat us like crap."

"Yeah, man, but they don't hit us; they can't beat us up like they do in the Iranian Army."

"For real?"

"Absolutely. I still have the scars to prove it. All these guys do is shout at us and make us do push-ups. It's a piece of cake; I'm loving every second."

—

Ricardo made many friends during basic training. He fondly remembered the same feeling in the Iranian Army: that he was part of a family, bonding with friends and colleagues, and he felt secure and comfortable. It would pass many of the other recruits by, but when Ricardo woke up in the barracks after the first few days of training, he appreciated that he wasn't lying in the cold mud of a trench or wrapped in a blanket beneath a highway overpass. The surface beneath him wasn't cement or dirt but a firm, sturdy, reliable mattress. And above him? A roof. Not the kind of makeshift shelter made from cardboard or a discarded tarp but solid walls and a ceiling that didn't leak or creak with every gust of wind. He felt . . . safe.

The sound of footsteps and voices came from outside the door of his barracks, and as he sat up, the smell of breakfast drifted in—eggs, bacon, coffee. He hadn't smelled food like that in ages. Real food.

He stretched his arms, savoring his muscles' warmth and the sheets' soft weight still clinging to his legs. He had forgotten what it felt like to wake up knowing that the day wasn't a battle to survive. He had a uniform now, folded neatly at the foot of the bed. It had his name stitched onto it—*Rosen*—marking him not as another nameless face in the crowd but as a soldier, part of something bigger. The US Army had taken him in when he thought no one else would.

He remembered the recruiting officer's words: "The Army isn't just about fighting; it's about brotherhood."

He swung his legs over the edge of the bed, his bare feet touching the cold floor, but even that was a welcome sensation. It was something solid, something real. He glanced around the room. The other men were waking up, too, some still groggy from sleep, others already lacing up their boots and cracking jokes. These weren't the hostile stares of strangers on the street, eyes that glanced past him as though he didn't exist. These were his brothers now. They shared the same space, the same mission, the same trials.

—

But not everybody sailed through basic training. Almost daily, some men were sent back to their hometowns. The drill sergeants showed no mercy. If they didn't think a recruit was up to the task, they were told to pack their things and issued travel documents to wherever they had come from.

Malcolm struggled with discipline; he hated being shouted at, but Ricardo told him he would get through it.

"You're so damn calm, Ricardo," he said. "You don't let them get to you."

"And neither should you. It's small stuff; why should you sweat about it? They are looking for negative reactions; it's what they must do."

"What do you mean?" Malcolm said.

"Sticks and stones: They can shout and scream at me all they like; it ain't ever going to hurt me."

Malcolm jabbed a finger at him. "And you, they call you the Terrorist; they insult you. Doesn't that bother you?"

Ricardo burst out laughing. "Of course not. It gives me an identity; it's their way of telling me they love me. They call me a Jew Boy and a Spaniard, too."

Malcolm shook his head. "You're from another planet, man."

"You'd better believe it."

———

Several recruits were on "the fat boy" program. At the end of the six-week basic training, every recruit had to conform to a strict height-and-weight ratio. If the recruit was overweight, they were out, or they had to repeat the six-week training from the beginning, and nobody wanted to do that.

There were two men, Ethan and Clarence, who Ricardo liked and respected greatly. However, a regular diet of pizzas, hamburgers, and too much Coca-Cola had taken its toll on them, and they had been pushed into the fat boy program from day one. It meant extra physical training and limited the food they could eat. For the most part, it worked, but it would be touch and go in the case of his two friends.

Ricardo was determined that Ethan and Clarence would graduate.

He walked into the barracks early and woke the two men up. "Wake up. We are going to do some early morning exercise. I will make sure your metabolism is pumping like fuck when you sit down for breakfast. That way, you won't put on any pounds."

They followed Ricardo into the small basement gymnasium, and within a few minutes, all three men were doing a circuit of sit-ups, push-ups, and weight work.

A short while later, the drill sergeant burst into the gymnasium. "What the hell is going on here?" He pointed at Ricardo. "You, the Terrorist—what the fuck are you doing?"

Ricardo explained that he was helping the two men lose weight so they would graduate. "They are good soldiers, Drill Sergeant," he said. "They just need a little help."

The drill sergeant looked at his watch. "At this time of the fucking morning? I thought we were being attacked. Are you serious?"

"I am, Drill Sergeant. These are just the sort of men the US Army needs."

—

Later that week, the same drill sergeant stood before another recruit and pointed at his stomach, pushing his finger into the flab. "You, Private," he shouted. "You are too fat; you need to go and see the Terrorist. The Terrorist will take care of you."

"The Terrorist, Drill Sergent?"

"Yes, son, the fucking Terrorist."

Ricardo stood in the same line, just a few feet away. He couldn't help but smile.

—

During weapons training week, it was Ricardo's first time handling an M16, a stark contrast to the old G36 assault rifle he had used in the

Iranian Army. He quickly adapted to the M16 at the shooting range
and excelled, outperforming his peers. He was awarded a sharpshooter
badge, top in his class.

—

Throughout his basic training, Ricardo wrote letters to Martha, sharing
updates on his progress. Her return letters to him became increasingly
intimate.

During his basic training, Ricardo observed that the US Army operated differently from the civilian world he had experienced in Detroit.
In the Army, racial disparities were less pronounced. He trained under
Black and White drill instructors, and it became clear that respect was
based on rank rather than skin color, just as it should be. From the first
day, the drill instructors instilled a crucial ethos: Everyone wore green; it
was the only color that mattered. All soldiers were equal members of the
same team, committed to the same goals and standards.

—

After graduation, Ricardo was granted a few days off before heading to
Fort Benning, Georgia to Infantry School.

He dialed Martha's number, eager to share his news and hear a familiar voice.

Martha was thrilled to hear from him, but her voice carried a strain
of worry.

"What is it, Martha? What's wrong?"

"Nothing for you to worry about; it's just that I had to move back
home with my parents, and it's a little strained."

"But why? You had a nice place."

"Money, Ricardo. You wouldn't understand. I was managing OK,
but then the landlord increased the rent by a hundred bucks."

"That's it? You've moved back with your parents for a lousy hundred bucks?"

By the time the call ended, Ricardo had Martha's bank details and, at his insistence, had wired Martha three months' rent. He wouldn't take no for an answer.

—

The bus ride from Fort Jackson to Fort Benning lasted about five hours, and it was already late at night when they finally arrived. Ricardo and Malcolm, dressed sharply in Dress Green uniforms, stepped off the bus. They collected their duffle bags and were promptly greeted by a new team of drill sergeants.

The first four weeks of training at Fort Benning proved significantly more challenging than basic training. They tested every recruit physically and mentally, pushing them to their limits and beyond.

Malcolm slumped against the wall, wiping sweat from his brow. "Man, this is brutal. I don't know if I can keep this up."

Ricardo leaned in, a determined look in his eyes. "Hey, we've got to hang in there, man. It's all part of the game," he said. "Remember what the drill sergeants said? These first four weeks are critical. We get through this, and then it gets better."

Malcolm took a deep breath, nodding slowly. "You're right, Ricardo. It's just . . . tougher than I thought."

Ricardo clapped him on the back. "We'll make it, buddy; just keep pushing."

By the fifth week of training, the intensity began to ease slightly, and they spent more time in the classroom, reading maps and studying land and urban combat techniques.

There was a lecture on nuclear, biological, and chemical warfare. Ricardo's mind wandered back to his days in the Iranian Army. He thought about how different things might have been if he and his comrades had received the comprehensive training he was now getting. It dawned on him just how unprepared they had been during that war. They had faced threats they barely understood. The memories of Keavon haunted him; if they'd had US Army training and the right equipment, perhaps his friend would still be alive.

"Bastards," he cursed under his breath.

Ricardo's experience in combat set him apart from most of his fellow trainees. He'd witnessed the harsh realities of war firsthand and understood the critical importance of the training in a way that others could not. While many of his peers viewed the exercises and simulations as just another set of tasks to master, Ricardo saw them as vital preparation for the life-and-death situations he had already experienced. He had a deep understanding of war's cruelty and put 100 percent into everything they threw at him.

33

FOUNDATIONS
OF WISDOM

He who has a why to live can bear almost any how.
—Friedrich Nietzsche

Airborne School had been a brutal yet rewarding experience for Ricardo, surpassing the intensity of his previous military training. The program was designed to test and enhance soldiers' physical and mental endurance to prepare them for the demands of airborne operations. The training involved rigorous physical fitness sessions, demanding drills to master parachute landing falls, and multiple practice jumps from towers and moving aircraft.

Ricardo thrived, and when he completed his first jump from an aircraft, the exhilaration and sense of achievement were overwhelming. A surge of confidence and pride washed over him as he collected his parachute and walked away from the drop zone.

He spotted Malcom and ran toward him. "Hey, man, we did it."

"We did," Malcolm said, "but I was crapping myself at the doorway of that plane, weren't you?"

"Of course," he admitted. "But bravery isn't about not being afraid; it's about being scared and going through with it anyway."

Malcolm listened intently as he processed Ricardo's words.

—

The graduation ceremony marked the completion of another phase in Ricardo's military career. After completing their fifth successful jump, Ricardo and his fellow graduates stood in formation on the landing zone, their anticipation and pride evident. When it was his turn, Ricardo stepped forward. The company commander approached him with significant force and pushed the airborne wings onto his chest. The sting of the pin and the blood he felt on his chest were not just physical but deeply symbolic. It represented his hard work, dedication, and resilience to achieve this milestone.

Ricardo had earned his blood wings.

He stood on the hallowed grounds of the drop zone, acutely aware that this very spot was where US soldiers during World War II had trained and earned their wings before parachuting into France on D-Day.

It was a stark reminder of the courage of those before him and the sacrifices they had made for freedom and the defeat of tyranny. He'd uphold that honor until his dying day.

—

Ricardo was planning to be transferred to Fort Bragg in North Carolina for his permanent duty station. He called Martha and suggested they spend a few days together, and she readily agreed. Ricardo harbored feelings for Martha, but being good friends was as far as it would go; she wouldn't come anywhere near replacing Bahar. His brief encounter with Shahla in Brussels had reinforced a painful truth: No one could honestly fill the void left by his first and only true love.

—

Martha looked great. She had lost a few pounds. Her dress was more close fitting than she usually wore, and unless he was mistaken, her lipstick was a brighter shade of red than usual.

She threw herself into his arms when she stepped from the bus. "I've missed you so much, Ricardo, you've no idea."

As they walked away together, Martha reached for his hand. "Come on, show me your new apartment; I can't wait to see it."

—

They had barely made it through the front door, when, with a gentle smile, she moved closer to him, reaching out to take his hand in hers. His fingers trembled slightly, but he held on tightly when she squeezed them. She leaned in. "I can't wait any longer, Ricardo."

Her lips brushed against his, her tongue probed between his lips. The kiss deepened, her sweet breath mingling with his, and with deliberate slowness, she guided his hands to her breasts. His fingers fumbled at first, but soon, she felt the shirt sliding off her shoulders. Her gaze never wavered. She reached around her back and loosened her bra, letting it fall to the floor.

He wrapped his arms around her, pulling her close, and she embraced him. The rest of their clothes fell away. She kissed him again. "Take me to the bedroom, Ricardo."

There were no more words between them, only soft sighs and whispered breaths. They moved together. It was uncharted territory, and there was an awkwardness, but as the minutes blended into hours, there were few regrets.

And as they lay there in the afterglow, wrapped in each other's arms, Martha promised undying love and swore they would be together forever.

—

In Brussels, David sat with Shahla and Abbas in a spacious suite at Hotel Amigo.

He thanked them in near-perfect Farsi for their help with Ricardo and his journey to America. He remarked to Shahla, "Abbas has been telling me about your feelings for Ricardo. When I first contacted you about helping him in Turkey, I didn't anticipate that you would fall in love with him. But whatever happens, he must remain unaware of my role."

Shahla's response was firm. "I was already helping him long before you knew he was in Turkey. We crossed the border together, and he cared for me and my baby throughout our journey. Your financial assistance has been crucial for our operations in Europe, but rest assured, your secret is safe. My personal feelings for Ricardo have not affected my judgment. He remains unaware of your involvement."

"And Abbas," he said, "the blueprints we gave him have safely made it to the United States. That was a masterstroke, and now that he is in the US Army, he'll prove invaluable to us."

—

Malcolm and Ricardo were packing their bags, about to depart for Fort Bragg. The CQ corporal walked into the room. "Hey, Rosen," he said. "Report to the commander's office, pronto."

"What for?"

"I have no idea, man, but you better fucking hurry up. He didn't look too happy."

—

The commander's office door was ajar, and Ricardo knocked before standing to attention at the threshold. "Private Rosen reporting as instructed, sir."

The commander looked up. "Come in and close the door, Rosen."

Ricardo walked in and stood to attention.

"At ease. Private Rosen, it has come to my attention that you have excelled in your training up to this point. You can proceed with your plans to go to Fort Bragg as your first permanent duty station, or you can sign this paper now and go straight to Ranger School. The Army believes that you would make a fine Ranger. You have your maroon beret; you might want to consider getting a black one."

Ricardo didn't hesitate. Ranger School was an intense eight-week course that was one of the most challenging leadership courses the US Army offered.

"Take your time," the commander said. "It's a huge decision."

Ricardo needed just a second. "Sir, it is an honor to be selected, and I gladly accept the challenge."

Why not? he thought. *It's only eight more weeks of hell; I can get through it.*

After Ricardo had signed the necessary papers, the commander handed him a pass. "Take this weekend pass. Take time to relax, prepare yourself, and report to the 6th Ranger Training Battalion on Monday morning. Your orders will be waiting for you at the CQ desk."

Ricardo stood to attention and saluted the commander. "Thank you, sir. I'll be there."

Ricardo couldn't have been more excited. He couldn't wait to tell Martha his news and jogged to the phone center.

He picked up a receiver and dialed Martha's number. She answered in just three rings, and the call connected. "Hey, Martha, I have some great news: I've been selected for Ranger training."

"What does that mean?" she asked.

"It means elite status, Martha. Rangers are recognized and respected across the world; it's a real honor. It will mean another eight weeks of training, so we won't be able to meet up. I know it's unexpected, but it's a great chance for me. You can settle into the apartment and give it the woman's touch."

Eventually, she spoke. "How could you do this to me? It feels like all you care about is the Army, and to make this decision without considering how it affects me. . . . I can't believe how selfish you've been."

"But Martha, it's just eight weeks. After that we—"

She cut in, "Eight weeks here on my own, and you say it's just eight weeks."

"But, Martha—"

"Don't even think about calling me until you have left that damn base and you are on your way back."

Without another word, Martha slammed down the receiver.

"Wow!" he muttered. "What the hell was that all about?"

He walked back to the barracks with a heavy heart. Malcom was sitting on the bed, packing the last of his gear.

"Hey, buddy," Ricardo said. "I won't be going with you to Fort Bragg. I'm going to Ranger School."

Malcom jumped to his feet and ran over to hug his friend. "Man, that's fantastic! Ranger School, that's huge."

'Yes, but Martha . . . she isn't too happy."

"She'll come round; it's only eight weeks. You guys have got the rest of your life together."

"That's what I tried to tell her, but she wouldn't listen."

"She ain't happy for you?"

"Didn't sound like it."

Malcolm looked over. He was determined that the man who had helped him every step of the way during his training enjoy himself tonight of all nights.

"You deserve this, man. We both got passes, and we're going out on the town to celebrate. I won't take no for an answer."

34

RANGER SCHOOL

*I offer neither pay, nor quarters, nor food; I offer only hunger,
thirst, forced marches, battles, and death. Let him who loves his
country with his heart, and not merely with his lips, follow me.*
—Giuseppe Garibaldi

Despite everything life had thrown at him, Ricardo didn't mind admitting that those first few weeks were more challenging than he had ever expected.

It didn't make matters any easier how he had left things with Martha, and there were no telephones out in the fields and forests of Georgia, where they spent most of their time. There was nothing he could do about it. He recalled Malcolm's words: *It's just eight weeks.* But he reminded himself that it was her choice to move from Detroit; he'd hardly had a say. Before he'd known it, she'd parked herself in his new apartment with all her worldly goods and no return ticket home.

—

One hundred and eighty trained soldiers entered the initial stages of the course, and after just a few days, they started dropping like flies. Some called it a day voluntarily; others were told that they hadn't made the grade and were returned to their units.

Sleep deprivation exercises formed a large part of the training. The assessors wanted to see if the soldiers could handle pressure when they were dead on their feet, when every fiber of their body cried out for rest.

There were long-distance runs, swims, obstacle courses, ruck marches, combat drills, unarmed combat, boxing, and martial arts. They also practiced ambush scenarios, urban warfare, and navigation exercises with minimal equipment.

They were deprived of food and made to solve complex problems under time pressure. Once again, Ricardo found himself at the gates of hell, but he knew the exact direction to walk.

Three weeks into the eight-week program, they had lost nearly fifty soldiers.

During week four, they were only allowed one to two hours of sleep per night, often in short, interrupted bursts. The instructors randomly woke the soldiers for surprise drills and tasks, forcing them on night ruck marches. They pushed them to their mental limits and beyond.

The Rangers put each soldier through a timed physical training test every three days. There were no second chances; failure to make the time meant elimination.

—

Ricardo had buddied up with a soldier of Puerto Rican origin, Jose Martinez. There was a big macho culture among the trainees, testosterone in abundance, and both men were often ridiculed about their size.

"Hey, guys," a six-foot-four beast of a man from Cleveland said as they prepared a campfire. "You munchkins ready to quit yet? Mama needs help around the kitchen."

His friends joined in on the joke.

They stood, rippling muscles and broad chests, puffed out like strutting peacocks. Ricardo shook his head and smiled. "We'll be here at the end, Miller; don't you worry about that."

Miller slapped his thigh and screamed out loud, laughing.

Ricardo turned to Martinez and spoke softly. "Beneath their muscles and bravado, there's a fundamental flaw."

"Really?"

"Absolutely. They think their physique is a golden ticket. It's not what the instructors are looking for; it's about endurance, teamwork, resilience, discipline, and determination."

"I hope you're right, man."

"Trust me, I've seen it all before. There's no way the Clevelander will make the grade. If I was in charge, he'd have been RTU'd during week one."

—

Ricardo and Jose's friendship deepened, but Ricardo sensed that Jose was keeping something about himself hidden.

One evening, the two friends sat on the ground outside their tent, a rare moment of calm in their hectic lives. Ricardo sipped slowly from his canteen while Jose fiddled with a small pebble, tossing it back and forth between his hands.

"Ricardo," Jose said, finally breaking the silence, his voice low and hesitant. "There's something important I've wanted to tell you for some time."

Ricardo turned to look at his friend. "What's on your mind, buddy?"

Jose's eyes fixed on the pebble. "Back home, there's someone very special to me. Someone I had to leave behind."

"Yes?"

"My boyfriend. I'm gay, Ricardo. I haven't told anyone here. It's not exactly something the Army accepts, you know?"

Ricardo nodded slowly. "I appreciate you telling me, Jose. That's not easy to carry around alone, especially in this place."

Jose let out a shaky laugh. "Yeah, it's been tough. But I trust you, and I . . . I just needed someone to know the real me."

Ricardo reached out and placed a hand on Jose's shoulder. "You don't have to carry this alone, Jose. I'm here for you, just like you've been here for me."

They hadn't noticed Miller, who suddenly walked out of the shadows of the night. "So . . . we have a fag in our midst," he said.

"This is no place for queers," Miller continued. "you're either a man out here or you're nothing at all. I'll make sure you're kicked out of the Army first thing tomorrow morning."

Ricardo's heart sank; the thought of losing his friend was more than he could bear. He had never grasped why someone's sexual orientation should affect their ability to serve. He acted instinctively, standing up and confronting Miller—David and Goliath. "He's more of a man than you'll ever be; he had bigger balls than you the day he was born."

Miller edged closer. He towered over Ricardo and snarled through gritted teeth, "And you, little man, what are you going to—"

Ricardo's right hand shot out, holding Miller's balls in a vice-like grip. He reached around Miller's neck and pulled his head toward him with his other hand. He whispered in his ear, "Do you know what Article 112a of the Uniform Code of Military Justice is, motherfucker?"

Miller tried to speak, but he found nothing.

"Let me tell you: It states that any person who uses, possesses, manufactures or distributes opium, heroin, cocaine, amphetamine, methamphetamine, or marijuana shall be instantly dismissed from the US Army." Ricardo nodded and smiled. "That's right, man, you've abused Section 202 of the Controlled Substances Act, and I have all the evidence I need to get you kicked out of the Army for good."

Ricardo released his grip, stepped back, and pointed at Jose. "Now, all that remains is an apology to my friend here, and then we can all go about our business, and nobody knows anything about anybody."

Miller took a deep breath. "And if I don't?"

"If you don't, I'll kick your ass in front of your macho redneck buddies on the parade ground tomorrow morning. I'll put you in a coma before you even realize I've invaded your body space."

Miller stepped forward. Ricardo stood his ground. Ten seconds passed before Miller spoke in a barely audible whisper. "I'm sorry."

He walked away into the gloom of the night.

Jose stood, mouth wide open in shock. "What the hell?"

"He's a cokehead," Ricardo said, "and I know exactly where he gets it and where he keeps it. You won't be getting any more trouble from him."

—

Twenty-four hours later, a duty sergeant entered the camp and stood before the assembled men. He read out six names. The last name on the list was John Miller, from Cleveland, Ohio. "Return to your units, gentlemen; you haven't made the grade."

Jose cast a casual glance toward Ricardo. Ricardo winked.

—

Ricardo and Jose graduated fourteen days later, along with just sixteen other men.

35

AN UNYIELDING
HEART

Strength does not come from physical capacity.
It comes from an indomitable will.
—Mahatma Gandhi

Ricardo was sent to the 75th Ranger Battalion in Fort Benning, Georgia, the same base where he did his Airborne and Ranger training. Martha was far from happy; she'd had her heart set on Fort Bragg, one of the largest military installations in the world.

Nevertheless, he had already secured an apartment off base. It was spacious and pretty, but with very little furniture—just the basics.

Ricardo stood in the empty living room; Martha was visibly disappointed. "Don't worry," he said. "We'll save up, and we'll get there in time."

"There is another option," she said.

"And what's that?"

"The Army treats married couples so much better; they provide housing allowances, and if we were married, they'd even pay to move all of my furniture from Detroit."

"They would?"

"Yes, I've looked into it. If the Army treats married couples much better, why don't we get married?"

Martha's suggestion was practical, but Ricardo was taken by surprise.

"You don't want to marry me?" Martha questioned.

Ricardo opened his mouth to speak but was at a loss for words.

"It will put us in a better financial position," she continued. "You do love me, don't you?"

"Of course I do."

"Well then?"

Ricardo smiled and pulled her into an embrace. "Of course, I'll marry you."

—

After completing all the necessary paperwork the following week, Ricardo and Martha found themselves at the courthouse, ready for their marriage ceremony. The day was simple yet significant, marking a new beginning in their lives together. Jose, ever supportive, was there too, serving as a witness for the couple. As they stood in the courthouse, the ceremony was supposed to be a heartfelt affirmation of their commitment. It should have been one of the happiest days of his life. Ricardo couldn't quite put his finger on it, but somehow it didn't feel right.

Four months later, Martha announced she was pregnant. Ricardo was just twenty-two years old . . . but nevertheless excited about becoming a father.

—

Martha's wish to be transferred to Fort Bragg finally came to fruition when Ricardo received orders to join the 82nd Airborne Division's infantry unit. Fort Bragg was a much larger base, with better medical facilities, and knowing Martha's tragic history of losing her first son to SIDS, Ricardo knew the move would provide better support for her and their unborn child. He accepted the transfer, recognizing it as the best choice for his family's well-being.

—

But he wasn't expecting the phone call that came just two weeks after arriving at Fort Bragg. It was from his platoon leader, Lieutenant Baker. "You're to report first thing tomorrow morning. Tell your family you don't know where you're going or when you're coming back."

—

At 0530, his platoon was on the Green Ramp at Pope Airforce Base. A military transport plane with its engines running stood on the runway. The briefing was short and to the point: "You're going to Turkey."

—

The Lockheed C-141 Starlifter touched down seventeen hours later. It had been a nightmare of a journey, with troops, weapons, and equipment packed like sardines. Ricardo couldn't wait to stand up and stretch his legs.

When the doors opened, a blast of hot air hit the troops like a Scandinavian sauna. Ricardo lifted his head. His nose twitched as he picked up the scent of sand and the arid, dry landscape. He looked out and knew enough about Turkey to see that they weren't anywhere near the place.

"We've arrived," his buddy beside him said.

"We have," Ricardo said, "only not in Turkey."

—

It was the start of the First Gulf War.

Ricardo's team had been posted to a corner of the desert between Saudi Arabia, Kuwait, and the Iraqi border. It was the first of August, 1990. Iraq was just about to invade Kuwait. Ricardo's unit had been assigned to the 18th Airborne Corps HQ company. The commander looked nervous as he strolled past the assembled men. He turned to Ricardo. "Specialist Rosen," he said.

"Yes, sir."

He pointed to the highway that stretched out into the distance. It was devoid of any traffic. "Specialist Rosen, about four miles up that highway is an Iraqi tank division, and I'm taking a rough guess they're probably on their way toward us. What are we going to do when we see them?"

"We'll fight them, sir," Ricardo replied.

"Fight them, Specialist? We've got a few Stinger missiles and some small arms; we're talking about a fully prepared and well-armed Iraqi tank division."

"We'll still fight them, sir."

"And what happens when we run out of bullets?"

Ricardo shrugged and looked around at the terrain. "Then I guess we'll have to throw rocks at them, sir."

The commander grinned. "That's the spirit I want to see, soldier. That's exactly the sort of spirit I want to see from my troops."

—

The Iraqi tank division never appeared, and the Iraqis didn't invade Saudi Arabia, much to Ricardo's dismay. He was spoiling for a fight with the Iraqis. He sincerely believed it was the calm before the storm, but the storm never arrived. They sat around for weeks while America and its allies implemented Operation Desert Shield as they built up their troops and supplies on the Saudi border.

Ricardo was once again facing the vast expanses of the Iraqi desert, a terrain hauntingly familiar from his days fighting Iraqi forces during the Iran–Iraq War. Back then, he was a young soldier navigating the complexities of war with limited resources and training. Now, as part of the United States Army, he was equipped with advanced training, superior technology, and the latest equipment. The irony of fighting the same adversary under such different circumstances was not lost on him. Now, with the best gear at his disposal, Ricardo felt both a sense of empowerment and poignant reflection on the cyclical nature of conflict, where the enemy remained the same, but the context had drastically changed.

He often thought about Keavon, wondering what he would be thinking now if he could somehow see him transformed into a formidable soldier, an actual fighting machine, with skills honed to near perfection. The fickle hand of fate had spun its wheel of chance and returned him to these deserts, allowing him to confront the foes responsible for his friend's death.

Chemical weapons were, once again, a significant concern for the Allied forces as they prepared for the operation to retake Kuwait. It was common for Scud missile alarms to sound at any time, day or night, sending everyone scrambling to put on their NBC (nuclear, biological, chemical) gear. The constant threat that each incoming Scud missile might be carrying chemical weapons kept the troops on high alert.

—

During one particularly tense alarm, Ricardo found himself in a tent with two other soldiers. A large man, about six-foot-four and weighing around 230 pounds, was so overwhelmed by fear that he began to cry. As Ricardo tried to help him with his mask, a petite female soldier sprang into action with surprising speed. After quickly donning her gear, she effortlessly helped Ricardo secure the mask on the distressed soldier. The contrast wasn't lost on Ricardo: The physically imposing soldier was paralyzed by fear, yet the slight, unassuming woman displayed remarkable agility and composure. He had told Jose in Ranger School that being a good soldier wasn't about bulk and brawn.

—

Ricardo quickly discovered the Desert Shield operation's purpose: It was all about building up troops and protecting Saudi Arabia at the same time. The Saudi forces received training, but overall, there were extremely long periods of sheer boredom, sitting in warm tents drinking tea and warm water because there was no refrigeration or ice to cool much-needed drinks.

Ricardo spoke Arabic and was quickly assigned to reconnaissance work. One of the officers had commented that "a Chinaman would look more like an American than he did." He quickly took on his role and dressed up as an Iraqi Bedouin. Ricardo and two of his team were given a dirty old Toyota truck, half a dozen goats, and a map of Iraq's border towns and cities. The orders were simple: Locate Scud missile launch sites and antiaircraft guns without getting caught.

Their first mission to Baghdad was nearly their last.

Baghdad was a city caught between two worlds. Minarets and modern high-rises punctuated its skyline, with luxurious hotels and government buildings starkly contrasting the crumbling relics of ancient times.

As they drove through the streets, the goats bleated in the back of the truck, and there was a vibrant but chaotic energy. The *souks* bustled with activity as merchants hawked everything from fragrant spices and rich textiles to the latest electronics and contraband goods.

Ricardo sensed that the conflict had cast a long shadow over daily life. Saddam Hussein's regime maintained a tight grip on the people; propaganda posters and murals glorified his leadership, and the nation's military prowess adorned walls and buildings. It was a constant reminder of the State's dominance, and military intelligence said that the average family had stockpiled supplies, fearful of what the future might hold. Most civilian men were armed.

"We're lost," a voice sounded.

Ricardo looked across at the driver. "What do you mean we're lost?"

The driver held up the map. "It's useless; half of these streets don't exist."

"Stay calm, and put that fucking map away," Ricardo said. "If anyone sees we have a map, we are done for."

It would prove to be a prophetic statement.

They drove another five miles, and as Ricardo turned around and looked out the back window, he spoke. "OK, guys, we'd better get out of here as quick as we can. There are two truckloads of Iraqi troops behind us; we've been spotted."

To compound matters further, the driver spoke. "Iraqi checkpoint up ahead. What will we do, Sergeant?"

Ricardo didn't hesitate. "Run it down. We have no other option—put your foot on the gas and go for it."

The driver needed no further persuasion, and he floored the pedal on the Toyota truck and sped toward the checkpoint. The Iraqi soldiers dove for cover as the truck smashed through the flimsy barrier, and they sped west toward Abu Ghraib, in the direction of the Iraqi desert.

As the driver concentrated on the road ahead, Ricardo was the self-appointed rear gunner. He delivered the bad news within just a few minutes. "There's a whole battalion of Iraqis after us now. You'd better get on the radio and get us out of here, because there's no way we are going to be able to outrun them. You can rest assured they've radioed ahead and have a welcoming committee waiting for us."

Ricardo had to think quickly as he listened to his radio operator request close air support. He pointed to the map and read the coordinates: "Tell them we'll try and make it here, and we'll dig in and hold them off for as long as we can."

They ditched the Toyota at the side of the road and ran full sprint out into the desert, taking cover behind a natural rocky outcrop. The Iraqi vehicles had stopped within less than a minute, and a firefight began.

Ricardo heard the drone of the C-130 gunship before he saw it. Seconds later, it located the position of the Iraqi forces, and its Vulcan guns began to spray their positions with 75mm rounds. It was effective and deadly. The C-130 was joined by two Apache helicopters and two A-10 Warthog anti-tank planes. They made short work of the Iraqi battalion as the three men looked on in awe.

Behind the Apache helicopters, a Black Hawk helicopter landed, and the door opened. "Your carriage awaits you, gentlemen," a grinning .50-cal gunner said as he leaned out of the doorway.

36

BATTLING THE
BEAST WITHIN

*But she goes not abroad, in search of monsters to destroy. She is
the well-wisher to the freedom and independence of all.*

—John Quincy Adams

After another dangerous reconnaissance mission, Ricardo and a
Saudi colonel returned to the base camp, seeking respite. They settled into a foxhole, gazing at the stars scattered across the vast desert
sky, enjoying the calm after the day's tense activities. As they relaxed, the
Saudi colonel reached into his pocket and pulled out a short cigarette
filled with hashish. The unexpected sight of the joint in such a setting
caught Ricardo off guard.

"Try this," the colonel said. "It might take the edge off."

'No thank you, Colonel. I need to keep my head clear."

Before the colonel could respond, the sharp wail of the Scud missile
alarm pierced the calm. Ricardo sprang into action, scrambling for his
protective gear and mask. He glanced over to see the colonel calmly taking a drag from his cigarette, unfazed by the alarm.

"Colonel, you need to put your gear on now!" Ricardo snapped.

The colonel looked up at him with a resigned smile as he exhaled a cloud of smoke. "If there are chemicals on this Scud, I'd rather die with this in my hand."

Ricardo stared, momentarily stunned by the colonel's fatalistic, drug-induced calm. But in that moment, the penny dropped: This was precisely why the United States was there.

—

As the months dragged on, Ricardo became acutely aware of Martha's predicament in Georgia. In November that year, he had been notified that his baby daughter had been born. He had become best friends with the Signal units in the desert and the cooks from the mess hall. In exchange for extra food, the Signal guys bent a few rules, connecting him to Fort Bragg and from Fort Bragg to the civilian telephone lines, and he'd share a few precious moments over the airwaves with his new wife.

Ricardo knew it was not the ideal start to his married life or that of a young father with his first baby, but there was precious little he could do about it.

—

Martha held the phone close, the fatigue and frustration evident as she spoke from the hospital bed. "Ricardo, she's here. Our daughter's here," she said.

"Martha, I wish more than anything that I could be there with you," he replied. "How are both of you? Is she healthy?"

"We're fine. She's perfect, Ricardo, but . . ." Martha paused. "When are you coming home? I need you here."

Ricardo's heart sank. "I don't know, Martha. Everything is so uncertain . . . the war . . . and the Army . . ."

"It's hard, Ricardo. It's tough doing this alone."

"I know, and I'm so sorry. I'm doing everything I can to get back to you. I love you both so much. Tell me about her; tell me everything."

As Martha described their newborn daughter, Ricardo listened, clinging to every detail, wishing he could be there more than ever.

After the call ended, Ricardo felt an overwhelming sense of helplessness wash over him. The weight of his responsibilities as a soldier clashed painfully with his desire to be a good father. He didn't want to repeat his father's mistakes, yet the uncertainty of his return gnawed at him. Every moment away from his new family intensified his fear of becoming the man he had always vowed never to be.

—

David prided himself on always being one step ahead of the game.

Changing his identity was as easy as falling out of bed, because he had done it so many times. As he was now known, David Bennett was in his office at the US embassy in Amman, Jordan, reviewing documents when a Marine guard appeared at his door. The guard stood at attention, his expression serious.

"Mr. Bennett, you have a call on a secure line in the communications room."

David looked up. "Thank you."

He followed the guard out of his office. They moved quickly through the embassy's less frequented corridors, reaching the communications room, where privacy and security were ensured.

Once inside, he picked up the receiver. "This is David Bennett."

"Mr. Bennett, this is Major Stevens from Womack Army Hospital in Fort Bragg, North Carolina. I'm calling to inform you that your granddaughter was born today at 1830. This conversation is confidential; neither her mother nor her father will be notified of this call. You requested a confidential immediate notification."

Relief and a complex mix of emotions washed over David as he listened. "How are they?"

"Both are doing well, sir. The baby is healthy, and your daughter-in-law is recovering nicely. As a precaution, we will be sending your granddaughter home with a heart monitor, given the SIDS history."

"That's very good to hear. Please ensure they have everything they need."

"We will. They're in excellent hands," Major Stevens replied.

"Thank you, Major," he said before ending the call.

37

RISING TO THE CHALLENGE

The best way to find yourself is to lose yourself in the service of others.

—Mahatma Gandhi

As Operation Desert Shield morphed into Operation Desert Storm, Ricardo had no hesitation in volunteering for every mission, no matter what danger it brought. He questioned whether it was the adrenaline rush he needed or just a way to alleviate the boredom of playing cards in a tent for ten hours a day. Perhaps he was just plain crazy!

The US military needed twenty volunteers to parachute into Kuwait City under darkness. They were warned that it would be vicious urban warfare, and they were expecting many casualties. Ricardo's hand was first in the air.

The major explained that they would be the first men in before a ground invasion, and the ground invasion commanders needed to know the positions of the Iraqi troops before they went in.

—

Ricardo and his team parachuted into the shadowy outskirts of Kuwait City. His heart pounded in his chest—his first combat jump. As he gathered his gear, his eyes adjusted to the darkness. Thoughts of soldiers who had parachuted into Normandy on D-Day flooded his mind; he imagined they must have felt a similar surge of adrenaline-bolstered fear.

His team moved stealthily toward the city, careful to avoid detection. The goal was to gather critical intelligence so that they could minimize the destruction of civilian infrastructure and protect the city's civilians as much as possible.

—

The coalition forces advanced swiftly across the Kuwaiti desert and outflanked Iraqi positions, cutting off their retreat routes. The terrain was challenging, with treacherous dunes and the constant threat of landmines and booby traps laid by retreating Iraqi troops.

In Kuwait City, Ricardo's team of twenty worked well, but the Iraqi forces, though demoralized and weakened by weeks of bombing, still posed a threat.

The city's landscape of high-rise buildings and narrow streets complicated the mission. Snipers and machine gun nests were scattered throughout the city as they tried to search house by house.

Inevitably, they were spotted and came under intense sniper fire. Ricardo was trapped, with his platoon leader, against the side of a building.

Lieutenant Baker spoke. "We need to neutralize the snipers, Sergeant."

"I've spotted three positions, sir," Ricardo said. "That building across the street, the closest sniper is there. He needs to be taken out."

"You sure? It's open ground. We'll be sitting ducks."

"We don't have much choice, sir, but if we take that sniper out, we can hold the position and call for backup."

"Think we can do it, Rosen?"

"I do, sir."

"OK, we go on three. Stay low and move fast. Ready?"

"Ready."

"Three . . . two . . . one—go!"

Together, they dashed across the street in a desperate bid to reach safety and turn the tables on their assailants. Under a hail of bullets, they made it and burst into the building. The tension mounted. Room by room, they searched. Each room was empty; nothing but barren walls and peeling paint, a ghost of what had once been a vibrant place. On the second floor, broken furniture lay scattered in each room, a whisper of lost moments, memories abandoned as quickly as the building itself.

The deeper they ventured, the more the silence pressed in.

"You sure the fucker was in this building?" Baker asked.

"Yes, sir." They moved toward the last room. "He has to be in there, sir."

Lieutenant Baker nodded, pointed to either side of the doorway, and they took up their positions.

They worked in perfect synchronicity, and as Ricardo kicked the door in, Baker lobbed the flash-bang inside. The grenade exploded with a blinding flash, giving them the crucial seconds they needed to gain the upper hand. They burst into the room and opened fire, covering all directions to neutralize any threats.

But there was no threat; the lone sniper lay dead in the corner. The grenade had exploded just a few feet from him, and he was riddled with shrapnel wounds; blood covered his body from head to toe.

Ricardo moved swiftly and checked his pulse and breathing. "He's stone dead, sir."

"You don't say?" Baker grinned.

Lieutenant Baker was on the radio, updating the rest of their team as Ricardo picked up the dead man's rifle and positioned himself to get a clear line of sight on another sniper position two blocks away. He took a moment to steady his aim, held his breath, and discharged the weapon.

As Lieutenant Baker looked out the window, he watched as the sniper fell from the building and crashed onto the street below. "Man, Rosen," he said, "with a weapon you've never used before, that's really impressive."

"I adapt quickly, sir," he replied, his eyes never leaving the scope, scanning every window he could see.

"All right, the team is en route, and we've got support coming."

"Good to hear, sir."

At that exact point, he spotted the third sniper. Ricardo wondered if sniping might be his true calling. The focus, calm, and precision it demanded resonated with him deeply.

Just as Baker began to speak, Ricardo cut him short. "Number three: spotted him, sir."

"Where?"

"In the window of that minaret 9 o'clock as you stand, second window down."

Baker strained his eye., "Can't see him, Rosen."

"Keep watching . . . you will, sir."

Ricardo held his breath, counted to five, and squeezed the trigger. As the two men studied the window, they saw an almost repeat performance of the previous target as the unmistakable shape of a human body tumbled through the air and smashed into the courtyard forty yards below.

Baker shook his head. "Well, I'll be fuckin' damned."

———

After the successful operation in Kuwait City, there was a lull of sorts while the hierarchy decided whether to go all out and take Baghdad or structure a ceasefire with Saddam Hussein. There were still hundreds of thousands of Iraqi troops, most of which were hiding in the familiar terrain of the deserts, whole tank battalions dug in. They had no intention of surrendering.

—

Ricardo worked alongside the 4th Psychological Operations Group (4th POG). He quickly discovered a side to war other than bullets and guns. To minimize casualties on both sides, the US Air Force was called in to bomb the food and water routes.

After several days of prolonged bombings, the supply routes through the desert were paralyzed, and while the coalition troops enjoyed fresh food and water in abundance, the Iraqi forces were starving and thirsty.

The 4th POG team moved units as close as they could possibly get to the Iraqi positions and then waited until the wind direction was favorable. They built bonfires and threw steaks on top of the burning coals and wood. The beautiful aroma drifted across the desert.

They set up loudspeakers with microphones, dropped ice cubes into vast buckets of water, and called for the surrender of the Iraqi troops. It had more effect than a thousand bombs, as the Americans promised them as much ice-cold water and food as they wanted.

—

The Iraqis walked across the desert in droves, with their hands held high, and, true to their word, the Americans gave them everything they needed, albeit now as prisoners of war.

Another successful tactic was the leaflet drops. The coalition forces would drop leaflets from airplanes, warning that the position would soon be bombed and urging the troops to surrender or get the hell out of there. The first time it happened, the Iraqi forces took no notice of the leaflets, and consequently, several hours later, the area was pulverized from the air. Word quickly got around, and from that moment, there was no need for any aerial bombardment; the flimsy pieces of paper written in Arabic were more than enough to get the job done.

—

In mid-February 1991, Ricardo returned from Kuwait City to his base in Saudi Arabia. Lieutenant Baker had summoned him for a briefing.

"At ease, Rosen. I have a new assignment for you," he began. "You're to lead a team that will escort General Schwarzkopf to a meeting near the Iraqi–Kuwait border. We're flying out tonight on the next chopper. Prepare your gear, pick your team, and brief them. We'll discuss more details on the way."

"Yes, sir. I'm on it."

—

A few hours later, the Black Hawk helicopter touched down near the Iraqi–Kuwaiti border. Ricardo had given his team a thorough briefing on the route. They had to ensure the safety of the legendary general and his team. They were to collaborate closely with the military police units they supported, a critical element in the complex security arrangement.

An hour's drive to the negotiation site lay ahead, a journey through potentially hostile territory that demanded vigilance.

Ricardo emphasized the importance of securing the area upon arrival. "I want no Iraqi surprises," he said.

The team checked their gear, and Ricardo told them the stakes were high and the eyes of the world were on them. He had devised a strategic plan: The unit would split up and set up a secure route for General Schwarzkopf to reach the negotiation site safely.

Ricardo's thorough preparation and clear instructions had ensured that every segment of the operation functioned like clockwork. He escorted General Schwarzkopf and his Iraqi counterparts to the site, where he met Lieutenant General Sultan Hashim Ahmad. The talks were formally opened, and Ricardo stood at ease in a corner of the room while they discussed the terms and conditions for a formal ceasefire.

He was a little surprised when the coalition agreed to allow Iraq to fly its helicopters into its territory. *Just as well I'm not leading the negotiations,* he thought to himself.

Schwarzkopf was insistent that the Iraqis give him the location of mines and information on all chemical and biological weapons. The meeting eventually concluded, and as Schwarzkopf stood, he made a beeline for Ricardo.

"Thanks for all your help, Sergeant," he said. "We couldn't have done this without you."

38

BRIDGING
THE DISTANCE

There are places in the heart you don't even know
exist until you love a child.

—Anne Lamott

Several weeks later, Ricardo and his unit received welcome news: They were going home and had been granted a three-week leave. He couldn't quite believe it; he would finally get to meet his daughter, Stephanie.

—

As the chartered America West plane touched down at Pope Air Force Base, crowds gathered in large numbers to welcome the returning troops, their enthusiasm visible from the runway. American flags fluttered everywhere, creating a sea of red, white, and blue; people were sporting yellow ribbons, a symbol of support and solidarity that had become synonymous with the war effort.

Off to the side of the Green Ramp, the 82nd Army Band added to the celebratory atmosphere, playing stirring music as the plane rolled to a stop.

The troops quickly assembled into formation on the tarmac, standing to attention under the watchful eyes of gathered families and friends. The battalion commander stepped forward and made a short but impactful address, expressing his gratitude for the troops' bravery and dedication during the war.

"Each of you has demonstrated incredible courage and commitment," he said. "You have served your country with honor, and it is now time for you to enjoy the peace you helped secure. Take this time to reconnect with your loved ones," he concluded.

With a final salute, he dismissed the formation. Ricardo scanned the bustling crowd but couldn't see Martha and his daughter anywhere. As the people drifted away, he continued his search.

"Where is she?" he muttered to himself.

And then, at last, a familiar face.

The two friends embraced. "Malcolm, I can't believe it's you."

"I returned a few weeks ago; I heard about the new baby. Congratulations, man!"

"It's great to see you, Malcolm, but where's Martha? I can't see her anywhere."

"She's at home. She wanted to be here, but she had a bad headache and couldn't handle standing out in the sun. She asked me to come pick you up."

"Is she OK, though?"

"Yeah, she's fine; she didn't want to risk it. Let's get you home, buddy. She's waiting for you there."

—

As Ricardo stepped out of the car, his excitement surged, and he practically sprinted through the apartment door and into the living room. Martha stood motionless in the corner of the room as his eyes fell on his new daughter beside her. He crossed the room quickly, pulled Martha into a tight embrace, and cradled his daughter in his arms for the first time.

"She's beautiful," he said, kissing Martha.

She pushed him gently. "Wow, you stink; take a shower before you come anywhere near me or the baby."

He waited for a grin or a small laugh to indicate she was joking, but neither the smile nor the laugh materialized. She was deadly serious.

"Now," she said, "you remember where the bathroom is, don't you?"

Ricardo was momentarily stunned at her insensitivity. Nevertheless, he agreed that he probably did stink. He'd been cooped up in a plane for the better part of twelve hours. His eyes fixed on his daughter for a few precious seconds. "Your mom is right: Your daddy needs a shower. Don't run away; I won't be long."

It was the quickest shower he'd ever had, and he was back with his daughter in less than ten minutes.

Martha handed Stephanie to him.

"I need to pick up a few things, so you'll have some time to get to know her," she said. He nodded eagerly, happy to spend time alone with Stephanie and get acquainted with his new role as a father.

As Martha closed the door behind her, Ricardo found himself alone with Stephanie for the first time. He felt a mix of awe and nervousness. Her tiny form in his arms was so fragile and dependent. As she looked up at him with curious eyes, the weight of her trust was exhilarating and intimidating. He'd never done this before.

Each tiny movement she made fascinated him, and he felt an overwhelming surge of love that deepened his connection to the tiny, new life. It was a moment of pure, unguarded emotion.

As Stephanie drifted off to sleep in his arms, Ricardo leaned down and whispered, "I'll always be here for you, little one. I'll always protect you, no matter what happens. I'll never walk the walk my father took. I'll always be here for you, beautiful one."

—

Finances were tight, so Ricardo and Martha had no option but to prepare to drive the twelve-hours to Detroit instead of flying. The airfares were beyond reach, and the prospect of such a long journey with a baby was daunting. They prepared carefully for the road trip, packing everything they needed to keep Stephanie comfortable. They'd take in the sights along the way. It would be a mini adventure, Ricardo told himself. It would be fun.

It was anything but fun. Just an hour into the trip, Martha's mood changed, and she started to complain about the confined space of the car, the heavy traffic, changing nappies, and almost anything else she could think of.

Despite the tense atmosphere, Stephanie handled the long hours better than expected, adapting well to the long stretches on the road and the frequent stops.

—

Finally, after what felt like an eternity, they arrived at Martha's parents' home and pulled into the driveway. The two proud grandparents greeted them warmly, excited to meet their granddaughter for the first time.

The morning after they arrived in Detroit, Ricardo stepped into the quiet of the guest room and picked up the landline to make a long-distance call to his mother.

"Ricardo, my dear, is that you? I've been so worried."

"Nothing to worry about, Mom. I am back from Saudi Arabia, safe and sound and cuddling my beautiful baby girl."

After the phone call, Ricardo felt a renewed sense of family connection. He desperately wanted his mother to come to America to rebuild and strengthen family ties.

Later that day, Ricardo took Martha and Stephanie for a nostalgic drive around Detroit. He drove past Wendy's, where they had first met, and, without even realizing it, passed through the neighborhood where his cousin Baback lived.

"I have family in Detroit," Ricardo said.

"You have family here in Detroit? Why didn't you ever mention this before?"

"It's complicated, Martha; a long-standing family drama. But Mom tells me things are better now. We'll catch up with them soon, I'm sure. We . . ."

"What is it?" Martha said.

Ricardo was confused. "A police car. They are indicating that I should pull over. I wasn't speeding, was I?"

"I don't think so."

Ricardo brought the car to a steady stop on the side of the road. He wound down his window. The policeman approached him.

"Can I help you, Officer?"

"Driver's license, insurance, and registration, sir."

The arrival of a second police car heightened the tension. He watched with growing concern as another officer approached their vehicle.

"Please exit the vehicle, sir."

Ricardo did as he was asked, and suddenly, the atmosphere changed.

"You're under arrest, Mr. Rosen," the officer said as he produced a set of cuffs.

"There has to be some sort of mistake, Officer."

"No mistake, sir. You've been writing bad checks, and the warrant for your arrest is over twelve months old."

—

At the police station, they placed Ricardo in a holding cell; all the while, he protested his innocence but remained courteous. The police officers did likewise when they learned he was a serving soldier.

The most prolonged four hours of his life passed before an officer unlocked his cell and told him he was free to go. "You have a good lawyer; he's out front, and he'll explain the situation. Thank you for your service, Sergeant Rosen. It was nothing personal; we were doing our job."

"I understand, Officer; just a mix-up, I'm sure."

—

The lawyer introduced himself and led him into a small interview room. He explained that he had spoken to the bank and covered the cost of the two checks together with a minor inconvenience payment. The checks had been issued when he was on active duty; he couldn't have possibly written them. They were forged signatures, and the bank had dropped the charges.

He breathed a huge sigh of relief. "I knew it had been a mistake."

The lawyer handed him copies of the two checks involved in the fraud. "Do you recognize the signatures?" he asked.

A ball of ice formed deep in Ricardo's stomach. He swallowed hard. The handwriting was unmistakable, with familiar loops and strokes he had seen countless times.

"I do."

"Who signed these checks, Mr. Rosen?"

"My wife. That's Martha's handwriting."

—

Ricardo was shocked; the revelation that his wife had taken such liberties with his identity and finances was hard to accept.

She was full of apologies and said that she had intended to cover the money, but things had gotten on top of her, and she lost control of her finances.

"Martha, I wish you had told me; we could have figured something out. This could have ended badly for both of us."

"I know, and I'm so sorry. I was trying to keep everything afloat and made some poor decisions. I promise nothing like this will ever happen again."

—

Ricardo never slept that evening; a million different things were spinning around in his head. They weren't exactly rich; he knew that, yet he had sent home his monthly salary. Military pay wasn't the best in the world, but all of the other families seemed to manage, and Martha's situation was much better than it had been before he had met her. As he looked at the ceiling in the darkened room, he couldn't quite figure out how much she had spent. He was struggling with his feelings toward her, yet she was his child's mother; he had to make it work one way or another.

She needed a break, and he knew she hadn't had it easy. Ricardo hated her father and everything he stood for; he was a racist and a bigot, and he had never taken to him. Martha had told him countless stories of how he'd beaten her when she was younger. Ricardo mellowed and closed his eyes. *I have to get some sleep.* Perhaps there were things she had never shared with him.

—

Back at Fort Bragg, he quickly found where most of the money had gone. He checked the receipts on the grocery bills and found out that

Martha had spent a lot of time and money in liquor stores and sections of the supermarkets that sold alcohol.

Ricardo was determined to address this situation that evening as he returned home from work on the base. He walked into the living room. Martha was slumped in a chair, and the room was filled with the sound of his daughter's cries.

"Martha—what the hell? Stephanie is crying; she needs attention. What are you doing?"

Ricardo could see her eyes were glazed over as she looked at him.

She spoke. Her words made no sense; they were all slurred. Martha was dead drunk, and it was 4:30 in the afternoon. Ricardo picked Stephanie up, and her cries faded as she nestled into his chest.

Before he could say another word, Martha spoke. "Your daughter, too, soldier. Joint responsibilities and all of that shit."

Ricardo glared at her. "I'll speak to you in the morning when you're sober. You should be ashamed of yourself getting into that state when you have a young baby to care for."

Martha lifted her wine glass and took a long drink. "Cheers." She smiled and stood. "I'll get my coat. I'm going out; don't wait up for me."

—

Military life wasn't easy, and it was tough for the families. It wasn't just the loneliness that made it challenging; it was the constant undercurrent of fear. Every news report, every unknown number flashing on the phone, sent a shiver down the spine of all military wives. They had to live with the uncertainty, but Martha had also signed up for military life, and it wasn't all bad: The regular monthly wage and an apartment that was theirs was something she'd never had. Surely, she could appreciate that.

Malcolm's wife was a constant in their lives, and there was an on-camp sisterhood bound not by blood but by shared sacrifices. They gathered every so often, drank coffee, and shared stories. There were more than enough shoulders to cry on, and there were young, new mothers just like Martha. It was only a matter of time before Ricardo's next deployment or his next training exercise in the field, and he'd have to leave her again.

—

That day came quicker than he expected when the Special Forces recruiting team arrived at Company headquarters. The team had a small unit out in the field encouraging the soldiers to sign up for the selection process. Ricardo strolled over, picked up a leaflet, and read it. He shook his head; he had no intention of signing up for more of the same he'd had at Ranger School, so he returned the leaflet to the table.

"Not interested, Sergeant?" one of the men said.

Before Ricardo could respond, a lieutenant from his unit spoke. "Step back, soldier. I know your background; you're not the kind of man they want in Special Forces."

"And why is that, sir?" Ricardo said.

"This unit is comprised of America's finest; you couldn't handle the selection process," he scoffed.

Ricardo gently lifted the clipboard. "We shall see about that, sir."

The officer stepped forward, pulling the clipboard from Ricardo's hands. "Stop wasting my time; you will never make it."

Ricardo smiled and saluted the officer. "Unfortunately, sir, it's too late. My name is already on the list. I'll see you soon."

—

As he walked away, he wondered how he would tell Martha the news. It was a two-month selection in the field, and the Special Forces guys didn't get to go home at night.

—

His first stop would be the family support group; then, he'd need to call Malcom and his wife. He'd ask them to keep an eye on Martha and the baby. If he made it through, it was sixty-three weeks of training, with little time off, and he was worried. He'd signed up on a whim, determined to prove the lieutenant wrong. Had he done the right thing?

—

As he entered the living room back home, Ricardo hesitated. Martha was helping herself to a considerable measure from a bottle of whiskey. He looked at his watch: It wasn't yet midday.

No time like the present, he thought to himself as he took a deep breath. "Martha, there's something I need to tell you."

Martha glanced up, her expression already clouding over. "What is it now?"

"I've signed up for Special Forces training."

"And?"

"It's a two-month course. If I get through, it will take me away for over a year. There'll be very few breaks in between to come home, and not much more."

Martha slammed the glass hard on the counter. "You're leaving again?"

"I'm a soldier, Martha; it's what soldiers do. It's what you signed up for when you married me."

"But a whole year . . . you decided this without thinking about us?"

"It's crucial for our future. It's a promotion; we'll get Special Duty Assignment Pay, Proficiency Pay, and bonuses."

Martha cut him off, her anger boiling over. "Important for our future? What about now? What about your family now, Ricardo?"

"I know it's tough, but—"

"No, you don't know!" Martha cut in, her face flushed with anger. "If you knew, you wouldn't be doing this."

She stood, drained the whiskey from her glass, and threw it against the wall. Without another word, she stormed out of the room.

Ricardo collapsed into a chair and buried his head in his hands. He knew it wasn't about the career, the extra pay, or the bonuses. He had committed to Special Forces for no other reason than the bigoted lieutenant had bugged him. Ricardo was definitely stubborn, but he was a rebel with a cause. It was in his nature; he couldn't do anything about it.

39

THINKING OUTSIDE
THE BOX

Imagination is more important than knowledge.
For knowledge is limited, whereas imagination
embraces the entire world . . .

—Albert Einstein

His mother's voice floated on the warm breeze, calling him from the courtyard. He could smell the familiar scent of jasmine flowers mixed with the earthy aroma of bread baking in the kitchen.

He followed her voice, though he could not see her yet. His auntie's laughter echoed from the garden, and his sister ran ahead, her scarf fluttering in the breeze. He longed to reach them, touch their hands, and tell them he was home.

But as he turned the corner toward the house, a dark shadow loomed in the distance, growing larger with each passing second. Faceless men in black turbans surrounded the once gleaming dome of the mosque, their eyes cold, their mouths twisted in fury, and dirty, long beards hiding their faces. The faces of his family grew dim; their laughter faded into the wind as the Mullahs approached him.

A jarring vision of the American Embassy, the angry mob, the chants, the hostages dragged through the gates. He saw himself there, helpless, powerless, as his world spun out of control. He tried to run but couldn't; his feet were somehow glued to the ground. The crowd came closer until he could feel their breath on his neck. He turned; more black robes, swords raised, fists clenched, and they came for him, screaming, "Die, die, death to the Shadow Rider."

"Mom," he cried, "help me. Hannah, help me."

And finally, Uncle Masood was running toward him to help, until the crowd swallowed him up.

His heart pounded, his skin slick with sweat, the sharp taste of adrenaline on his tongue. He awoke with a start. The darkness of his tent wrapped around him, starkly contrasting the warm, sunlit Tehran of his dreams. His chest heaved as reality set in—he was not home. He was not in Tehran; there was no family.

—

The training camp was nestled in a rugged, secluded area with dense pine forests. The air was crisp, filled with the sounds of distant commands and the rhythmic stomping of boots, but although ready for the challenge, he worried about the domestic situation he'd left back home.

But he'd committed; it was too late to change his mind, and as always, he'd give it his all. He knew no other way.

Three days into the training, he knew he'd made the right decision, and nothing would stop him from getting the coveted green beret. The incredible intensity of the atmosphere was both daunting and invigorating, and it made the hairs stand up on the back of his neck.

—

During one exercise, Ricardo and his group were split into teams of three, each tasked with moving a heavy telephone pole up a steep, muddy hill. There was a fifteen-minute time limit.

From the outset, Ricardo could see that it would be impossible. Ricardo told his teammates to hang back as the dozen other teams sprinted toward the telephone poll on the whistle.

They watched as, from the outset, they floundered in the mud, struggling to make it even halfway up the hill before sliding back down to the bottom.

"What have you got planned, Sergeant?" one of his team members asked. "We're already six minutes in."

"Wait here," Ricardo said as he walked toward the driver of a Humvee parked nearby. "Do you mind if I borrow your truck for a minute?" he asked.

"Be my guest," the driver said as he climbed out of the vehicle.

Ricardo drove the Humvee to the telephone pole, attached the winch, and then drove to the top of the hill.

Within thirty seconds, the telegraph pole and Ricardo's team were at the top of the hill, cheering in victory while the other teams looked on in dismay.

As they made their way to the bottom of the hill, there were accusations of cheating; they argued that using the Humvee wasn't in the spirit of the challenge.

Eventually, one of the instructors stepped forward, surveying the group with a stern expression. He addressed them firmly. "We never specified any rules; we didn't say you couldn't use a truck. You imposed the limitations on yourself. Sergeant Rosen and his team were thinking outside the box. All the rest of you did was complain about how difficult the task was, and in reality, it wasn't. Being a soldier in the Special Forces is about adaptability and resourcefulness."

—

At the end of the two-week selection process, the 350-person group was reduced by nearly 50 percent. Names were called out each evening, and each person had to leave the training site immediately.

The ritual became known as the "duffle bag drag," a term that captured the sad moment of gathering one's belongings and exiting the training area, dragging their kit bags behind them.

—

Ricardo successfully completed the two-week selection and moved on to phase II, known as the Q course. The training was designed to deepen their skills and officially qualify them as Special Forces operators. Much time was spent in the classroom, and second languages were essential. Ricardo was already fluent in Farsi, so he didn't need to take any language courses. Instead, he requested to join the Special Operations Sniper School.

—

In the US Embassy in Tel Aviv, David was studying a large map of south Lebanon when a knock at the door interrupted his focus.

As David opened the door, General Carter, a seasoned Special Forces officer, entered the room. "David, I've got news about your son," he said.

"Tell me."

"He has passed selection and requested to attend Sniper School."

General Carter smiled. "It's quite ironic: the same path you took."

A broad smile spread across David's face as he processed the news. "Like father, like son, eh? And tell me, has his request been accepted?"

"Of course; he was one of the best candidates out there."

"Fantastic! He'll be a great asset to the team one day. Special Forces and the CIA go back a long way."

General Carter nodded. "We'll ensure he receives all the support he needs. He has a bright future."

"Thank you, General," David said.

"I'm sure he'll be successful at Sniper School," the general said. "We've already heard about his shooting in Kuwait City from Lieutenant Baker. Ricardo picked up a rifle he'd never set eyes on before and took out two snipers. Baker said he'd never seen anything like it."

David wanted to say, "That's my boy," but he held his tongue.

The general continued. "The instructors are confident; he's good, David. After Sniper School, it's the Robin Sage exercise, and then your son will receive his green beret. After that, he can return home to his wife and your granddaughter for a while."

"Excellent. How are they both, General? It's been a while since I've heard anything."

A frown crept across the general's face. "Well, David, I think we have a little domestic problem back at Fort Bragg."

—

Ricardo was in the final stretch of his training. He'd breezed through Sniper School; qualified in high-altitude, low-opening parachute school; unconventional warfare; guerrilla warfare tactics; infiltration; tactical weapons; operational planning; surveillance; survival skills; and leadership.

And now, there was only one final discipline between him and the coveted green beret: one exercise involving carrying a fifty-pound rucksack across rough terrain, combat movements under simulated enemy fire, and a few obstacles thrown in for good measure.

He was a mile from the finish, and he looked up. He felt good. He could see the two brightly colored pillars that signified the end. His green beret was tantalizingly close. And then, as he lurched forward and fell, he heard a sickening crack, and the pain registered immediately.

"Shit! Shit!" he cursed.

He looks down at the hole in the ground he'd missed. He looked at his leg; it was twisted at a grotesque angle, broken—no doubt about it.

A Humvee pulled beside him before he had time to assess the situation. General Carter was in the passenger seat. "What's up, Sergeant Rosen?"

Ricardo could hardly speak; the nausea was building, his body had begun to tremble, and the sweat stood out on his brow. "Problem with my leg, sir."

Carter looked. "Sergeant Rosen, it shouldn't be bent like that; it's broken. Get in, and let's have the medics look at it."

"But I'll be disqualified, sir."

General Carter pointed up ahead. "So tell me, how do you plan to run the last mile with a broken leg?"

Ricardo checked his watch. He still had thirty-five minutes to complete the run. "Don't need to run, sir; I'll get there, even if I have to crawl," he said.

"Get in the fucking truck, soldier; you have a broken leg."

"Sir, is that a direct order?" he asked.

General shook his head. "No, it's not a direct order."

"Then I'm OK to continue, sir."

General Carter shook his head and spoke to the driver. The Humvee pulled away.

The pain in his leg was unbearable; his progress slowed to an agonizing crawl. In a desperate bid to lighten his load and preserve any remaining strength, he removed his rucksack from his back, attached it to his good leg, and started dragging it behind him. He was going to get there, no matter what.

As Ricardo struggled forward, his vision was blurred from the intensity of the pain. He vomited every few minutes, his body's reaction to the shock.

He rested for a minute, concentrating on getting his breathing into a rhythm he could control.

He checked his watch: He was progressing. He had time.

General Carter's Humvee appeared again. "Half a mile, Rosen. You ain't gonna make it; get in the fucking truck."

Ricardo lay in a pool of his own vomit and looked up. "With respect, sir, I ain't going fucking nowhere." He lifted himself onto his knees. "Nothing's gonna stop me making it over that line."

"Your leg, you idiot: It's bleeding," General Carter said. "I can see the fucking bone. You'll get an infection; we'll have to amputate it."

Ricardo threw the general a weak salute. "I want that beret, sir; it's as simple as that."

He set off at a snail's pace once again, the pain so severe that he nearly passed out several times. He pushed on, yard by yard, the finish line getting ever closer.

He checked his watch: ten minutes left. Progress was painfully slow, and Ricardo became aware of the Humvee roaring toward him again.

It pulled up beside him; the general stepped out, his expression serious. "Get in the truck now. I do not want a dead soldier on my hands."

Ricardo crept forward and crawled another six yards closer to the finish line. "I'm nearly there, sir; so close. I'll do it."

Ricardo's words were slurred, every natural drug in the human body pumping through his system, working together so that he would not lapse into unconsciousness.

General Carter said something to the driver.

Ricardo looked up. Carter had a green beret in his hand.

"Sergeant Rosen, listen to me very carefully. I can see how badly you want this. I've never seen a soldier more deserving of it; it's yours. You've earned it."

"Sir, I'm confused," Ricardo said. "I have to get over that line."

"You don't. I've moved the fucking line, and it's right here."

"But you can't do that, sir."

"Oh yes I can. With my rank, I can move mountains, so moving a line a couple hundred yards is well within my power."

Ricardo shook his head. "But . . ."

"But nothing. Congratulations, Rosen, you're one of the finest, most determined soldiers I've ever met, and I'm honored to present you with your green beret."

The general stepped from the Humvee, placed the beret on Ricardo's head, and a spontaneous burst of applause came from the driver's seat.

The general smiled and spoke. "Now get in this fucking truck; that's a direct order."

40

THE PRICE OF DUTY

The more you sweat in peace, the less you bleed in war.
—Norman Schwarzkopf

Ricardo's doctor was amazed by his dedication and resilience. He was determined to regain full fitness and pushed his body beyond what was expected. Within three months, he could complete a light jog on the treadmill; a few weeks later, he could sprint around a two hundred-meter circuit.

He was assigned to the 7th Special Forces Group at Fort Bragg.

—

In the early morning hours, the phone's shrill ringing cut through the bedroom's silence like a sharp knife.

Ricardo reached for the phone, and the man on the other end barked out the order before he could speak. "Lieutenant Smith here. Report to company HQ with full gear in two hours."

"Yes, sir."

Martha was groggy and irritated; she'd heard everything in the silence of the darkened room. "Why can't they just wait until morning? What's so urgent that they need you right now?"

Despite her complaints, Ricardo felt a surge of excitement. This was his first mission as a Special Forces soldier, and he couldn't wait. As he jumped out of bed, he was already picturing how to prepare his gear. As he moved around the bedroom, gathering his equipment, he tried to soothe Martha's concerns. "It's how these missions go; timing is critical. It's what I signed up for."

"You keep saying."

———

Within the hour, he stood in the living room, every gear item perfectly packed and in place, enjoying a black coffee and wondering what excitement lay ahead. He was focused and excited, eager to meet the challenges of his new role.

Ricardo felt a pang of guilt, but he knew the urgency of his mission left no room for delay. He disappeared into Stephanie's bedroom, kissed her, and whispered, "Daddy's a soldier, my child; you know how it is." He kissed her again. "When you are older, you'll understand. You'll be as proud of Daddy as he is of you." He could do nothing to prevent the solitary tear running down his cheek.

As dawn's soft, golden light seeped through the curtains, it cast a gentle glow over the room. Ricardo knelt beside the crib. His daughter's tiny chest rose and fell with each breath, blissfully unaware of the world beyond her dreams. He brushed a tender kiss against her forehead, his voice hushed. "I need you to be brave for me, OK? Like I'll be brave for you." He stroked her soft, downy hair; his fingers trembled slightly. "I want you to know how much I love you. Whenever you feel the sun's warmth on your face, my love surrounds you. Whenever you hear the wind whisper through the trees, I tell you how special you are." His eyes glistened. "You're my little miracle, Stephanie. I promise to carry your photo with me, to keep your laughter in my heart, and I'll return as soon as possible. There might be nights you miss me, but remember, I'm always with you."

He paused, taking a deep breath to steady himself. "If you ever feel scared or lonely, just remember that Daddy is out there. You're the reason why I fight the bad guys. I never want you to see the shadows that I had to battle."

With one final kiss, he stood, took one last look at her peaceful form, and, with a heavy heart, turned and walked out of the room.

He grabbed his keys and headed out, his mind switching to the mission ahead.

—

At company HQ, he went directly to the mission briefing room. Lieutenant Smith was already there, waiting for the rest of the team to assemble. The room buzzed with a quiet tension.

Lieutenant Smith began the briefing, his voice steady but firm. "Gentlemen, we are facing a challenging mission that demands precision and flawless execution. At 0800 hours, we depart from Pope Air Force Base on a C-141 Starlifter, heading to MacDill Air Force Base in Florida. Once there, we'll prepare our equipment and await further orders. At 2100 hours tomorrow, we'll reboard the aircraft and head toward a location just outside Bogotá, Colombia." He pointed to a specific spot on the map pinned on the wall behind him. "The aircraft will reach the drop zone at approximately 0100 hours. Our task is to perform a HALO jump into this clearing." He pointed to the map, to a small open area surrounded by dense jungle. "Our RV point will be here." He pointed to the map again. "We're scheduled to meet with CIA operatives already there. They will provide further details on the ground."

Lieutenant Smith's expression grew more serious. "Our primary objective is a rescue mission; the cartel has taken a CIA agent hostage.

We are also tasked with destroying a major cartel drug warehouse where we believe our hostage is being held."

—

Within the hour, Ricardo and his team were assembled at the Green Ramp, geared up and ready to board the plane.

—

As the team boarded the second flight out of Florida, a heavy silence settled among them, only broken by the steady hum of the aircraft's engines. They sat in the dimly lit cabin, each member lost in their thoughts. Three hours into the flight, Ricardo noticed the tailgate red light, signaling they were approaching the drop zone.

The Air Force loadmaster began to lower the tailgate, and a rush of cool night air filled the cabin. Outside was only pitch-black darkness—no lights, no visual clues, just a vast open sky and the dense jungle somewhere below.

The team lined up. Ricardo took a deep breath as the jumpmaster gave the signal, and they jumped into the unknown.

He was all alone. He couldn't see any of his team as the cold wind whipped his face, and the dark void below seemed infinite. His heart pounded as he counted the seconds, and then he yanked the rip cord. The parachute unfurled, snapping him back, and he felt a strange calmness as he descended toward the ground.

As he landed, he felt a rush of relief and satisfaction; his extensive training had paid off, and he had landed precisely in the designated clearing. He gathered his gear and met up with the rest of the team.

They moved swiftly through the dense jungle, the mission now fully underway. Every step took them deeper into the heart of enemy territory.

—

By the break of dawn, they had reached the rendezvous point and met with their CIA counterparts. One of the agents approached Ricardo and extended his hand. "Sergeant Rosen?" he said. "It's nice to meet you finally."

Ricardo was puzzled; why had the agent singled him out?

The group gathered closely around a map the agent had placed on the ground. He pointed out the location of the cartel's warehouse. "It will take most of the day to get there, and the jungle is a bastard. We must avoid any clearings and roads; this is cartel territory, make no mistake about it."

The stakes were clear; the journey was fraught with danger. With a final nod of understanding, they began the next part of their critical mission.

The team pressed forward through the dense jungle toward their target, maintaining a relentless pace. As dusk began to settle, they finally neared the cartel's heavily fortified warehouse.

They settled down in the foliage of the jungle floor while Lieutenant Smith observed the enemy camp through binoculars.

After several minutes, he addressed the team. "Two machine gun nests are perched on two towers, and all the guards are armed." He turned to Ricardo. "You're the team sniper sergeant. You need to take out the tower guards, and you'll need to use a silencer."

Ricardo nodded; he knew a silencer would compromise his accuracy.

"Take your time, Sergeant." Lieutenant Smith handed him the binoculars.

Ricardo surveyed the area, calculated shooting positions, and ran through the ballistics in his mind. He nodded firmly. "Absolutely, I can take them out, sir."

Lieutenant Smith outlined the next steps of their plan. "Once the tower guards are down, we'll move quickly to neutralize the outer guards.

We'll place our charges and force entry. Once inside, our priority is to locate the hostage, and once we've got him, we'll blow the fucking place to kingdom come. We'll destroy their entire operation and every gram of coke in there."

—

The team waited until night fell over the dense jungle, and Ricardo was given the nod to get into position. He was acutely aware that his team depended on him; failure was not an option.

Ricardo settled into the optimal shooting position, ready for the kill. His heart weighed heavy with the burden of taking a life, the guilt a shadow he couldn't shake. Yet clarity cut through the doubt; the man in his sights had endangered countless innocents. He was the bad guy.

With a deep breath, he steadied himself as he aimed at the first guard. With a gentle squeeze of the trigger, he watched through the scope as the guard slumped over the rail a split second later, suspended like a lifeless mannequin.

Ricardo waited a minute or two, repositioned himself, and brought the second guard into the scope of his sights. He held his breath and brought the trigger slowly toward his body. Another silent shot, and the second guard was down.

—

From his vantage point, Lieutenant Smith monitored the situation through his night vision binoculars and gave Ricardo a thumbs-up. Despite the high stakes, Ricardo felt an unexpected calmness; he was focused, methodical, and ready for whatever came next.

As the team began their advance toward the warehouse, Ricardo stopped them. "Down, sir, three more guards."

The team dropped to the ground. As Lieutenant Smith viewed the three men emerging from the central warehouse, Ricardo already had the first guard in his sights. The man dropped to the ground; the other two guards stopped dead in their tracks. The silent kill had confused them. As the man on the right bent down to check on his friend, his head exploded in the darkness. The remaining guard froze as his body stiffened in shock. A second later, he was also lying dead on the ground.

Lieutenant Smith lowered his binoculars. "Fuck me, Sergeant, I've never seen anything like that in my life. When we get out of this shithole, I'm going to buy you the biggest beer you've ever had."

Ricardo lowered his rifle and spoke. "Mission cleared to continue, sir."

—

The silence of the night was shattered by the explosive blast that breached the warehouse door. The team burst into the building, their movements swift and coordinated as they searched for the hostage, ready to take out the guards inside.

As Ricardo and his team entered the illuminated warehouse, weapons drawn, they were prepared for anything—except what they found.

The stench of chemicals and fear hit them first. In the dim light, they saw small children, no older than ten years old, chained to workbenches. Tiny hands trembling, they had been cutting and bagging cocaine for their cruel overseers. Their cheeks were tear-streaked and dirt-stained; their eyes hollow, devoid of hope. The sight was a nightmare come to life, a scene of unimaginable horror.

Ricardo's resolve hardened, fury boiling inside him. The guilt he'd felt at taking out five members of the cartel, men who would never return to their families, evaporated in a cloud of anger and disbelief. "How can humans do this?" he mumbled to himself.

A sound from the far corner of the warehouse brought them back into operational mode. A door was flung open, and half a dozen armed men burst on the scene. They stood no chance, as the highly trained Special Forces team quickly took them out before they could pose a threat. The enemy had made a fundamental mistake: They were all grouped together, barely an inch or two between the six-man target. They were cut down like freshly mown grass.

The children were terrified and screamed and cowered under the tables. A few team members who spoke Spanish gently reassured the frightened children, explaining that they were there to help and that no harm would come to them.

In one of the back rooms, they found the hostage—badly beaten, but he'd recover. As the team medic began to administer first aid, it was clear that the MO had now changed.

"What are we going to do?" Lieutenant Smith asked of nobody in particular.

Ricardo was the first to speak. "We can't leave them, sir. You can bet your last dollar that the cartel reinforcements are coming, and we need to act quickly."

Lieutenant Smith nodded. "Free them, talk to them, tell them they will be fine."

The team worked at breaking the chains with anything they could find.

Amid the chaos, Lieutenant Smith contacted headquarters for guidance. He quickly relayed the unexpected situation, describing the children's presence and the urgent need for a revised extraction plan.

As he awaited instructions, the rest of the team secured the area, keeping a vigilant watch for any signs of incoming cartel forces.

After a tense radio exchange, Lieutenant Smith returned to his team with updates. "HQ's in contact with the US State Department; they've already contacted the Colombian government. They've agreed to send military support, but they will take a few hours to arrive. Until then, we're on our own. We need to secure the warehouse and prepare for the possibility that the bad guys might arrive before the Colombian military does."

—

Within five minutes, the team was in place, working cohesively, their training and instincts guiding their every move in preparation for what might come next. The safety of the children added a profound sense of duty to their task.

—

As dawn broke, the team remained vigilant, but there was no sign of the Colombian Army. The children had been moved to a secure room, and a Spanish-speaking team member was assigned to stay with them. He gave them chocolate and other rations; there was plenty of water. In a bizarre spectacle, as Ricardo looked on, his colleague began translating and recounting some of the bedtime stories he had once told his own children. His calm and steady voice wove tales of adventure and bravery, capturing the children's attention and providing a much-needed distraction from the terrifying situation.

The soft sound of his voice provided a soothing contrast to the tense atmosphere outside, where his teammates continued to watch the perimeter, ready and waiting for any sign of trouble.

Ricardo watched in quiet admiration as his teammate worked his magic with the children. The terror and chaos they had just experienced were momentarily pushed aside by the gentle tones of a fatherly figure providing comfort. It struck Ricardo profoundly; a simple act of kindness amid the horrors they had uncovered not only helped to calm the children but also served as a powerful reminder of the resilience of the human spirit and the importance of tenderness in the face of brutality.

Ricardo felt a renewed sense of purpose and a deep respect for his teammate's ability to bring a moment of peace to tiny innocent lives that had been shattered by violence. This underscored the dual nature of their mission—not just to confront and eliminate threats but to protect and restore, to bring a sense of safety where there had been fear.

His thoughts drifted to Bahar and Shahla. He remembered his promises to them to be a voice for the voiceless and bring light to the world's darkest corners.

The Special Force's motto was *De Oppresso Liber* (To Free the Oppressed). It had always been a guiding principle, a distant ideal. But in this moment, it became a tangible reality. It was about more than fighting enemies; it was about alleviating suffering, rescuing the vulnerable, and restoring justice where it had been denied. Each word of that motto reinforced his belief that he and his colleagues could make a difference. It was precisely why he had fled Iran and was here now, in the moment.

—

The ominous rumble of trucks rolling toward the compound broke the silence outside, and the atmosphere tensed. Every man had his weapons drawn, not knowing whether the approaching vehicles were friend or foe. The familiar rush of adrenaline sharpened Ricardo's senses. Were these the reinforcements promised by the Colombian government, or was it the cartel coming to defend their territory and reclaim their assets?

The sounds grew louder, and the first vehicles became visible through the gaps in the warehouse's entrance.

A crackle of the radio. Lieutenant Smith spoke. "Stand down, men. The Colombian military has intercepted the cartel reinforcements on the ground, and with support from our gunships, they've wiped the bastards out."

There was a collective sigh of relief and a few cheers, and they slowly lowered their weapons. Now, they could prepare for extraction.

—

They coordinated with the Colombian military and helped the children onto military trucks, preparing them for transport back to Bogotá. The children, visibly shaken, were now safe from immediate danger. Miraculously, more chocolate appeared, and rations of biscuits, nuts, and raisins were emptied from each man's ration pack; Ricardo even noticed a smile or two on some of the children's faces.

The team provided the security for their onward journey to Bogotá. They accompanied the children out of the compound and from the life they'd known only as *hell*.

It was tense. They remained highly vigilant, scanning the surroundings for any signs of trouble. The collective goal was clear: Get the children safely to Bogotá, where they could receive proper care and be reunited with their families or placed under protective custody.

—

In Bogotá, the team received a comprehensive debriefing about the rescued children. They learned that most of the children had been abducted from their villages by the cartel, a common tactic for recruiting forced labor. The gangs didn't care; they had no compassion, and they exploited the children because the end justified the means. One of his team commented, "How the fuck can a grown man exploit a child in such a way?"

Ricardo knew better than the next man that adults could use children for a purpose, regardless of the ethical or moral implications. Ricardo shed a tear as he bid goodbye to each child and turned away.

"Why, Father," he mumbled. "Why would you do it?"

—

After their rest period, it was time to prepare to return to Fort Bragg. The team gathered their equipment and made their way to the airport. Despite the mission's success, it was a quiet flight; few words were exchanged, and every man was lost in his own thoughts.

41

A SOLDIER'S BURDEN

The true soldier fights not because he hates what is in front of him, but because he loves what is behind him.

—G. K. Chesterton

Back in Fort Bragg, Ricardo headed straight home, eager to reunite with Martha and Stephanie; he longed for the comfort of his family. As he walked through the door, he scooped Stephanie into his arms, his emotions overwhelming him as tears streamed down his cheeks.

The haunting images of the frightened children were etched deep in his memory, a stark reminder of the brutal realities of life at the rough end. His daughter was nearly three years old now; he was struck by the thought of her ever witnessing such horrors.

The relief of being home safely was tinged with the responsibility he felt as a father and a soldier. It was a poignant reminder of the ongoing struggles against violence and exploitation around the world. Now more than ever, he was committed to his role in Special Forces, driven by a personal and professional mission to prevent such tragedies and protect the innocent. It had been a tough start—mainly as he had no support from Martha—but now he knew he had made the right decision.

But he knew it was an ever-growing chasm that seemed to widen with every deployment. Each time he left, he wondered if this was the time the gap would become too wide to bridge, if this would be the time when the life he was supposed to be living slipped too far from his grasp.

He had chosen this life—no one had forced him into it. But the choices he made weighed heavily on him. The longer he stayed away, the more he felt like a stranger to his family.

He could handle the physical strain, the long hours, and the uncertainty of each mission. But knowing he wasn't there for Stephanie when she needed her father was what ate away at him in the quiet moments. He couldn't shake the feeling that he was losing something precious with every day he spent away.

Yet tomorrow, he would do it all again, because it was right, and he was making a difference to the world. But the most brutal battles weren't fought on foreign soil—they were fought in silence, in the mind, in dreams and nightmares.

—

In Amman, Jordan, David's phone rang. He glanced at the caller ID, and a brief smile crossed his face: Mike Kapplen, an old friend and colleague from his days in the field. David picked up the phone, eager to hear from him.

"David, it's Mike." The voice was warm with familiarity and the shared bonds of past experiences.

"It's good to hear from you," David said. "What's new on your end?"

"A little bit of this and a little bit of that. You know me, never a dull moment."

"Join the club."

"Actually, David, there's a reason I called: I've just returned from the mission in Colombia. I finally met up with Ricardo."

"How did it go?"

"Your boy did good. He's a fucking living legend; he took five guards out single-handedly. If it hadn't been for him, the mission would have stalled right there and then."

"That's great to hear."

"Your suggestion to send in Ricardo and his team was spot-on. They played a crucial role in the mission. The bad guys were wiped out, and they rescued Charlie."

David felt a mix of pride and relief. Charlie and he went back a long way; his safety was a great relief. "That's fantastic news. I'm glad he's safe, and it sounds like the boy stepped up."

"Absolutely; he did you proud."

"He doesn't know about—"

"Of course not," Mike interrupted. "My word is my bond, remember?"

"Thanks, Mike. Ricardo has to carve out his own path."

"He was like a seasoned pro, David—kept his cool under tremendous pressure and made some sharp decisions. The kid's got a bright future ahead of him."

"Keep me posted on any further developments, Mike, and let's try to catch up next time."

"Definitely, David. I'll keep you in the loop. Take care."

David said goodbye, placed the receiver on the hook, and leaned back in his chair.

Things were going exactly as he had planned. He was very proud of what he had achieved with this young man. It had nothing to do with the family aspect, though he could never forget that Ricardo had his DNA: the same genes, the same makeup. No, it was because David had been his guiding light from the very beginning, and the best bit was that Ricardo knew nothing about it.

42

BEYOND THE HORIZON

Uncertainty is the only certainty there is, and knowing how to live with insecurity is the only security.

—John Allen Paulos

Martha was drinking more than ever, and it affected not just their marriage but also the family atmosphere for young Stephanie.

Each attempt at conversation about the future or discussions aimed at addressing Martha's drinking seemed to end in frustration, creating an ever-growing chasm between Ricardo and her. There were no tender kisses or intimacy, no declaration of love or romantic dinners at fancy restaurants.

Martha complained about everything and said she was lonely, and that's why she drank.

"How can you be lonely?" Ricardo said. "Linda calls in nearly every day; there are social clubs, gyms, coffee mornings, holiday parties, mother's clubs, educational classes, and, if the fancy takes you, even churches. You're only going to be lonely if you want to be lonely.

Twenty thousand other wives and girlfriends are on the base; surely you can find a few friends?"

"You wouldn't understand."

Nothing made any logical sense.

"I wonder why you ever married a soldier," Ricardo said.

Martha just smiled, nothing more.

Their future was clouded with uncertainty.

—

Each time he returned home, the worries seemed to build as he mulled over his options into the early hours of most mornings. His duty as a father was paramount, yet he couldn't help feeling the best course of action for everybody concerned was some form of separation. He explored all possible options and sought advice from some of his most trusted colleagues. It was good to talk things over; it cleared his head, yet as soon as he walked back into the house and saw Martha, the black cloud descended again.

—

When he returned home that night, Martha was asleep on the couch, clearly intoxicated. His immediate thoughts were of Stephanie. But after walking to the bedroom, he found his daughter was fast asleep, tucked up in bed, knowing nothing about the chaos around her. Ricardo walked back through the living room and into the kitchen. It looked like a mini tornado had breezed through the window, with dirty dishes piled high and the kitchen table littered with leftover food, plates, and at least a dozen cups and glasses. As his eyes scanned the kitchen countertops, a dark reminder of Martha's ongoing battle was evident, with two empty whiskey bottles sitting behind the microwave.

As he started to tidy up the mess, Martha stumbled through and joined him.

Any thoughts that she was about to lend a hand were quickly dashed.

"What the fuck are you doing? You want to clean the kitchen at this hour?"

Ricardo snapped, "I am done with this, Martha. I can't take your drinking anymore. This has to stop, or I am taking Stephanie and leaving."

Martha's reaction was immediate and alarming. Her face flushed red with a mix of anger and desperation—a look Ricardo had never seen before. She grabbed a knife from the counter and held it in her outstretched arm.

Ricardo stepped forward. "Put the knife down!"

She thrust it out toward him. "Stop! Stay away."

Ricardo was more than confident about disarming his wife; he'd spent countless hours training in unarmed combat, but his instincts told him to play the waiting game.

"Put the knife down, Martha," he repeated.

She extended her left arm and placed the blade against her wrist. "If you are going to leave me, then I don't want to live anymore," she cried out.

Before Ricardo could react, she pulled the knife sharply toward her, and Ricardo looked on in disbelief as her flesh parted like the Red Sea. The first drop of blood emerged, dark and rich, then, like a dam breaking, the arterial spray was an arc of crimson.

Martha fell to the floor, and with each heartbeat, the sticky lake she lay in grew bigger.

Ricardo stood in shock for a second before his training took over. He pulled a towel from the back of the chair and tied it tightly across the wound. He ran to the phone, called the emergency services, and sat with Martha until the ambulance arrived. Thankfully, he had stemmed the flow of blood.

—

As he sat in the hospital waiting room, with a sleeping Stephanie on his knee, he questioned himself over and over again. How had his life come to this point? Was he somehow to blame? The medical staff were efficient and professional, but he was also aware of their coldness toward him, wrongly assuming that Martha's injury was a result of domestic violence. He couldn't blame them; they had likely seen their fair share of domestic violence during their careers. He sat there for hours, trying to work things out in his head. He needed to get professional help for Martha. That was the first step, and despite the late hour, he phoned Malcolm and explained everything, chapter and verse.

—

Later that morning, a doctor walked toward them and said that Martha was fine physically, but she would be staying another night and needed to undergo a psychological evaluation. "Our priority is to ensure Martha receives the best care for her physical and mental health. We also recommend a family counselor."

Ricardo listened, nodded, and agreed with everything the doctor said. Strangely, he felt better knowing that everything was out in the open.

He was prepared to do whatever it took to rebuild their lives with the help of the Army professionals. He would stay with Martha and work it out, if for no other reason than Stephanie needed a mother. He guessed that some marriages were like this: The love had left their relationship, but he had made his bed, and now he had to lie in it for the sake of Stephanie.

—

Malcolm and Linda had arrived. Linda announced that she was taking Stephanie back home with her. "She can stay with us as long as necessary; you stay with Martha."

Ricardo was lost for words. With friends like this, they would pull through.

—

Ricardo was sleeping in a chair when he heard a familiar voice and felt someone shaking him gently.

He opened his eyes and focused. It was his company commander, Captain Hood. Instinctively, Ricardo jumped to his feet and saluted.

Captain Hood smiled. "No need for that, Sergeant; we're in a hospital."

Ricardo looked around. There were more people there: First Sergeant Jackson and his wife, and now Captain Hood's wife too.

Ricardo was confused. "Sir, it's great to see you, but why are you here? Why are your wives here?"

"Why do you think we're here, Rosen? We're here to support you. Remember, you signed up for this when you joined the Army; you are all in with the biggest family in the world, and don't ever forget it. We've already spoken with the doctor, and they will keep Martha here for observation for a few days. I've granted you an additional week's leave. My wife and Mrs. Jackson will ensure Martha receives the care she needs. Don't worry about anything for now. Just go home and get some rest. We'll keep in touch and call you with any updates."

Ricardo was stunned. He'd heard a lot of the guys talking about the "family," but until now, he never really knew what it meant.

—

Captain Hood, First Sergeant Jackson, and their wives spent the next few hours supplying Ricardo with coffee, offering reassurance and kind words. Their compassion touched him; he knew that they were all gen-uinely concerned. He realized the military was a close-knit community, and his superiors had gone beyond the call of duty.

It was a leadership model that resonated deeply with him, an exam-ple of how leaders can impact the lives of their team members. The military was not just about taking out the bad guys; it was about look-ing after the good guys and lending a hand when times got tough. There were days when every moment felt like a sun-drenched afternoon, warm and endless. Yet, inevitably, there were stormy days and nights of doubt. With the help of his second family, he'd get through it. For the sake of Stephanie, he had to.

As he walked along the hospital corridor with yet another cup of coffee, he reminded himself of his favorite quote from *The Count of Monte Cristo*. He mumbled softly to himself, "Life is a storm, my friend; one day, you will be basking in the sunshine, and the next, you will be dashed on the rocks. What makes the man is what he does when the storm arrives."[1]

—

The doctor had diagnosed Martha with a form of narcissism. It was not her fault, the doctor kept saying, and while cautious, Ricardo felt a glim-mer of hope as Martha signed up for counseling. She promised to stop drinking, and the extended military family pledged to play a significant role, providing them with the resources and encouragement needed to start the healing process and begin a new life.

---

1   Alexandre Dumas, *The Count of Monte Cristo* (New York: Penguin Classics, 2003), 102.

43

SEEDS OF HOPE

Hope is being able to see that there is light despite all of the darkness.

—Desmond Tutu

Two weeks later, at 5 a.m., as Ricardo walked into the gym and began to get changed, Lieutenant Smith walked over to him. "No PT today, Sergeant. We have a mission. Head to the briefing room."

"Yes, sir."

The camaraderie and focus were palpable as they awaited Lieutenant Smith's arrival.

Lieutenant Smith entered without delay, his expression serious.

"Gentlemen, we are heading to Somalia in a few hours as part of Operation Restore Hope. Our primary mission is to secure safe routes for the UN aid trucks that are bringing food and supplies to the country during the civil war. Most of the population is on the brink of starvation; we need to ensure the safety of these convoys. We are accompanying a Civil Affairs unit that will supply and manage the aid distribution, and we need to take care of them. We'll also be working with the British SAS, and I don't need to tell you anything about those guys. This operation is about more than just military objectives; it's about delivering stability and hope to a people desperately in need."

The briefing lasted less than an hour. "OK, gentlemen, that's it," Lieutenant Smith said. "Remember, it's about making a difference in the world."

As the men stood up to leave, Lieutenant Smith called Ricardo over and told him he had an additional covert role. "You'll be meeting one of our undercover guys. He'll explain everything. I'm just telling you so there are no surprises," he said.

"Yes, sir. Thank you, sir."

—

Ricardo's gear was packed, and, as always, during a quiet moment of reflection, he prepared himself mentally and remembered the past promises he'd made. He took a moment to call Martha, explained the situation, and reassured her he'd return home safe and sound. He hung up the phone and walked outside.

First Sergeant Jackson pulled him to one side as he boarded the truck. He whispered, "Rosen, don't worry about anything at home; we've got this. My wife and the commander's wife will check on Martha and Stephanie. They'll make sure everything's OK while you're gone."

Once again, Ricardo was at a loss for words.

—

After a grueling sixteen-hour flight aboard a C-141 Starlifter, the team finally touched down in Mogadishu.

Shortly after their arrival, they were introduced to the Civil Affairs team and their British SAS counterparts. Ricardo sensed they were experienced and battle-hardened.

The initial briefing outlined a seemingly straightforward task: They were to act as escorts for a convoy from the airport to several villages, ensuring the safety of the supplies and the personnel involved. They'd need to neutralize any militia threats that might attempt a hijack or sabotage. The potential for conflict with local militias was a significant concern.

Ricardo was aware of a man approaching him. The face was vaguely familiar.

"Sergeant Rosen?" he said.

"Yes, can I help you?"

"Hi, my name is Charlie. We met before, but I wasn't in excellent shape the last time you saw me."

Ricardo's mind raced.

And then it came to him. "Charlie." Ricardo held out a hand. "The warehouse in Colombia."

"That's me."

"Wow, you're looking good, man."

"Thanks to you and your team. I owe you my life."

He surprised Ricardo by embracing him. "I mean it," Charlie said. "I owe you big time. Those bastards were ready to execute me."

The small talk and pleasantries were over as Charlie discussed the brief. "We'll meet at 0600 hours tomorrow morning. We'll work with Sergeant Gand from the SAS and review all the details in the morning. I don't need to tell you any more at this stage."

—

At precisely 0600, Ricardo was in the briefing room, prepared and focused on the details of a critical side mission. As Charlie entered the room, he was accompanied by Sergeant Gand and a woman introduced as Dianna, to whom Ricardo felt an instant, raw attraction. As the woman looked over at him, there was a brief flicker of a smile.

Much to his surprise, Dianna chaired the briefing.

She pinned a black-and-white photograph on a corkboard behind her. "This man here is the bad guy," she said, "a Russian arms dealer with the morals of a starving rat. He's connected to the Russian government, and they've been supplying the militias who have been disrupting our aid routes."

She continued, pointing to a map on the wall. "Your drop zone will be here, and you'll be on foot for the rest of the day. I'm sorry to tell you, but you'll leave your ID and dog tags back here. This is very much a black operation, and if you're caught, you're on your own, and you'll be treated as a rogue operative. We'll deny that you're even there."

The SAS man turned to Ricardo. "They tell me you're a bloody good shot, Rosen. I hope so, because we don't want to hang around there too long. We're relying on you."

Ricardo grinned. "No fuckin' pressure, then."

The room's atmosphere was charged with determination and the underlying tension of the risks involved. Ricardo's attraction to Dianna added a layer of complexity to his mental state.

As the briefing concluded, he stepped outside into the early morning sunshine.

A few minutes later, Dianna emerged from the building. She pulled out a cigarette, lit it, and took a long, steady drag.

Ricardo couldn't help but comment, a half-smile on his face. "You know those things will kill you."

Dianna returned his smile. "I know, but we all have to go someday. Besides, I'm a bit nervous since I'm running this op."

"I didn't get your last name," he said.

"I didn't tell you, Sergeant Rosen. In the agency, we don't do last names. Perhaps if I get to know you a little bit better, I might tell you."

That smile again—the smile that started an involuntary movement of serotonin and phenylethylamine from the brain. Ricardo wanted to fight it, but he could do nothing about it.

As Dianna took another drag of her cigarette, Ricardo nodded, understanding the boundaries, yet intrigued by the woman who now stood before him.

—

At precisely 1800 hours, the airfield buzzed with the sound of a small propeller airplane warming up on the tarmac. Ricardo and Sergeant Gand were fully geared up.

Just as they began to climb aboard, Dianna dashed toward the plane, a map in her hand. She made a beeline for Ricardo. In a surprising move, she stepped forward and hugged him tight. The hug lingered slightly longer than was normal in this professional capacity.

"You get your pretty ass back here safe and sound, soldier; that's an order," she said.

As they settled into their seats on the plane, Sergeant Gand turned to Ricardo. "I think you have a secret admirer, mate," he teased.

He was as surprised as Sergeant Gand at Dianna's gesture. "Maybe," he replied. "You never know your luck."

—

As the small aircraft neared the DZ, the darkness outside was absolute, a thick blanket of night broken by the occasional flicker of distant lights. Inside the plane, the atmosphere was tense but focused. The pilot signaled with a thumbs-up that they were approaching the jump point. Sergeant Gand moved confidently toward the plane door, pulling it open against the roaring wind. The cold air rushed in, filling the cabin with the harsh reality of the mission ahead.

A minute later, the pilot's voice cut through the noise, a simple command over the intercom: "Go!"

The men leaped from the aircraft without hesitation, plunging into the icy night air. They deployed their parachutes and drifted gracefully toward the ground into thick vegetation. Their location had been strategically chosen: a position in the trees adjacent to an airstrip, the site of their mission's focal point.

They dug in and settled down for the night.

The timing had to be perfect. Intelligence indicated that the Russian arms dealer's plane would arrive at 0700. The hours of darkness would give them time to survey the airstrip, plan their approach, and prepare for the critical moments of engagement and escape.

As dawn broke, Sergeant Gand scanned the early morning sky with binoculars. He pointed up to the sky. "Another fifteen minutes, we're being told; it's flying in from the west. We'll probably hear it before we see it."

—

Gand grabbed the binoculars and positioned them with a clear view of the airstrip as they heard the unmistakable sound of an approaching aircraft.

The plane landed, turned around, and taxied to a stop. A minute later, the aircraft doors opened, and half a dozen people started walking down the steps.

Gand spoke in a barely audible whisper. "Target confirmed, at the bottom of the steps now: a sky-blue shirt and dark blue jeans. Take the fucker, Rosen; send him to meet his maker."

"You sure?"

"Hundred fuckin' percent."

Ricardo focused and caught the target in his crosshairs, slightly to the left of the middle of his chest. He held his breath, counted to four, and squeezed.

The target dropped to the ground. He lay motionless on the airstrip as all hell broke loose, bodies running in every direction; some fell to the ground instinctively.

"He's down, Rosen. Great fuckin shot. Now let's cause some real trouble."

Sergeant Gand quickly armed his grenade launcher and focused on the lead truck of four militia vehicles speeding toward the plane.

"Second truck, Rosen; do your fuckin' magic."

A split second later, the cab of the front truck exploded into a ball of fire, bodies and pieces of bodies scattered on the runway.

The second vehicle had veered off to the right, seeking shelter. As it turned in a 180-degree arc, Ricardo had a clear line of sight. As he squeezed the trigger, he watched through the scope as the driver's head took the full impact of the round, and he flopped forward into the steering wheel as the driverless truck veered off its intended path and crashed into the plane. A split second later, the truck and the plane erupted in a ball of flames, and the remaining two trucks sped off into the distance.

Gand looked at Ricardo, a big grin on his face. "Fuckin' result, soldier boy. Everything I've heard about you is fuckin' spot on. Now, let's clean this place up and get the fuck out of here."

As they retreated from their position, Ricardo reached for his radio, his voice steady despite the adrenaline coursing through his veins. "This is Rosen. Target neutralized, secondary threats contained. We're moving to the extraction point now."

They moved through the jungle stealthily and quickly, gaining the advantage of natural cover and the early morning light.

The tension did not wane as they made their way through the rugged terrain, every sense heightened and alert for any sign of pursuit. Their extraction was as critical as the mission itself, and the knowledge that each step brought them closer to safety was their only reassurance as they pressed forward to the rendezvous point where their team awaited to bring them home.

Exhausted but relieved, Sergeant Gand and Ricardo climbed aboard as the helicopter touched down. It was a welcome sight, and they headed for base camp. The rumble of the engines gradually subsided into the quiet of the early evening.

As the helicopter touched down, they approached the building for some much-needed rest, and Charlie and Dianna were waiting to debrief them. They were both smiling.

"Well done," Dianna said. "A textbook execution." She stepped forward, her demeanor subdued but her eyes bright with admiration. Leaning closer to Ricardo, she spoke in a low, flirtatious tone that only he could hear: "I have some vodka with me; maybe I'll stop by tonight, and we can have a drink. I might even tell you my last name."

It carried an unmistakable hint of intrigue.

Ricardo surprised himself. "You're on."

The prospect of a quiet evening sharing a drink with Dianna offered a rare moment of relaxation, a brief escape from the relentless pace of their operations. It had been some time since any woman had given him that sort of attention.

—

Ricardo sat alone on his cot, the room silent, as he reflected on the day's events, the successful operation, and his unexpected interactions with Dianna. The knock on the door snapped him out of his reverie.

"Come in," he called.

The door opened and Dianna stepped in, a bottle of vodka in one hand and two glasses in the other. Her appearance was strikingly different from earlier in the day; her hair was no longer in its usual bun but flowed freely, enhancing the soft glow of her features in the dim light of the room. She also had applied a little makeup. She looked good.

"Are you ready to celebrate, soldier?" she asked.

"Absolutely," he replied.

Dianna closed the door gently behind her and made her way over, setting the bottle and glasses down on the small table next to the cot.

She poured the vodka, the clear liquid catching the light as it splashed into the glasses. Handing one to Ricardo, she raised her own in a toast.

"To successful missions and new friendships," she said.

"To new friendships," he echoed.

As they both took a drink, the sharpness of the vodka seemed to mark the beginning of a new chapter, one that Ricardo was now surprisingly eager to explore.

They began talking. Ricardo showed her a picture of Stephanie. "She's my life," he said. "I miss her so much. I love my job, but . . . I wish I could spend more time with her."

"And your wife?"

Ricardo drained his glass. "Pour me another."

The question went unanswered.

Dianna said that her job was her life; it left little room for family. She gazed at Ricardo. "You know, what happens here stays here," she whispered. "Your team won't be back until tomorrow afternoon; we will have the whole night together."

She couldn't have been more obvious.

He wanted to fight it—he did—but he also knew he could do nothing about it. He was attracted to everything about her and sensed the feeling was mutual.

It was a momentary escape from his troubled marriage, yet he knew he should stick to the rules. A quotation came to mind, often attributed to Douglas Bader: *Rules are for the obedience of fools and the guidance of wise men.*

He leaned across and kissed her. It felt like an electric charge coursing through his body, a mix of excitement and apprehension. She responded with equal passion.

The isolation from the rest of the world and the excitement of knowing it was wrong of both of them amplified the intensity of their encounter. As the passion increased, they tore at each other's clothing, and within seconds, they were both naked.

"Are you sure?" Ricardo whispered, his voice barely audible.

"Yes," she whispered back, her voice steady. "I'm sure."

He led her to the bed. They lay down together, their bodies fitting together perfectly, like two puzzle pieces. He wrapped his arms around her.

As they kissed and explored each other's bodies, they talked in hushed tones, sharing memories, dreams, and fears. Each confession brought them closer, the intimacy deepening with every word. As the conversation lulled, they joined together, their movements instinctive and unhurried.

And when the final barrier fell away, it was with a sense of beauty at their connection. They held each other close, their hearts beating in sync.

—

As the first light of dawn began to creep into the room, they lay entwined, the world outside slowly coming back into focus. Something had changed; Ricardo had crossed a forbidden threshold.

Dianna dressed quietly. They were both processing the whirlwind of emotions. With a look that held both warmth and a hint of sadness, she gave him a passionate goodbye kiss. "I'm heading back to the United States today," she said.

As she walked toward the door, he called out, "You never told me your last name."

As she reached the door, Dianna paused and turned to look at him with a mysterious smile. "Maybe next time," she said.

She left the words hanging in the air as she closed the door behind her.

"To next time," Ricardo said.

44

DIRTY DEEDS

*People sleep peaceably in their beds at night only because rough
men stand ready to do violence on their behalf.*
—George Orwell

D avid entered the US Embassy in Abuja, Nigeria. He presented his
ID to the guard, who waived him through.

When he reached the front desk, he said, "Can you direct me to
the secure communications room, please?"

The receptionist recognized him. "Good morning, Mr. Bloom. We've
been expecting you. Take the door over there on the left; the communications room is at the end of the corridor."

"Thanks."

David followed the instructions. The communications room door
was unlocked, and he walked in and sat at the desk. He dialed the number, and the call was answered almost instantly.

"Charlie, David here. How's it going?"

"Good to hear from you, David. I guess you're calling about the
mission?"

"I am. How did it go?"

"It was executed perfectly," Charlie said. "Dianna did exceptionally well on her first operation with Ricardo."

David listened intently.

"Even the British SAS were impressed."

"Good, I knew he would pull this off. And he still thinks that this was just about an arms dealer, right? Nothing more?"

"Absolutely, as per your instructions." Charlie paused for a second. "And there's a bit of a twist, just so you are aware: Dianna told me that she and Ricardo spent the night together. She had to report it, so I am letting you know."

"Good; she follows directions well."

"Yes, it appears the ladies like your son; he has a certain charisma. It seems she enjoyed herself a little too much."

"As long as she doesn't fall for him. Tell her to be careful next time. This has happened before. I'm not sure what it is about him and women. They keep falling in love with him."

The call lasted another fifteen minutes. Charlie told him every detail of the mission, from start to finish.

David ended the call, returned the receiver to the hook, and left the embassy for the next part of his plan.

—

Ricardo stayed in his room, waiting for his team to return. Around noon, his teammates finally arrived at the base camp. Lieutenant Smith walked into the room and spotted him. "Rosen, I have no idea what you were up to yesterday, but I heard it was textbook. Glad you're back safe."

Ricardo nodded. "Thanks, sir. It went well, but I'm ready to rejoin the team and finish what we started."

"No need, Sergeant. We ran into an ambush. It was a tough fight, but we completed the mission and got the supplies to the village. The mission is complete."

"That's good. No casualties?"

"Sergeant Bell was injured. It's nothing serious, but he'll be out of commission for a few days. You take another day's rest, and we can prepare you for the next village rescue, and then we'll head home."

"Yes, sir."

—

Their next mission brought them into a small village, and the extreme starvation and lack of basic needs were evident. The women and children were scared, thin, and tired. Some of them looked like they hadn't eaten for days, and most of their pitiful homes were in ruins, some burned to the ground; the scene hit Ricardo hard, as they poured forward toward the convoy, begging for food and water.

The crowd of villagers was desperate, and it took all the efforts of the Civil Affairs team to keep control. His thoughts filtered back to his childhood in Iran and his family life at Fort Bragg. Despite his troubles, they still had the basics they needed to survive, and even the torment he had suffered at the hands of Reza paled into insignificance as he looked into the hopeless eyes of the small children. He had seen war before. He had seen the destruction it left in its wake, the broken bodies of soldiers, and the devastation of towns shattered by conflict. But this was different. This wasn't a battlefield abandoned by its soldiers; this was a village with real homes, and what he saw before him weren't enemies or allies but children, too young to understand the politics of war. They were too young to know why their bellies were swollen with hunger and why their eyes looked more like hollow craters than windows to a future. A small boy, no older than eight, wandered aimlessly toward him, his ribs clearly visible through his bony chest. The boy's eyes were distant, unfocused, as though the weight of hunger had long since robbed him of the energy to care. He clutched a rusty tin can in his tiny hands as though it were a treasure. He held it up, begging for something. Ricardo gave the boy his pack of biscuits and some dried fruit. He had nothing else to give.

There was no doubt about it that his life had been a challenge. But at least when the mission was over, he'd be returning to a life of normalcy, returning to familiar places and faces, where a quick visit to a supermarket would give him everything he needed to keep his family fed and watered and a roof over their heads.

—

The ridiculously long sixteen-hour flight landed just before midnight eastern time. He had been able to call Martha the previous day, and she had agreed to meet him.

But once again, despite dozens of family members waiting for the soldier's return, Martha was not one of them.

He caught a ride home from one of his teammates, and as his house loomed in front of him, he felt the heavy weight of depression descending upon him. He exited the car, said goodbye, and crept quietly toward the front door.

He opened the front door and tiptoed into the house. It was late; he chastised himself for feeling upset that Martha hadn't been at the base. He walked upstairs to Stephanie's room and found her sleeping soundly, her breathing soft and steady. He kissed her on the forehead, whispered goodnight, and walked to where Martha was sleeping. She looked peaceful. He had mixed feelings, and as he crept back through the house, he noticed it was unusually clean and tidy, with no empty booze bottles.

He dared to hope that she had changed; she was trying.

He collapsed into one of the sofa chairs and started to breathe hard. He fell asleep, but the nightmares were ready and waiting for him, quick to make themselves heard. He relived each moment of fear, the death and destruction, the bad guys he had killed. And yes, those eyes of the small children in the villages he had left behind on his latest mission were ingrained into his psyche; it was something that couldn't be unseen.

He awoke with a start, took a few breaths, and his thoughts drifted to Dianna and their encounter. A wave of guilt washed over him. He knew deep down that what had happened between them crossed a line, yet he couldn't help but rationalize it, given the emotional distance in his marriage with Martha. The internal conflict of right versus wrong was genuine, but he reminded himself that his job wasn't a run-of-the-mill office job or that of a mechanic in the automobile factory down the road. He was one of the wolves who kept all the other wolves at bay.

—

He took a shower, washed his thoughts away, and lingered a lot longer under the hot water than usual. He changed into civilian clothes and contemplated returning upstairs to sleep with Martha. Instead, he made up his usual spot on the couch, a symbol of the rift in his marriage. It was his safe place; strangely enough, the sofa was more comfortable. He lay his head on the cushion, and within seconds, he was out for the count.

—

This time, he slept like a baby.

His daughter woke him, jumping over him and calling his name. Her smiles and giggles filled the room with joy. He opened his eyes, embraced her, and then looked at Martha, who sat in the chair nearby, sipping a cup of coffee.

"What time did you get home?" she said.

Ricardo wiped the sleep from his eyes as he wrapped his arms around Stephanie. "I think it was around two. I didn't want to wake you," he said.

Ricardo jumped from the couch, lifted his blanket, and folded it. He felt a surge of enthusiasm.

"Why don't we all get dressed and eat lunch together?"

Martha's response was curt. "I already have plans."

"What do you mean you have plans?" Ricardo said. "I've been away for weeks, and I called you beforehand. You knew I was coming home last night."

"It's unavoidable," she said "Meetings and appointments. I'll be home late, but don't worry; it will give you quality time with Stephanie. She's missed her daddy."

Ricardo masked his disappointment with a smile. He turned his full attention to his daughter. "Well, it looks like it's just you and me today. Let's make it fun, shall we?"

—

Despite the strained circumstances, he couldn't wait to spend the day with his daughter.

There wasn't a lot of interaction while Martha got ready, and within the hour, she had left the house. Ricardo focused his attention on Stephanie and took her up to her bedroom. He opened the wardrobe doors and picked out a pink dress with a bow. "Let's get you changed," he said. "This will be perfect. It's such a pretty dress; it will make you look like a princess."

Stephanie's expression fell, her face clouded over with her sadness, and a solitary tear rolled down her cheek. "I don't want to wear that, Daddy. Don't like it."

Her reaction surprised him. The dress had been a present from Malcolm and Linda. It was expensive, and the label was still on it.

"I choose, Daddy."

"That's fine, darling. You can wear whatever you want," he reassured her.

She smiled again, wiped her tears, and ran to the closet. She returned with a pair of her favorite jeans and a dark button-up shirt.

Ricardo nodded in approval, smiling and supporting her choice. Today was about making her happy and comfortable.

He left his daughter playing with some toy cars as he went to get changed himself.

—

Nothing could have prepared him for the shock he got as he opened the wardrobe and lifted a pile of paperwork on one of the shelves. He didn't know what made him lift the first few pieces of paper from the file—an electric bill, a gas bill, and the third piece of paperwork down, a credit card statement from American Express. He frowned. He didn't have an American Express card, but his name and address were on the top of the statement.

"What the hell!"

But it was at the bottom of the statement when he read the figures that hit him harder than a prize fighter's right hook. In bold letters, the word *balance*, and then—$10,637. He almost couldn't stand.

"No fucking way," he mumbled to himself.

Confusion set in. He picked up the statement and scanned it again. Surely there had to have been some mistake?

—

The statement and the balance at the bottom of the statement were on his mind even as he enjoyed a fabulous day out with his daughter. They visited the mall, and he bought her a few small presents. They had food together and, later, ice cream. They enjoyed the simple pleasures of playing in the park, and the sound of her laughter was intoxicating. But

despite the fun they were having, the weight of the credit card discovery
lingered in the back of his mind.

—

Martha arrived home just before midnight. Stephanie had been in bed
for hours. There was only one way to approach it: He threw the statement on the table and asked her to explain it.

She was caught off guard. Her demeanor shifted dramatically, and
her voice, which was usually assertive and harsh, softened as she realized
that she'd been caught out.

"I was lonely," she said. "I fell in with a lovely group of people, and
they organized trips to a casino in South Carolina."

Ricardo was dumbfounded; he hadn't expected anything like this.
"You're gambling?" he said.

"I won a lot of money, Ricardo. I was very good at it, but I made
some bad decisions, and the casino made me open an account and—"

"You've gambled away $10,000 of our money?" Ricardo said in
disbelief.

"I'm sorry, Ricardo. It won't happen again. I don't go anymore. We'll
find a way to pay this back."

He was ready to explode. The sheer enormity of the sum of money
blew him away. It was nearly half his annual wages, and they'd be in debt
for years.

But instead, he counted to ten and took a deep breath.

She was struggling with mental illness; all he could do was encourage
her to move on. Perhaps she had changed: There were no empty bottles
around the house, and it was clean and tidy. Perhaps her meetings and
appointments today had been with therapists and professional people.
He had to give her the benefit of the doubt.

"Don't worry, Martha, we will work this out between us."

45

RETURNING TO
THE HOMELAND

You gain strength, courage, and confidence by every experience in
which you really stop to look fear in the face . . . You must do the
thing you think you cannot do.

—Eleanor Roosevelt

n Langley, Virginia, David walked toward the conference room with a
determined stride. As he opened the door, he was composed and confident to address the serious matters at hand. Dianna, Charlie, and
Mike were already seated at the table. Dianna appeared particularly agi-
tated and nervous.

She confronted him. Her tone was sharp. "For my life, I can't understand why you'd choose him for this," she said.

David half expected the reaction and took a moment to choose his
words. "I am fully aware of what I am asking him to do. He has a choice;
he doesn't have to accept it."

"You know your son, David. For fuck's sake, he won't say no, and you
know it. That's what makes me so angry."

David responded. "I repeat: He has a choice, and this situation is bigger than you, him, and everyone here. We must stop them before it's too late, and he is the perfect man for the job, regardless of our personal feelings."

"Fucking hell, he's your son, David. Don't you feel anything for him? Are you even human?"

"I know he's my son better than anyone else in this room, but this mission is critical, and he can handle it." He looked her in the eye. "Perhaps if you had kept your feelings in check, this might have been easier for you."

"You bastard, I should—"

"Enough," David interrupted. "Your damned hormones are running away with you; you aren't thinking straight. You're in charge of this mission, and I expect you to do your job. Tell me now if you think you can't handle it, and I'll find someone else."

Charlie was on his feet, trying to calm her down. "David's right, Dianna. Forget the family ties, forget the romantic liaisons. Can you honestly say we have a man more suited to this job than him?"

Dianna sat in silence.

Charlie continued. "Tell me, Dianna, tell me honestly: With his recent track record and his Iranian background, is there another man in America who could pull this job off?"

A warm, smug feeling passed over David. Charlie had taken the words right from his mouth. He waited in silence for nearly a minute before Dianna stood. She gathered her papers, picked up her handbag, and walked toward the door.

"I'm done here," she said. "Whatever I say won't make any difference, and I will do it. It's my job, but that doesn't mean I have to like it." She paused briefly at the door. "But I must tell you, David, you are one heartless bastard."

She slammed the door behind her.

David leaned back in his chair and placed his hands around the back of his head. "And she's good, too. I'm glad to have her on board. Just don't fucking tell her, will you? Keeping that bitch on edge is exactly what she needs."

—

It was an all-too-familiar feeling—a soldier's life.

They had planned an evening out and had even managed to arrange for Malcolm and Linda to babysit Stephanie. It was just after midday, and as Ricardo picked up the telephone, he recognized the voice of First Sergeant Jackson. "Full gear and ready in three hours, Sergeant Rosen," he said.

Ricardo groaned.

Martha was standing in the kitchen. She'd heard the all-too-brief conversation and walked back through into the living room. As he opened his mouth to speak, she turned swiftly to her right and walked silently up the stairs.

—

"Commander's Office," First Sergeant Jackson said as soon as he saw him. "You know where it is."

As he climbed the stairs, Ricardo's mind raced. The lack of information added to the tension. This was different; he felt alone. There were no other team members and no gear bags in the building.

He knocked on the commander's office door.

"Enter."

They were familiar faces. He saluted the commander. "Good afternoon, sir." He turned to the commander's left. "Charlie, Dianna, it's good to see you again."

They both nodded. Ricardo's curiosity notched up to the highest level possible.

"You'll be working with Charlie and Dianna again. They are calling you the 'dream team,' and I can't disagree. But this operation is a little bit different. It's very sensitive, and I must tell you, you can decline."

"And why would that be, sir?"

"Because of the danger level. We are sending you to a country where there's an execution notice on your head. If your true identity is found out, you will be arrested and executed within twenty-four hours."

"You're sending me to Iran?"

"If you accept the mission."

It was Dianna's turn to speak. She told him that the operation was connected with the Russian arms dealer who had been eliminated in Somalia. "That bad guy was just the tip of the iceberg, and he's been replaced. We'll fly you by helicopter into Iran." She unfurled a map and smoothed it out on the table. "You will contact our man here"—she pointed—"and they will provide you with everything you need. The new Russian agent is scheduled to meet with Iranian officials, and our intel tells us they are discussing nuclear capabilities. I don't need to tell you that if Iran gets the bomb, then we might as well sign the declaration for World War III and Armageddon, which will surely follow. But as the commander says, it's your choice. Saying no will not count against you; we will completely understand."

Her words were ice cold, yet there was a slight tremor in her voice, and she deliberately lingered on the dangers involved. If Ricardo was to take a wild guess, he figured she wanted him to say no.

"I echo Dianna's words," Captain Hood said, "but we don't have much time, and you must decide quickly. There's a plane leaving tonight for Ramstein Air Base in Germany, and I need a man on it."

"Tell me a little more about the operation, sir," Ricardo said.

"Well, you'll be flying into Turkey, and from there, you'll fly across the border into Iran. You will assume an Iranian identity. The man has been dead for a few weeks, but his death has not been registered with the authorities, and your paperwork is good. It's probably one of the trickiest operations we've ever pulled together. The target knows he's a target, and he has security. His plane flies into Tabriz Airport from Murmansk. We estimate the flight time to be around twelve hours. We don't know which runway he'll be coming in at; a shot at him at that point is almost impossible. The plane taxis directly into a hangar, and he climbs into a bulletproof car, and it doesn't stop until he pulls into an underground car park. I don't know if taking him out is even possible because once he's in the building, he doesn't leave."

"Almost impossible," Dianna reiterated. "The decision is yours, Ricardo."

Captain Hood, Dianna, and Charlie said nothing.

Ricardo should have said, *Thanks, but no thanks, I'll go back home to my family.*

Traveling back into Iran undercover was ridiculous; he'd be on edge every step of the way. "How long do you expect the operation to last, sir?" Ricardo asked.

"How long is not determined," the captain said. "That's entirely up to the man on the ground."

"Me?" Ricardo questioned.

"Yes, if you decide to take the operation."

Ricardo nodded just once, stepped forward, and saluted the captain. "Then I'm in, sir. It sounds intriguing, and I've always liked a challenge."

He could see Dianna's head drop from the corner of his eye, and her hands slapped against the tabletop. She was trying hard not to cry.

—

As they flew out of Pope Air Force Base aboard the Agency's Gulfstream jet, Dianna took the seat next to Ricardo; Charlie sat a few seats behind them.

Breaking the silence, Dianna glanced at Ricardo. "You are one crazy son of a bitch, you know that?"

"I've been in tougher situations and always found a way out. This is no different."

"But back to Iran?"

"Yeah, but this is different. This time, I've got real training, backup, the best intel money can buy. I'm not just a teenage boy on a motorcycle with a team of teenagers throwing Molotov cocktails."

—

As the plane touched down at Ramstein Air Force Base, Dianna and Ricardo disembarked and walked toward the hangar. Dianna briefed him on the plans for the next few days and said she was leaving him for now.

Early the following day, Ricardo boarded a flight to Izmir, Turkey.

His passport bore a new name: Paymon Atarie. Despite living in Iran for many years, Ricardo had never adopted an Iranian name; he was constantly teased as the "Spanish Jew boy." But now, operating undercover, he fully assumed an Iranian persona. The change was more than symbolic; a practical measure to blend in seamlessly during the mission, yes, but it was more than that. Every minute he spent in Iran was like giving the regime the finger, and that fact wasn't lost on him.

Ricardo was met at the airport and driven to a village near the border. He joined an Air Force team equipped with a specialized helicopter unlike anything he had seen before. The team briefed him, assuring him their technology would allow him to enter Iran undetected. However, they clarified that he would be alone once on the ground. He'd heard that before. He was in familiar territory.

The helicopter flight lasted forty-five minutes.

Ricardo landed in the darkness and gathered his gear, and a car pulled up within a few minutes.

After a brief greeting from the driver, he introduced himself as Paymon.

—

The following day, Ricardo and the driver embarked on the seven-hour drive to Tabriz.

Just one hour into the drive, they encountered their first checkpoint, manned by Revolutionary Guards. Ricardo flipped into acting mode.

He wound the window down and gave the guard a big smile. "Good morning to you, sir. You're doing a fine job," he said.

"Papers."

"Yes sir, happy to do so."

Ricardo spoke fluent Farsi, and the Iranian documents were good. The man studied the documentation for a few minutes and then returned it to Ricardo.

"Keep up the good work," Ricardo said. "Allahu Akbar."

"Allahu Akbar," the guard responded.

The surroundings were familiar, evoking memories of a past life. The sights and smells of the country overwhelmed him but added an intense layer to his experience, reminding him of his deep connections to the land he had once called home. He thought of his family—Samira, Hannah, Masood, his aunts—so close yet so far.

When they arrived in Tabriz, the driver stopped the car at a large apartment complex. He pointed to one of the buildings. "You must go to that building, fifth floor, unit 543."

After exchanging brief farewells, Ricardo climbed from the car and walked toward the building.

He took the lift to the fifth floor, found the apartment, and knocked on the door. A strikingly attractive woman opened it, asked him his name, and beckoned him inside.

The apartment was modern and adorned with expensive decorations and furniture. Opulent drapes framed large windows, creating a stark yet elegant aesthetic. There was a familiar aroma of Persian cuisine; Ricardo couldn't believe how much he had missed that aroma. The woman introduced herself as Laleh and introduced him to a man called Sassan and another man named Ari, who declared himself a Mossad agent. They got down to business immediately.

Their intelligence told them that the Russian was expected within the next four weeks.

"We won't know when he's coming until his airplane takes off from Murmansk," Ari said, "and then you'll have no more than twelve hours before his plane touches down. I believe Dianna has already briefed you on how complicated this one is; there is no possible shot on the runway, and he'll be in an armored car that will be moving all the time. If he lands in rush hour, then obviously the car could be held up, but we don't know; he could be landing at any time."

"But you know the building he'll be staying in?"

"Yes, but again, they have underground parking that is well protected, and if he does venture out, it will be in that bulletproof car."

Ari pointed to Laleh. "It's important you maintain your cover. You and Laleh will be posing as man and wife. You'll be staying here until the mission has been completed." Ari sighed. "If the mission is completed at all."

"You don't sound too hopeful," Ricardo said.

"I'm not overly optimistic, if I'm honest. It seems almost impossible. They tell me you're good, but I have to say, if you can carry this out, you deserve a medal. It's all up to you: the planning, the execution, the escape. It's your call; all we can do is tell you when the man is in the air." Sassan handed him a photograph. "And there he is, and even that photograph isn't perfect."

—

They sat for the next two hours as Ari discussed the operation in more detail and handed Ricardo maps, documentation, and the exact address of where they believed the Russian would be staying.

Ari and Sassan left, and Lalah presented a simple Persian meal. Lalah opened up and told him about her family. "These Mullahs are murderers, savages; they killed my father, my mother, my sister."

"I am so sorry. I had no idea."

She explained that her father had been part of the Imperial Guard during the Shah's regime and was executed following the revolution. Her older sister, devastated by their father's death, joined an anti-government group. During the crackdown of 1988, she, too, was arrested and executed a few months after their mother died of all the pain and heartbreak.

Her personal history gave Ricardo a deeper understanding of Laleh's motivations for her involvement in such dangerous activities; she was driven by a profound sense of loss and a desire for retribution against the regime that had destroyed their family.

—

Ricardo and Laleh settled into their roles, introducing themselves to their neighbors as a newly married couple. They established an ordinary but unremarkable routine. For the next few weeks, they diligently maintained the facade. Laleh dressed conservatively and adopted the demeanor of a religious woman, which helped her blend into the community. With his understanding of local customs, Ricardo convincingly portrayed a religious-minded businessman. Together, they managed to navigate their surroundings without drawing attention, keeping their true intentions well hidden from prying eyes.

—

In the fourth week of their mission, there was an unexpected knock on the door around midnight. It was Sassan, breathless; sweat stood out on his brow. "He's in the air; he'll be landing in exactly eight hours." He handed Ricardo a case. "And here's the weapon you requested."

Ricardo checked his watch and smiled. "Perfect timing." He had been preparing for this moment. For weeks, he'd surveilled the route from the airport, identifying the best positions for the operation.

Ricardo needed to act. "Vehicle?"

Sassan handed him some keys: "A black Mercedes, parked outside. I'll get a taxi back."

"Great. Call Dianna and tell her we are operational. Prepare my exit plan."

Sassan stood for a minute. "Well?"

"Well, what?" Ricardo asked.

"Well . . . aren't you going to get going?"

Ricardo looked at his watch. "No need. I have everything in hand. Laleh and I will have something to eat. I'll catch a few hours of sleep and then be on my way."

Sassan shook his head. "Fucking hell, everything they say about you is right; you are one strange dude."

—

Ricardo had mapped the route from the airport, meticulously studying the path the car carrying the Russian operative would likely take. He knew there would be options, but the nearer they reached their final destination at Baran Avak, where the Russian was planning to stay, the more they would be limited. There was only one road into the apartment building on 1st Entezam Street. He'd walked it more than a dozen times. It was the prominent place to strike.

He picked up the phone in the living room and dialed the number. "It's time," he said. "ETA between 0830 and 0900."

—

The Russian agent was tired. It had been a long flight, and as the airplane taxied into the hangar, the aircraft doors opened. He climbed to his feet and made his way to the steps and his driver. He smiled; the car was his favorite, an American Cadillac with military-grade armor plating, five inches thick, a combination of steel, aluminum, titanium, and ceramic. The windows were multilayered bulletproof glass, and the wheels were reinforced with Kevlar to keep the car running even if the tires were shot out.

He climbed into the car and felt as safe as he would have felt inside the Kremlin's inner sanctum.

The traffic was light, and the early morning dawn cast shadows across the streets as the driver took the Chaykenar Highway, which ran right into the city's heart.

As instructed, the driver took a slight detour and cut through the Kuchebagh district, adding another fifteen minutes to the journey; he wouldn't tell anyone about his movements. They passed a mosque and an impressive-looking hospital and, at last, turned into 1st Entezam Street. The apartment building was at the bottom of the one-way street.

As the agent collected his things, the driver slammed on his brakes and cursed—the Russian shot forward in his seat. The driver apologized, and as he looked out the window, he noticed a heavy dump truck blocking the street.

"Reverse out," the Russian instructed. "Reverse out; we can go another way."

The driver applied the hand brake and put the car into reverse. He looked in his rearview mirror. The traffic was thick, and more than a dozen vehicles were lined up behind them. "Nowhere to go, sir," he said.

Looking ahead, the agent noticed that the dump truck driver had climbed out of his cab and appeared to be running away.

"What the fuck . . ."

The agent was a sitting duck, and every instinct he possessed screamed at him to get out of there. He was tantalizingly close to the entrance of the underground garage. He could make the five yards. He flung the door open and jumped out, then hesitated for a split second. It would be a final and fatal mistake. Ex-military, he recognized the unmistakable sound of a rifle a split second after the round pounded into his chest. As the searing pain spread through him, he found it difficult to breathe, and he noticed that he had lost the power to stand. As his knees buckled, there was a second impact to the left of his breastbone, and he closed his eyes and collapsed in a heap.

The meticulously planned operation had reached its grim conclusion.

Ricardo carefully packed his gear and descended from his vantage point in the empty apartment. He crossed the street, walked the two miles back to Sassan's car, and then drove back to the apartment he shared with Laleh. Knowing the importance of maintaining their cover, Ricardo stayed in Tabriz for another week to avoid suspicion arising from a hasty departure.

46

INTIMATE LIAISONS

We always long for the forbidden things,
and desire what is denied us.

—François Rabelais

A s they neared the border, a faded signpost told him they were nearly there.

"Laleh," Ricardo said, "could you stop the car?"

Laleh slowed the car to a gentle stop on the gravel shoulder, the engine's soft rumble fading into the stillness of the surrounding hills. Without a word, he opened the door and stepped out.

He crouched down, his fingers digging into the earth, and grabbed a small handful. He held it momentarily, staring at it in his palm, symbolizing a place he had never indeed known. He kissed his knuckles and tucked the earth carefully into his pocket as though it were the most precious thing he'd ever owned.

—

Laleh, watching him from the driver's seat, couldn't hide her curiosity any longer. "What are you doing?" she asked.

He straightened up and smiled almost sheepishly. "To be quite honest, I don't know. This is my homeland . . . and I tell myself my family has walked this land, that they've touched this soil at some point, even if I'll never know for sure." His voice faltered. "This is my way of bringing a piece of them back with me. It's all I have left to hold on to."

He climbed back in the car. They didn't say another word until they reached the border.

—

Their goodbyes were heartfelt. They had become allies and friends; she embodied the spirit and courage he admired. He told her she was a true heroine of Iran.

At the designated meeting point, the same helicopter that had delivered Ricardo to the mission area was waiting to transport him back.

—

An hour later, he landed in Izmir, and a car drove to the Hotel Izmir, a luxury establishment in the city's heart.

After freshening up, Ricardo headed to the hotel lobby to meet Dianna, as planned. He spotted her sitting near a window. Dianna saw him as he approached, and her face lit up immediately. She rushed over to him, enveloping him in a warm, enthusiastic hug.

"I am so glad to see you, soldier boy. That was a hell of a job, you crazy bastard."

"It wasn't the easiest. It might never have happened if he hadn't landed in rush hour."

"Drinks on me after the debriefing?" she said.

"How can I refuse?"

After the debriefing ended, Charlie congratulated Ricardo again. "And I'd love to join you two for dinner, but I have to head back to the United States in a few hours, so enjoy your evening." He handed Ricardo an envelope. "You're flying back to the United States tomorrow on a commercial flight. Here are your tickets."

—

Dianna and Ricardo had dinner at the hotel restaurant, and she introduced Ricardo to European wines. As they sipped their wine, their conversation turned intimate; Ricardo shared stories about his childhood in Iran, while Dianna spoke about growing up in Nebraska as the youngest of five siblings.

After dinner, Dianna flashed Ricardo a playful smile. "Can we take the last of this wine somewhere more comfortable?"

"Let's do that. Show me your room," he said. "You're more senior than me, so I'm guessing it's much more spacious."

As they entered the room, they pounced on each other, kissing passionately before tearing off their clothes. They never made it to the bed, their first lovemaking session taking place on the floor.

They couldn't get enough of each other as Ricardo felt the tension of the past few weeks melting away.

Dianna nudged him awake in the early morning hours, and their bodies intertwined once again, and she climbed on top of him. As her rhythm built to a climax, she looked him in the eyes. Between breaths, she spoke. "I think I'm falling for you, and that's not good for either of us."

Ricardo gripped her hips and moved her a little quicker. "Quiet," he said.

As Dianna moved faster and their rhythm synchronized, she fell forward and cried out as they climaxed together.

Ricardo took a while to catch his breath. "I like you a lot, Dianna, but what happens here stays here, remember? We need to be professional about this."

Dianna smiled. "You see, this is why I'm falling for you. You don't hold anything back, just like someone else I know."

Ricardo prodded, "And who might that be?"

Dianna rolled off him. "I think you should go; I've said too much. You have a long journey tomorrow, and I must be in Germany by tomorrow evening."

The sudden shift surprised him. Something was clearly bothering her, but he didn't want to overstay his welcome. He dressed quickly and kissed her goodbye. He walked toward the door and turned. "Until next time."

47

ECHOES OF EMPIRES LONG GONE

Africa has her mysteries, and even a wise man cannot understand them. But a wise man respects them.

—Miriam Makeba

ort Bragg was sweltering on a hot spring day. Ricardo was busy at company headquarters, organizing a close combat training exercise scheduled for the following week. The phone on his desk rang, and a foreboding feeling fell over him.

He lifted the receiver. "Seventh Group, Sergeant Rosen speaking."

"Captain Hood here, Rosen. Alert all active teams to meet at company HQ at 1700 hours. Make sure everyone brings their gear. I'll brief the teams myself."

"Sir."

"That's all, Rosen. See you there."

"Wow!" Ricardo mumbled under his breath as he replaced the handset. "Not often that happens."

His first call was to Martha. "Looks like we are being deployed again.

It's big. Captain Hood wants all of the active teams there, and I have to tell you, there was a lot of urgency in his voice. Something serious is happening, but I—"

Martha cut him short. "I know, we signed up for this."

"I'm sorry, Martha."

"No need, we'll be fine. We are used to it by now."

The guilt washed over him. It was the same every time. Yes, he had signed up for the US military's terms and conditions, but it didn't make it any easier.

—

At 1700 hours, the briefing room was packed. Silence fell over the room as Captain Hood entered. Everyone stood to attention, and more than a few soldiers noticed Captain Hood's expression was rather solemn.

"At ease, gentlemen; as you were," he began. "I'll get straight to it. There's no easy way to tell you this, but we have a mission of the utmost urgency. As some of you may be aware, a civil war has broken out in Rwanda."

"Where the fuck is Rwanda?" a soldier sitting next to Ricardo said.

"Africa," Ricardo whispered.

The soldier winked. "Sending us to a place I've never heard of. Typical."

Hood continued. "US Army Special Operations Command has tasked us, along with the 5th Group, to evacuate all NGOs and missionaries from Rwanda. It's a dire situation, and we do not intend to interfere in the civil war in any way. We are not taking sides. A UN peacekeeping force will also be deploying soon, but our role is separate from theirs. Our only job is to get our citizens out of that war zone. On the ground, it's an absolute slaughter; you may witness things that will stay with you for a lifetime, and the body count is already in the tens, possibly hundreds, of thousands."

Captain Hood gave a background and an overview of the civil war. He explained in detail about the colonial legacy of Rwanda and how the Germans and, later, the Belgians exacerbated ethnic divisions. The Belgians had favored the Tutsi minority for administrative roles, creating resentment among the Hutu majority. When Rwanda gained independence in 1962, the newly established Hutu-dominated government implemented policies that marginalized the Tutsis. Many Tutsis fled the country due to persecution and violence. Many were exiled to neighboring countries like Uganda, and they formed the Rwandan Patriotic Front, with the aim of overthrowing the Hutu-led government. The captain announced that the Rwandan Civil War had officially started on October 1, 1990, when the RPF launched an invasion from Uganda.

"Intel reports tell us that the war is heading toward genocide and ethnic cleansing. The Hutus are killing the Tutsis, and the Tutsis are killing the Hutus; even the government is encouraging Hutu attacks. It's imperative you understand that you should not intervene in the conflict, regardless of what you see or how it makes you feel. Your sole objective is to rescue our citizens, using force if necessary."

Ricardo processed the briefing. Yet another war, yet another government creating division. He sometimes wondered if certain world governments planned for war and conflict—if there were hidden agendas. As the briefing ended, something deep inside told him to prepare for the worst horrors imaginable.

—

The C-17 Globemaster landed in Nairobi, Kenya. Everyone on board was unsure of what to expect from the mission. Ricardo sat with his eyes closed, thinking deeply and preparing himself based on what the commander had told them.

His team was well trained for this type of mission, but there were certain things the best training in the world couldn't foresee. Something was gnawing away at his insides; it was something that Captain Hood had said about walking away, about only evacuating US citizens. And yet the captain had said that the two different sides were killing one another en masse. As he walked down the steps of the plane, he was painting pictures in his head of walking away from people who needed him the most.

It was the story of his life.

—

After a few hours of rest, they boarded a US Army helicopter bound for the Rwandan border. During the briefing, they were informed that Hutu armed groups were aware of their mission but would not attack unless provoked. However, the teams were cautioned that the Hutu militias were well armed and capable of overwhelming them if the situation escalated.

As they disembarked from the helicopter, dusk settled in, casting a breathtaking sunset over the jungle ahead. The helicopter's departure left a palpable silence.

Darkness took over as Ricardo and his team walked toward their target village. With minimal light pollution, the African night sky was dense with countless stars, and the constellations were vividly clear.

Despite the beauty, Ricardo remained acutely aware of the dangers ahead as he scanned every tree and bush. His training had drilled into him the mantra of never letting your guard down.

As they approached the village, an unsettling stench of death grew stronger, and eventually, they came across the first dead body by the side of the road. As they walked farther, the body count rose, and the road into the village was lined with bloodied bodies, a reminder of the brutal reality of the conflict they had come to navigate.

As they entered the village, the devastation was stark. Most of the huts were burned to the ground; the remaining few were severely damaged. Inside each hut were the dead and charred bodies of men, women, and children. It appeared that the entire population had been wiped out for no other reason than historical, socioeconomic roles. There were no significant biological or racial differences in either tribe.

Lieutenant Smith ordered an inspection of the village. "We need to find those missionaries; that's why we are here."

After an hour of searching every hut and the surrounding jungle area, it was clear that there were no survivors.

It was decided they would stay overnight in the village. Lieutenant Smith organized rotating guards to ensure their safety. They'd resume the search in daylight, and the team prepared to spend a tense night among the dead bodies, the charred human remains, and the still-burning embers of what had once been people's homes.

Ricardo was assigned the last shift for guard duty, and he did his best to ignore the haunting images engrained in his mind.

A few hours later, a noise suddenly jolted him as he scanned the immediate area; something was rustling in the bushes ahead.

He hunkered down and held his breath, wondering if he had imagined it. Thirty seconds later, he heard it again, and this time, he quietly alerted his team. He explained the situation and quickly pointed to where the noise was coming from as the team formed an arc, weapons drawn, and crept quietly toward the bushes.

Three yards away, Ricardo spoke. "This is the US Army. Identify yourself!"

The bush moved and parted, a dark shape crept toward them, and eventually, Ricardo made out the shape of a woman's body as she stood with her hands held aloft. "Don't shoot; I'm American!"

The woman's clothes were soaked in blood. She walked toward them, stumbled, and began to cry uncontrollably. Ricardo reassured her. "You're safe now; we're here to help. I'll get the medic. You're in a real mess; where are you hurt?"

The woman shook her head. "I'm fine; this isn't my blood. The Hutus attacked, and they killed everyone—men, women, and children; it made no difference."

Ricardo wiped her face with a field cloth. "You're safe; take your time."

"They called the Tutsis cockroaches. They said it was the blade for the Tutsis and the flame for the Americans. They piled the missionaries into a hut and said they were going to burn it."

The woman explained that she had heard the terrified screams of the villagers as the slaughter carried on. "We waited there for some time, then suddenly the door was flung open, and I recognized one of the local men who had escaped hours earlier. He led us into the jungle. Every few yards, there were dead bodies and injured people who couldn't walk, and we did our best to help them. In the chaos, I fell and cracked my head against a tree. When I came around, everybody had disappeared."

Lieutenant Smith had appeared. "Do you know where the rest of the missionaries are?"

She pointed down the road. "I can only think they are headed to the next village, a few miles away."

"OK," Lieutenant Smith said, "you've been very helpful. Now, I need to get you out of here. I'll arrange for some air support, and you'll be evacuated."

The woman shook her head. "I'm going nowhere without my friends. You need me to find where all the other villages are; I know this area like the back of my hand."

Despite Lieutenant Smith's protests, the woman refused to move, and eventually, he gave in. The medic bandaged her head and cleaned her up as best he could, and within half an hour, they were on the road, walking toward the next village.

As they walked into the village, it was a déjà vu moment: dead bodies, huts burned to the ground, and the stench of death hanging in the air.

"We'll need to check every hut," Lieutenant Smith said. "We might get lucky."

The team spread out. Ricardo walked toward the first hut. It was one of the few that hadn't been razed to the ground. The door swung loosely on one hinge.

As he walked into the hut, nothing could have prepared him for the sight that would be forever etched into his mind.

In the far corner of the hut, what looked like a young woman lay flopped to one side. She was motionless, soaked in blood, holding something to her chest. As Ricardo edged forward, he could see it was a baby. As his eyes grew accustomed to the dark, he noticed two shapes on the ground. He walked over and knelt down. It was clear that the young woman was dead and had been for some time. He leaned forward and touched the baby. It was still warm. He desperately searched for a pulse. Nothing—the baby was dead. He was aware of the missionary who had appeared beside him, and she let out a gut-wrenching wail. "Not again. Not again. Those animals."

Ricardo pieced the scene together: The two shapes on the ground were the woman's breasts, which the militia had sliced off. They hadn't bothered to kill the baby or the mother. Instead, they had allowed the young mother to hold her child, knowing she'd eventually bleed to death. The baby had clawed at the breasts that weren't there, desperate to feed from his mother as he had done since birth. The baby had starved to death.

The missionary had collapsed in a heap, and between tears, she explained that in the eyes of the Hutus, this was payback, and sheer torture for mother and baby. They'd both die a slow, lingering death.

It was cruelty beyond belief; no other creature in the animal kingdom could dream up such depravity.

He walked outside, stunned. He looked up at the sky. "Why?" he muttered to himself. "Why, God, why would someone do this? If you exist, why would you allow this to happen?"

The old feelings of loss and anger were back. He leaned back against the hut and slid down onto his backside. He felt the tears building. He prided himself on his strength: the man who had endured so much but still came through the other side. His presence was a fortress, an impenetrable wall against the chaos that often threatened those around him. But in the privacy of his own thoughts, that strength began to crack.

He tried to swallow, fought the tears, and had to bury them with the rest of the emotions he had locked away in that deep, dark place within him. But this time, the feeling was relentless, rising with each breath, pushing against the dam he had so carefully constructed.

He wiped the tear away hastily, almost angrily. He wanted to erase the evidence of his weakness. But the more he fought it, the stronger it grew. Another tear followed, and then another, until they slipped through his fingers as the memories surged forward—of losses endured, of burdens carried alone, of love lost. His defenses finally shattered, and he cried like a baby.

The missionary walked out into the sunlight and sat down beside him. She was crying, too, and between the tears, she told him her name: Mary.

"You're a good man," she said.

—

There were no survivors anywhere in the village; every man, woman, and child had been hacked to death with machetes. There was clear evidence of torture, dozens of people being decapitated, and women and girls raped.

—

Mary led them to the next village, just a few miles up the road.

The scene was overwhelming, but there were survivors. The village was bustling with activity, and injured people were being treated in a makeshift hospital in a large hut. He stepped inside to a scene from the worst horror movie he could have ever imagined.

The sheer scale of human suffering laid out before him was almost too much to process. Once more, the weapon of choice was the machete. There were men, women, children, and even babies with limbs missing and deep wounds on almost every part of their bodies. One small boy sat bleeding from the head, holding one of his ears in the palm of his hands as his tears mixed with the blood. He was no older than six or seven years of age; what possible danger could he have been?

Lieutenant Smith entered the makeshift hospital and quickly located Ricardo, who stood with Mary. "Rosen, we've found the missionaries. We need to get out of here now." He looked at Mary. "You too, ma'am."

"Lieutenant, we can't just leave these people here," she said. "What will happen to the injured if we go?"

"I understand your concerns, ma'am, but my orders are clear. We can only evacuate US citizens and other Western nationals. I don't have the authority to extend our mission to anyone else."

"And just leave them here to die?"

"I'm not saying it's an easy choice, but it's the only one we have right now. The situation is deteriorating, and staying here puts everyone's lives at risk."

"But these people are my friends. I've been with the mission for years, and some of these young boys and girls are like my family."

"Prepare to evacuate," Lieutenant Smith said. "I won't tell you again." He turned to Ricardo. "Rosen, all the missionaries we were looking for are here. Go outside and find a suitable landing area for the rescue helicopters. Call in the grid coordinates."

"Yes, sir."

He turned to Mary. "You heard the lieutenant. We need to go now. The Hutu militia group is heading this way, and you know what that means."

"And this is a Tutsi village," she said, "and you know what that means; you've seen it with your own eyes."

Ricardo had no answers. He felt a deep conflict within himself because, as his badge motto said, he was there to protect the oppressed, and now he had been given the order to walk away from them.

He reached for Mary's hand. "You are a United States citizen, and my orders are to get you out of here. You know we can't save everybody's life, but if you believe you're carrying out God's work, we must rescue his missionaries."

Mary looked around the hospital, nodded just once, and took Ricardo's hand as they walked outside together.

—

As the rescue helicopters touched down to pick up the missionaries, the group started moving toward the landing zone, knowing they were leaving behind hundreds of people to a certain death. They had to hold back the villagers who desperately wanted to join them on the helicopters. It was a heart-wrenching scene, which Ricardo knew he would never forget.

As the team loaded the helicopters, Ricardo noticed Mary was nowhere to be seen. He turned to Lieutenant Smith and said, "Sir, have you seen Mary? I don't see her on the chopper."

Lieutenant Smith scanned the area. "That stubborn fucking woman . . ."

Ricardo was already running back to the hospital. "I'll look for her, sir."

"You've got five minutes, no more."

His heart pounding with urgency, he caught a glimpse of her as he ran into the hospital. He said, "Mary, what the hell are you doing? We have to go now!"

Her expression was resolute and unwavering. "Sergeant, I can't leave these people here; I'm staying because God is with me."

He admired her; she reminded him of the Basij boy during the Iran–Iraq War. He had run through a minefield, believing it would lead him to heaven. She believed in her god and her faith, she had a profound commitment to what she believed was right, regardless of the danger, and he had a split decision to make.

He approached Mary and said, with a heavy heart, "Mary, I am so sorry for doing this."

Mary shrugged her shoulders. "Sorry for . . ."

Ricardo's punch to the sweet spot on the chin was a very practical, calculated movement. As she lost the power in her legs and headed toward the ground, he caught her before she fell, scooped her up in his arms, and headed back to the helicopter.

Lieutenant Smith stood in the doorway and shook his head. "You haven't done what I think you've done, Rosen?"

"I had no choice, sir; it was the only way."

"Well, she's gonna fucking love you when she comes around."

—

As the helicopter lifted off, Mary regained consciousness and turned her attention toward Ricardo. "How could you do that? How could you remove me from my family?"

The tears streamed down her face as she grappled with the reality of being taken against her will. Ricardo looked out the helicopter window; he saw Hutu militia trucks rolling into the village. One stopped beside the makeshift hospital, and the sight filled him with dread. At least a dozen men jumped out of the truck and walked toward the door, each carrying a machete.

Overwhelmed by guilt and helplessness, Ricardo closed his eyes, attempting to block out the desperate faces and the harsh reality of the conflict below. He struggled to convince himself that he had made the right decision for Mary's safety, even if it went against her wishes, knowing he was powerless to stop the massacre on the ground that was beginning.

48

BULLETS FOR REDEMPTION

The line separating good and evil passes not through states, nor between classes, nor between political parties either, but right through every human heart . . .

—Aleksandr Solzhenitsyn

The team ventured deeper into the jungle to locate a camp where an NGO group was working to provide water to a nearby village. The day was sweltering, and as the helicopter set down in a small clearing, it stirred up clouds of dust and leaves.

The heat was oppressive as they navigated through the lush foliage and trekked toward the camp's coordinates.

Everyone on the team hoped the militia hadn't reached the village and they could reach the NGO workers without incident, secure their safety, and escort them back across the Kenyan border.

—

As the team approached the village, the sounds of screams and gunshots pierced the air. The noise grew louder and more distressing as they drew closer, confirming their worst fears—the Hutu militia had already reached the village ahead of them.

On high alert, the team moved with increased urgency. As they neared the village, it was engulfed in chaos, Hutu militia members running amok with machetes as the carnage unfolded in real time before their eyes. They readied themselves to intervene. Ricardo and Lieutenant Smith, leading their team, burst from the cover of the bushes, firing shots into the air to announce their presence.

A militia leader, covered in blood, emerged from a hut and stared at them. His eyes showed no fear; he knew the US team was under strict orders not to engage.

With a cold, calculated look, the militia leader signaled to one of his men, directing him toward another hut. The man obeyed and quickly moved toward the hut. Moments later, he paraded six NGO workers in front of the hut. Their faces were etched with fear, but they were undoubtedly relieved to see the US military.

Lieutenant Smith directed the NGO workers to walk toward them. As they reached the clearing, Ricardo and Lieutenant Smith began retreating backward, maintaining a watchful eye on the militia. They moved steadily toward the location where the rest of their team was waiting, ready to extract everyone to safety.

As they regrouped, one of the NGO workers approached them, out of breath and clearly distressed. "I really appreciate you guys coming to rescue us, but Jennifer is missing. She was with us until they herded us into the hut, and then they took her away. She's still in the village."

"OK," Lieutenant Smith said, "let's get everyone to the landing point and on the chopper. The rest of us will go back for the girl."

"What does she look like?" Ricardo asked.

"White with long, blonde hair; should be easy enough to spot."

The team of six moved stealthily back into the woods. Time was of the essence, and the militia expected them to return: The US rescue teams don't leave anyone behind.

They moved closer to the village as darkness enveloped it. Ricardo surveyed the village through night vision binoculars.

"What do you see?" Lieutenant Smith asked.

"Dead bodies everywhere. There are women in cages."

"Cages?"

"Many young women in cages, but there is no sign of a White woman. What will we do, sir?"

"We wait," Lieutenant Smith said. "Let's watch for an hour; find yourselves a spot, but stay hidden."

After an hour, Ricardo reported back. "There's a hut, sir. One of the militia leaders keeps visiting it. Two guards are on either side of the door. There's something precious in there; it might be our girl."

"And militia numbers?"

"About twenty."

"OK, we'll give it a go. We don't have much time, so, Rosen, up in the tree. I know your capabilities—as many quiet kills as you can. As soon as they raise the alarm, we go."

Ricardo took his position in the branches, ten feet from the ground, while the rest of the team prepared for imminent action.

Ricardo worked on the lone guards on the perimeter of the small village. The silent shots to the head dropped the militia, and they fell quietly to the ground. Ricardo took five guards out without any disturbance, but the sixth man fell noisily into a fence, which was lined with earthenware pots. The guard crashed to the ground.

A cry went up, and Ricardo jumped down hastily. "That's it, sir. We need to go now. A dozen of them are running around like headless chickens, some coming this way."

They met the militia head-on; they were armed with nothing more than machetes, and they stood no chance against the heavily armed Americans. They killed nearly a dozen militiamen before the remainder fled into the jungle.

As Ricardo burst into the hut, the militia leader stepped into his boots, the belt of his trousers in his hand. He raised both hands above his head. "No shoot, no shoot," he said. As Ricardo looked into the corner of the hut, he saw the precious cargo: a small girl no more than eleven years old, completely naked, her crotch stained with blood. Ricardo pointed his rifle at the rapist's chest and pulled the trigger three times.

Ricardo grabbed the clothes that lay on the ground and told her to put them on. The child's face was streaked with dirt from the floor and tears. He took her hand, and they ran out of the hut toward where the women were caged. Ricardo broke the lock on the cage; a dozen half-naked women poured through the gap, and one of them reached for the girl, who fell into her arms.

They found Jennifer in the next hut. She was in a cage, also naked, her clothes on the ground next to the cage. The hopeless look in her dead eyes told Ricardo everything he needed to know about what had happened to her.

"Put your clothes on," he said as he opened the cage, and she crawled through the gap. "You're safe now, you're going home.'"

"The other women?" she inquired.

"They're free; they've all run off, but they're safe."

Jennifer nodded as she buttoned up her dress. No words were said; Ricardo and Jennifer both knew that the women were anything but safe. The surviving militiamen were still out there.

The mission had been a success in the eyes of the US military. They'd rescued dozens of US citizens, but all Ricardo could think of was the people they'd left behind.

49

A BROKEN TRUST

It is easier to forgive an enemy than to forgive a friend.
—William Blake

I t had been forty-five days of hell. There were things the men had seen that couldn't be unseen, the images forever etched into some distant corner of their brains.

And there were sounds, cries of anguish, of desperation, of torture and death. The horrors they had witnessed were beyond what any of them could ever have imagined, and despite heading home, there was no sense of celebration.

—

Only the thought of seeing his daughter's face and holding her again kept him going. He felt guilty; he didn't feel the same way about Martha.

But when he arrived home, Martha surprised him with her positivity. For once, she was very talkative, even animated.

Martha shared her progress as Stephanie sat on her father's knee, her arms wrapped around his chest and her head buried into his neck.

Martha had made financial arrangements to service the debt and had maintained her therapy sessions. These were significant steps forward. Things were looking up.

—

About a week after Ricardo returned home, he received an unexpected call from Malcolm and Linda. They wanted to meet up, just the three of them. Martha was not on the invite list.

—

In Malcolm's house that evening, the atmosphere was tense. Malcolm and Linda were visibly anxious. Linda hesitated momentarily, then met Ricardo's gaze. "There's no easy way to say this, so I'm just going to come out and say it: Martha is having an affair."

"What?" Ricardo said. "Are you sure?"

"Positive. Ricardo, I'm sorry. I saw her kissing a man the other day at the mall. Thank god Stephanie was in the playhouse with the other kids and didn't see anything. We couldn't keep this secret from you; we're your friends—you need to know."

Ricardo sat back on the sofa. "Thanks. I've suspected something for a while now."

"Really?" Linda said.

"Yes, she's been coming home late, not picking up the phone when I called. But honestly, I'm more relieved than hurt right now." He looked up. "Just keep it between us for the time being. I need time to work things out, and Stephanie needs her mother. I don't want to do anything too hasty."

"Of course," Malcolm said.

—

As Ricardo drove away from the house, a surprising sense of calm settled over him, especially in light of his recent encounter with Dianna. It made him feel less alone in his own complexities. Should he confront Martha? His mind buzzed with what to do next.

No, he wouldn't. He'd focus on co-parenting Stephanie and maintaining stability at home. That was the only thing that mattered.

—

In a guesthouse on Ft. Bragg, Dianna had just stepped out of the shower when the phone started to ring. She wrapped herself in a towel and answered it. "Hello."

"It's David. Are you ready for tonight?"

A chill coursed through her. "I guess I have to be if I want to keep my job."

"It's all about the job, Dianna."

"So you keep saying. I'd call it straightforward blackmail. You played me from the beginning. I was right about you; you don't belong to the human race."

"It's not about emotions, Dianna. It's about what needs to be done. He is not focusing enough, and I need him to be focused."

"Seducing him was one thing, but this . . . this takes it to another level."

"Just do it and cut the dramatics. Call me afterward and let me know how it went."

—

Ricardo's return home was jarring. He froze at the sight of Dianna sitting casually on the couch with Martha. The unexpected scenario sent a rush of conflicting emotions through him. Confusion, suspicion, and a hint of betrayal swirled inside him as he tried to process the scene before him.

"Why are you here?" he asked.

The room fell silent as both women looked up at him.

Martha's words cut through the tense silence. "She told me what happened in Somalia and in Turkey; a full, blow-by-blow, fucking confession."

He struggled to find his voice. His gaze shifted to Dianna. He felt disbelief . . . hurt. "How could you betray me like this?"

Dianna found no words.

He gathered his thoughts. "I won't deny it, Martha, but you must take some of the blame; you and I haven't been man and wife for a long time. There was nothing there, and I can't remember the last time we shared a bed. But I take full responsibility. I was out of order."

Martha should have kept quiet.

She stood up and started shouting, berating both of them. In her last sentence, she threw the sanctity of their marriage vows at him. It was the straw that broke the camel's back.

"You have the nerve to talk about marriage vows. Do you think I don't know what you've been up to?"

Martha's face fell. "What do you mean?"

"You were spotted, Martha, at the mall: you and your boyfriend."

Ricardo was conscious of Dianna throughout the exchange. Something wasn't quite right. It was as if she didn't want to be there, yet that didn't make sense. She was here, her car was parked outside, and it wasn't as if she had been dragged kicking and screaming.

Dianna was anxious to get away. She stood. "I'm sorry, I guess I need to leave and let you two talk things over," she said as she headed toward the door.

Ricardo caught up with her outside, grabbed her arm, and looked her in the eyes. "What the hell was that? Why would you do this to me? Just because I told you I didn't want a relationship, you go behind my back like this? I trusted you, and this is how you repay that trust."

"But, Ricardo, I . . ."

"Don't ever talk to me again. I won't be on any mission you are part of. I never want to see you again."

Tears welled in her eyes as she met his gaze, her voice breaking. "I'm sorry, Ricardo. I had no choice."

"No fucking choice—are you kidding me?"

"Maybe someday you'll understand and forgive me."

"I'll never forgive you. I trusted you, I . . ."

She broke down, the floodgates opened, and she ran to her car.

She drove away. He watched the car disappear from view and then turned and walked back into the house, shaking his head. He still couldn't get his head around what had just happened.

Ricardo paused at the kitchen's entrance, watching Martha momentarily as she moved methodically, wiping down the counters. He cleared his throat, breaking the silence that had fallen between them. "Do you want to talk about this?" he asked, unsure what to expect.

Martha didn't look up from her cleaning, her voice flat and emotionless. "No, not really," she responded briskly. "There's not much to talk about. You do your thing, and I do mine. We have a daughter together, and you need me since you're always deploying to some godforsaken place and aren't around. I need a stable home, and I like not having to work for that. Like I said, you do you, and I'll do what I want. It's that simple. There is no need to make this more complicated than it needs to be."

The bluntness of her words stung, but they also laid bare the reality of their relationship: a partnership held together not by love but by necessity and mutual convenience, especially for the sake of their daughter.

With everything out in the open, Ricardo felt relieved. The tough conversation with Martha had cleared the air, even though it was hard. Now, with Dianna gone and the understanding with Martha, he felt free to focus all his energy on his job without worrying about unresolved issues at home.

This shift was just what he needed. It allowed him to dedicate himself fully to his work, free from the personal distractions that had been weighing him down.

—

Dianna's tears started when she pushed the car into gear, but they didn't stop until she reached the guesthouse.

She composed herself just enough to make the call. The phone rang briefly before David answered; his voice was cold and emotionless. "Is it done?" he asked directly.

"Yes, it's done. They reacted exactly as you said they would." Her voice trembled slightly. "I want to know how he knew about the guy you set her up with."

David's reply was chilling in its detachment. "You don't need to know anything. I call the shots, and you follow orders. That way, you keep your lifestyle. I don't need to tell you I could have you out of the country before your next paycheck arrives."

Before she could say another word, he ended the call.

Dianna stood, phone in hand, speechless. She felt fear and desperation . . . totally under the control of a man she hated with all of her heart.

She had been played like a pawn in a complicated chess game, but a willing pawn at first. She had feelings for Ricardo. Deep feelings. But as the game had developed, she had lost control of the situation, and David lined up the big players. Her lone game piece was surrounded by the bishop, the castle, and the queen, and the king was lining up behind them to pounce. She was on her own; she was in checkmate, and surely, it was only a matter of time before the game ended.

50

ABDUCTED AT
GUNPOINT

Evil is unspectacular and always human, and shares
our bed and eats at our own table . . .
—W. H. Auden

I t was late when Ricardo arrived at company HQ. The late-night vis-
its to Captain Hood's office were becoming routine. He knocked and
entered, saluting the commander as he stepped into his inner sanctum.

Captain Hood returned the salute. "Good, Rosen; glad you're here.
We're heading to USASOC. Follow me."

"Yes, sir."

They left the office together, and as Ricardo followed Captain Hood
into the briefing room, Mike and Charlie were already seated. Dianna's
absence was conspicuous.

A sense of relief washed over him, knowing she wouldn't be involved.
He could concentrate fully on the mission ahead.

Lieutenant Smith was also present. He looked up and smiled. He
was his usual composed self, standing beside a woman Ricardo hadn't

seen before. She introduced herself as Adara, a liaison from Mossad who would be part of their operation.

Adara's demeanor was serious and direct as she began the briefing. Her strong Hebrew accent colored her English as she spoke. She directed Lieutenant Smith to dim the lights before presenting the first slide, which showed a man with blond hair and blue eyes.

"This is their man," Adara announced, pointing to the image. "He is the key supplier of centrifuges Iran is attempting to acquire. We have intelligence from sources in Beirut and Moscow that indicate Russia is using Hezbollah as an intermediary to bypass sanctions on these parts."

She changed the slides, displaying several metallic components. "As you can see, Iran plans to reward Hezbollah with newly developed missiles in exchange for their role in this scheme. This is where our operation comes in. Mossad needs someone who can convincingly portray an Iranian agent in this deal, and we would like Sergeant Rosen. He performed exceptionally well in the last operation in Iran. We've evaluated all of our agents of Iranian descent, but Sergeant Rosen is by far the best and the most experienced. The fact that he is an Iranian by birth is a bonus we cannot ignore. It has been said around the world that the Jews favor their own race, but I'm afraid with Mossad, it boils down to who was the best, and we don't care what race, creed, or religion they are. The fact is that Sergeant Rosen is the best man for the job, and we want him."

Mike brought the room up to speed. "And his cover is already established. He's known as an international businessman living in Tabriz with his wife, Laleh. His role is more than established; there are no indications of any suspicions among the local authorities. The Russians believe he is simply a go-between, ready to sell anything if it means a substantial profit."

—

The briefing lasted three hours, after which Ricardo, Adara, and Lieutenant Smith boarded a US C-141 Starlifter en route to Istanbul. As the aircraft's engines hummed steadily in the background, Ricardo attempted to engage Adara in conversation to learn more about her.

"Where in Israel are you from?" he asked.

Adara maintained a typically serious demeanor. "I'm from Haifa."

"Your accent—it's not quite pure Israeli, is it?"

"You're shrewd, Sergeant. My grandparents were originally from Poland. They lived in Iran briefly during World War II before moving to Israel. It's a shame what has become of Iran; my grandfather often talks about the incredible hospitality they received while they were there."

Adara's mention of Iran reminded Ricardo of times long past, specifically the hours spent in his uncle Masood's bookstore in Tehran. He fondly remembered the smell of old books and their engaging conversations about the children of Tehran. It seemed like a lifetime ago. Those days shaped who he was, how he thought, how he viewed tyranny and oppression and the world in general. It was far removed from his current military missions and secret operations life, yet those conversations with Masood still held a significant place in his heart.

—

They landed in Istanbul, and Ricardo took up his alias and prepared his documents for the flight to Beirut.

Ricardo walked down the aircraft steps. It was a bright, sunny day, and something about the atmosphere of the Middle East almost made him feel like he was home again.

As he walked through the bustling airport, a man approached him. "Mr. Atarie, welcome to Lebanon. We've been expecting you," he said.

Ricardo followed the man to a waiting car, its engine idling. They drove through the city's lively streets.

Despite the briefings and the intelligence, the uncertainty of what lay ahead always lingered in his mind. He carried all the necessary documents to make the deal and sabotage the Iranian operation.

Ricardo and his escort arrived at an apartment complex and were quickly ushered inside. The apartment was filled with several men, including the Russian contact he was meant to meet. One of the men, speaking Farsi, informed Ricardo that he would act as his translator. Despite being deep within enemy territory, Ricardo maintained a casual air.

The Russian began the discussion, outlining that the centrifuge parts would be shipped to Iran via a cargo vessel from Uzbekistan. He stressed that the Russian government knew nothing about the meetings, emphasizing the necessity for "clean" money. This, he explained, was why all financial transactions would be routed through Hezbollah agents in Turkey and Lebanon, to avoid leaving any trace.

One of the men, clearly affiliated with Hezbollah, handed Ricardo several documents detailing the shipping routes and banking information—exactly the intelligence he needed. The man elaborated on their gratitude toward Iran for its support. He expressed a sincere hope that, with Allah's will, they would succeed in overthrowing the Zionist regime and unifying the Muslim world. "And, of course, Mr. Atarie, you will be well rewarded for your role in all of this." He handed Ricardo another document, listing the ships designated to transport missile components to Lebanon for use against Israel.

They talked for several hours and told him everything he needed to know. His cover wasn't ever questioned, and he never felt threatened.

Ricardo stood and announced he was leaving. He pointed to the documentation on the table. "I'll need to take the documents back to Turkey with me; otherwise, I won't be able to do anything."

The Russian nodded.

—

He took out a tiny camera in his Beirut hotel room and photographed each document individually. It was the only way to share the intelligence quickly with Adara. The plan was in place, and within ten minutes, he had left the apartment, heading for the restaurant. Within just a few minutes, he realized he had a tail. It wouldn't stop him. He needed to get the information to Adara; otherwise, the mission had failed.

He walked into the restaurant, ordered a coffee and a pastry, and sat down.

The man following him strolled in and sat in the far corner of the restaurant. Ricardo would not deviate from the plan. The waitress brought his coffee and the pastry in a brown paper bag. He let the small camera slip inside as he reached into the paper bag. After a few minutes, the waitress returned, picked up the bag, and walked back behind the counter. Ricardo lingered in the restaurant for an hour, drank a solitary glass of wine, paid his bill, and stood up to leave.

He returned to his hotel room, ready for the next phase of his mission with the documents safely at hand.

—

The next day, Ricardo boarded a plane back to Turkey. He had checked the secret documents in a hold bag under a different name. Another agent would collect them in Istanbul.

As he walked through Istanbul's airport, he knew two men were walking behind him. As he stopped, so did they, and as he walked on, they did likewise. There was no doubt they were following him.

As he reached the exit doors of the airport, one of them pressed a gun against his side and instructed him in fluent Farsi to keep walking. A black Mercedes with tinted windows pulled up beside them in seconds, and the men ordered him into the car. As they closed the door, they placed a hood over his head, and the car sped off.

The car ride took about an hour. They had tied Ricardo's hands behind his back with a rope. Throughout the ride, nobody spoke. Ricardo never uttered a single word. Eventually, the car stopped, and the men led him into a building. They tied him to a chair, securing both his hands and feet, then left him alone for several hours.

The men who spoke at the airport had accents; they hadn't spoken in Khorasani Persian like the men in the room the previous evening. Khorasan was spoken in the northeastern provinces, which Turkmen and Lor influenced, but the men at the airport spoke Tehrani Persian. Something wasn't right.

Ricardo lost track of time before he finally heard footsteps. Someone came and removed the hood from his head. As his eyes adjusted to the light, he looked around the room.

An Iranian man stood before Ricardo, scrutinizing him closely before breaking the silence. "Well, if it isn't the Shadow Rider of Tehran."

Ricardo breathed a sigh of relief. The mission was still on track, the documents were safely delivered, and these men were from the Iranian secret police and had nothing to do with the Russian operative.

Another man, who had been standing silently to the side, stepped forward and delivered a hard punch to Ricardo's stomach. The blow forced the air from his lungs. He regained his composure; it was time to start acting. "I don't know who the Shadow Rider is. My name is Paymon, and I'm a businessman."

The second punch came swiftly, and the man spoke as Ricardo tried to recover. "You need a few hours with my men to jog your memory about who you really are," he said sternly. "Let me tell you, we have eyes everywhere, and we know who you are."

—

For nearly two days, Ricardo endured beatings and relentless questioning, steadfastly denying his real identity throughout the ordeal. They allowed him only occasional sips of water, and he began to feel the physical toll of the abuse. He suspected his jaw was broken and a few ribs as well; he had even lost a couple of teeth. His body was weak; they hadn't fed him anything, but he would hang on. They wouldn't break him.

A sliver of hope remained—he hoped that whoever was meant to pick him up from the airport had witnessed his abduction and that a rescue mission was being arranged.

He was confident his team would retrieve the bag at Istanbul airport, ensuring the mission's crucial intelligence wouldn't fall into the wrong hands. This small but critical detail gave him a slight edge, fueling his resolve to withstand the interrogation and maintain his cover.

Ricardo was confined in a windowless room, losing all sense of day and night, and time seemed to blend into a continuous loop of uncertainty and pain. He clung to hope, though the words *you are on your own* echoed ominously in his mind, a stark reminder from his briefings before embarking on such black operations.

Toward the end of the second night, one of his captors told him they planned to transport him back to Iran. "You will stand trial for crimes against the Islamic regime."

"I'm a businessman," Ricardo repeated. "My name is Paymon."

Ricardo's battered body ached with every movement, and he drifted in and out of consciousness, the pain often too much to bear.

—

He was blindfolded when the team moved in. He was disoriented and didn't know what was happening. He recognized the sound of gunfire outside in the corridor, loud shouts and screaming, and the sound of bodies falling to the floor. He instinctively threw his chair to the ground and made himself small. His heart raced at the chaos unfolding just beyond the walls of his cell.

The door burst open abruptly and was followed by footsteps, then someone pulled at his blindfold, revealing a silhouette against the harsh light flooding in from the hallway.

"Lieutenant Smith," Ricardo said. "So nice to see you again."

Smith helped him to his feet, draping Ricardo's arm over his shoulder for support. "You've seen better days, Rosen; you look like shit."

"That's good, sir, because I feel like shit, too, but you're the best sight I've seen in a long time."

"Let's get you the fuck out of here before these jokers regroup."

They ran from the building, and Smith helped Ricardo into a waiting truck, where a medic was waiting to attend to him.

As they drove away at speed, Lieutenant Smith watched him. He asked the medic, "How is he?"

"I need to stabilize him, and he needs an IV, but he'll live. I'm told this motherfucker is a tough cookie."

"That's good," Lieutenant Smith said. "We can't afford to lose men like him; they don't grow on trees."

—

A few days later, Mike, Charlie, Lieutenant Smith, and Adara walked into Ricardo's room in the military hospital at Ramstein Air Base in Germany. They all looked relieved to see him relatively stable and conscious, albeit surrounded by medical equipment.

Ricardo listened intently as Charlie explained the rescue.

The hospital room was quiet, filled only with the occasional beep from the monitors. "When you were spotted at the airport, we immediately knew who had you," Charlie said. "Dianna was in the airport; she alerted the team, and they were mobilized and, with Captain Hood's unofficial blessing, flew to Turkey to find you." Charlie paused momentarily. "Dianna was key in this; she worked tirelessly to get Mossad's assistance to pinpoint your exact location. It wasn't easy: At first, they said you were on your own, but she wouldn't let it go. She was like a dog with a bone, and eventually, they caved in."

"And Dianna, is she here?" he asked.

"She went back to the States yesterday," Charlie replied. "She did everything she could here. We recovered all the documents you obtained in Lebanon; it's just a shame you paid such a heavy price. You've lost a lot of blood, have six broken ribs and a broken jawbone, and you've got internal organ damage. You have swelling on the brain and a fracture of the skull, and on top of that, you've lost four teeth."

"But I'll live."

"You'll live," Adara said. "Thank you, on behalf of the State of Israel and our people. We really appreciate what you have done for both of our nations."

—

After six weeks in the hospital in Germany, Ricardo was ready to return home and resume light duties. The ordeal had taught him a powerful lesson about the unwavering support within his team. Despite the circumstances, he found holding a grudge against Dianna hard. He was puzzled by her parting words, claiming she had no choice in her actions. The confusion lingered in his mind, leaving him with an unresolved mystery about her motives. For now, he focused on the solidarity and trust he shared with his team, leaving the questions about Dianna for another time.

51

BOSNIA

The world will not be destroyed by those who do evil,
but by those who watch them without doing anything.
—Albert Einstein

One of the team leaned back and stared out at the gray sky. "Man, Rosen, I didn't even know Bosnia existed until a month ago."

"You're telling me," Lieutenant Smith said. "I thought it was some kind of new Italian pasta."

Ricardo laughed. "It's in Europe, part of the former Yugoslavia."

"And how do you know that?"

"I read books," he replied. "My uncle had a shop in Tehran and—"

"Yeah, we know, but why are we going to Bosnia?"

Ricardo shrugged. "Peacekeeping, they say."

"Peacekeeping from what? What's going on over there?"

Ricardo sighed, pulling out a crumpled map. "Something about ethnic conflicts. Serbs, Croats, and Bosniaks."

"Bosniaks? Sounds like a fucking race of aliens."

"All I know is we're supposed to keep them from killing one another."

"Great," he muttered. "Play referee in a game we don't understand."

Ricardo folded the map and tucked it away. "Orders are orders, and we're flying into Ramstein, Germany. From there, we'll pick up the vehicles for another two-hour flight to the Austrian border."

"Ramstein. Familiar territory, eh, Rosen?" Lieutenant Smith said.

"Sure is, sir."

Ricardo looked out the window, memories flooding back. It had only been a few months, but now he was back, almost 100 percent fit, and ready for the next mission. This mission aligned more closely with his envisioned work when signing up with the Army—it was a real war. They were to support Operation Deliberate Force, part of a fifteen-nation peacekeeping force in Bosnia.

The intel had been brutal; the Serbian forces had committed the largest massacre in Europe since World War II. A place called Srebrenica. Women, children, and the elderly were put on buses and driven to Muslim-controlled territory. The men and boys of "battle age" were separated from the women and children after seeking refuge in an area that had been declared a UN "safe area."

Despite the presence of Dutch UN peacekeeping forces, the Bosnian Serb forces had overrun the town. The men and boys had been taken to isolated locations, where they were executed by firing squads. After the executions, the bodies were buried in mass graves to conceal the crimes.

Ricardo's team was also acutely aware of the recent tragedies where Bosnian Serb forces had overrun another UN-declared safe haven at Zepa and dropped a bomb in a crowded Sarajevo market.

They would be the first team on the ground. They had minimal backup, and he knew the conflict had rapidly evolved into a sniper war. Serb snipers would position themselves and target anyone venturing outside. Men, women, children, and the elderly were fair game.

—

Ricardo's team arrived at the base camp and subsequently moved into a nearby village in the Prijedor region, under UN protection. He sensed the subdued atmosphere among the residents; they had been notified that Serb forces were approaching.

They positioned their initial setup just outside the village, which gave them a strategic advantage in monitoring approaching troops.

As dawn broke, Ricardo was positioned atop a building, overseeing the village's streets. He caught a fleeting glint of light through his scope: a Serb sniper.

As his focus shifted, he noticed a man stepping out of a house. Suddenly, a gunshot rang out, and the man fell to the ground. Ricardo quickly adjusted his position to where he had seen the flash of light. He picked out the sniper's silhouette, gauged the distance, held his breath, and fired. He watched as a split second later, the man's head exploded in a burst of red mist.

—

They had been defending the village for three weeks when Lieutenant Smith approached the team. "We're going to evacuate the town. There's a big Serb force heading this way. We need to get the civilians to safety; there's not enough of us to protect them."

They quickly worked with the UN evacuation team and moved all the civilians to UN camps in just a few days.

As the last of the civilians were evacuated, the Serb forces arrived.

Lieutenant Smith, Ricardo, and his team, alongside Dutch troops, took up a defensive stance to cover the retreat. With the civilians safe, they began strategically withdrawing to the designated helicopter landing zone.

Amid the chaos, a shot rang out, and Ricardo saw Lieutenant Smith fall to the ground. Within seconds, he was kneeling by his side. Ricardo gave a fake smile, trying to make light of the situation. "You've seen better days, sir; you look like shit."

Lieutenant Smith grimaced. "I feel like shit, Rosen; the bastards have shot me in the back."

Ricardo checked the wound; it was bleeding profusely. "I've got you, sir. We're getting you out of here."

He wrapped the wound tightly with gauze from his kit and lifted the lieutenant in a fireman's lift around his shoulders. He moved toward the helicopter while his team lay down, covering fire. He focused solely on getting his injured commander to safety. He kept talking to him. "Hang in there, sir, we're almost there."

As he heaved Lieutenant Smith toward the waiting helicopter, the roar of the blades cutting through the din, a sudden, searing pain tore through his leg like fire. He staggered but kept moving. He reached behind and wiped his hand down the back of his leg—blood, lots of it. He'd been shot. Then came another sharp sting and another, each one more vicious than the last. His heart pounded in his chest. *Keep going,* he told himself. *Don't stop; keep going.*

He could feel the blood running freely down his legs. Panic clawed at him, and his breath grew heavier and heavier. His legs were trembling; they were failing him. *Just a little more, just a few yards.* But as his vision blurred, he lost sight of the helicopter, and the ground rushed up to meet him. The darkness swallowed him whole, and the two men crashed to the ground.

—

The medic from the helicopter leaped out and shouted for cover. A US gunship helicopter swooped in and attacked the advancing Serb forces. Seizing the opportunity, the team quickly moved the two men into the helicopter, and it took off toward the base camp.

Lieutenant Smith was drifting in and out of consciousness; they had already stemmed the bleeding and inserted an IV. The medic treating Ricardo was cursing, in a state of panic. He had attached a cardiac and pulse monitor. He had also attached a central venous catheter. "He needs more blood; he's losing it rapidly."

Another medic was attending to his legs, trying desperately to stem the rapid loss of blood.

Ricardo had suffered multiple gunshot wounds: four in one leg, two in the other, and two in his back.

"Were losing him; his pulse is dropping!" the medic shouted.

"No heartbeat," the other medic shouted. "He's going; we're going to lose him. More blood—get me the fucking defibrillator!"

Ricardo showed no signs of life; his vital signs flatlined on the monitors. The two medics worked on him for ten minutes. Ricardo was dead.

—

In Zurich, Switzerland, the phone on David's desk rang. He picked up. "Hello?"

"Hi, David, this is Mike. I'll get straight to the point: I've got some bad news."

"Ricardo?"

"Yes."

"How bad?"

"Pretty bad, I'm afraid."

"Tell me."

"He was shot up pretty bad in Bosnia—multiple gunshot wounds, both legs and two shots in his back."

"Fucking hell."

"I'm getting reports that he died in the helicopter, but the information is sketchy, communication poor. They're telling us that he didn't make it."

"What do you mean *sketchy*? What the fuck does that mean, Mike? Is he dead or not?"

"We're not 100 percent sure. You know how it is, how good the medics are at resuscitation. We haven't heard anything since the helicopter landed."

David was shouting; he had completely lost control. "For fuck's sake, Mike!"

"Don't shoot the messenger, David, I'm—"

"Then call me when you have a better update on him."

Before Mike could offer anything else, David slammed down the handset.

52

BACK FROM
THE BRINK

Our greatest glory is not in never falling
but in rising every time we fall.
—Confucius

Ricardo's eyes fluttered open. Confusion clouded his mind as he tried to piece together his last memories. The room was filled with the constant beeping of monitors, and his body ached intensely. He attempted to move but found himself heavily bandaged, immobilized by the swathes of gauze and apparatus holding his legs together.

A nurse approached, her face breaking into a relieved smile. "Look who's back with us," she said warmly. "So glad to see you awake."

Ricardo's lips moved weakly, but no sound emerged.

"You gave us a real scare. They thought they'd lost you out there. You were pronounced dead for ten minutes in the helicopter. Not many people come back from that."

"Keep walking," Ricardo whispered.

"Don't try to talk just yet," the nurse said. "Just rest. You've been in an induced coma for four days. Give it some time before trying to talk."

Her soothing words settled over him like a blanket.

"You're at Walter Reed Hospital in Maryland. They transferred you from Germany after a week in ICU."

He tried to speak with all his strength; only one thing was on his mind.

He opened his mouth and tried to form the words.

The nurse frowned. "I've told you, don't try to speak. Get some rest."

One word. "Lieutenant."

The nurse's eyes lit up. "Ah yes, your friend Lieutenant Smith."

"How is . . ."

"He's fine; he survived too. He should arrive here by week's end. I daresay he'll want to thank you for saving his life."

—

Major Allen, the Army doctor overseeing Ricardo's recovery, entered his private room. "Sergeant Rosen, how are you feeling today?"

Ricardo smiled weakly. "OK, I guess, given the circumstances."

Major Allen sighed; his expression was laden with concern. "Well, Sergeant, I'm afraid I have some bad news for you. We don't think you'll be able to walk again. Despite the surgeries, the artificial knees, and the rods, we aren't sure you'll regain full movement in your legs."

Ricardo looked the doctor in the eyes, his voice steady. "I don't think that will work for me, Major. We'll need a new plan."

"What do you mean it won't work for you? I'm a doctor; this is just how it is."

"But there's a chance?"

"Well, there's a slim possibility, but the odds are not good. Your legs were shot to pieces."

"That's good enough for me, doctor. I'll take the slim chance as long as it's not a done deal. I'm not giving up this easily."

"Soldier, I admire your resolve, but—"

"With all due respect, sir," Ricardo interrupted, "I've been in tougher spots than this; I've stood at the gates of hell more times than you'd care to guess. Churchill once said, 'If you're going through hell, keep going.' I've always done that, sir. I'll keep going until the devil drags me in there."

The major lowered himself slowly onto Ricardo's bed. He shook his head. "I don't believe it, Sergeant. I wish all my patients had your resolve. If you're prepared to fight ten times harder than on any battleground, you'll have my full support. I'll do everything in my power to help you. You have my word."

—

The days blurred together in a haze of pain and sweat as Ricardo clawed his way through recovery. Each morning began with the same ritual: a slow, agonizing shuffle from his bed to the therapy room, hanging on to a mobile frame. The hospital corridors echoed with the sounds of his struggle, the relentless march of a soldier who refused to surrender.

Physical therapy was a fight all on its own. The major had been right: It was far more challenging than anything he had faced on any battlefield. He faced it with the same grit and determination that had carried him since childhood. Every stretch, every lift, every agonizing step was a battle cry, a defiant roar. The therapists, kind and patient but firm, watched him with a mix of admiration and concern as he pushed himself beyond the limits they had set for him. His muscles screamed, and his bones ached, but Ricardo didn't care. He would walk again, no matter the cost.

"Take it easy, Ricardo," they'd tell him, their voices constantly murmuring in the background. But he didn't hear them. The only sound that mattered was the breathless grunts as he forced his legs to move, trying to remember the strength they once held.

He lived for the small victories—the day he managed to stand without support, those first dozen steps without resting—but with those victories came defeats, and Ricardo knew them well. The day he fell from the frame was a harsh reminder that the road to recovery was far from a straight path. He had been pushing himself too hard, as always, driven by the fire that burned in his chest, a fire that refused to be extinguished.

—

After three months, Major Allen came into the room. "I have some good news for you, Sergeant. We've had some results, and we can't quite believe them. You've built up some new muscle, which means you are ready to start more advanced therapy. There's much better movement in your toes."

—

Two months later, Ricardo took three steps without his frame. Three weeks later, he was discharged from the hospital on crutches and returned to Ft. Bragg, where the military therapists continued where Major Allen's team had left off.

His first visitor was Lieutenant Smith, who visited him daily for almost a year. They shared a bond that would never be broken.

—

Lieutenant Smith had arranged a night out in one of the local bars. He watched as Ricardo walked through the door. Lieutenant Smith stood as Ricardo walked toward him. He studied him as he walked over.

"Barely a limp now," he said. "You're not walking like a robot anymore."

"I feel great, sir," Ricardo said. "I can even manage a light jog. I can't wait to return to the team."

Ricardo noticed Lieutenant Smith's reaction; his expression gave it away. "What is it, sir?"

"It's that obvious, huh?"

"I can read you like a book, sir; you should know that by now."

"Well, I'll just come out with it. I'm leaving the Army. Getting shot up took a lot out of me, and I've realized I'm not as young as I once was. It's time to move on."

Ricardo said nothing.

"I've agreed to take a civilian job at IBM."

53

A PATH PAVED WITH DOUBT

*Boredom is the root of all evil—the despairing
refusal to be oneself.*
—Søren Kierkegaard

He had put off the meeting too long. He walked toward Captain Hood's office and knocked on the door.

"Enter," Captain Hood called from inside.

As Ricardo entered, he saluted.

"Wow, Sergeant Rosen, I'm so glad to see you here and walking without crutches, no limp, nothing. That's amazing."

"I'm progressing well, sir."

"What brings you here? You're still on medical leave."

Ricardo looked him straight in the eye. "Sir, I think I'm ready to return to work."

The captain looked anxious. "I knew this day would come."

"I'm running more than five miles, I feel—"

Captain Hood held up a hand. "Let me stop you there, Rosen. There's a big difference between a normal soldier and what we do. No easy way to say this, but I've contacted your doctor. He doesn't think you can return to a specialized team."

"He also said I would never walk again, but I proved him wrong."

"That may be the case, Rosen, but this is different."

"With respect, sir, in what way?"

Captain Hood took a deep breath. "You had extensive injuries. Your recovery has been amazing, but I'm afraid you can no longer be on jump status."

"But, sir—"

Captain Hood interrupted him. "I'm not saying you must leave the Army, but you can't be on an active team. You jump out of a plane and land a little too heavy, and your legs will shatter like a glass vase."

Captain Hood let the news settle in. "We don't want you to leave the Army, Rosen. You're everything a good soldier should be, and we think it's time for you to move up the ladder."

"In what way, sir?"

"I've been talking to Major Beck, and there's an instructor position at Psychological Operations Group. I can't see anyone more qualified to teach that course."

There was an uncomfortable silence. Ricardo's world suddenly crumbled. It was as if the room's walls were closing in, suffocating him. He had known his legs weren't what they once were, that he was a little slower than he used to be, but he had healed. He had fought the pain, determined that it wouldn't slow him down. He was a soldier, not a teacher. Soldiering was his life. Without that, who was he?

"There's a place for you; it's an important role," Captain Hood continued. "We need experienced men like you to train the next generation, to pass on what you've learned."

But Ricardo wasn't listening. His thoughts had drifted, carried away by memories of battlefields, nights under the stars with his comrades, the deafening roar of helicopters, and the crackle of gunfire. He saw the faces of the men he'd led, the ones who hadn't made it home. He thought of the camaraderie, the unspoken bond between soldiers who had faced death together. How could sitting behind a desk ever compare to that?

"I'm not a teacher, sir," he said. "I'm a soldier."

Captain Hood sighed and leaned back in his chair. "I know this isn't easy, Rosen. But you've done your part. You've given enough. It's time to step back."

Step back. The words hit him harder than the bullets in Bosnia had. The Army was supposed to be his family, his home. He had given it everything, and now it was casting him aside like a worn-out piece of equipment. His hands clenched into fists, the knuckles white with tension. He wanted to shout, protest, and demand that they give him another chance, but he knew there was no point. He was just another broken soldier.

"Well, Rosen?" Hood asked.

"Can I think about it, sir?"

"Of course you can, but I need an answer in a couple of weeks; we need to fill the position."

—

A month later, Ricardo began his new role as an instructor at the 4th Psychological Operations Group. This was different from the path he had envisioned for himself. His new role focused more on psychological tactics than direct combat, a significant shift from his previous field experience.

Although he quickly became one of the top instructors, deep down, he was restless. The routine of going to work and coming home daily lacked the adrenaline rush he craved and had thrived on in the field.

—

By now, Stephanie was nearly ten years old, growing into a strong, independent personality with a penchant for jeans, T-shirts, and short haircuts, every bit the tomboy. Ricardo adored her; she was his entire world.

Life with Martha had settled into a tolerable routine, but there were still problems.

She had managed to control her drinking, but there were still occasional displays of drunkenness, and she continued gambling. The situation could have been better. The mundane life of teaching and returning home daily, devoid of the adrenaline-pumping action he was accustomed to, left him feeling unfulfilled. The stability he had achieved felt more like a trap than a comfort. He felt that he needed to do more to keep his promise to Bahar.

—

In Langley, Virginia, David walked briskly into the conference room where Mike, Charlie, Adara, Dianna, and the newest team member, Matt (formerly Lieutenant Smith) were waiting.

David was clearly in a hurry as he addressed the group. "Well, it's been long enough. Matt, it would be best if you made contact. We have much work to do, and I can't wait any longer."

Mike sounded concerned. "Are you sure he's ready? His injuries were quite extensive; he can't possibly be the same person he was."

Matt responded. "Well, it's true, he won't be running the half marathon in under ten seconds ever again, but he's a rock. I've never met a stronger man in my life, and no matter what life throws at him, he'll face it head-on. I'm with David on this: It's been long enough, and I'm sure he's ready."

David was nodding in agreement. "Let's do it, Matt. Approach him and see if he goes for it. I'd guess that he's itching to get back into the field. Just be careful that you don't give too much away."

54

MASKS AND
MIRRORS

*Once you've lived the inside-out world of espionage, you never
shed it. It's a mentality, a double standard of existence.*
—John le Carre

Ricardo was surprised to see a familiar face waiting for him as he
stepped out of the classroom. Now a civilian, Matt stood before
him with a big, welcoming smile. They embraced warmly. "How
are you, sir? It's great to see you."

Matt chuckled, shaking his head slightly. "I'm a civilian now, so no
more of the *sir* or *Lieutenant*. Just call me Matt. I'm in town tonight and
thought we could grab dinner and a beer or two."

"Absolutely, I'm in."

"Great, I'll book a table out at Laguna Point. I know it's a great place."

—

As they settled into their seats at the restaurant, Matt looked at Ricardo. "So, how are things going for you?"

Ricardo sighed, half smiling. "It's been tough. I lived for the adrenaline rush—you know that. Not being on a team anymore is killing me. You know, I thought getting shot was hard, but living this nine-to-five life might be worse."

"It doesn't have to be like this. You have options."

"And what options would they be?"

"Well," Matt said, leaning forward, "I told you I'm working with IBM, right?"

"You did."

"Well, we just landed a new project with Riyad Bank in Saudi Arabia. They've asked me to find a project manager. You speak Farsi and Arabic and know the culture, which seems a good fit for you. The job is yours if you want it. Saudi is an incredible place; it would be a whole new change of scenery."

Ricardo raised an eyebrow. "A project manager, huh? Is that what I've become, project-fucking-management material for a fucking computer company? It sounds about as exciting as manning the McDonald's drive-through. I miss the team—don't you understand?"

Matt nodded. He said nothing.

Ricardo continued. "You know, even when they jammed that gun into my ribs at Istanbul Airport, I felt that familiar tingling. It spread from my fingertips to my chest, and I vibrated with energy. My heart knew what was happening; it started to pound, hammering against my ribs like a drum. My lungs expanded, and I sucked in the oxygen that my brain craved. Everything around me sharpened into focus, every detail in super clarity because, once again, it was me against the bad guys, and I loved every fucking glorious second." He looked across the table. "You know how it feels."

"I do." Matt nodded. ". . . I still do."

Ricardo looked up. "What . . . what do you mean?"

"IBM," he said. "I still get that rush because I still get to fight the bad guys."

"What are you telling me?"

"Come and join us at IBM, Ricardo. We need specialist people with specialist skills—men like you, my good friend, because people need to sleep sound in their beds at night . . ."

Ricardo finished the quote for him. ". . . because we are the wolves that keep other wolves at bay so the sheep can sleep easy."

Matt grinned. "That kind of sums up what we do."

"So as a project manager at IBM, you are in the perfect position to . . ."

"Let's just say there are side jobs that have nothing to do with IBM."

"But I—"

Matt held up his hand. "No more talk, Ricardo." He reached into his inside breast pocket and placed a document on the table. It was labeled:

1000 Colonial Farm Road

Langley, VA 22101

USA

"Here's your contract: sixteen pages long; terms and conditions; blah, blah; details; death in service; rules and regulations; financial package; confidentiality and nondisclosure; operational secrecy and legal immunity."

Ricardo pulled a pen from his pocket, turned to the last page, and signed.

Matt spoke. "You're not gonna even read it, talk to Martha about it?"

He slid it back across the table. "No need, sir. I'm all in and reporting for duty."

———

To be continued.

ABOUT
THE AUTHOR

Nick Berg is an American author whose life has been marked by tragedy and resilience. Born in Tehran to an Iranian mother and American father, he experienced Iran's vibrant culture and violent political upheavals. These events deeply influenced his worldview and literary voice. In his autobiographic novel, *Shadows of Tehran*, Nick mirrors his life through the protagonist, Ricardo, reflecting his struggles with identity, betrayal, and redemption.

Nick moved to the United States, served in Special Operations, and transitioned to a successful tech executive career after an injury. *Shadows of Tehran* is his first novel. Post-military, Nick has focused on writing, speaking, and coaching on diversity and servant leadership. He is also a music enthusiast, finding creativity and renewal in producing electronic music. Nick's work bridges cultural gaps and emphasizes resilience and hope.

SHADOWSOFTEHRAN.COM